TREASURES OF THE TWELVE

CINDY LIN

HARPER

An Imprint of HarperCollins*Publishers*

Treasures of the Twelve
Copyright © 2020 by Cindy Lin
All rights reserved. Printed in the United States of America.
No part of this book may be used or reproduced in any manner
whatsoever without written permission except in the case of brief
quotations embodied in critical articles and reviews. For information
address HarperCollins Children's Books, a division of HarperCollins
Publishers, 195 Broadway, New York, NY 10007.
www.harpercollinschildrens.com

Library of Congress Cataloging-in-Publication Data

Names: Lin, Cindy, author.
Title: Treasures of the Twelve / Cindy Lin.
Description: First edition. | New York, NY : Harper, an imprint of
    HarperCollins Publishers, [2020] | Sequel to: The Twelve. |
    Audience: Ages 8-16. | Audience: Grades 4-6. | Summary:
    "Usagi's quest to save her younger sister, Uma, and save
    Midaga from the Dragonlord continues in this sequel to The
    Twelve"— Provided by publisher.
Identifiers: LCCN 2019056123 | ISBN 978-0-06-282130-0
    (hardcover)
Subjects: CYAC: Fantasy. | Sisters—Fiction. | Orphans—
    Fiction. | Astrology, Chinese—Fiction. | Magic—Fiction. |
    Adventure and adventurers—Fiction.
Classification: LCC PZ7.1.L553 Tr 2020 | DDC [Fic]—dc23
LC record available at https://lccn.loc.gov/2019056123

Typography by Molly Fehr
20 21 22 23 24 PC/LSCH 10 9 8 7 6 5 4 3 2 1

First Edition

To my sister, Wendy—
for listening to my stories
from the very start.

To knowingly destroy any one of these artifacts would remove the protection of concealment, resulting in grave consequences for the kingdom. The Twelve Treasures must remain a part of the Warrior Circle, or the power of Mount Jade—and Midaga's strength—will be lost.

—Council Testament, Eighth Month of the Earth Boar, Second (Fire) Snake Cycle, from *Annals of the Warrior Council*

CHAPTER 1

THE PEN OF TRUTH

USAGI WINCED AT THE SCREECH of seabirds and hurried along the harbor's busy waterfront, squinting against the reflection of the morning sun as she followed her target. A crisp spring breeze, sharp with the tang of salt and fishrot, threatened to blow off her headwrap and expose her dark braids. She shifted the pole across her shoulders, empty baskets dangling from either end, and tugged the white kerchief down more securely. While there were girl porters working the docks here in Port Wingbow, they were few and far between, and the last thing she wanted was to call attention to herself.

"To your left, Rabbit Girl," said a familiar voice, twenty paces back. Most passersby would think that Nezu was just muttering to the other young porter hauling a basketload of packages beside him, but Usagi could hear the Heir to the Rat Warrior loud and clear, thanks to her ability to hear as

well as a rabbit. She didn't dare risk trying to reply to him and her friend Tora, neither of whom shared that particular animal talent. Raising her arm, she scratched her shoulder to show that she'd heard, then veered across the crushed-shell path toward the main pier.

"Tell her the Guards have arrived," hissed Tora, who was keeping a lookout with her sharp tiger vision. *"We're too late. We'll have to wait till the harbormaster's done for the day and his Guard detail goes away."*

"You can tell her yourself," said Nezu. *"Are you forgetting she hears us?"*

"I've known Usagi a lot longer than you—I know exactly how well she can hear. You're the one who insisted on a protocol. 'Everything must go through the head of the mission!'" Tora mimicked. Usagi heard her best friend stroking imaginary fuzz on her upper lip, something the Rat Heir often did when he was pleased, nervous, or deep in thought.

"Stop it, Tiger Girl. I've been doing this for a few years now."

"Doesn't mean you know everything, Rat Boy."

"You're just upset about not wearing the belt, but I'm telling you, it fits me better—and as head of the mission, why shouldn't I?"

Usagi groaned. In all her thirteen years, she'd never known anyone to squabble as much as this pair. She turned and retraced her steps, pretending to look for something she'd dropped, until she bumped right into them, knocking some of their decoy parcels to the ground. Usagi yelped a false apology, and as they all bent down to collect the scattered packages, she glared at them.

"What's wrong with you two? We're close to getting one of the Treasures back, and you're arguing!"

Looking abashed, Nezu reached up and tugged at the barest wisp of whiskers on his upper lip. It didn't help them get any longer, but he'd been doing it since he first sprouted peach fuzz, and now it was a habit. "Sorry, Rabbit Girl. You're right. We're just on edge after waiting for so long—and now we have to wait some more." He flashed an apologetic smile, his usual grin dimmed somewhat. At sixteen and the seniormost Warrior Heir on the mission, he was responsible for leading them, and the difficulty they'd had securing their target these last few days was wearing on him.

"If you'd only trusted me the first time I said I saw the harbormaster, we might have gotten to him sooner." Tora's amber eyes flamed with indignation. She was a year older than Usagi but wasn't yet a Warrior Heir. She was hoping to become one by proving herself on this assignment.

Long before Usagi had become the Rabbit Heir, before ever meeting Nezu and the other Warrior Heirs, Tora had been by her side. For years after the Dragonlord's overthrow of Midaga's king and the Warriors of the Zodiac, she and Tora had been orphans in the forest. Along with Usagi's sister, Uma, the three of them had been just trying to survive and keep their zodiac powers hidden. Until—

Until . . .

Usagi pushed the painful thought of her little sister away and handed over a stack of parcels to her friend. "Can the two of you please behave?"

"Of course," said Tora, baring her sharp white canines. They were snaggleteeth that stuck out from the rest of her smile, making her look extra fierce even when she wasn't annoyed. When she was truly furious, her tiger teeth would grow till they protruded from her upper lip. Thankfully they were currently in check. An angry youngling sprouting long fangs would draw attention—too much attention on a mission to steal back the Pen of Truth.

One of twelve Treasures that once belonged to the Warriors, the pen was now in the possession of a man who ran the kingdom's main seaport—and he was using its powers for profit.

"You said you saw the Guard?" Usagi asked Tora. Her stomach clenched at the thought of the armed troops who kept order for the ruler of Midaga. Though she'd bested one in a fight once, it was always better to avoid tangling with the Dragonlord's men.

Her friend nodded. "Two of them, right as the harbormaster got to the dock."

"So we wait until he's alone again. Might as well stick together till then." Usagi straightened. "My apologies!" she said loudly. "Let me help you." She made a show of taking some of their bundles—mostly just straw wrapped in squares of cloth—and putting them in her empty baskets. She hoisted her pole over her shoulders, making sure the sword hidden inside was secure. Nezu's walking stick also hid a blade, as weapons had been forbidden for all but those serving the Dragonlord. Since Tora was not yet an Heir, her pole was just solid wood. She was eager to earn her place as the Tiger Heir, and with it, a hidden weapon of her own.

Together they headed toward the largest pier in port, where the harbormaster's station was perched. Weaving between rumbling ox carts, they ducked and dodged as bales of wool, cords of exotic woods, bundles of sharkskin leather, and other imports were unloaded from the myriad ships docked along the piers built all throughout the cove. Though they'd been on Feather Island for nearly a week, Usagi was still dazzled by the sight of all the boats. Who knew there could be so many types of vessels to travel across water? There were ships with battened sails that folded like fans, sloops with white canvas billowing from the masts like puffed-out frogs' throats, flat-keeled boats propelled by paddlewheels, longships that sported rows of oars manned by oarsmen, squat boats with chimneys that belched smoke, armored ships bristling with firecannon.

Before the fall of the Shield of Concealment, the kingdom of Midaga had never seen so many visitors to its shores. It had remained hidden from the rest of the world, safe and protected by the Warriors of the Zodiac, until Druk the Dragon Warrior betrayed his oath to the Circle of the Twelve. He shattered the Shield, allowing invasion and war to devastate the land, and seized the throne as Dragonlord.

Now, seven years into his reign, ships from lands near and far came to Midaga, eager to see and trade with the kingdom that had been but a myth for hundreds of years. The port in the Bantam Islands, once the only part of Midaga that the world was allowed to see, had been expanded by leaps and bounds, per the order of the Dragonlord. A harbor that had received at most four ships a year when the Shield was up now saw many times that each week. And from his spare wooden lean-to on the main pier, the harbormaster ruled over it all.

They drew close and saw the line of ship captains and various agents waiting to report their cargo to the harbormaster. The front of the shanty was wide open, flanked by two armored Guard. They glowered beneath metal helmets that sat on their heads like overturned cookpots. Their burly torsos were shielded by iron breastplates, and their leather-sleeved arms cradled firecannon. At the sight of them, Usagi quailed. It was an old reflex. She forced herself to hold her head up. She was the Heir to the Rabbit Warrior, after all. She'd spent months training and could handle them both if need be!

She spotted the harbormaster's bulky form and tall

official's hat but was unable to see the Treasure. Fortunately, they had Tora's tiger vision, just as Usagi's sharp ears listened for them all. "Is it there?" Usagi whispered.

Tora's eyes narrowed. "On his desk there's a pen, in a brush stand beside the cargo registry. It's bigger than an ordinary ink brush, with a gold handle decorated with the twelve animals of the zodiac. It's got a gold cap, but he's taken it off. I see the bristles. They look like ox hair."

"Ox—the animal embodying truthfulness," Nezu said. "That's the Treasure, all right." They continued farther down the pier until they came to the last ship, which looked nearly deserted, its cargo unloaded, most of its crew likely in one of the port taverns. They set their baskets down. Nezu took his headcloth off and wiped his face, then retied it around his close-cropped hair, taking care to tuck in the long, thin rat-tail braid at the base of his skull. He flashed a smile at Usagi. "How are your rabbit ears from here?"

She tilted her head and squeezed her eyes shut, listening. Out of habit, Usagi reached for the pendant she wore around her neck and rubbed the little silver rabbit with its chips of green jade for eyes. Over the cries of seagulls, the shouts of dockworkers, the splash of seawater against ships and dock pilings, the creak of wooden hulls, the clattering of wheels on cobblestones and planks, Usagi located the gravelly voice of the harbormaster, which she'd come to recognize after several days of surveillance. He was interrogating his latest quarry in the line of ship captains and cargo masters waiting to report to him.

"Name and vessel name?"

"Captain Golae of the Fleet-Finned Whale*."*

"Home port?"

"Port Busana in Solonos."

The harbormaster would always ask about the cargo, and then hand over the Pen of Truth to sign off. That was the part that always made Usagi feel a little sorry for the harbormaster's prey.

"Oh! Wait! I—I didn't mean to write that! Th—that's a mistake!"

"Is it really, Captain? You aren't trying to skimp on paying your import duties, are you? If I have the Guard go to your ship right now and search it, do you swear on your life we will only find ten *bales of cotton for trade instead of* fifteen*?"*

After some threats detailing what could happen to those caught trying to cheat the Dragonlord, the harbormaster would then offer the hapless victim an opportunity to buy his way out of trouble. In this way, Usagi noticed, the harbormaster was becoming a very rich man.

"He's up to his usual tricks," she reported. "Just got a Soloni ship captain to hand over five gold mon for lying about his cargo."

Nezu whistled. "That's more than some people make in a lifetime." He peered into the water. "Anyone getting hungry?"

8

Glancing around to make sure no one was looking, he made a little swirling motion with his hands until a small cyclone of water rose from the sea. Knitting his brow, he gestured sharply upward, and the cyclone spat a silvery fish onto the pier, where it flipped and flopped at their feet.

"Mealtime!" Tora exclaimed. She pounced on the wriggling fish and dispatched it with a quick thump against the dock. With his knife, Nezu cleaned the fish, slicing it into neat filets. He portioned it out between the three of them and pulled out fist-sized balls of salted rice wrapped in seaweed.

"It's too bad none of us have a fire gift," he remarked. "A little blast of flame would sear this fish nicely."

Usagi couldn't help but think of Uma at that moment. Her sister was able to conjure fire with her bare hands and had used her elemental gift to cook whatever they could scavenge, back when they lived with Tora in the forest outside Goldentusk. Now Uma was part of the Dragonlord's troops, a prized cadet in a corps of younglings with zodiac powers, her fire gift and horse speed to be used by the Dragonlord as tools in maintaining order over all Midagians. Usagi's rabbit locket felt heavy at her neck, and she rubbed its hollow belly. It contained the charred remains of the wooden rabbit she used to wear—until Uma had burned it in a fury. That was the last time Usagi had seen her sister.

With a sigh, she sat with the others on the edge of the

dock, dangling their feet over the swirling seawater. Clumps of kelp drifted on the surface while a pair of black-tailed gulls bobbed alongside, staring up at their meal with hungry yellow eyes. She was about to take a bite of her rice ball when Tora stopped chewing and squinted down the pier.

"There's the harbormaster's daughter," she muttered. Usagi turned and caught a bit of movement as a small figure ducked behind the railing of a docked ship. Since coming to Port Wingbow, they'd seen the girl hanging around the docks—the only youngling who wasn't a porter, though she might as well have been one, dressed as she was in a ragged tunic and pants, a grimy white kerchief tied over a frizzled braid.

Nezu draped a piece of fish over his rice ball and took a bite. "Are you sure she's his daughter? Seems like more of a servant to me. He's always ordering her around."

"And slapping her if she's too slow," said Tora with a frown. They had witnessed the harbormaster boxing the girl about the ears when he wasn't in his shed extorting payment from ship captains. It had disgusted Usagi—the girl couldn't have been more than seven or eight and was spindly with large dark eyes that reminded her of Uma.

Usagi got to her feet. "I'll be right back."

"Where are you going?" Tora cocked her head.

Waving a vague hand, Usagi headed for the ship, eyes on where she'd last seen movement. As she drew closer, she heard the growling of an empty stomach—only for once it wasn't hers. She stopped at the base of the lowered gangplank. "Merciful spirits! What a lot of rice and fish," Usagi exclaimed. "I can't eat all of this by myself! What to do?" As a dark head with wide eyes peered out, Usagi smiled. "Oh, hello!" She held up her rice ball. "I've got a little too much here. Would you like some?"

The girl hesistated, then nodded. Usagi waved at her to come down, and she crept down the gangplank. Her face was smudged with dirt and soot, and she smelled like she'd been sleeping in a pile of fishnets. Usagi broke her rice ball in half and gave her most of her raw fish. Shyly, the girl took it, then stuffed everything in her mouth all at once, as if she were afraid Usagi would change her mind. Usagi laughed. "Slow down! You'll give yourself a bellyache." She took a bite of her own and then looked at the girl chewing mightily, eyes half-closed in relief. It reminded Usagi so much of Uma that a lump came into her throat. Swallowing hard, she held out the rest of her food. "Here, why don't you have some more?"

Eyes shining, the little girl took it. She bobbed her head in thanks.

"What's your name?" asked Usagi, and pointed to herself. "I'm Usagi, born in the year of the Wood Rabbit."

The girl paused in her chewing and mumbled through a mouthful of rice. "Ji. Year of the Rooster."

"I knew a boy back home who was born a Metal Rooster," Usagi said. "Jago was always full of energy, as Roosters often are." She took care not to mention that little Jago had developed the talent of flying or had been hauled away by Strikers to serve the Dragonlord. She waved a casual hand at the harbormaster's station. "So, is that your father in there?"

Ji stopped chewing, startled. Slowly, she nodded.

"You know that gold pen of his?" Usagi pressed. "It's so pretty. Do you know where he got it?"

Shaking her head, Ji backed away, eyes wide.

"No, wait!" Usagi hadn't meant to alarm her, but the girl turned and ran back up the gangplank, disappearing onto the ship. She'd said too much. *Spit and spleen.* Usagi stood there a moment, cursing herself, then returned to her friends.

Nezu looked at her curiously. "What were you trying to do there?"

"I remember what it's like to be hungry," said Usagi with a sigh. "And I thought maybe she could tell me a little bit about the pen. But she ran away before saying anything."

"Better to leave her alone," Nezu advised. "The fewer people we speak to today, the better. We don't need anyone recognizing us after we've lifted the pen." He polished off the last of his rice ball and licked his fingers. "Spirits. I could've eaten five of those." He tightened the leather belt at his waist. Decorated with silver, wood, and horn fittings, the Belt of Passage was a precious heirloom passed down from warrior to warrior in the Circle of the Twelve. That was, until the war had decimated their ranks and scattered their treasured artifacts around the kingdom. The belt had only recently been recovered, and the other Warrior Heirs had insisted that Nezu wear it on this mission, in case its powers were needed.

Tora stiffened. "The harbormaster's leaving his station and dismissing the Guard. He must be off to the teahouse for midday meal. Should we try for the pen now?"

"Is it on him?" asked Usagi. From where she stood, more than two hundred paces away, she saw the harbormaster closing the doors to his shed but couldn't see much more than that.

Narrowing her eyes, Tora nodded. "He's sticking it in the back of his belt, just as he has for the last three days. He's consistent, at least."

"Perfect." Nezu rubbed his hands and flashed a grin. "I think we've watched and waited long enough."

He and Tora lifted their poles onto their shoulders, balancing their baskets of decoy parcels. They waited for Usagi to pick up her own baskets, then followed her off the pier. They hurried after the official with his tall winged hat. Usagi kept her eyes on the wide cloth belt where he'd stashed the pen. The harbormaster lumbered toward the main thoroughfare, where shops, teahouses, and taverns had sprung up to offer goods, food, and drink to the countless crews coming through Port Wingbow. All throughout the port were Guard patrols, swaggering in pairs, or small teams of armored men, crunching along streets paved in crushed shells.

"Okay, Rabbit Girl," said Nezu. "You know what to do. Be quick before he gets too far away—there'll only be more of the Dragonlord's men around at the teahouse."

Taking a deep breath, Usagi nodded. She could hear the harbormaster jingling a few coins in his hand. Several of the gold mon he'd gotten that morning, it sounded like. She was half-tempted to try for them, too, but shook off the impulse. They were here for one thing only.

Boldly, she trotted after the harbormaster. "Honorable sir? Your Excellency?"

The harbormaster's belly bulged over his belt like a giant steamed bun. He frowned at her, his large jowls drooping. "Yes?"

Usagi held up a small drawstring sack. "Did you drop this, sir? I found it on the dock." She shook it and it jingled. The harbormaster's eyes grew keen and he stopped, giving her a fake smile.

"Why yes, I believe I did," he said heartily. As he reached for it, he lurched forward and nearly fell onto Usagi. She threw her arms out to steady him, just as Tora piped up.

"Oh! My apologies! I didn't see you, sir!"

Red-faced, the harbormaster turned. "Why don't you

watch where you're going?" he bellowed. Usagi saw the glint of the pen poking out of his belt. Tora hadn't managed to nab it when she bumped into him—she'd only dislodged it. *Spit and spleen.* Usagi was going to have to get it herself.

Nezu began alternately scolding Tora and apologizing to the harbormaster. Tora bowed her head, flicking a glance at Usagi.

Heart pounding, she reached for the pen. The harbormaster half turned, and she snatched her hand back. His long billowing sleeve flapped in Usagi's face as he gestured in the direction of the docks. "I am the master here, and we do not suffer this kind of incompetence gladly!"

Tora dropped everything and got on her knees. "Please, sir! It was an accident!" She pressed her forehead to the ground at the harbormaster's feet. Pawing at his robes, she began to wail. "Forgive me!"

"What are you doing? Don't touch me!" He kicked and Tora ducked. The pen slid higher out of his belt, gleaming.

Now. With a swift movement, Usagi nicked the pen and shoved it into her tunic.

"Sir?" She jingled the small cloth sack. "You said this was yours, sir?"

He turned his attention back to Usagi and took the sack. "Yes, it's mine," he grunted. He glared at Tora and Nezu. "Get out of here, before I call the Guard on you."

Taking up their loads, they thanked the harbormaster

profusely and scurried away. Usagi bowed slightly and backed away. "Have a good day, sir."

As she turned and walked rapidly after Tora and Nezu, she could hear the harbormaster impatiently tearing at the knots holding the sack closed. Nezu steered them down a busy side street. "Do you have it?"

With a grin, Usagi patted herself. "Right here."

"Gods' guts!" The harbormaster cursed behind them. *"There's no money in here!"*

Usagi quickened her pace. "He just discovered the nails."

"No running," Nezu warned. "Just act normal."

"My pen. Where's my pen?! Oi!"

"And now he knows the Pen of Truth is gone," said Usagi, clutching her tunic and hunching her shoulders.

Tora glanced back. "He's coming this way."

"Come back here! Guard! After those porters!"

Looking over her shoulder, Usagi saw the harbormaster with several Guard, pointing at them. "He's sending the Guard after us."

"This way," said Tora. They ducked around a corner— and ran straight into a wall of tall, beefy armed men. It was a full squad of Guard.

"Flying fireballs," groaned Nezu. "We're trapped!"

CHAPTER 2

ESCAPE FROM FEATHER ISLAND

EIGHT SCOWLING GUARDS BLOCKED THE way, with more coming up to join them. They stared at Usagi and the others suspiciously. A few of them reached for their swords, while others swung their firecannon off their shoulders.

"Run!" said Nezu. Ditching their baskets, they took off at a sprint.

A shout went up. "After them!" An alarm bell began to ring insistently, answered by other bells across the port. The burst of clanging pierced Usagi's eardrums. Dropping her walking stick, she doubled over, clapping her hands over her ears. Nezu and Tora stopped and grabbed her.

"Don't worry about me!" Usagi shook them off.

"We're not," said Tora briskly. "But you've got the pen."

Usagi laughed in spite of herself. They had the Pen of

Truth at last! There was no way she was going to let the Guard catch her. Steeling herself against the clanging of the bells, she picked up her stick and sped off, leaving Tora and Nezu to scramble after her. The three of them raced through the streets, dodging everything and everyone crossing their path, as more Guards responded to the alarm and joined in the pursuit.

"I thought you said not to run," she shouted as they dashed down a small lane away from three Guards.

Nezu flashed a grin. "Plans change." He vaulted over a wheelbarrow pushed by a porter.

"Watch out!" cried Tora. An ox cart blocked their way as it trundled down the narrow lane. It was piled so high with crab cages, each crammed full of snapping, clicking crabs, that its cargo nearly grazed the shop signs hanging from the storefronts flanking the street.

Usagi didn't even stop to think. With a bounding leap, she launched high into the air. As she sailed over the cart, she caught the astonished stare of a woman hanging nets to dry from a second-story window. "My stars! Zodiac powers," the woman gasped. Usagi gave a little wave.

"A freakling!" shouted the pursuing Guards. "Alert the Dragonstrikers!"

Boils and blisters, Usagi swore silently. The Dragonstrikers were searching for the Twelve Treasures too. As the Dragonlord's elite forces, they were far more skilled and fearsome than the Guard. And now Usagi had given herself away—she wasn't supposed to be using her animal talents so openly, but she'd forgotten in the moment. Nezu was going to be furious.

Landing neatly in front of the ox cart, Usagi turned to see its driver standing beside his team of oxen, his mouth agape. She gave him a sheepish smile. The cart jostled a bit, and then Usagi heard howls of pain. "My nose!" bawled a Guard. "Get these crabs off me!"

Squeezing their way into slivers of space on either side of the cart, Tora and Nezu scuttled through and joined Usagi. "We set some of the crabs free to slow the Guards down," said Tora, smirking. Her headwrap had gone missing, and her unruly dark locks had sprung free.

But Nezu's usual grin was also missing. "Rabbit Girl, that was unwise."

Usagi grimaced. "Plans change?" she offered.

He shook his head and hustled them out of the alley. They didn't get very far before another group of Guard spotted them and gave chase. They tore through the streets, swerving around sailors and fishermen, winding about merchants and dockworkers, turning corners at the sight of a helmet or firecannon, veering around barking dogs and wagons pulled by plodding horses, till they were spit back out onto the harborfront.

Wildly, Usagi looked about. The Guard were coming

from all directions—except for the docks ahead. "That way!" she shouted.

They careened down the main pier, dodging porters and stacks of cargo as the shouts of the Guard and the pounding of their boots neared.

"Now what?" panted Tora. "We can't just jump into the water!"

Nezu reached for the belt at his waist. "Yes, we can."

Usagi stopped him. "Wait—I hear something." She looked around. A voice was calling from the end of the dock.

"Over here!" It was the harbormaster's daughter, waving frantically from the deck of a ship. "You'll be safe up here!"

Usagi started toward the ship. "There's a place to hide!"

"With her?" Tora fretted. "Her father's the one who's after us."

"I've got a good feeling," Usagi said firmly, and ran up the gangplank.

With a sigh and a grunt, Tora and Nezu followed. The little girl looked at them with wide eyes. "This way," she whispered, and scurried to the door of the hold. She held it open. "It's empty—the crew won't be loading till tonight."

Usagi smiled at her and began to climb in. She looked up at the others, who stood unmoving on the deck. "What's the problem?"

"She's not going to lock us in, is she?" Tora demanded.

Nezu flashed a grin at Ji. "We appreciate the offer, but

some of us aren't comfortable in the dark." Tora snorted and he elbowed her.

"You don't have to go in there if you don't want," Ji said in a small voice, rubbing her dirt-smudged nose. "I can make the Guard go away."

Crossing her arms, Tora hunkered down by a stack of barrels. "That sounds good to me."

Exasperated, Usagi climbed back out. "The Guard are getting close. If I hear them set one foot on the gangplank, we're going down into the hold."

"Wait here," said Ji. She went to the ship's stern, which was tied in at the dock, and crouched below the railing so she couldn't be seen.

Then Usagi started. Her own voice was coming from the direction of the pier—but she wasn't talking. Nezu and Tora looked at her as if she'd sprouted another head—then Nezu's voice answered, as if they were both somewhere down on the dock. Nezu put a hand to his throat, eyes wide.

"This way! Bring the pen!" called Tora's voice. But Tora's lips hadn't moved. Usagi stared at her.

"Are you . . . ?"

Tora shook her head. "It's not me!"

Nezu pointed. "It's her!"

Out of sight of the Guards swarming on the docks, Ji was throwing her voice—or rather, the voices of Usagi, Tora, and Nezu—so that it sounded as if they were far from the ship. She cupped her hands around her mouth and imitated them, their three voices moving farther down the pier. Usagi listened with astonishment, watching tensely as the little girl called out an entire decoy conversation. "Quick, get off the pier! . . . The Guards think we're on the ships! . . . To the Rat's Run!"

"They're headed for the bridge to the mainland, those little sneaks," shouted a Guard, and the heavy footfalls stepped away from their ship. Usagi's shoulders loosened as if a wire between them had been cut, and she breathed a sigh of relief. Ji peered out over the docks, watching for a long moment. Then she smiled.

She returned to their huddle, face aglow. "I told you I'd get rid of them."

"You certainly did." Usagi beamed at her, then introduced the little girl to the others. "Ji is born in the year of the Rooster."

Nezu flashed a grin. "And what an animal talent that was! Thank you for getting the Guard off our tail."

"I've met Rooster younglings with powers, but I've never seen that," marveled Tora. "Have you been doing it long?"

"My rooster crow?" asked the little girl. She pinched her bottom lip, thinking. "Since last year, I guess. It started in the summer. I was making seagull sounds at first. It's lots more fun trying to sound like other people."

"Does your father know you can do that?" asked Usagi.

Ji shook her head. "If he did, he'd hand me over to the Dragonstrikers for coin. I've seen him sell off other younglings." She glanced around. "He also doesn't know that I can do this." Furrowing her brow, she snapped her fingers, and a flame appeared between them.

"Spirits!" said Nezu. "You're a Fire Rooster!"

The little girl snapped her fingers again, and the flame disappeared. "I guess so. I can't do anything more than that, though—nothing like the way you caught that fish." She smiled shyly at Nezu.

He nudged Tora with his elbow. "Talented *and* observant."

"If you practice, I'm sure your gift of fire will grow," Usagi told Ji. The sight of her conjuring fire struck Usagi with longing. Uma had been so proud of her elemental gift. Usagi thought of her face, alight in the glow of a flame in her hands, then straightened and pushed the memory away. Her sister was lost to her now.

A black-tailed seagull flew to the railing and nuzzled Ji's ear. "Say hi, Nabi," Ji cooed, stroking its feathers. A second gull circled over their heads before swooping down and landing on Ji's shoulder. "Neko, are you jealous?" she teased. The two birds had wingspans that dwarfed Ji's scrawny frame, but she giggled as they preened her hair with their long beaks. She turned back to Usagi and her friends. "It's nice to be around others who aren't afraid of zodiac powers."

"That's because we know there's nothing to be afraid of," said Tora briskly. Shading her eyes, she squinted up at the sun, which was well past its midday peak. "It's the hour of the Ram. We'd better get out of here while the Guards are off our trail."

"Except now they're swarming all around Rat's Run," said Usagi. "How are we to get off Feather Island and back to the mainland if they've got the bridge surrounded?"

"We'll just wait until dark and sneak over," Tora said.

Nezu grinned. "Why do that when we have a bridge of our own?"

Usagi regarded the belt Nezu wore. "I don't think the Belt of Passage can bridge a gap that wide." On her first mission as the Rabbit Heir, she'd gone to track down the lost Treasure with Nezu and Inu, the Dog Heir. They'd found it in a remote valley, in the form of a small footbridge that spanned a deep ravine. It had been hidden there by Horse Warrior Mori the Seventh, the very last Warrior to wear the belt. The bridge had silver-capped posts and a wooden deck bound with leather and trimmed with horn inlay. When they'd located the buckle underneath and unhooked it, the bridge had transformed into a belt. It had been wondrous to behold.

Groves of trees lined the ravine the belt had bridged, so Usagi had laid her hands on one particularly large banyan tree and coaxed it into stretching its tangled, thick roots across the gap, weaving them together until a living bridge had formed. "Spirits," Nezu had said, impressed. "Now the local villagers can still get to their hunting grounds, and we can return the Treasure to its rightful place. That's the best work with your wood gift yet!"

"You mean second-best," Inu had corrected. "Or have you forgotten how she freed us from an underground prison in the Dragonlord's compound?"

Usagi had gotten to wear the Belt of Passage all the way back home to Mount Jade.

Looking at the belt now, she thought of the ravine where they'd found it, and shook her head. "The bridge to the mainland is a hundred times longer than the one in Godsbridge Valley. There's too much water between Feather Island and the rest of Midaga."

Nezu shrugged and winked. "Good thing it's more than just a bridge, then." He removed the belt at his waist and tossed it over the side of the ship. Usagi gave a startled shriek. Tora quirked an eyebrow at her.

"My heart stops when he throws it away like that," Usagi confessed.

With a chuckle, Nezu glanced into the water. "Don't worry. It's not going anywhere yet. Look!"

They all peered over the side of the boat, Ji on tiptoe. The belt floated on the surface of the sea for a few moments, then began to expand, rippling and twisting as if it were a dried sponge soaking up water. Within seconds it had transformed into a long, low boat. At its stern was a wooden horse head with a flowing mane, flared nostrils, and teeth bared in a warning scream.

"Now that's a sea horse!" said Nezu with satisfaction. He flashed a grin at Ji. "Thank you, Rooster Girl, for your help." He threw a leg over the railing, preparing to jump down into the boat. "I'll go first, and Usagi, you help Tora."

The little girl tugged at his sleeve. "Wait! Could I go with you?"

The Rat Heir paused. "You don't even know where we're going."

"Anywhere would be better than here," Ji said. She twisted the hem of her tunic with dirty, calloused fingers, her eyes wide and pleading.

"Won't your father miss you?" asked Usagi.

"And send Guard after you?" added Tora. Her hand strayed to the slashing scars that covered one arm, tokens from an old encounter with the Guard.

Ji's gaze dropped to her feet. Rubbing her nose, she left more smudges of dirt on her face. "He's not really my father—he just took me in when I was little. He always says I should be more grateful. But he doesn't much care for me. All he cares about is how much work I can do and how much money he can get."

Nezu pulled at the whiskers on his upper lip, thinking.

"She's too green to come all the way to the shrine with us, but we could take her to stay with Yunja."

"There're already some younglings with him," Usagi agreed. "He won't mind another."

Tora frowned. "The harbormaster knows we've taken the pen from him. If we take his daughter too . . ."

The little girl squared her shoulders. "I'm not his daughter—and you wouldn't be taking me. I'd be going with you."

Nezu grinned. "Well then, come along. We know a place where you won't have to hide your powers."

"Oh, thank you!" Ji clapped her hands. Nezu extended his arm and pulled her up beside him.

"We'll jump into that boat together," he said. "Ready?"

After they leaped off the ship, Usagi helped Tora onto the railing and linked arms with her, their walking sticks in hand.

"Shall I count to three?" Usagi joked.

Tora shook her head. "I don't know about this," she muttered.

"Don't worry. I'll leap for the both of us," Usagi reassured her.

Tora waved an impatient hand. "I don't mean jumping. I mean bringing along a youngling—especially one who's part of the harbormaster's household."

"You've seen how he treats her," said Usagi. "We can't leave her here."

With a reluctant sigh, Tora nodded. "You're the Heirs. You know best."

Usagi squeezed Tora's arm. "Ready?"

They leaped off the ship's railing, straight into the narrow longboat bobbing on the sea. Nezu had settled Ji in the stern, right by the screaming horse head, and sat himself at the other end. There were wooden paddles lying in the bottom of the boat, tethered with thin strips of leather. Usagi put down her stick and reached for a paddle, as did Tora.

"Hold on," called Nezu from the bow. "I don't think you'll need to use them." Sticking a paddle in the water, he wiggled it gently, frowning in concentration. Before Usagi or Tora could even get their paddles wet, the boat began to move. Water foamed up and a small wave pushed them along, away from the docks and into the open water of the harbor. Usagi gave a small whoop. What a blessing to have his water gift!

Nezu steered the boat with the paddle and used his powers to churn the wave at their back. The cold salty sting of sea spray lashed their faces as they gathered speed.

Skittering over a wake, the boat went airborne for a brief moment before landing back with a splash, and Ji's startled squeal dissolved into delighted giggles. Her two seagull friends dipped and swooped in the air, skimming alongside them. The afternoon sun bounced off the surface of the sea, sunlight scattering into diamonds on the water. Usagi tilted her face toward its warmth and basked in the glow of their success. They'd recovered another Treasure, and *she'd* been the one to nab it. On top of which they'd found another youngling with talents and were saving her from being sold into the Dragonlord's forces. Gods be good, another mission would soon be complete.

They moved out of the harbor and around the tiny island to the narrow strait that separated it from the rest of Midaga. A wooden bridge, more than a thousand paces long and wide enough for three ox carts, ran across the shallow water, connecting Feather Island and its port to the mainland. They'd crossed Rat's Run on foot last week dressed as porters.

"The Guard have set up three checkpoints on that bridge," Tora said, pointing.

Squinting into the distance, Usagi thought she saw movement on the span, but the people were as small as ants. "Glad we're not anywhere close." She swiveled back to warn Nezu. "Definitely keep your distance from Rat's Run—Tora says it's overrun with Guard."

Nezu made a curt nod, his brow furrowed with the effort of controlling the water around their small craft. Usagi bit her lip as she turned to face the mainland. Keeping away from the bridge meant that they were taking a longer route back. He was going to be tired when they landed.

But the sun hadn't moved too far by the time they neared the Midagian coast, only just entering the hour of the Monkey. As the wave they were riding ebbed, the longboat slowed. Nezu steered toward a small cove that Tora pointed out, with a shallow beach that would make it easy for them to disembark. With a final grunt, Nezu made the water surge, pushing them well up onto the sand. The two seagulls circled overhead, wheeling and diving, making a show in the sky to go along with their mewling cries. Ji watched and laughed, clapping her hands.

After they hopped out onto dry land, the boat began to shrink, the head of the sea horse rearing as if it were neighing one last time before melting away. As it transformed back to its original state, Usagi looked up at the bluffs surrounding them. Plenty of footholds and potential pathways crossed the craggy rock. It would be a bit of a climb, but from here they could get to the Ring Road, which was the main thoroughfare that encircled the island, and into the wilderness beyond.

Nezu scooped the belt up and fastened it back around his waist. "Spirits, I love this thing. It almost makes up for losing the Bowl of Plenty."

Click-clack. Click-clack.

Usagi stiffened at a noise in the distance. "Oh no."

"You hear something?" asked Tora. "What is it?"

It was the telltale clatter of the special armor worn by

the Dragonlord's elite strike force. Formed from shiny dark plates of lacquered leather, it made them look like giant bugs. The clacking sound twisted Usagi's stomach into knots. "Roaches," she whispered. "Hide!"

CHAPTER 3

FIGHTING THE WIND

OVER THE CRASH OF WAVES on the shore, Usagi could hear a troop of the Dragonlord's most feared forces nearing the cove.

"Dragonstrikers are on the march," she said. Frantically Usagi secured the Pen of Truth, tucking it snugly beneath her wide cloth sash. The last thing they needed was for Strikers to see that they had one of the Treasures, let alone two. "Sounds like they'll be here any minute."

They looked around the sunwashed beach surrounded by rocky bluffs. There was nary a tree, bush, or boulder to hide them on this curved strip of sand. The only way out of the cove seemed to be by sea or climbing up the steep bluffs.

"We're dead fish standing in this spot. We need to get out of view at least," Tora said, and headed to the bluffs with Ji in tow. Usagi and Nezu hurried after them, and they pressed themselves against the rock face.

Nezu gave a wry chuckle. "This isn't much of a hiding place, Tiger Girl."

"I know," snapped Tora. "But I don't have any better ideas. Do you?"

Usagi gazed up at the cliff edge. "They might miss us if they don't look down." She stole a glance at Nezu. His tanned face was gray with fatigue. Steering the boat through the waves had been a tremendous effort. "Water Rat, are you okay?"

He flashed a weak smile. "As long as the Strikers march on by, I'll be just fine."

Tora groaned. "Too late. The roaches are here—and they're staring right at us."

Dragonstrikers had appeared on the bluffs. Nearly a dozen stood at attention, clad in elaborate suits of scaly black armor. Their horned helmets gleamed in the afternoon sun. Usagi tried to see if a familiar figure was among them, but it was hard to tell—especially with their helmets pulled low over their foreheads.

"You were right about the unusual seagull activity, Striker Teo." Usagi heard the one with the largest set of horns grunt in approval as he pointed to Ji's two seagulls flying in wild patterns above the cove. *"Well spotted. Go down there with Striker Mayan and interrogate those porters. Find out if they're connected to*

the bandits with powers that we're looking for."

"I can hear the commander," she reported. "It's definitely not Tupa."

Tupa—the former Ram Heir—was an imposing young man Usagi had once regarded as a big brother. He had betrayed them and become the head of the Dragonstrikers, and he was the Dragonlord's chief aide.

"Thank the gods for small favors," said Tora. "Tupa would recognize us immediately. What are they saying up there?"

Two Strikers saluted and began making their way down the bluffs. Usagi tightened her grip on her walking stick. "They saw Ji's birds and came to investigate. They're looking for bandits with powers—but for now they think we're porters. Their commander is sending those two roaches down to check us out."

Nezu stepped forward. "Good," he said. "We can talk ourselves out of this." He waved. "Ah, hello!" he called. "Can you tell us which way is the Ring Road? We've taken a bit of a wrong turn!"

"He's lying," Usagi heard one roach say to the other. *"See the marks on the beach? They came by some sort of boat."*

"Yes, but where is it?"

Usagi poked Nezu. "They see our tracks coming from the water—they already know you're lying."

"Spitting spirits." Nezu swore softly. He put a hand on the top of his walking stick, ready to draw out the blade hidden within. "We may have to go back the way we came."

"How?" asked Tora tersely. "You're not suggesting that we use the Belt of Passage in front of them?"

Nezu looked back at her, his expression grim. "We might not have a choice."

Feeling small fingers clutch at her arm, Usagi glanced down to see Ji trembling, her troubled gaze on the wheeling seagulls. She grabbed the little girl's hand and squeezed. "It's not your fault. Just stay close, okay?" They edged toward the sandy beach, taking slow steps back.

The Strikers drew closer, firecannon in hand. "Halt!" ordered one. "Don't move. Show us your travel papers."

With a shrug, Nezu handed over a set of forged papers. "Is there a problem?"

Usagi and Tora exchanged glances. How were they going to get out of this? Usagi couldn't see how they could leave the cove without getting into some sort of fight.

Looking over the documents, the Strikers frowned. "Wait here," said one, and climbed back up to his commander. The other roach, a young woman, stared at them from under the brim of her helmet, with hazel eyes that looked almost green. Usagi was reminded of the Tigress. Her teacher. *May her spirit rest.* Was this Striker one of those with zodiac powers? She prayed to the gods that they wouldn't find out. Nezu kept up a steady commentary with the remaining Striker, sounding friendly and unconcerned.

"Everyone said we just had to follow the Ring Road to get to Feather Island, so we didn't expect to get lost! A map would have helped, but our masters never gave us one, since the only port for ages and ages was Port Wingbow. By the gods, it was never easy reaching the Bantam Islands—I should have asked for a map. Oh, they're going to be so angry we're late . . ."

As he prattled on, he gestured behind him, signaling to Usagi and the others to move back. Slowly, they shuffled a few steps. The Striker narrowed her eyes and raised her firecannon. "We said halt. Don't go any farther."

"Sorry," said Nezu. "We're just trying to keep away from the bluffs. So many of you standing up there—it's dangerous! What if someone slipped and fell? What if a rock was kicked loose? Someone could get hurt . . ."

"Ow!" exclaimed Tora. She crouched and grabbed her foot. "I stepped on something! I think I cut myself!"

Nezu broke off his stream of chatter. "Spirits save us! Are you okay?" He huddled with Usagi and Ji around Tora.

"I see blood!" Tora wailed. With a glint of her snaggleteeth, she whispered, "Get ready to run for the water. Nezu, can you lure the Striker over here?"

He smoothed his whiskers and gave a tiny nod. Then he turned and addressed the Striker. "Excuse me, you wouldn't happen to have any bandages on you? As a warrior I expect you might know something about injuries. Could you take a look at my friend's foot?" Tora began to keen.

The roach scowled. Lowering her firearm, she walked up and peered at Tora's foot. "What's the problem?"

Tora threw a handful of sand in the Striker's face and kicked the muzzle of the firecannon away. An errant shot blasted into the air. Tora leaped at the Striker and wrenched the weapon from her hands. "Now!" she shouted.

They whirled and ran as the Striker clawed at her eyes and shrieked.

A shout went up. Usagi glanced back to see the rest of the Strikers launching themselves straight off the bluffs. They landed easily, as if the jump from the heights was nothing, and barreled after them.

Boils and blisters. "Those Strikers all have zodiac powers!" Usagi cried. "Watch out!"

They dashed for the sea, racing across the sand. Nezu fumbled for the Belt of Passage and was nearly to the surf when a gust of wind walloped them like an enormous invisible fist, knocking them all to the ground.

Scrambling back up, they made again for the water—and another blast of air hit them. Usagi screamed as it lifted them off their feet and tossed them farther from the waves. Landing with a violent thud in the sand, she groaned and looked behind them. The Striker commander stood on the bluffs alone, holding something in his hand. He raised it above his head.

"What is that?" Usagi cried.

"It's a fan," said Tora. "A folding fan of wood and metal." Her eyes narrowed. "It has twelve spokes and there's a swirling gold circle painted on it."

"That's no ordinary fan," said Nezu, looking stricken.

Usagi's heart sank. "It's not . . ."

Nezu nodded. "They've got the Winds of Infinity."

"No!" gasped Tora. "They found another one of the Treasures?"

The commander flicked the fan, and a whirling wind drew a cloud of sand into the sky. It bore down on them like a storm and whipped into their faces, the sand stinging like a swarm of bees. As the others threw their arms up and hunched over, Usagi yanked her headwrap off and tied it around her nose and mouth. She helped Ji do the same with her kerchief and pulled at Tora and Nezu. "Get to the water," she wheezed, tears streaming from her eyes. She could barely see outside the sandstorm, but shadowy figures were approaching—the Strikers! Their footsteps crunched on the beach, closer and closer.

Nezu straightened. "Of course! The water!" He raised his arms and shook his hands as if he were trying to dry them off. Sheets of sea spray blasted from the ocean and collided with the cloud of sand. It washed out of the sky and rained down in wet glops that coated everything it touched.

"Son of a spirit—that youngling's got powers!"

"*Get him—get all of them! Take them, alive! I want them for interrogation and inspection.*"

"*Yes, sir!*"

Gasping for air, Usagi pulled down her makeshift mask. "They definitely know you have powers now."

"They were going to find out anyway." Nezu flashed a smile and then flicked his fingers. Pellets of water shot from the ocean and exploded in the Strikers' faces. As they jerked back, spluttering and blinded, Usagi and the others turned for the sea.

With a wave of his arm, the Striker commander sent another gust of wind through the cove. They staggered, and Ji fell facedown in the sand. Usagi and Tora ran to pull her up.

Nezu gathered a large, shimmering ball of sea water and threw it at the commander. The Striker commander swept it away with the fan, and the water splashed harmlessly against the rocky bluffs.

A firecannon went off, aimed by a Striker down on one knee. A fly-net came sailing through the air, opening wide like a hungry jellyfish. Upon landing on them, it became sticky, plastering itself to their heads and shoulders. Ji screamed and began to thrash about.

"Don't panic—hold still!" ordered Nezu, reaching for his knife.

With a roar, Tora ripped at the fly-net, her fangs out and

her nails hardened into curved claws. By the time the Strikers ran up, the fly-net had been reduced to gummy shreds. Tora launched herself at a Striker, biting and scratching at any part that wasn't protected by armor. But the Striker's neck seemed to grow over with shiny scales, like his *skin* was his armor. He grabbed for Tora, who leaped off with a curse. "Boils, a snake talent!"

The other Striker raised a hand, which glowed with flame. Her long braid hung over one shoulder. Usagi started, thinking for a moment that it was Uma. But though the Striker's helmet was pulled low over her forehead, the young woman was taller and clearly at least twenty, twice the age of her sister. Usagi shook herself. Uma was too young to be out with the Dragonlord's troops—she was still a cadet.

The Striker threw a ball of fire at them. Ji jumped up and caught it. Clumsily, she tried to throw it back, but it hit the wet sand and rolled a few times before disappearing with a sizzle.

"Leave them to me!" Nezu sprayed the Dragonstrikers with another round of water pellets, driving them back. A new blast of wind swept through the cove, but they leaned into it and managed to stay standing. "Spitting spirits—I don't know how long I can hold them off when they've got the Winds of Infinity."

A wild thought struck Usagi. What if they could get the fan away from the Strikers? What if they could bring home *two* new Treasures instead of one? She looked at the commander, surveying the scene from up high, the Treasure in his hand. Usagi clutched her walking stick.

"I'm going after it," she said. "Stay here and keep the Strikers busy."

"No, wait, not by yourself—" Nezu broke off as he deflected another ball of flame. "Usagi, stop!"

"I know what I'm doing!" Without a look back, Usagi ran and vaulted for the bluffs, soaring through the air and landing neatly at the top. She faced the Striker commander, whose eyes were wide with surprise. He was an older man whose gray-flecked beard was worn in the style of the Wayani invaders. He didn't look Midagian, so there was little chance he possessed zodiac powers. But he did have the fan. He stepped back and raised it, preparing to call forth another gust of wind. Usagi sprang at him, swinging her stick straight at his head.

He snapped the fan shut and used it to block the blow. The fan's outer ribs were made of enameled iron and deflected her stick with a sharp crack. Usagi shook it off and went on the attack, trying to get him to drop the fan. But her strikes glanced off his gauntlets and did little more than rattle his armor. He returned her blows, wielding the closed fan like a club.

"Not bad, youngling," he grunted. "You'd do well to join the Dragonstrikers with those powers. Surrender, and I'll put in a good word with the captain."

Tupa. The mention of the Striker captain made Usagi grit her teeth. "That won't be necessary. He already knows me well." She dodged a clout to her head, then charged, swiping her stick at the roach with each step, spinning and twisting to keep him off balance. At the point of her sword, the commander might give up the fan. But each time she paused to draw out the blade hidden within her stick, the roach attacked, frustrating her attempts. At least she was preventing him from using the fan against Nezu and the others.

She glanced down into the cove and saw them struggling to hold off the roaches, who were responding to Nezu and Tora with equal feats of strength and speed, and knocking Ji's birds away as the seagulls dove at their heads. Usagi heard the folded fan whistling through the air as the commander took another swing. She ducked a little too late, the edge of the fan catching her chin. Stumbling, she took a hard step to catch herself.

Then came a new sound. Over the rattle of Striker armor, the shouts of Nezu and the others down on the sand fighting off the roaches, the shushing of ocean waves and the screams of Ji's seagulls, Usagi heard a tiny clatter at her feet. With horror, she saw that the Pen of Truth had fallen out of her belt. It was rolling away. All thoughts of getting the other Treasure vanished, and she scrambled after the pen.

The commander snapped the fan open. "Drop something

important?" With a sneer, he sent out a puff of wind and the pen skittered along the ground.

"No!" Usagi ran and dove for the pen as it trundled to the edge of the bluffs. A giant gust of wind slammed into her, knocking the air from her lungs and sending her and the pen flying. Usagi tumbled through the air, head over heels, out of control, buffeted like a falling leaf. As the wind died down, she hurtled toward the ground and barely managed to right herself before crashing into the sand.

"Usagi!" The others came running to haul her up, pursued by the Strikers. She looked around frantically. Where was the Pen of Truth? Glancing back, her heart sank. The commander stood atop the rocky bluffs and was examining the pen in his hand.

"The . . . the roach got the pen," Usagi gasped. "I have to go get it."

Tora turned and raised a firecannon she'd taken from a fallen Striker. "There isn't time!" she shouted, squinting at the approaching roaches.

"Just give me a minute—"

Tora fired, and an explosion of sand flew up at a Striker's feet. Her amber eyes were fierce. "If we don't get off this beach, we'll be captured."

"I'll have to bring the water to us," said Nezu grimly. Jaw clenched, he thrust his arms toward the ocean. The surface of the gray-green water began to bulge, becoming a small bump on the horizon that rapidly gathered and grew. He squeezed his eyes shut in concentration, and a bead of sweat rolled down Nezu's temple as the hillock of water swelled out of the sea, rising higher and higher until it was a great cresting mountain that blocked out the afternoon sun.

With a growl, the Rat Heir yanked at the enormous wave. A snowy cap of foam appeared and began to tip, curling toward the shore. It quickly collapsed into a churning white wall of water nearly as high as the bluffs. Usagi could hear cries of astonishment by the Dragonstrikers, but as the giant wave gained speed, the roar of the rushing water drowned out all else. The cove was thrown into shadow as the towering wave crashed onto the sand.

The water raced onto the beach, knocking Strikers down and swamping everything in sight with a blanket of foam. Icy cold waves rose to Usagi's neck, squeezing the breath out of her as they lifted her off her feet. With astonishing speed, the swirling tide swept her farther into the cove. Ji and Tora shrieked and spluttered, while Nezu unleashed the Belt of Passage. As it grew, he scrambled onto the boat and reached for Ji and Tora, hauling them on board.

There was a shift as the waves began to recede toward the sea. Usagi felt the pull as the ocean sucked the water back out of the cove, carrying the boat along with it. She paddled hard, desperate to get onto the boat, but the initial wave had pushed her far from the others. The water rushed out faster than she could swim, and within seconds she was flat on her belly, scrabbling in a rapidly growing hollow of wet sand. The boat bobbed away on the outgoing waves, edging out to sea. Usagi staggered to her feet.

She heard the Striker commander shouting. "That boat is one of the Dragonlord's Treasures! Don't let them get away!"

Usagi couldn't let herself be stranded. She had to follow. With one last despairing look back at the roach on the bluffs, she leaped. But her heart was heavy and her mind fixed on what was being left behind, and she missed the boat entirely. She splashed into the sea, sinking into the murky green water. A part of her wanted to keep sinking, down into the dark depths. After all they'd gone through to find it, the Pen of Truth had been theirs. Now she'd lost it.

Clean the Pen of Truth as you would any ordinary brush pen:

Rinse bristles gently in cool water until the water runs clear. It may take longer than a regular pen due to its size, but *do not let ink remain in the brush hairs.* It may contaminate what is written the next time it is used, layering one truth onto another, obscuring all understanding.

Shake off excess water and shape the bristles into a point.

Hang the pen brush-side down on a stand to dry, or place the handle in a brush cup, bristles pointing heavenward.

One note of precaution: When doing test strokes, even when the bristles are wet with nothing but water, be prepared for the possibility of writing hard truths about yourself that you might not want others to see. Keep a rubbish bin handy, or use the nearest lantern or candle to burn the test paper.

—Care and Maintenance, from *Warrior's Guide to the Treasures of the Twelve*

CHAPTER 4

YOUNGLINGS OF
THE LAKE

"USAGI? USAGI!"

Wearily, she turned and gave Tora a baleful stare. "What?"

"You need to dry off. Please? It'll make you feel better." Tora's fangs had disappeared, but her amber eyes were troubled. They had been struggling through thick brush and steep terrain for the better part of an hour, and Usagi's clothes were still soaking wet.

She shrank away, hunching her shoulders. Despite the miserable chill, her cheeks burned with shame. "Leave me alone." Unless there was a way to get back the Pen of Truth right at that moment, she didn't want to feel better.

"Blasted blisters, do you want to get sick? Just let Nezu get the water out of your clothes. It's cold and the sun's going down. Your lips are starting to look like the Blue Dragon's."

Ordinarily, Tora's use of the Dragonlord's forbidden nickname would have made Usagi smile, but with their defeat fresh in her mind, all she could do at the moment was shiver. If the Dragonlord got ahold of all the Treasures before the Heirs did, there would be no hope for Midaga, for Usagi's sister, for humankind.

"I don't care." Usagi forged ahead and whacked morosely at wayward bushes and scrub with her blade. Nezu's admonishment after he'd dragged her onto the boat still burned in the pit of her stomach.

"What'd I tell you?" he'd scolded. "You shouldn't have tried to go after the fan on your own."

"I was trying to help," Usagi had protested, but Nezu's and Tora's disappointed faces were too hard to argue with. Their mission had been completely ruined. They'd set off to recover the Pen of Truth, they'd managed to get it—and then Usagi had lost it.

She kept going over the fight in the cove. If Usagi had only tried to get Nezu and the Belt of Passage to the water, maybe they'd still have the pen and could stalk the fan, awaiting the right moment for a raid. But if she hadn't distracted the commander, would they even have had a chance against a dozen Dragonstrikers with zodiac powers *and* the Winds of Infinity?

"Okay, stop," commanded Nezu. "Enough with the

moping. This is ridiculous." He caught up to Usagi in a few long strides, and before she had a chance to object, he waved his hands, pulling the seawater from her clothes and hair in a fine spray that flew over his shoulder and splattered a nearby tree. Usagi was left coated in a thin layer of sparkling salt, as if it had been snowing. The Rat Heir brushed the salt off her sleeves and looked her in the eye. "I know you feel bad about what happened, but there's nothing to be done about it now. We have other things to worry about." He nodded behind her. Ji had plopped on the ground, stroking one of her seagulls as it waddled around her, hardly noticing as the other nibbled at her hair. The youngling was exhausted, and they'd barely started on their journey.

"You're right. I'm sorry." With a frown, Usagi shook off the rest of the salt. Since Ji was so new to her abilities, they couldn't use their powers to traverse by spirit speed. They had to journey through the kingdom on foot like regular folk, one small step at a time, and that would be challenging even for adults. Just trying to get to the Ring Road was taking longer than expected. The little girl was nowhere ready to ascend to the shrine on Mount Jade, but they could take her to an old friend at Sun Moon Lake, where he was looking after some other younglings with powers. It wasn't as hard as climbing to the shrine, but it still wasn't going to be an easy trip.

As they resumed their trek, Usagi thought about the last

time she had gotten into trouble over one of the Treasures, and felt as shriveled and salt-bitten as if she were still soaked in seawater. The Coppice Comb, which could turn into a copse of trees; the Bowl of Plenty, which would fill to the brim with whatever you put in it; the Mirror of Elsewhere, which showed you distant people and places; and the Apothecary, a pillbox holding the cures to every ailment—all had fallen to the Dragonlord, thanks to a trap set by their former friend, Tupa. While on a mission to spy in the capital, he had secretly joined the Blue Dragon's cause, renouncing his position as Heir to the Ram Warrior, and becoming head Dragonstriker instead. He'd only returned to the Shrine of the Twelve to lure its priestess—the Tigress—away. A retired Warrior named Horangi, the Tigress had been the last living Warrior of the Zodiac. Usagi had been so gullible then, helping Tupa spirit four recovered Treasures from the shrine. She'd managed to take back two of them—the Apothecary and the Mirror of Elsewhere—but had had to fight her sister to get them. Now, losing the Pen of Truth and failing to get the Winds of Infinity meant the Heirs only had four Treasures, and the Dragonlord had just as many—maybe even more. What were they going to do?

If only the Tigress were still with them. Usagi remembered having to confess to her teacher how she'd unwittingly helped the Dragonlord. The old warrior's croak echoed in her memory. *What is fated to be yours will always return to you.*

The Treasures belong to the Twelve. It just may take longer than we thought to see their return."

How she missed the Tigress's steady gaze and calm presence. Whether her green eyes glowed with approval or disapproval, they were filled with wisdom, for she had seen much in her years as the 42nd Tiger Warrior, and later as the guardian priestess of the sacred shrine on Mount Jade.

Usagi sighed. She still had so much to learn. But Nezu was right: they had a job to do, and moping over mistakes wouldn't help. She owed it to the memory of the Tigress, may her spirit rest, to keep on. She couldn't let her teacher's death be in vain. Even if Usagi were as old as the Tigress by the time the Treasures were safely back in their rightful place at the Shrine of the Twelve, she would not stop trying.

Around the hour of the Dog, well after the sun had gone down, they finally reached the Ring Road. The moon hovered over the eastern horizon like a round paper lantern, casting a silver glow over the wide thoroughfare that connected all the kingdom's villages and towns to the capital of Dragon City. On this stretch at night, far from any major settlements, there were few travelers. They scurried across the empty road into the safety of the wilderness.

Finding shelter in a little wood, they got to work setting up camp for the night. Usagi gathered kindling and dry branches. She began digging a firepit while Nezu examined their meager rations.

"If only we still had the Bowl of Plenty," he remarked, counting out some dried rice cakes. "We'll have to go about getting more food the old-fashioned way."

Bowing her head, Usagi dug harder at the dirt. Tora gave her shoulder a little squeeze. "I'll take care of it. After a whole week in Port Wingbow, I'm a little sick of fish." She went off to hunt, carrying a slingshot and a snare, undaunted by the dark. It wasn't long before she came back triumphantly with a few flying squirrels.

"These will make a fine stew!" said Nezu happily. He pulled a metal pot from his pack and poured in some water from the drinking gourd he wore at his hip. With his water gifts, he'd contained a wisp of cloud from Mount Jade inside the battered flask, and now it conveniently never ran dry. "Where'd my firestarter go?" He rummaged through his pack.

Ji stopped him with a snap of her fingers. She held up a bright orange flame that lit the darkness. "May I?" she asked shyly.

"I was looking in the wrong place!" Nezu smacked his forehead. "My firestarter is right here!"

The little girl giggled. Reaching toward the wood in the firepit, she sparked a merrily crackling fire. They huddled around as the chill of night settled in, and the pot began to bubble. A delicious smell filled the air, and their stomachs all growled in a loud chorus. To thicken and season the broth in the pot, Nezu stirred in the rice cakes and spices, and added generous pinches of sea salt. "I saved some salt from your clothes," he told Usagi with a laugh.

At last Nezu distributed feedsticks. They dipped them into the savory stew for pieces of meat and pillows of rice cake, eating in contented silence. Ji offered bits of her food to her seagulls, feeding them like they were mere chicks.

Full and drowsy, they relaxed around the fire, staring into the flames. Ji's seagulls settled by her side, preening their feathers. She pointed at Nezu's belt. "These things you call the Treasures—how did they come to be?"

Nezu grinned and leaned forward. "It's a tale that's been passed from Warrior to Heir for centuries." He cleared his throat and began to sing, his once-squeaky voice now a steady tenor.

> *"Long, long ago when the world was quite young*
> *And the gods walked among man and beast*
> *The Warriors did gather twelve objects far-flung*
> *To protect both the strong and the least."*

As Ji listened with wide eyes, Nezu sang of what led the Treasures to be made.

"Strangers arrived on our shores in a quest
For great riches and youth eternal
Spurning our efforts to treat them as guests
They told us that we were infernal."

He chanted about how the Twelve had united the Midagians to expel the explorers from across the sea, and how the kingdom's finest artisans created their best work.

"The treasures were brought from all over the land
As off'rings to sacred Mount Jade
Great power was lent by the goddess's hand
A shield of concealment was made."

Raising his voice, Nezu belted out the new powers possessed by each object, and how together, they were strong enough to protect the entire island.

"Midaga was safe from being overrun
Outside trouble would thereby cease
As long as the Treasures and Warriors were one
The kingdom could flourish in peace."

The last notes faded into the night air. "That's where the song ends," said Nezu. "But not the story." He explained that the Treasures had been scattered about the kingdom when the Shield of Concealment and the Warriors of the Zodiac were felled by one of their own.

"Thanks to the Dragonlord, all of Midaga is exposed to the outside world again, and unable to keep outsiders away," Tora added.

Nezu rubbed at one of the fittings on his belt. "We have to find every item before the Dragonlord and his forces do. For whoever controls the Treasures of the Twelve controls the power of the mountain and the future of the kingdom."

Feeling her cheeks warm, Usagi stared into the flames. She prayed to the gods that she wouldn't make any more mistakes—and the Dragonlord wouldn't get any more of the Treasures.

They moved farther inland, heading for the island's interior. Ji's seagulls became increasingly restless, taking off and flying off for longer and longer periods before returning.

"Will Neko and Nabi stay with you if they're not by the sea?" Tora asked, eyeing the gulls. They shifted from foot to foot, one on each of Ji's shoulders, occasionally stretching a wing.

"I don't know," said Ji, and burst into tears. "I've never been far from the sea before." Her ears turned red and then erupted into flame, and both birds leaped off her shoulders, screeching. That was something Usagi had never seen, not even in her sister. It was as if, once Ji no longer had to hide her zodiac powers, her talents and gifts were starting to emerge more fully. It took some distraction, including Nezu performing a juggling routine with three balls of water poured from his gourd, for Ji to calm down and the flames to subside.

"We're headed to a great big lake," Usagi soothed. "I'll bet they'll like it there."

Upon getting their feathers singed a couple of times, the seagulls stopped perching on Ji's shoulders, which seemed to upset her even more. By the time they were in the highlands leading to the lake, the seagulls had taken off and failed to return. The little girl was crushed, and the tips of her ears reddened till they were perpetually smoking. Usagi did her best to divert her with stories about the Twelve and their adventures.

At last, they reached the cloud forests around Sun Moon Lake, after more than a week of hard travel. It would have taken just a couple of days had they been able to use spirit speed. Usagi had almost forgotten what it was like to go without it. Propelling themselves over long distances quickly, whether by jumping through treetops, running at high speeds, or leaping enormous strides, was one of the great advantages—and joys—of having zodiac powers.

The mists that hung about the cloud forest thickened along with the foliage, and the sounds of chattering monkeys, booming frogs, and twittering birds filled Usagi's ears.

More than a year and a half had passed since she'd last been here—in fact, at the time she'd hardly believed that Warrior Heirs still existed, nor understood that they were fighting for their survival. So much had changed.

They approached the great lake that sat in the crater of a former volcano, the morning sun creeping higher in the sky. Usagi listened carefully for any trace of the old friend she'd encountered on her first journey to Mount Jade. Before long she was rewarded with the sound of several animals snuffing and padding toward them. She smiled. "Yunja's dogs have found us."

Three wild mountain dogs emerged from the underbrush, their pointed ears erect and their sickle-shaped tails wagging. They ran up to Usagi and Nezu and licked their hands, then sniffed at Tora and Ji. The dogs cocked their heads.

"I'm sorry Inu's not here to speak dog with you," the Rat Heir laughed, patting the brindled back of one and scratching the base of its tail. "But first let me introduce our new friends. This is Tora, who's born in the year of the Wood Tiger, and a candidate for Tiger Heir. We found her at the Dragonlord's compound. She's with us now." Tora's eyes were wary as she held out a hand for the dogs to sniff. Nezu put an arm around Ji and knelt as the three dogs circled round and inspected her. "And this is Ji—she's going to be staying with you for a while." One of the dogs made a huffing noise and trotted into the cloud forest, followed by its companions. Nezu got to his feet and shrugged. "I have no idea if they understood me. Inu was here last time to talk with them."

Tora looked around the dense growth of the cloud forest and flinched as a drop of moisture splatted on her nose. She wiped it with her sleeve. "When you found younglings who weren't ready for Mount Jade, what made you decide to bring them here?"

"It's isolated, far from the Ring Road, and hard to get to," said Nezu. "It's the perfect place for a youngling with zodiac powers to hide."

"More importantly, they're under the care of someone who can help teach them a little about their talents and gifts," Usagi said. "Wait till you meet Yunja. He's born in the year of the Wood Dog, and was the first one to teach me how to fight—using a stick."

Tora gave her wooden staff a twirl. "The invaders slaughtered all men and women with any hint of animal talents or elemental gifts. It's a wonder that old man managed to survive." Her face clouded over. Absently she rubbed at the scars slashing across her forearm. Usagi knew she was thinking of her father and older brothers. Her own parents had been caught in the brutal purge. They had *not* survived.

"Becoming a hermit is what saved him," Usagi replied.

She heard an indignant snort in the trees. "Good morning, Yunja!" she called.

A shaggy man dressed in barkcloth and moss shambled onto the path before them, a stout leafy branch slung over his shoulder like a club. He shook it at Tora. "Old? I'll have you know, in some parts of the world, being in your fifties is considered young."

Tora put her hands on her hips. "Where, in some magical land where everyone lives to be a thousand? You've lived for more than half a century!"

"Well," growled Yunja, "when you put it that way…better old than dead." He made a rusty coughing noise that Usagi recognized as his laugh. His eyes twinkled at her. "Rabbit Girl, your friend is a fierce one, I can tell!"

Usagi threw herself at him and gave him a big squeeze. "This is Tora—I've told you about her!"

"I gathered this was your Tiger friend," he chuckled. "One of the new Warrior Heir candidates, eh? No doubt she'll be promoted from Heirling to full Heir soon enough."

Nezu grinned at Tora. "Heirling—I like that. That's what I'm going to be calling you and the other candidates from now on." Rolling her eyes, Tora shrugged, but the glint of her snaggleteeth betrayed her.

The hermit held Usagi at arm's length. "The boys told me you're Rabbit Heir now." He gave her a wide, gap-toothed smile. "That's just as it should be."

Beaming, Usagi looked at her old friend. His hair was as long and tangled as ever, still littered with leaves that flecked his equally long and tangled beard. But though he still blended into the cloud forest, his face and hands were no longer smeared with mud, and he seemed less gaunt and haunted than he had the first time they'd stumbled across him. He greeted Nezu with a hug, pounding him on the back, and then turned to Tora and Ji.

"So, who's coming to stay this time?" Yunja's voice boomed through the trees. He looked at Ji, who was shrinking back behind Tora, and instantly softened. "No need to make yourself small, youngling. Here you can be as big and as loud as you want! Come meet the others and you'll see."

The hermit led them through the cloud forest, giving them updates on the progress of his charges and their zodiac powers. "Biri's getting quite strong—I swear she set off a small earthquake the other day. And the twins—I think they're almost more Dog than my dogs!"

Nezu told the hermit about their latest mission, and how Ji had helped them escape the Guard with her rooster talents. "But we had a close call with some Dragonstrikers. They were on the hunt for bandits with powers. You haven't been taking the younglings onto the Ring Road for some mischief, have you?"

Coming to an abrupt halt, Yunja shook a long finger at the Rat Heir. "You should know me better than that! I'm insulted."

"Right, sorry," laughed Nezu. "You'd rather eat your own slippers than leave Sun Moon Lake. But hearing about these bandits worries me. It means younglings with zodiac powers are attacking and robbing others. Which will only make Midagians without powers fear and mistrust anyone with gifts and talents."

The hermit grunted. "The Blue Dragon makes no distinction between those with powers and those without. Whoever isn't with him is his enemy, and everyone else is a tool for his own gain." He smacked his club against his palm, thinking. "There must be a way for those without powers to see that we're nothing to be afraid of."

"It would certainly help if all Midagians joined in fighting him instead of turning against each other," said Nezu.

They reached the lake, where an encampment of snug huts had been set up, built of wood and vines. Around a central firepit, half a dozen younglings were laughing and tussling, while Yunja's dogs romped at their feet.

"Oi," called the hermit. "Come meet our new friend!"

The younglings stopped and stared. Then the oldest, a girl of about nine, caught up the hands of two small boys, and they raced over. The younglings were dressed in barkcloth and jackets of moss, blending into their surroundings like Yunja, and wore sturdy sandals of woven reeds. Usagi smiled in recognition. Yunja had made a similar pair for her that she'd worn for months on end. She'd been so sad to outgrow them. The younglings bobbed their heads in greeting, and the littlest boy lit up at the sight of them. "Nezu's here!"

"Daga!" Nezu crouched and embraced him, then lifted him up and tossed him in the air. "How's my fellow Rat?" The little boy squealed with delight. Daga was barely four when the Warrior Heirs found him, caged by his stepfather after his powers had been discovered. He had nearly gnawed his way through the bars with no apparent harm to his teeth, much to the stepfather's horror, and was about to be handed over to the local Guard, who would have had him carted off by Dragonstrikers.

Usagi had heard all about it from Nezu and Inu, the Dog Heir, when they'd returned from a mission. Nezu had been shaken. "We couldn't just leave him—but we couldn't bring him to the shrine either! Thank the gods Yunja was happy to look after him."

On a different mission led by Saru the Monkey Heir, she and Inu had come across a young girl born in the year of the Ram, living on the outskirts of a village with her small brother, born of the Water Boar. The two of them were fending for themselves—much like Usagi had done with her sister and Tora. The Warrior Heirs had noticed them using their powers and quickly convinced them they would be better off under Yunja's care.

Over time, the Heirs had found an eight-year-old girl with monkey talents similar to Saru's and a pair of identical twin boys born in the year of the Dog. All of them were just starting to display their powers but hadn't yet been caught by the Blue Dragon's Strikers, so the Heirs spirited them away to the safest place they could think of outside of Mount Jade.

Now the younglings stared at them with eager eyes. Usagi nudged Ji forward and introduced her. "Ji can do amazing things with her voice—and she can create fire!"

"Ooh!"

"Can she show us right now?"

"Yes, please show us!"

Ji's face reddened, and for a moment Usagi feared she would burst into tears and her ears would flare again, but then she hesitantly snapped her fingers and sparked a small flame between her thumb and forefinger. The other younglings shrieked with excitement and applauded, the two littlest boys jumping up and down.

"How useful is that?" Yunja chortled. "We're growing a little army of talents here!"

The oldest ones, both girls, sidled up to Ji. Biri, born in the year of the Ram, stared at the flame in Ji's hand. "I'm so glad they brought you. No one here has a fire gift."

"Plus it will be nice to have another girl around," added Hanuma, born in the year of the Monkey. A small monkey scampered out of the underbrush and leaped into Hanuma's arms. It chattered at the visitors, its curious eyes bright in a pale face framed by golden fur.

Ji smiled shyly. "I wish my birds were with me. They're girls too."

"We've got plenty of birds around here," Yunja interjected. "I bet you'll be making friends with them in no time."

Usagi's ears pricked at a sound in the distance. It was a cry she hadn't heard in a few days.

Kaa-oh . . .

Ka-ohh ka-ohh ka-ohh ka-ohh . . .

"I hear seagulls!" she shouted.

Ji's eyes brightened. "You do?" She scanned the clouds eagerly. They parted to reveal a patch of blue sky, and two figures in flight, black and white feathers lit by the sun. They called out, their sharp cry growing louder as they approached. "Neko and Nabi!" Ji ran to the lakeshore. "You're back!" As she hopped and waved her arms, they circled about her until one landed on her shoulder and the other on her head, grandly flapping its wings. She turned to Usagi and the others, her face aglow. "They came back!"

One of Yunja's dogs got up, barking, but the old hermit hushed it and then rumbled and grunted in his own throat until the dog whined and sat back down. "When Rooster Girl said birds, I was thinking along the lines of chickens. The gods take my pants, I don't think I've ever seen seagulls so far inland before." He chuckled. "Well, the lake has fish enough."

They watched the gulls nuzzle Ji's ears, and she giggled. Usagi had never seen the little girl look so happy. She looked over at Nezu and Tora, who were smiling. "I think it's safe to say she's going to be okay here."

Nezu nodded. "It's time we get back to Mount Jade."

CHAPTER 5

THE SHRINE OF THE TWELVE

"TWELVE HUNDRED TEN, TWELVE HUNDRED eleven, twelve hundred twelve!" Tora panted, reaching the top of the Steps of Patience where Nezu waited. She glanced back at Usagi. "Good thing we didn't try to bring Ji up here."

Staggering up the last few steps, Usagi groaned. "I've climbed this staircase four times now, and it never gets any easier."

"It's not supposed to." Nezu flashed a grin. "At least you're not trying to take shortcuts anymore."

Usagi laughed, remembering her very first time on Mount Jade. When she'd attempted the climb, the staircase had unceremoniously bounced her back each time she tried skipping its steps with her rabbit leap. She hadn't yet understood that the sacred mountain demanded her effort. Her honesty. Her perseverance. "I learned my lesson."

The bracing alpine air was tinged with warmth, and the snow around the shrine had recently melted away, leaving patches of damp on the ground. They made their way through the Singing Bamboo, the grove filling with melodies from the swaying stalks as they passed. Nezu hummed along happily with the bamboo's flutelike song. The light from the midday sun filtered through the towering columns, their sword-shaped leaves a luminous haze of green. The color reminded Usagi of the Tigress's eyes, and once again she felt a pang at the old warrior's absence. More than a year had passed since they'd left the shrine with the Tigress to Dragon City, only to return without her.

From the shrine's main courtyard, Usagi's rabbit ears heard voices raised in excitement.

"They're back! The mission team has returned!"

"Oh Inu—are you sure? Have you caught their scent?"

"Yes, they've just reached the Singing Bamboo. They smell of the sea still—and are in need of a bath."

"Gods be good! I can't wait to see the new Treasure!"

Usagi stopped in her tracks, her feet stuck fast at the thought of breaking the news to the others. Tora turned, knitting her brow. "What's wrong?"

"Everyone is going to be so disappointed," Usagi said.

Wearily, she leaned against one of the twelve stone animal lanterns standing tall in the middle of the grove. It happened to be the rabbit, her own insignia. Reared on its hind legs, the stone rabbit snarled. Usagi held fast to it, wishing she could absorb its fierceness. Its hollow eyes and open mouth were aglow from a flame within. She stared up at the flickering light.

Tora shook her head. "Of course they'll be disappointed, but only for a minute. Then we'll figure out together what to do next." She gave Usagi a little push. "Come on."

They'd only gone a little way when an enormous wild cat came racing through the bamboo. A cloud leopard. It leaped over Nezu, who ducked and swore. "Flying furballs!"

"Kumo!" Tora shouted. The leopard pounced and Tora went down. "Silly boy!" she cooed, the two of them wrestling and tumbling on the ground. "Did you miss me? You did, didn't you? Fluffy monster!" Kumo's deep rumbling purrs filled the grove, almost drowning out the silvery melodies of the bamboo.

Usagi couldn't help but laugh. "I can't imagine what he must have been like while we were gone." For years, Kumo had been the Tigress's constant companion. The old warrior had found the orphaned cub, and when they'd left him behind on Mount Jade for the capital, he'd been anxious and unsettled. When they'd returned without the Tigress, the big cat had been despondent, stalking about and yowling, unable to eat. Only Tora had been able to comfort him, and since then he'd been like her shadow.

"He was mostly grumpy, I'd say." They turned to see Inu, the Dog Heir, smiling at them. "It's been a long month."

Nezu greeted Inu by throwing an arm around his neck in a headlock. "Brother Dog!" He ruffled Inu's shaggy, dark hair till it stood in unruly spikes. "Watching over the shrine! On the alert and first on the scene!"

The Dog Heir extracted himself from Nezu's hold with a good-natured grunt. "If you're trying to take me out, your stink will do it. Gods, you need a bath!" He gave Usagi a hug. "Welcome back, Rabbit Girl."

Weakly, she returned his smile. They passed through the Singing Bamboo and entered the main courtyard of the shrine, where three figures waited. They were sitting before the enormous building that was the Great Hall, on a low wooden platform that edged the courtyard.

"There they are!" cried Saru. The Heir to the Monkey Warrior leaped up and hurried over. Strands of chestnut hair had come out of her topknot, framing her pale face. The oldest Warrior Heir at twenty, she was the closest they had to a leader now that the Tigress was gone. She swept Usagi and Tora in a warm embrace, her wiry arms wrapped tight around them. "Are you hungry? Shall we get you something to eat?"

Nezu chuckled. "Who cooked while I was away? Did you put these Heirlings to work in the kitchen?" He flashed a grin at the two candidates who'd stayed at behind at the shrine.

"Show us the new Treasure!" Goru, a giant of a boy, big and strong as the Ox that ruled his talents, rose and loomed over them. He peered eagerly at their packs. Rana, a lithe girl nearly twelve, poked her face around his bulk. Her dark braids were coiled about her head like the sign she was born under, the Snake. She wriggled with impatience.

"Yes, let's see it!" Rana cried. Along with Usagi's sister, she, Goru, and Tora had been captured by the Dragonstrikers and forced to train as cadets in the Dragonlord's academy. The three of them had managed to slip away with Usagi and the other Heirs the previous spring. Since arriving on Mount Jade, their powers had steadily strengthened. Goru had grown even taller and wider than before, and some new talents had emerged for Rana and Tora. All three were now candidates, working hard in hopes of becoming Heirs as well.

"The Treasure." Usagi swallowed hard. "We uh . . . we don't have it."

Goru's face fell. Despite being fifteen and bigger than three men put together, he looked in that moment like a tiny youngling whose favorite sweet had just been snatched away. "Oh," he said in a small voice.

At first glance, Goru looked ready for his Warrior Trials, which once had been administered by the Warriors when an Heir was ready to carry a weapon. But Goru still hadn't found a weapon that suited him as well as his fists. After all, why bother with swordwork or the fiddly parts of archery when your hand was big enough to palm a man's entire head? Tora had been chosen for the mission instead, and when he'd argued that he'd make a great porter in Port Wingbow, the Heirs had overruled him. "You'd make *too* good a porter, and they'd never let you leave," Saru had insisted. "We can't risk you getting stuck there." Goru had been disappointed, but was cheered when Usagi and the others promised that he could be the first to try out the pen when they brought it back. "So . . . you never got it?"

Shaking her head, Usagi tried to speak, but her mouth seemed to dry up.

Tora exchanged a look with Nezu. "We ran into Strikers," she said.

Rana gasped. "Was Captain Tupa—I mean, Tupa the traitor—with them?"

"No, Snake Girl. Lucky for him—he would've have had to answer to me." Nezu's usual cheerful expression was stormy. "But their commander had another one of the Treasures— the Winds of Infinity."

"The fan!" Saru's pale face grew even paler. "The Dragonstrikers have found it?"

Usagi finally found her voice. "The commander was using that fan to blow us every which way," she blurted. "So I went after it." She hung her head. "But I was carrying the pen, and it fell when I was trying to fight the commander. He took it and blew me away with the fan."

"So, the Blue Dragon's forces got to the Winds of Infinity? *And* they took the Pen of Truth?" Inu scrubbed a hand across the back of his neck, looking troubled. "Stars."

"Someone was being ambitious, trying to face down a Striker commander on her own," said Nezu, glancing sideways with a raised eyebrow. "Or maybe a little greedy for the extra Treasure."

Greedy! Usagi couldn't bear it anymore. "I was only trying to help," she insisted. "That fan could have killed us."

Shrugging, Nezu smoothed the fuzz on his upper lip. "I guess we can be glad we're in one piece."

"So what happens now?" asked Rana, her dark eyes filled with dismay.

With a sigh, Saru put a hand on Usagi's shoulder. "Let's get the mission team settled first. Go wash up for midday meal, and we'll discuss it in the Great Hall after we eat."

But hardly anyone had any appetite. The mood at the dining table was gloomy, so different from past meals when mission teams had come back triumphant. They'd celebrated then. No one was celebrating now. Usagi picked at a bowl of rice topped with pickled vegetables and a fried egg, its yolk still runny and the edges browned crisp. It was a simple dish that was one of her favorites, but she might as well have been swallowing sand. Each bite stuck in her throat.

After a subdued meal, they went to the Great Hall, a cavernous space with sparring mats and weapons against one wall, and a lacquered wooden chest housing the Treasures against the other. Above the chest hung a scroll with a poem extolling the Treasures and their powers. Staring up at the first stanza, Usagi silently read it over and over.

"Together they will help the power of the Twelve to shield
The island will be safe from harm and never have to yield
In turn the Twelve must keep them close and treat them
*   with great care*
For should the bond be broken then Midaga is laid bare."

Kumo padded in and settled on his haunches next to Tora, who rubbed the cloud leopard's ears. Goru and Rana stood with her, the three Heirlings waiting while Usagi and the other Warrior Heirs returned the Belt of Passage to the shrine. Nezu removed the belt from his waist and folded it carefully. He placed it in one of the chest's twelve drawers, whispering a prayer of thanks to the mountain goddess. He pulled out the other three drawers that held Treasures, and everyone gathered round to look.

There was the Apothecary, a cunningly carved pillbox filled with many compartments. It could conjure antidotes to all known ailments. In the next drawer, a gilded metal disk known as the Mirror of Elsewhere gleamed up at them, its polished surface able to show faraway things. The Fire Cloak shimmered in its drawer, its golden silk weave almost too delicate to imagine as a shield against fire. And then there was the Belt of Passage, which had been so vital to them in their getaway from Port Wingbow and beyond. Had Usagi not dropped it, they would have added the Pen of Truth to the chest—and if she'd only fought better, they would have had the Winds of Infinity as well. She sighed.

"We know the Strikers have the fan and the pen," said Saru. "What else does the Blue Dragon have in his collection?"

Nezu ticked them off on his fingers. "The Coppice Comb and the Bowl of Plenty, which we had to leave at the Palace of the Clouds last year."

"That's four," Tora said.

"But there's also the Jewels of Land and Sea," said Inu, his dark eyes flashing. "Two-faced Tupa brought it here to be fixed by the Tigress, at the bidding of the Blue Dragon."

Saru nodded. "Although the Tigress swallowed the jade replacement bead instead of giving it over."

"He might still find a way to repair the necklace. Even if they don't have the Land Jewel, they have the pearls that make up the rest of the Treasure, which is more than we have," said Nezu. The Rat Heir smoothed the whiskers on his upper lip, calculating. "So let's say that's half a Treasure. Including the Pen of Truth, the Blue Dragon's got his filthy hands on four and a half of the twelve Treasures."

Goru sat down heavily on the sparring mats in the Great

Hall, jolting some of the weapons hanging on the wall behind him. He stared up at the scroll. "And we have four. There's only three Treasures left to be recovered. The flute, the ring, and the hammer."

"If the Dragonlord hasn't already found them," said Usagi, despondent. "We didn't know they had the fan till they used it on us."

"Well, until we know for certain, we can't worry about that," said Nezu firmly. "As far as I'm concerned, three Treasures are still out there, and we have to get to them first."

Inu nodded, his dark eyes fierce. "And once we do, we'll find a way to get the ones in the Blue Dragon's possession, too."

The Monkey Heir slid all the drawers shut. "Then we'll need to plan our next mission quickly," she said. "There's no time to waste when the Strikers are out looking for the Treasures too. But some of us have actually been around the Treasures and seen them used. That's our advantage. We know more about these items—their history, their appearance, their powers—than they do."

"There's the flute, which belonged to the Snake Warrior," said Inu. He pulled his own flute from his belt and examined it. "What I wouldn't give to try playing it to the Dragonlord! I'd make him dance off a cliff into a nest of vipers."

Frowning, Nezu tugged at his whiskers. "If only the Snake Warrior had done that. But during the terrible final battle we'd fought at the Palace of the Clouds, he wasn't carrying the flute."

"I remember." Saru shook her head sadly. "The Snake Heir told me that they'd hidden it, but Brother Hemi was struck down before he could say where." She hesitated, then opened the drawer nearest her and removed the Mirror of Elsewhere. "Maybe this will give us some clues." The Monkey Heir gave Tora, Goru, and Rana a chance to try looking in the mirror. "Think of the flute and what you know about it."

But the Mirror of Elsewhere remained frustratingly blank for them. "Guess I wasn't paying enough attention when the Dragon Academy headmaster was going over the Treasures," Goru said ruefully.

"What *did* you Heirlings learn about them?" asked Nezu.

Rana looked down at a ball of clay in her palm—she carried it in her pocket and liked to play with it when she was thinking. She squeezed it between her fingers. "That there were twelve Lost Treasures—but Master Douzen never said they belonged to the Warriors of the Zodiac. We were taught that these powerful items had been stolen or hidden from the Dragonlord." With each squeeze of Rana's hand, the clay became a replica of a different Treasure: first a miniature fan, then a small bowl, then a little comb.

"They never belonged to the Dragonlord—they can't really be stolen from him," sniffed Usagi. She wrinkled her nose at the memory of the Academy cadets, including her sister, bowing to the wizened old Hulagan who'd been appointed headmaster. In a deal struck with both the empire of Hulagu and the neighboring empire of Waya, the Blue Dragon had brought down the Shield that protected Midaga, allowing their invading forces to overwhelm the kingdom. The Blue Dragon took the throne as his reward, paying annual tributes to the twin empires and installing their people as advisers and teachers at his Academy.

Nodding, Rana held a tiny clay mirror in her palm. "We know that now." She closed her fingers around it and opened them to reveal a miniature flute. "About the flute—they said if you played it, anyone who heard the tune would do whatever you wanted."

"And that while it looks like an ordinary bamboo flute, it does have some special markings on it," Tora added.

"At least the Academy got that right," said Nezu, sounding surprised. "Whoever hears its song falls under its spell, and can be made to dance, fall asleep, or go into a trance."

Saru handed the mirror to Usagi. "Take a look, Rabbit Girl. Maybe the flute will reveal itself to you."

Angling the bronze disk just so, Usagi gazed into its polished face. She'd only seen paintings of the flute, along with some descriptions and stories, in the scrolls kept in the shrine's library. Hopefully that would be enough to bring forth some sort of image in the mirror. She thought about the flute's lacquered body, the design of twelve zodiac animals dancing around it, and recalled that the end was painted to look like a hissing snake.

An image appeared in the mirror. She squinted. "I'm thinking about the flute, and it's showing me something moving like a slithering snake. How strange—I'd say they're hills or mountains, but they keep shifting."

"Oh!" cried Saru. She took the mirror from Usagi and gazed into it, then smiled. "Those aren't mountains, Rabbit Girl. They're sand dunes."

Nezu and Inu looked at each other with wide eyes. "The Dancing Dunes," they said in unison.

"For the Flute of Dancing Dreams! Of course!" said Usagi. "That must be where it's hidden. How very clever of the Snake Warrior!"

Then and there it was clear that the next mission would be to find and retrieve the flute. Usagi immediately wanted to go, in hopes of redeeming her terrible failures, but the others agreed that they needed the team small and more experienced. Since Saru and Inu were the oldest and had been Warrior Heirs for years, they would be the ones on the mission. Nezu and Usagi would keep the Heirlings practicing and training.

But which Treasures should be brought along to help? As the others chimed in, Usagi objected. They couldn't risk losing another one.

The Monkey Heir disagreed. "If we stick to the plan and

work together, whatever we carry will be fine. We've done it before, Rabbit Girl."

"Besides, what's the point of having these Treasures if you don't use them?" asked Rana.

Saru gave her an approving nod. "You shouldn't keep something from its true purpose because you fear losing it."

Nezu stroked his lip thoughtfully. "They're right. If we hadn't had the Belt of Passage on us, we might not have made it back here. It got us out of trouble twice."

"Maybe just bring one," suggested Tora. "The Fire Cloak might be of good help."

Goru scoffed. "The Dancing Dunes aren't made of flame—it's a bunch of blowing sand."

"True, but the cloak could protect us from that too," said the Monkey Heir. "It's light but surprisingly strong." She put the Mirror of Elsewhere back in the chest of Treasures. "It's settled, then. Inu and I will go after the flute, and we'll take the Fire Cloak with us."

Usagi hung her head. She would only wait for their return.

CHAPTER 6

A DISCOVERY

THE TARGET SWUNG BACK AND forth, waving like a disembodied hand from across the courtyard. Left, right, left, right. Inu squinted at the swaying piece of white cloth, pinned to a weighted board, a constellation of stars painted on the cloth in dark ink. Standing tall before the Great Hall, he pulled an arrow from the quiver slung across his back and nocked it to his bow. Hooking the string with his thumb, protected by the archer's ring he always wore, he drew the arrow back, then let it fly with a twang of the string.

The arrow whistled toward the target, while Inu reached for another arrow. As the first arrow sank into a star with a resounding thunk, he shot the second arrow just as the target changed direction, then another, and another.

Twang! . . . thunk. Twang! . . . thunk. Twang! . . . thunk.

"Looks like someone's ready to go after the next Treasure," said Usagi. She and Tora were perched on the wooden platform behind him, watching Inu practice while they cleaned and inspected gear for the mission. Beside them, Kumo licked his furred paws and groomed his face, pausing to gnaw at sharp claws that were as long as Usagi's fingers.

"You don't even know if he's hit every star," Goru countered. He hefted a couple of heavy straw bales overhead, working on his arm strength.

Inu rolled his eyes. "Go ahead, check."

Tora stopped counting arrowheads and glanced at the target. With a nod, she announced, "He hit them all."

"No! Impossible!" Goru dropped the bales of straw with a thump and lumbered across the courtyard to examine the board. "Flying fireballs, he did!" He plucked out the arrows and brought them back. "I can't even hit the target when it's still."

"It's not that hard," scoffed Tora. "All it takes is a good eye and steady hand."

Inu barked a laugh. "Not that hard? I'd like to see you do the same. Don't forget, I'm the one who taught you to shoot."

"Ho, that sounds like a challenge," Goru hooted.

Springing to her feet, Tora dusted off her pants. "You'll see all right, Master Archer. This student will match every shot you make."

"Challenge accepted!" hollered Goru.

A slow smile spread across Inu's face. "Let's make this interesting, Tiger Girl. Every star hit on the target is a point. Whoever gets fewer points will have to do the other's chores."

Tora's snaggleteeth gleamed. "Good. I've been sweeping out the goat pen this week."

"And I've had to clean out the outhouses," Inu laughed.

Goru rubbed his massive hands. "Are you sure you want to do this, Tora? The bow is one of Inu's favored weapons."

"And I'm going to make it one of mine," replied Tora firmly. "Want to join us? You can help Inu with my chores once I've beat you both—I've been cleaning up after the chickens too."

As Goru began to stammer, Usagi giggled. "Let's make it a team effort," she suggested. "Whichever team gets the most points can give their chores to the other team."

"That'll be fun. A team competition it is." Breezily, Inu tossed the hair out of his eyes. "I'll even give Tora first pick."

"I'm picking Goru—for your team," said Tora, her smile widening. "Sorry, Ox Boy."

"Well, that's just cruel. I'm *terrible* at archery," Goru grumbled. "I'll wind up doing everyone's chores."

Inu thumped him on the back. "Don't worry. I'll rack up enough points for the both of us." He turned to Tora. "I'm taking Usagi, then. You can have Rana and Nezu. We'll get Saru to judge."

"I think I can get us a few points as well," Usagi told Goru. But Tora was becoming an excellent archer, thanks in part to her tiger vision. Secretly, Usagi wondered if she'd be adding the goat pens and hen hutches to her chores for the week.

They called everyone from around the compound and explained the challenge. An amused Saru agreed to act as judge. "A little competition never hurt," she said. "That, and the threat of cleaning toilets."

As they debated on the number of targets, teased each other about their archery skills and compared chores, Kumo got up from the platform, tail twitching. Disturbed by all the commotion, the cloud leopard stalked off. Inu distributed bows and Saru drew up the target patterns, using a brush and ink on pieces of cloth. She pinned them on various bales of straw, as well as some target boards that waved back and forth, bobbed up and down, or spun in a circle. Pointing, Saru said, "Hitting the target mark is ten points. If you hit the cloth but not the mark, you get one point." She raised her ink brush. "I'll tally."

Goru set up the bales all around the shrine compound, wherever there was enough space to shoot. "Minimum distance for shooting is thirty paces," he informed everyone. "No getting closer than that."

"And hitting the target from a farther distance will earn you more points," added Saru. "Five points for every ten extra steps back." Tora's eyes brightened at this, while Goru looked up at the sky, muttering to himself.

Nudging him, Usagi whispered, "At least we won't get points taken away for bad shots."

To see which team would go first, Inu and Tora played earth-wood-metal. "Earth, wood, metal," they chanted, before throwing out their fists. "Wood beats earth!" cried Tora, her open hand covering Inu's closed fist. "Paper covers rock!"

Smiling, Inu twisted his thumb ring. "Good luck, Paper Tiger."

"I don't need luck, Rock Dog," said Tora loftily. Hefting her bow, she walked to the first target. It was a straw bale with a simple circle drawn on a piece of cloth. She selected an arrow from a bucket at her feet and aimed, her eyes narrowing as she gazed down her left arm. *Twang! Thunk!*

Saru went and examined the circle. "Right in the center. Ten points to Team Paper Tiger!"

As Nezu and Rana cheered and congratulated Tora, Inu took his bow and made a show of stepping farther from where she'd stood. Usagi and Goru egged him on and taunted the other team until Saru signaled for Inu to shoot. He fitted an arrow to his bow and let it fly. *Thunk!* His arrow quivered in the bale. It had split Tora's in two. "Ten points to Team Rock Dog, five extra points for shooting from ten paces farther—and a ten-point bonus for splitting an arrow!"

"Look at that," said Goru, relieved. "Maybe *I'll* be giving my chores away."

The rest of them had a turn before they moved on to the

other targets around the shrine. Though nearly everyone managed to hit the target enough to gain a stray point here and there for their teams, the match was clearly between Tora and Inu. When it came time for her to shoot again, she insisted that Inu go first. "I'd like to have a chance to score bonus points too," she said—and proceeded to jog as far away from the bale as she possibly could, nearly doubling the distance. She then hit not just Inu's but other arrows that had reached the target. Even on the moving targets, Tora held her own, matching Inu shot for shot, and quickly racked up points.

The two teams were tied, 183 to 183, when Rana stepped up for another go at a target. She was still very much a beginner and had to wear a special training glove on her right hand. The leather sleeve had just one finger covering her thumb, to help her with pulling on the bowstring. Raising the bow in her left hand, Rana drew the string back. Her left arm wobbled as she strained to keep the bow in place against the string's tug. "It's really tight!" she exclaimed.

"She looks tired," Nezu muttered to Tora.

Ignoring the fact that Rana was on the other team, Inu went into teacher mode, offering advice and encouragement. "Drop your shoulders, Snake Girl—your neck's disappeared. Focus on your form, and don't worry about the target. Correct shooting is correct hitting."

Rana nodded, then loosed her arrow with a snap of her

string. She cried out in pain and dropped her bow.

"Oh no, string slap!" Usagi grimaced. She knew the feeling. It happened whenever she gripped her bow too tightly or got tired and let her posture go. She hurried over to take a look. Sure enough, an ugly red welt bloomed on Rana's left forearm. "Shall I go get the Apothecary?"

"Let me see." Saru gently pushed Usagi aside. She examined Rana's wound, then put an arm around her shoulders. "I'll take care of this. Let's go make a poultice." The Monkey Heir looked around and shook her head. "Fun's over, everyone. Inu and I are leaving the day after tomorrow, so we all should get back to work."

As she led Rana away, Usagi felt a strange pang in her chest. Saru and Rana seemed to be growing quite close and shutting her out. Worse, since returning to the shrine, Usagi had been feeling a strained distance from the others. Everyone was so disheartened over the failed mission. They must be blaming her for the loss of two Treasures. But what could she do now? Reaching for her rabbit pendant, Usagi worried it with her fingers.

"Boils and blisters." Goru looked let down. He headed for the target bales and began to remove arrows.

"We were so close to deciding the winning team," Nezu agreed.

But Inu shrugged and tossed back his shaggy hair. He turned to Tora and bowed. "Excellent showing, Tiger Girl," he said. "Call it a draw?"

"I guess." Pursing her lips in disappointment, Tora bowed in return.

"We can still trade chores if you like," he said with a smile.

Laughing, Tora demurred. "That's all right—I'll stick with the goats. I'll have plenty of chances to clean the out-houses when you and Saru leave."

Soon the time came for Mission Flute to leave for the Dancing Dunes, down on the southern tip of Midaga. Tucked in their clothing and in their backbundles, Inu and Saru carried what had become essentials on these missions: a firestarter; a cloth that could be used as kerchief, scarf, towel, or sling; a slate pencil rolled in a strip of paper for taking notes or writing messages; and select medicines from the Apothecary in case they got into trouble. They also had their hidden weapons in their walking sticks, Inu's unstrung bow stored in his pack along with a bundle of arrows, and a set of throwing blades that Rana had enhanced with venom. It was a newly developed animal talent of hers, producing a venom that could paralyze, and Saru was eager to see whether it would work better than the sleeping potion they usually used. She'd sewn the shimmering Fire Cloak beneath a plain dun-colored wrap. Dressed as traveling peddlers, they had a selection of trinkets that everyone had had a hand in creating.

"Think anyone will buy them?" Rana asked, polishing the tiny grooves in the shell of a cherry-sized tortoise she'd fashioned out of clay.

Saru took it and held it up by its bright silk thread. "Get your long-life charms here! A long life and good fortune, yours for two coppers!" she called. She stopped and raised an eyebrow. "What do you think?"

"I think you should take my money!" drawled Goru. "Nice work with your earth gift, Snake Girl. That tortoise looks like it'd walk off if it weren't on that cord."

Coming out of the kitchen, Nezu brought Inu and Saru a string of rice balls tied up in bamboo leaves and filled with bits of mushroom, sausage, and salted egg. "A little something for your first evening meal tonight."

The Monkey Heir's pale face lit up. "I'm drooling already!" As she put them in her backbundle, she reminded everyone that Nezu would be in charge, and Usagi second-in-command. "Everyone keep studying—and practice the stealth arts that the Tigress taught us," Saru urged. "We're going to need them more than ever if we hope to get all the Treasures back."

"There may not be enough of us to take things by force," Nezu agreed, "but we still have ways to outsmart the Dragonlord." He flashed a grin.

The two senior Heirs looked around at the five who would remain: the Rat Heir, the Rabbit Heir, and the three

Heirlings who'd escaped the Dragon Academy. "In the name of the Twelve, we leave the shrine in your care," Saru said.

"May the spirits of the Twelve be with you and guide you until we are together again," Usagi replied.

Inu gave a solemn nod, then his dark eyes crinkled. "Try to stay out of trouble, the lot of you."

Life around the shrine settled into a new routine. As the Heirs in charge, Usagi and Nezu would lead the others in mind-the-mind sessions each morning to prepare for the day. They would sit quietly with their eyes closed, breathing slowly and evenly, letting their thoughts settle. There were chores both before and after their morning meal, then intensive study in the shrine library. It was urgent that they go over the Treasures that were still missing and memorize what they looked like and how they worked, especially since the Heirlings had done so badly trying to see the Flute of Dancing Dreams in the Mirror of Elsewhere. Nezu began quizzing them on a manual known as the Warrior's Guide, which included stories and cautionary tales recorded about each artifact.

"Why must we always carry waxed cotton wool around the Flute of Dancing Dreams?" he demanded of Rana.

Rana didn't hesitate. "To plug the ears of anyone who should not fall under its spell. Unlike what happened to the 31st Snake Warrior, who accidentally made a whole village sleep for an entire year."

"That doesn't sound so bad," Goru scoffed. "Who doesn't like a good nap?"

"Except their crops went untended and all their animals ran off," Usagi said. "The Warriors had a lot to make up for with that village."

Nezu nodded. "With any tool, mistakes can be made and its power abused. Each Treasure is only as good as the person using it—so it's important you learn all this. Can't have Inu and Saru bringing back the flute only to have one of you accidentally force us to dance till our feet bleed."

In the afternoons, they worked on drills. After stretching and warming up their muscles, they focused on stealth techniques, like misdirecting attention to enter forbidden territory or make a quick escape. "If you're on a rooftop trying to run away, throw a pebble down one side—then head down the other side. Whoever's in the building won't know which way you've gone," advised Usagi.

They studied spy tactics that would help them on their missions. Usagi was especially good at them, since her rabbit hearing allowed her to eavesdrop easily on conversations, and Tora's tiger vision meant that she had a good view on things, but spying, as Nezu was fond of repeating, meant gathering information, and there was more than one way to do that.

"Talk to people! It's amazing what people will tell

someone who asks, if they think they're interested and are harmless. Everyone likes to tell stories about themselves."

They worked on disguises to help them hide in plain sight, mixing face paints and applying them so that Usagi looked like she had a scruffy beard, Goru appeared to have only one eye, and Tora's tiger teeth were blacked out so she had wide gaps in her smile.

"I don't know if that makes you look harmless," Usagi laughed. "But it definitely makes you look hilarious!"

Tora waggled her eyebrows. "I could say the same about your beard!"

Along with their disguises, they practiced acting, to help them blend in wherever they went. Nezu would point to one of the three Heirlings and suggest a possible character, and then Usagi would pretend to be a stranger, challenging them to pass as a "rich merchant's son," a "traveling entertainer" or an "old blind beggar."

"Use what the other person says to build on your story," Nezu advised. "If someone mistakes you for somebody else, or thinks you're a peddler when you really meant to be a fisherman, go along with it instead of saying, 'No, you're wrong.' It's easier than having to come up with an elaborate cover story—just say yes to whatever they say to you."

Goru scratched his shaved head. "I don't know—what if they catch you in the middle of a lie?"

"I'm not saying that you shouldn't prepare a story for

your disguise," Nezu said. "It's always better to be prepared. But sometimes things will happen that catch you off guard, and it doesn't have to throw everything else you've planned into doubt. You can still make it work."

Usagi had never considered that before.

Things didn't need to go perfectly to work out. The thought gave her hope.

One morning, a few weeks after Inu and Saru had set off from the shrine, Usagi and Tora were elbow-deep in chores. As they wiped down the expanse of wooden floor in the Great Hall, Tora suddenly stopped scrubbing. She looked around, then spoke in a lowered voice. "I saw something in the Mirror of Elsewhere the other day."

"What do you mean?"

"When Saru had us look for the flute. I—I didn't focus on the flute. I actually tried looking for something else."

"What? What did you look for?"

"My father," confessed Tora. "I thought I started to see something, but it went cloudy very quickly. I want to take another look."

Usagi sat back on her heels. "You really think you saw him?" She chewed her lip, doubtful. "It's not good to look at that Treasure too often. There are consequences for using the mirror without care. It's quite powerful."

"Yes, yes, 'You'll get stuck looking Elsewhere all the time

and stop paying attention to what's right in front of you'—all you Heirs keep saying that. But I remember you telling me that you used it all the time to check on me and Uma when Strikers took us to the Dragon Academy."

"Not *all* the time," Usagi protested. "I mean, I did sneak peeks at it, but I made sure not to look for too long whenever I did. Besides, I saw you both captured, and the mirror showed you clearly. I knew I had a chance of finding you. I worry that you'll wind up staring into that thing for hours, trying to look for your father when he's dead . . ."

Tora's amber eyes flared. "You don't know that he's dead. You don't know for sure." She went to the weapons wall. The simple sword that Tora had been given as a cadet from the Dragon Academy hung there, along with some of the more legendary blades that had been wielded by Warriors of old. She brought the steel blade to Usagi. It had an unadorned hilt and simple scabbard, but the edge of the sword was finely wrought, with wavy lines visible in the metal. "These lines show how many times the metal has been folded and beaten—just look how many there are! And this mark—it's supposed to be Wayani, but I swear it looks like the stamp my father used to brand his pieces." Her jaw set. "I'd know his work anywhere."

"So you—you think your father has been taken to Waya and is making swords for the Dragonlord and his army?" Usagi's voice trailed off. Tora had spoken of this before, but it always seemed dangerous to Usagi to hope, even as she secretly wished for it to be true. If it were, perhaps her parents were being held prisoner somewhere too. Anything would be better than what they'd always believed, which was that their parents had been callously murdered and buried in a mass grave so vast it formed a hill outside their hometown of Goldentusk. "I just wonder if maybe you're seeing something that's not there—something you want really badly."

Tora snorted. "You're saying it's all in my imagination? Here, I'll test it by thinking of something else—something that I know won't show up." She fetched the mirror from the chest of Treasures, then plopped down before Usagi. She gazed into it, then grew pale. "That can't be."

"What do you mean? What are you seeing?" Usagi leaned over to look, but Tora pulled away, staring intently.

"The Tigress! She's in the mirror."

Usagi whispered, "*Tigress?* She's . . . alive?"

CHAPTER 7

THE SECOND TIGER

THE HAIRS ROSE ON THE back of Usagi's neck. Though it was nearly summer and the weather had finally warmed, the Great Hall suddenly felt ice cold. "How? How can you be seeing the Tigress in the Mirror of Elsewhere?"

It was impossible. With her own eyes, Usagi had witnessed the Blue Dragon striking down the Tigress. Whenever Usagi thought about their mission to the Palace of the Clouds, she could still picture the moment when the Dragonlord had brought down his sword on his old teacher, and the explosion that had sent them all sprawling when he'd struck the former Tiger Warrior. "She's dead. You were there."

"I know!" Tora was still staring, eyes wide, into the mirror. "That's why I was asking the mirror to show her to me—I thought nothing would come up. But here she is."

It was too much for Usagi to grasp. "Give me that," she demanded.

Tora handed over the gilded metal disk, her tawny cheeks ashen. "I swear on the Twelve, I'm not making it up."

A beam of sunlight from the open doors of the Great Hall struck the mirror and bounced into Usagi's eyes in a dazzling flash of light. It reminded her of the blinding flare that had gone up when the Blue Dragon killed Horangi. Blinking, she waited till she no longer saw spots, then held up the mirror. Usagi thought about the Tigress's gnarled hands, how healing they were when she'd attended to a cut on Usagi's arm, how gentle they were when she stroked her cloud leopard's great furry head. She remembered the priestess's penetrating green gaze whenever she was teaching them, and how she shuffled around the shrine with the help of her long wooden staff, twice the height of the diminutive old warrior. And yet how gracefully she'd moved when she was battling the Blue Dragon, with nothing but the wood staff to protect her.

The image of the banners fluttering above them in the Great Hall grew cloudy in the mirror, then changed. A shrunken figure appeared, crumpled and motionless. Long hair, snow white with a streak of black, hung in a ragged curtain, obscuring the figure's face. But Usagi would recognize that hair anywhere, even out of its usual braid. "Teacher?" she breathed. She examined the figure, still as stone. Was the Tigress truly *alive*? Usagi wished she could reach through the mirror and touch the gnarled hands. They appeared bound, attached to a chain of some sort.

Her heart leaped at the sight of movement, the chain shifting. The gnarled hands came up and parted the curtain of hair. A single eye peered out, a slashing scar just below it. It was the Tigress, all right, and she was alive.

"Stars and spirits," Usagi gasped.

Tora grasped Usagi's wrist. "You see her?"

"Yes." Usagi blinked hard several times, half expecting the image of Horangi to disappear from the mirror. But it remained steady and clear. The Tigress was alive, and she was a prisoner.

"Where are you?" Usagi whispered.

As if in answer, the mirror clouded over, then cleared to show an image of a squat central tower with long buildings radiating from it like the spokes of a wheel. The buildings' windows were slits too narrow for even a bowl of rice to pass through. It was a prison of some sort, but where? Was it in the capital? Out in the countryside? The image in the mirror shifted again, and Usagi was startled to see a complex of grand buildings with elaborately decorated tile roofs, surrounded by a great white wall on a misty hill.

Tora nudged her. "What are you seeing?"

Dazed, Usagi let the mirror drop in her lap. "I think she's at the Palace of the Clouds." In her mind's eye, she could still see the Blue Dragon roaring and shaking his fists in triumph. It had seemed clear the old warrior was dead. But it didn't line up with what Usagi was seeing now.

"Bulging blisters," said Tora. "We've got to tell the others about this!" She got to her feet and looked at Usagi expectantly. "Come on!"

They rushed out of the Great Hall to find Nezu and the Heirlings. Usagi felt both hot and cold, and she was dizzy, as if the blood had rushed from her head. Her limbs tingled, and she stumbled a little as they ran through the shrine compound, looking for the others.

Down by Crescent Lake, they found Nezu, Goru, and Rana by the Tigress's Nest, a prayer pavilion on the edge of the water where the old warrior had often spent time when she was alive. Usagi corrected herself. The old warrior was *still* alive.

Within sight of the ornate open-air pavilion, Rana was busily moving mounds of dirt and rocks with her elemental gift. As she frowned in concentration, a winding trench formed in the earth, the dirt flying into piles on either side, stray small stones lining up to form an orderly border. Goru, wearing heavy clogs made of iron, stomped on the piles of earth and packed them down tight. He looked up and waved. "All done with cleaning the Great Hall? We're building a new obstacle course. Nezu had the idea to install some water features for training after what you encountered in the last mission."

The Rat Heir stood knee deep in the water at the shore,

where he was anchoring several lengths of bamboo in various thicknesses, floating them in place on the lake's surface. "Want to try running across these poles? I think they're going to improve everyone's balance."

"We saw something in the Mirror of Elsewhere!" Tora blurted. "The Tigress is alive!"

Goru stopped stomping, his mouth agape. Several rocks Rana was moving rolled back into the trench as she turned and stared. Nezu let go of a bamboo pole, which began to drift away.

"What in the name of the Twelve are you talking about?" he demanded. "What were you doing with the Mirror of Elsewhere?"

Usagi shook her head. "That's not important. What matters is that we both saw the Tigress in it. Tora's right— Horangi's not dead."

Dumbfounded, Nezu stared at them, then at the Tigress's Nest. He started to speak, then sloshed out of the water, not bothering to dry himself off. Leaving a trail of wet footprints, he hurried to the main part of the shrine compound, followed close behind by Usagi and the others. In the Great Hall, he went straight to the chest of Treasures and yanked out the Mirror of Elsewhere. He gazed into it, his back turned to the rest of them. After an agonizing silence, Usagi heard a tiny sniffle. "Great glorious ghosts," said Nezu. He rubbed his eyes with the back of his hand. "That really is the Tigress."

"Does the mirror ever lie?" asked Rana.

Nezu shook his head. "No, the Mirror is a window—it shows what's happening elsewhere, just as that poem says." He pointed to the scroll hanging above the chest. "That's not to say the window always gives a clear view. It's possible to mistake what you see for something else." At that, Usagi couldn't resist a sidelong glance at Tora, but her friend's gaze was fixed on Nezu.

Frowning, he tugged at his upper lip. "But who else could that be but Horangi? I asked to see her, and there she is. If someone's dead, the mirror won't show them alive and moving—no matter how much you wish it."

"She might be at the Palace of the Clouds still," Usagi told him. "When I asked where she was, the mirror showed what looked like a prison, and then the palace compound."

Goru straightened and snapped his fingers. "The Sunburst! It's the lockup where people are taken when they displease the Dragonlord. He built it in an isolated corner of the palace grounds. I remember coming across it when I was looking for a way out."

"Sunburst?" said Nezu. "A rather pretty name for a lockup."

Goru shuddered. "Pretty grim is what it is. It's named after the shape."

"That's what I saw," Usagi exclaimed. "It looked like a

wheel—there were these long buildings that fanned out from a center tower like spokes. Or rays of the sun, I suppose."

"How did she wind up there?" wondered Rana. "I saw what the Dragonlord did."

"We all saw it," said Tora. "He brought his sword down on an old woman."

Nezu pulled at his lip so hard several whiskers came out. He winced. "I don't know—some sort of sorcery must be at work here. I knew Druk before he became the Dragonlord. Instead of killing the Tigress, he must have made everyone think he had, in an illusion. When all this time, she's been his prisoner."

"But why?" Rana asked.

Tora rubbed the slashing scars on her arm, left there long ago by the Dragonlord's troops. "I'm sure he has his reasons."

"This is more important than any Treasure," said Usagi. "We need to get her out!"

Nezu nodded. "But we'll need Inu and Saru—we shouldn't do anything until they get back."

An idea struck Usagi. "Why don't we try to Summon them?"

"With the bell?" Rana clapped her hands. "I've always wanted to see how that worked!"

"Me too," said Goru.

Tora nodded, a spark of excitement in her eyes. "We've never seen a Summoning, but Usagi's told us enough. We have reason for one now."

Flashing a grin, Nezu put the mirror back in the chest. "We haven't had a Summoning since we lost the Tigress. To think that she might be alive!"

They went across the courtyard to the wooden stand that sheltered the great bronze bell beneath a thatched roof. A small wooden log was suspended from the frame, one end resting against a raised circle of swirling shapes—the symbol of the Twelve. Cast-metal images of the animals of the zodiac marched across the bell's surface. Nezu glanced up at the sun, still climbing toward the high point of the sky. "Snake hour," he muttered. "I hope they've made progress in finding the Snake Warrior's flute."

In the shade thrown by the Singing Bamboo, they stood in a circle near the bell. Usagi had never actually seen the Summoning Bell rung either, but she remembered all too well the sound. "Get ready," she told the Heirlings. "It's going to be loud."

Nezu pulled the end of the log hammer away from the bell. He glanced over at Usagi, who nodded. He swung the log forward, striking the mark of the swirling circle. A huge metallic clang erupted on impact, then grew into a reverberating hum that throbbed like a heartbeat, sending powerful vibrations that shook the ground and rattled them to the bone. Usagi clenched her teeth to keep them from chattering and bared them at Tora, Goru, and Rana in a semblance of an encouraging smile. Their faces were scrunched up at the thrumming noise. Then their eyes flew open and their jaws dropped.

Tiny specks of light glimmered in the midst of the circle, like dust motes lit by a sunbeam. They grew till they looked like fireflies, then continued to expand, swelling into balls of light that began to morph and twist as the reverberations from the bell lengthened and faded. A glowing dog took shape, becoming ever larger, until they were gazing directly at its sniffing snout. Its ears were pointed and alert, and a shaggy tail curled over its back. A great shining monkey formed of pale light sat back on its haunches, its long tail swinging back and forth. And a third figure of light emerged. It didn't glow as strongly as the others, but it was clearly an enormous tiger, sprawled on its side as if it were trying to cool off on a hot day. Its eyes opened, and Usagi saw with a shock that they were green.

"Teacher?" she whispered.

"Teacher!" Nezu shouted.

The tiger raised its enormous head. "Younglings," it croaked.

"Nezu, Usagi, what's happening?" cried the luminous monkey. "Why are we seeing two tigers?"

Tora's eyes grew even wider. "Spirits!"

"Saru, is that who I think it is?" asked the glowing dog. Its ears had flattened back, and the shaggy tail had drooped down, nearly tucked between its legs. "But it—it can't be . . . Horangi is dead."

The pale tiger, transparent and glimmering, raised its head a little higher. "Almost, but not quite, young pup." It gave a dry chuckle that quickly became a hacking cough. The light of the tiger flickered as if it were a sputtering candle.

The circle erupted in a chorus of exclamations, cries of joy and shock, and questions.

"Oh, Teacher!"

"It's true! It's really true!"

"How did . . . wh-what happened to you?"

"When did you find out she was alive?"

"Why didn't anyone tell us about this sooner?"

"Gods be good—it's the Tigress!"

Nezu motioned for them all to be quiet. "Where are you, Teacher?" he asked. "Usagi said the Mirror of Elsewhere showed you at the palace. Are you in the Sunburst—their lockup?"

"I do not know where I am, exactly," the tiger rumbled. It closed its eyes. "To be honest, I do not always know who I am. You have found me at a rare moment of clarity."

The shining monkey reached out to the tiger, as if trying to embrace it. "We all believed you were dead. We'll come for you straightaway."

106

"I will take care of myself," said the tiger wearily. "I will not have you younglings worrying about an old, retired warrior who has lived long past her fighting days. You must find the Treasures! They cannot fall into Druk's hands."

The dog's ears had perked forward, and its tail wagged slightly. "We've just secured the Flute of Dancing Dreams, Teacher."

"That is good to hear." The tiger made a satisfied chuffing sound, and its tail flicked. "Continue with the work of recovering the Twelve Treasures, which has been our mission from the start. I did what I could to prevent Druk from restoring power to the Jewels of Land and Sea, and hid the jade bead."

Nezu started. "I thought you swallowed it, Teacher."

"Perhaps I did—or perhaps I did not." The Tigress coughed a chuckle. "What is crucial is that Druk has not yet found the bead. And no matter how angry he gets, I will never reveal its location to him."

"So where is it?" asked Usagi.

"I am not quite sure myself. When I found myself alive after our duel, hiding the bead was my first priority, and I buried it deep in the earth. But I have lost track of all the holding cells where they have kept me," said the tiger. It sighed. "If the Mirror of Elsewhere is showing me at the palace, then the Jewel that will restore the necklace is likely somewhere here too."

"We need to track down that bead before the Blue Dragon does," said Nezu. "We can't let him possess the necklace's powers—or the powers of any of the Treasures."

"Yes. That is all I ask." The glimmering beast laid its head down, its light beginning to fade. "Save the Treasures—and save Midaga."

"Wait!" cried Usagi, as the giant tiger's light grew faint, its shape beginning to dissolve. "Are they hurting you? How will we find you? We have to free you!" Though the Tigress had appeared in the Summoning, she seemed terribly weak, as if she could barely hold on to consciousness to allow her spirit form to talk to them.

"Do not worry about me—and do not try to contact me again," the tiger grunted. "It is unsafe." She fixed her green gaze on them. "Have heart and be brave, younglings. Remember what I said. You have an important job to do." The glowing twin orbs were the last part of the tiger to fade away.

CHAPTER 8

AN UNEXPECTED DANCE

STUNNED, THEY ALL STOOD IN silence in the shadows
cast by the Singing Bamboo. No one moved. Even the spirit
forms of Saru and Inu were left mute and still, glimmering
as if they were actual lanterns like the ones standing guard
in the grove. Finally, the monkey spoke.

"My stars—I can hardly believe it. The Tigress, alive!"
it said. "Finding the Flute of Dancing Dreams was already
a miracle."

Nezu flashed a grin. "The spirits of the Twelve have
blessed us twice."

A frantic huffing sounded as the cloud leopard came
racing across the courtyard to their Summoning circle,
tail held high. Kumo's long whiskers bristled, and his eyes
were intently searching as he sniffed the air. He stalked all
around them, then stopped. His ears flattened and his tail
lashed in confusion.

"Poor Kumo," Tora crooned. "You heard the Tigress's voice, didn't you? I'm sorry, big fellow. She couldn't stay."

With a mournful moan, the cloud leopard stalked off. Nezu's expression turned sympathetic as he watched the big cat slink behind the Great Hall. "What should we do about the Tigress? We can't just leave her, wherever she may be."

"No, we certainly can't." The glowing dog cocked its head. "But I think we'd best follow her wishes and find the remaining Treasures before we attempt a rescue."

The image of the Tigress in the mirror, crumpled and helpless with her hands bound, was lodged in Usagi's mind. "You saw her just now—she barely had the strength to be visible. But I saw her in the Mirror of Elsewhere—she's not well. We can't wait. There's no time."

Tora nodded. "In the mirror she looked even worse."

"We have to save her," Usagi said, her voice rising.

"No one's saying that we won't," replied the shining monkey. "But the Tigress has had us on a mission to recover the Treasures since before we met you, Usagi. We need to complete that task—for her."

"And what good will that do if she dies?" demanded Usagi. "Isn't her life more important than a bunch of . . . *things*?"

The glowing dog flared a little. "Of course her life is important. Her wishes are important too. Have you forgotten that a good warrior follows their leader's orders? She's right about the Blue Dragon—we have to get to the other Treasures before he does. Recovering these mere *things* may save this kingdom and everyone in it."

Nezu put a hand on Usagi's arm. "We will find the Tigress, I promise. Let's figure it out when Inu and Saru return with the flute. Arguing will only delay them."

"Fine." Usagi gave a reluctant nod. Her anxious fingers rubbed at her rabbit pendant.

"Where are you now?" Goru asked the dog and monkey loudly.

Rana nudged him, her dark eyes full of amusement. "I don't think you have to shout."

"Yes, we can hear you fine," said the shining monkey.

The giant boy smiled sheepishly. "Sorry. It's my first Summoning."

The monkey bared its glittering teeth, then leaned forward. "We left the Dancing Dunes this morning. We're still in the province of Pearl Sands. Going at spirit speed, we expect to be back at the shrine by the end of the week."

"Travel safely, you two," said Nezu. "We'll see you here soon."

The glowing dog's tail wagged. "Guard the shrine well. A new Treasure is coming."

With that, the light of the dog and monkey blazed brighter, then disappeared. Usagi blinked till she could see clearly again. Tora, Goru, and Rana stood dazed, their mouths agape and their eyes wide. Nezu grinned at the sight.

"Come on," he said. "We have work to do."

Over the next few days, they continued to practice stealth skills and strength exercises, now with a newly sharpened sense of purpose. They also honed their abilities by building out the obstacle course by the lake, creating a new training ground. As they worked to install a target range in the course, the five of them discussed the remaining two lost Treasures, debating where they might be hidden.

"We know that the Ring of Obscurity was worn by Pom, the 46th Tiger Warrior," said Nezu. "He was one of the Tigress's favorite successors. He and his Heir were trapped in battle with a horde of Wayani soldiers down on the eastern side of the island. They never made it to the Palace of the Clouds to help defend the king."

"And the Conjurer was carried by Yagi, the 48th Ram Warrior," said Usagi. "Tupa was his Heir."

Goru dropped two bales of straw with a thump. "If Tupa was the Ram Heir, then he must know where the Conjurer is. Shouldn't he have recovered the hammer by now?"

"I doubt it. Right after the war, we went with him to retrieve it," said Nezu. "Tupa swore on the Twelve that he'd helped his master hide the hammer near the Eastern Mines. But our search turned up nothing. He'd lost track of it somehow. Tupa was devastated." He gestured to Goru to move the bales. "A little more to the right. Perfect. I'm sure you remember all the chaos of the invasion. And after the war, a lot had changed. Some parts of the landscape were altered by fighting, and the Blue Dragon soon started expanding the Eastern Mines. So even if a Treasure was carried by one of our masters, we still had to hunt around to find it—and we weren't always successful."

He leaned over the trench that Rana had been working on. It had become a little moat around a small island, the moat surrounded by ramparts of earth that Goru had tamped down. "It looks great, Snake Girl."

"Thanks!" said Rana. "I think it's ready to be filled with water. Would you mind using your water gift?"

With a flashing grin, Nezu pointed to several handle-less jugs. "Use those to fill it the regular way," he told her. "It'll help strengthen your hands."

As Rana groaned, Usagi gave her a sympathetic smile. "I had to use these too. They really do work, though. Your grip will become like iron." Rana sighed, then took a jug in each hand and trudged off to the lake.

Tora laughed and grabbed a jug, fitting her hand over its narrow mouth and lifting with her fingertips. "I'll help you, Snake Girl."

As she and Rana sloshed back and forth between the lake and the new feature in the obstacle course, Usagi joined Nezu and Goru in hanging an archery target from a tree. She sprang onto Goru's shoulders and stood on tiptoe, trying to fasten a rope to a high branch. "It's a little too high," she grunted. Usagi touched her fingertips to the branch. With her wood gift, she got the tree to sway and bend toward her with a creak, lowering the branch to where she needed it. As she finished tying a firm knot, her ears perked.

"They're here!" she exclaimed, and leaped down from Goru's back. "Inu and Saru—they've come home!"

Dropping their tools and all thoughts of their lakeside project, they ran back to the shrine, dashing through the trees on white gravel paths. Usagi's heart raced. She couldn't wait to see what the two Heirs had brought back.

They got to the main courtyard just as Saru and Inu did, looking tired. The Dog Heir smiled at the sight of them. "Well, aren't you happy to see us!"

"It's just the Treasure we're excited about," Usagi teased. "But really, welcome back!" She gave Saru a hug. The Monkey Heir smelled of dust and sweat, and her clothes and hair glimmered strangely. When Usagi looked closely, she saw that it was grains of pale sand, so white they appeared almost like salt crystals, lodged in Saru's hair, the creases of her ears, the folds of her tunic and the crevices of her back-bundle. "You're covered in sand!"

Saru sighed ruefully. "Still?" She brushed at her sleeves to no avail. "We got caught in sandstorms every day."

"Here, let me!" Rana piped up. She furrowed her brow and waved her hands over Saru and Inu. With the force of her earth gift, the sand rolled off them in shimmering ripples to the ground, where it collected in a pile. The two Heirs smiled in relief, exclaiming at the amount of sand.

Inu ruffled his shaggy hair. "You got it all out! Thank you, Earth Snake. If I never see sand again, it will be too soon."

Crouching, Usagi scooped up a handful, letting the fine white grains run through her fingers. They sparkled in the sunlight. "You brought a whole dune back with you! Did they really dance?"

"Twice a day, every day," said Saru. "Each time the winds kicked up, the sand would start moving, and it was hard to see or even stay upright."

"So how did you manage to find the flute?" asked Usagi.

"We were looking for markers that might have been left behind," said Saru. "The problem is, the Dancing Dunes are constantly shifting. We searched for days. Finally, we found part of a long stake that bore the mark of the Snake Warrior and the Twelve, but it had been broken off. Thank the gods, Inu caught the scent of the rest of it, buried in the sand."

The Dog Heir shook his head. "We had to dig down deep. It would have been a lot easier if we'd had Rana with us."

Blushing, Rana ducked her head and toed the pile of sand. "Can I have this?" she asked.

"Take it!" Saru laughed. "I'm with Inu—I'd be happy never to see sand again."

Rana hurried off and fetched a bucket. She tilted it on its

side, and the sand swirled into the container. Watching the grains follow her every command was like watching Nezu with his water gift.

"What are you going to do with all that?" Tora asked curiously.

With a smile, Rana shrugged. "I don't know yet, but it's too pretty to throw away."

"It's not so pretty when it's in your eyes," snorted Inu.

Nezu slung an arm around him and Saru. "So are you two going to complain about the sand all day, or are we going to get a look at what you suffered for?"

"All right, all right," said Inu. "Keep your tea in your cup."

They crowded around as he and Saru shrugged off their packs and settled themselves on the platform edging the courtyard. Inu dug into his backbundle and pulled out a battered metal box with a tarnished coiled snake as its clasp. He opened the box to reveal a long, cloth-wrapped object. Unwinding the wrapping, he exposed the flute. Made of lacquered bamboo, the end was carved to look like the head of a snake, its mouth open wide in a hiss. The twelve zodiac animals were painted up and down the sides. "It used to be carried by the Snake Warrior," Inu said. He smiled at Rana. "We'll have to teach you to play, Heirling."

"Do you think it really works?" asked Tora.

Goru reached out to touch it, his finger nearly as thick as the flute. "Did you try playing it?"

With a frown, Inu pushed his shaggy hair out of his eyes. "Not yet," he admitted. "We wanted to bring it to the safety of the shrine first."

"It's better to test the more dangerous Treasures here," added Saru.

The Dog Heir looked around and raised an eyebrow. "Shall I play it now?"

With nervous titters, Tora and Rana nodded, while Nezu and Goru enthusiastically agreed. "I have to admit I'm curious," confessed Usagi. "Just go easy on us."

Putting the flute to his lips, Inu nodded. He took a breath, then began to play. A warm, low note sounded, and as it washed over Usagi, she felt her limbs grow numb, as if they weren't connected to her body. The note turned into a soothing lullaby, one that Inu often played before they went to bed, but this time its effect was instantaneous. Usagi slumped to the ground, the world going black.

The next thing she knew, a bright jaunty tune was ringing through her head, and she was on her feet, wide awake. Usagi still couldn't quite feel her arms and legs, but her feet were tapping and kicking while her hands waved wildly. The others were dancing about the courtyard alongside her, while Inu stood on the wooden platform, playing the flute with a look of glee.

"What just happened?" she cried to Tora, who was dancing in a little circle.

"That is definitely the Treasure." Tora's eyes were round. "I think he put us to sleep."

"Well, we're certainly not sleeping now!" Usagi bowed to Inu, and then bowed to the others, who bowed in return.

Nezu rolled his eyes. "Is that really necessary?" he shouted. Inu tootled on the flute in reply, and Nezu bowed again. "Oi!" he cried indignantly. Rana giggled, and a dimple appeared in Inu's cheek.

They danced in formation, moving back and forth in complicated patterns. All the while, there were exclamations of awe and nervous laughter.

"I'm trying to stop but I can't!"

"I can't even feel my legs!"

"Me neither!"

It reminded Usagi of the various holds that could be applied on pressure points all over the body—she'd experienced the freeze hold before, and it had been frightening to lose all control, to be at the mercy of someone else. A drop of sweat trickled into her eyes, and she blinked at the sting, powerless to wipe her face. She clasped hands with Rana and danced round and round, unable to pause even as she grew tired. Usagi felt the stirrings of alarm. "I think that's enough, Inu," she called over her shoulder.

"I don't usually move like this," huffed Goru as he leaped about on tiptoe and twirled. "I'm ready for this to be over."

But the Dog Heir didn't seem to hear, and the more he

played, the more Usagi's insides clenched. She tried to get his attention over the lively whistling of the flute. "Inu?" He kept going, the notes pouring out faster and faster, their steps becoming frenzied.

She could stand it no longer. Panic rose to the surface and burst out of Usagi in a shriek. "Inu, STOP!"

The music came to an abrupt halt as Inu looked up, slack-jawed. Usagi and the others stopped dancing. She felt her legs give way beneath her, and she collapsed to the ground, as did the others, panting.

"Scabs, Inu," groaned Nezu. The Rat Heir rolled over and rubbed his legs. "She told you to go easy!"

Shamefaced, Inu raked a hand through his hair. "I'm sorry—I thought everyone was having fun. Weren't you all laughing?"

"Only in the beginning," growled Tora. She lay back on the stone tiles. "I will never question the authenticity of that flute again."

Heart pounding, Usagi rested her forehead on her knees. Goru put a giant hand on her shoulder. "Are you okay?"

She raised her head. Inu had jumped down from the platform, hangdog and worried. Saru was patting Rana's back as she retched. "I'll be fine," Usagi replied tightly. Inu should have listened to her. "What about Snake Girl?"

Saru gave Inu a reproachful look. "A little too much spinning."

"It's more powerful than I remembered." Chastened, Inu wrapped up the flute and put it in its case, snapping the coiled-snake clasp shut. "I'm putting this away. Sorry, everyone."

Nezu shakily got to his feet. "Well. After all that whirling about, I think we need a little something to settle our stomachs. I'll make us rice porridge and we'll drink some honey-ginger tea."

Over the meal, they heard more about the flute mission's discoveries in the Dancing Dunes.

"We thought the dunes would be deserted, but Inu caught the scent of people living nearby," said Saru. "And when we went to investigate, we found a group of younglings—all with Earth gifts."

The Dog Heir wolfed down a tea-stewed egg. "Their gifts allowed them to live among the dunes without being bothered by the sand. They'd dug a network of deep pits that sheltered against the winds. With their powers, the walls of the pits stayed intact."

"That's amazing," marveled Tora. "Usagi and I hid with a dozen younglings after the war ended, but every one of us ended up being caught by Strikers."

"Almost everyone," Usagi reminded her. "Thanks to you and Saru, I escaped." She put another hard-boiled egg on Inu's plate. "So did you take these dune younglings to Yunja?"

He shook his head. "We offered, but they weren't interested in going to Sun Moon Lake. They're a group of five, all around our age or so—the youngest was an Earth Ox—and they've been living undetected there for years." Inu gave a wry smile. "They're pretty tough, the Dunelings. They were ready to bury us alive when we found them."

"They hurled hot sand from their firepits at us." The Monkey Heir poured herself another cup of tea. "Thank the gods we had the Fire Cloak to shield us. Once we proved that we meant them no harm, they were actually quite kind."

Rana bit into a pickled sour plum and smacked her lips. "I probably wouldn't want to leave the dunes either, if I felt safe there."

"You left the Palace of the Clouds," said Goru. "That place is a fortress."

"Yes, but not for our protection," Rana replied. "All those armed Guard and Dragonstrikers are for Lord Druk—and if there's ever an attack, even the youngest cadets are expected to fight for him."

"Speaking of the palace, the Tigress needs us. There are only two Treasures left to find, and we first need to track them down so we can help her. Where should we look next?" Usagi asked.

"Our traitorous Ram Heir always insisted that the Conjurer wasn't far from the Eastern Mines," said Nezu. "But even though Tupa helped hide it, we never found the hammer. It drove him mad—maybe that's why he joined the Blue Dragon."

"I don't think it will be any easier to find now. The Eastern Mines have only expanded, and the number of Guard will be high," Inu pointed out.

"What about the Ring of Obscurity?" asked Tora. "Nezu said it was last seen on Pom, the 46th Tiger Warrior."

Saru turned her teacup in her hands, thinking. "Pom and his Heir took their final stand in Woodwing, a town not far from Butterfly Kingdom on the eastern side of the island. Presumably the ring was lost there."

"Butterfly Kingdom!" Rana's dark eyes sparkled. "My mother used to tell me stories about that valley. It's in Flower Song Province, where she was born."

Slurping up the last of the porridge, Goru wiped his mouth and raised his hand. "I vote that we try for the ring first, since you've had no luck hunting for the hammer. Besides, a town near Butterfly Kingdom sounds a lot better than the Eastern Mines."

Tora's snaggleteeth glinted. "I second that vote. Let's go on a little trip to Woodwing."

Mirror Precept: The Mirror of Elsewhere should only be used for brief stretches under the watch of others, lest the user lose track of time and self.

Gowa the Third, 19th Dog Warrior, would forego meals and sleep to gaze in the Mirror of Elsewhere, and became alarmingly thin and short-tempered. When he could no longer put the mirror down to practice mind-the-mind, it was clear he had lost his ability to serve as Warrior. The Treasure had to be prised from his hands. He did not take kindly to losing possession of the mirror and was banished from Mount Jade. His Heir, Jindo the First, assumed the mantle of Dog Warrior, and this new precept was issued.

—Excerpted from the "Metal" chapter in *The Twelve Treasures*, from *Compendium of Consequences, Volume I*

CHAPTER 9

VENOM AND VISIONS

A SQUEAK AND A BANG echoed through the sleeping quarters. Usagi awoke with a start. Raising her head, she squinted through the dark. The long room was still. The only noises were coming from the snoring lumps in their bedrolls, neatly lined across a platform covered in thick straw matting. *Squeak. Bang.* One of the latticed wooden shutters was creaking in the breeze and knocking against the window frame. With a groan, Usagi got up and went to secure the shutter. She glanced out the window and froze.

Tora was crossing the courtyard, padding across the stone tiles with Kumo beside her. The moon was past its apex and sinking toward the horizon, signaling the hour of the Tiger. What was she doing up before dawn—and where was she going? Frowning, Usagi stepped around the snorfling mountain that was Goru, slid past a curled-up, softly whistling Rana, and tiptoed out.

When she got to the courtyard, it was empty. But over the musical sighs of the Singing Bamboo, Usagi caught the sound of Kumo's purr. She followed the cloud leopard's rumbling to the Great Hall, where the massive doors were ajar. Usagi slipped inside, and in the dim cavernous space, she saw Tora at the chest of Treasures, the cloud leopard flopped at her feet. Kumo got up when he saw Usagi, purring louder.

"Are you looking at the Mirror of Elsewhere?"

Startled, Tora hunched over something cupped in her hands. Her eyes met Usagi's. Guiltily, she revealed the mirror in her palm. "I thought it might help. I keep having these strange dreams." In the moonlight slanting through the high windows, her snaggleteeth gleamed.

Usagi sighed. "Is this about your father again?"

"What if it is?" Tora shrugged. "Something's going on—I can feel it. I just need to figure out what." Her jaw set. "Don't look at me like that. If it weren't for me, we wouldn't even know that the Tigress was still alive."

"Finding out about the Tigress was an accident," Usagi reminded her.

Tora put her hands on her hips. "So it doesn't count? Maybe I didn't *exactly* know about the Tigress, but I was the first to discover that she wasn't dead." She began to pace. "Look, in my dreams I keep seeing my family, and the Mirror once showed me something that must have been about my father. I'm not going to stop until I figure out what it is." She turned her attention back to the polished disk in her hand. "Besides, how can you not want to use this? You can look for anything with this mirror. You can explore the whole world."

"That's exactly the problem," Usagi warned. "You won't want to do anything else but look in that thing. That's why it's not good to use it too much. At least you should have someone around to stop you when you've been staring at it too long."

"I can stop whenever I want." Tora deposited the mirror back in the chest and closed its drawer with a huff. "Come on, Kumo." The cloud leopard stretched and yawned, then followed Tora as she stalked out of the Great Hall.

Frowning, Usagi contemplated the chest of Treasures. Could the mirror really have shown Tora her father when he'd been gone for so many years? It was hard to believe, but then again, they hadn't expected to see the Tigress alive either. Usagi decided to take a look, dismissing her own warning to Tora. She was a Warrior Heir, after all, and had used the Mirror of Elsewhere many times. *She* knew how to control herself.

Usagi slid the shining disk out of its drawer. She gazed into it, trying to recall Tora's father through hazy memories. She had been only seven and Tora eight when the invaders had come and rounded up all the adults with powers. But he had been the blacksmith in their town, and Usagi's father had often taken his woodcarving tools to him for fixes and sharpening. She struggled to remember the blacksmith's face. He had been a Metal Snake, more than ten years older than Usagi's father. Tora's four big brothers, all of whom had been blessed with metal gifts, had worked alongside the blacksmith in a foundry that Usagi remembered as being quite hot. She tried to feel the heat on her skin. . . .

The image in the mirror shifted, changing from a reflection of the Great Hall to the burned-out shell of the smithy, its furnace smashed across the stone floor.

"No, no, no," she muttered impatiently. It was the blacksmith she was trying to see. But her mind kept drifting back to the memory of arriving at the blacksmith's shop with her father, his chisels and saws wrapped in a square of leather, and running off with Tora to play. The mirror clouded and cleared, showing Tora back in the sleeping quarters, Kumo curled at her feet.

Usagi gave up. "Spit and spleen." It wasn't working. Or maybe that was all that was left to see. She turned the disk over and over in her fingers, fighting an old impulse. It had been a long time since she'd checked in on Uma. After her sister had chosen to stay with the Blue Dragon, Usagi had avoided looking in the mirror for months, too afraid of what her sister had become. If she asked to see Uma in the mirror now, what would it show her?

After a moment's hesitation, she returned the Treasure to

its drawer. She wasn't ready to know. She wondered if Tora was just longing to believe that her father was alive, so much so that she imagined seeing him. Usagi couldn't even look at her sister, let alone ask the mirror for a view of her parents. The last thing she wanted to be shown was the giant mound where they were buried with so many others.

The next morning, when Usagi got up, Tora was nowhere to be seen. Usagi ate her morning meal quickly, cramming down a steamed turnip cake and gulping a cup of sweetened milky tea before joining Inu and Rana by the weapons wall in the Great Hall, where they were in preparations for the next mission. Rana sat on the sparring mats and sorted metal arrow tips, separating them into piles of pointed cones, flat diamond shapes, dagger-like blades and little spade heads. "Which ones did you want poisoned, Inu?" she asked.

The Dog Heir looked up from the bamboo arrow shaft he was oiling and considered the piles Rana had made. "The long-range points."

While Usagi helped Inu prepare a bundle of arrow shafts, Rana carefully spit a bit of venom into a small dish, then began dipping the metal cones into the venom. After she had been on Mount Jade for a while, Rana's animal talent of producing poisonous venom had emerged, much like Usagi's elemental gift with wood—but the discovery had been rather unpleasant.

At their Harvest Moon feast, when Goru had gobbled all the extra mooncakes, Rana had shared hers. Upon taking bites of Rana's mooncake, both Usagi and Tora had been struck by nausea and unable to move. It had taken an antidote from the Apothecary to restore them to normalcy. But the Heirs didn't make the connection until there had been several more incidents in which Rana's generosity in sharing food and drink had left someone paralyzed.

Now Rana was careful not to share her food with anyone and avoided sharing cups as well, especially since there was a good chance her venom would become deadly as her powers grew. She'd cried when they first realized what was happening. "It doesn't feel like a talent. It feels like a curse." But the upside of being able to produce venom was that she could help make their weapons even more effective. It was still not terribly strong—it wouldn't do much more than stun, according to Saru's reports on the venom-tipped throwing blades they'd brought on the last mission. But it was easier than mixing up potions from scratch.

Rana lined up the metal arrow tips on a tray to dry, then brought them over to Inu. He accepted them with a brief smile. "Thanks, Snake Girl." Looking proud, she skipped off to look for the other Heirlings.

With a frown of concentration, Inu picked up an arrowhead with a pair of feedsticks and examined it. He glanced up at Usagi. "Want to help me with these?" He touched the base of the metal cone to a dish of glue, preparing to attach it to a bamboo shaft.

Usagi eyed the poisoned cones. Having experienced the effects of Rana's venom, she was in no hurry to come in contact with it again. But she was the Rabbit *Heir*. She shouldn't be afraid of anything. And they had the Apothecary besides. Not for the first time, Usagi thanked the gods that she'd managed to nab it before they escaped the Palace of the Clouds. Amid poisonings, various winter colds, several injuries, and even the ache of growing pains when Goru had become several heads taller and quite a bit wider after arriving on Mount Jade, the contents of the pillbox had gotten them through many rough moments.

She scooted closer to Inu and took up an arrow shaft and a pair of feedsticks. Copying everything Inu did, Usagi used the feedsticks to pick up an arrow tip, dip its base in a dish of glue, and slide it into the hollowed end of the arrow shaft. He handed her a small rag to wipe off excess glue. As they worked, Usagi longed to raise her concerns about Tora. "Do you believe that if you want something badly enough, it will happen? Or is wishing just a way to avoid facing reality?"

The Dog Heir inspected the arrow in his hand. "The Tigress liked to say, 'Weave a net instead of just praying for fish.' If there's something you want, you don't just wish for it—you work for it. Because no one gets everything that they want." He looked up with a sardonic smile. "Not even the Blue Dragon. Why do you ask?"

She told him how Tora had been having dreams, seeking out the Mirror of Elsewhere to find answers, and insisting on ideas she couldn't prove. "I'm a little worried about her, to be honest."

"Hmm." He tossed his shaggy hair out of his eyes. "You know, right before the mission to Port Wingbow, Tora told me that she'd had a dream of seeing the Pen of Truth flying through the air. Neither of us knew what to make of it at the time, but you can't say it didn't come true. What if her tiger vision has expanded since coming to Mount Jade?"

Usagi stopped in the middle of wiping glue off an arrow. "Expanded? You mean she can see not just in the dark but *into the future?*"

"It's possible." Inu plucked the arrow out of her hands and checked it, then secured the arrowhead more firmly into the shaft before putting it aside to dry with the others. "It's a talent not many possess—but there were Warriors in the past who had visions and premonitions."

Pondering the possibilities, Usagi reached for her rabbit pendant and rubbed it. If Tora could see into the future, what would that mean? Would she be able to predict what would happen to them? What if it were something bad? Would they want to know?

Kaa-oh . . .

Ka-ohh ka-ohh, ka-ohh ka-ohh . . .

132

Usagi's head snapped at the sound of a seagull. "What in the name of the Twelve . . . ?" She jumped up and stared into the sky.

"What are you hearing?" asked Inu.

As she put a hand over her eyes to shade them, Usagi's ears remained pricked. "A bird. But one that's far from where it's supposed to be."

Inu scratched his head, baffled. Then his nostrils flared. "Fish. A fish eater. Is that what I think it is?"

The white-and-black form of a seagull appeared, soaring gracefully above them. Usagi waved, and the seagull wheeled about before descending. It came into the courtyard, its wings held aloft, and landed on the platform, flapping as it stepped to a halt. It turned and looked at Usagi with a piercing yellow eye and held out its leg. There was a small scroll tied to it.

"I think this is Neko! Or Nabi—I'm not sure which." Usagi shrugged. "Sorry, bird." She removed the scroll from the proffered leg and began to unroll it.

"Who?" asked Inu. He stared at the bird, bewildered. "What?"

Usagi laughed. "Remember the youngling from Port Wingbow we brought to Yunja? The Fire Rooster? She had a couple of pet seagulls, and this is one of them." Scanning the scroll, Usagi smiled. "It's Neko, with a message from Yunja. He says that Ji's doing well, and that he's got her and the other younglings at Sun Moon Lake working on a project they're very excited about. They want us to visit."

"Flying featherbombs," muttered Inu. "A seagull at the shrine. This has got to be a first."

Reaching out a tentative hand, Usagi stroked the seagull's back. "I wonder if Neko will take a message back for us."

"It couldn't hurt to try," said Inu. He pulled out a scrap of paper and a slate pencil from his belt. "What do you want to say?"

Usagi chewed her bottom lip, thinking. "Let's just say that we'll come visit as soon as we can, so they know Neko did her job." She smiled at the bird. "A seagull certainly beats any of the messenger pigeons that the Dragonlord uses."

Rolling up the paper slip, Inu handed it to Usagi with a flourish. "They're definitely a lot bigger. Imagine having a whole flock."

"I just wish one of us could speak bird. I don't suppose birds understand your dog-speak?" Usagi asked. As Inu snorted and shook his head, Usagi tied the note onto the seagull's leg. "You must be tired, Neko," she cooed. "There's a lake just through those trees, and it's full of fish. Think you can find it?" The seagull took a few steps around the platform and stretched out the leg with the replying note, as if testing it. Then it took off, circling around them once before flying off in the direction of the lake.

"Looks like it understood you just fine," said Inu. "Or at least scented the water."

Usagi rolled up Yunja's message scroll. "I'm going to go find Tora—she'll be happy to know about Ji."

Trotting off, Usagi kept her ears pricked for signs of her friend. She hadn't seen Tora all morning. As she wound through the trees that surrounded the shrine compound, she could hear Goru and Nezu working on the new training course by the lake.

"Is that a seagull?" observed Goru. *"What's one doing up on Mount Jade?"*

Usagi smiled. Wait till they found out exactly where the gull had come from. She heard Saru join Inu in the courtyard, and him telling the Monkey Heir about the message from Ji and Yunja.

"Maybe we should check on them soon," mused Saru.

"After we've secured the missing Treasures, we'll go," agreed Inu. *"I'm curious to see how the younglings' powers are developing."*

Inu's remark about Tora's expanding powers came back to Usagi. Her friend had seemed so certain about her father. Was it because of tiger vision—a new kind?

What if Tora was right? If Tora's father was alive, then perhaps Usagi's was too. It was a hope that Usagi had buried under layers of purpose and distraction. There were missions to train for, Treasures to recover, Heirlings to help.

The notion that perhaps her parents might still be alive—that remained locked in a corner of her heart. If she allowed the key to turn, the door to open, then everything behind it might overtake her, and there was no telling what would happen then.

She was nearing the Tree of Elements, an ancient cypress in a rocky grotto not far from the compound. The roaring crackle of an eternal flame, burning over a trickle of water flowing from the rock, tickled Usagi's ears. She stopped and caught another sound—two people, silent but for the whisper of their breath.

Usagi quickened her step. Approaching the hollow that sheltered the tree, she saw both Tora and Rana sitting quietly beside the fiery spring, their eyes closed. The bent and twisted tree, its trunk warty with chunks of ironstone buried in the wood, was propped on a sturdy log like an old man and hovered protectively over both girls. Their legs were tucked beneath them and their hands were folded in their laps as they practiced mind-the-mind, allowing their thoughts to settle while breathing deeply and evenly. It was rude to interrupt someone while they were in mind-the-mind, so Usagi sat down beside them and closed her eyes as well.

Inhaling slowly, she counted to six, then exhaled, counting to six. After breathing and counting for several rounds, she felt herself becoming calm, less troubled. Whatever was happening with Tora and her tiger vision, with her dreams of her lost family, was not something that Usagi could control. And if Usagi's parents were truly still alive, she would find a way to help them—and her sister too. She wasn't giving up on any of them, even if she had to tamp down her hopes and fears at times. The words of the Tigress came to her. Usagi could almost hear the old warrior's croak, offering her guidance as always. *Do not let uncertainty bar the way. Steer your boat in the right direction, and the streams of time and destiny will carry you through.*

At last, she opened her eyes, and found both Tora and Rana smiling at her. Usagi smiled back, relieved that Tora didn't seem to be upset anymore. "I have good news—Ji sent one of her seagulls here with a message." She held up the scroll and let it unfurl. "She's doing well."

"Gracious gods! That's good to hear." Tora took the scroll from Usagi and examined it.

"Have you been here all morning?" asked Usagi.

Tora shook her head. "I was in the library, looking through the *Compendium of Recorded Talents and Gifts*. I was trying to find out if all my dreams and hallucinations could be linked to anything." She handed back Ji's message.

"I mentioned it to Inu, actually, and he seemed to think that your tiger talents are expanding," said Usagi.

"Really?" Tora brightened. "The compendium did say that tiger vision could include being able to see into the future."

Rana coiled a loose braid, pinning it in place. "How wonderful! If you could tell us what was going to happen, we'd always be prepared. Better off than any foe. Can you imagine? Nothing and no one could ever surprise us!"

"I don't know for sure if that's what's going on," said Tora. "Besides, are surprises so terrible?" She got up, putting a hand on the Tree of Elements to steady herself. Upon touching the gnarled trunk, she stiffened. Her legs crumpled and she collapsed. Her amber eyes turned white, as if they'd rolled back in her head. Rana cried out.

"Tora? Tora!" Usagi had never seen her friend like this. She grabbed Tora's arm, trying to pull it away from the tree, but it was stuck fast. She couldn't tell if it was because the tree had a hold on Tora, or if it was the other way around. Usagi had tried before to communicate with the Tree of Elements and had never had any luck. But she didn't know what else to do. She placed her free hand on the tree's trunk, the other grasping Tora's arm, and desperately felt for the tree's life force, hoping to connect with it. *Please,* she begged. *Let my friend go.*

"What do we do?" Frantic, Rana shook Tora. "Wake up!" She dipped her hand in the spring, dodging the flames that shot from the crack in the rock, and splashed water on Tora's face. But Tora remained still, her eyes wide and white.

Usagi stopped her. "Please, let me talk to the tree." She searched for a vibrating hum that in ordinary trees she found right away. At last she detected what seemed like a thready pulse. Silently she implored the ancient tree for help. *Please don't hurt her. She's to be the next Tiger Heir.*

With a whispering sigh and a groaning creak, a piece of ironstone fell from the trunk. It bounced off Usagi and landed on Tora. Tora's hand came off the tree and she blinked, her eyes returning to normal.

"What . . . just happened?" She sat up, assisted by Rana, who wiped Tora's face.

Usagi picked up the ironstone, which had tumbled to the ground. "You went somewhere else when you touched the tree, and seemed trapped. When I asked the tree to help, it dropped one of its ironstones—and then you came to." The stone, striped red, gold, and black, was weighty and rough in her palm. It felt warm, almost alive.

With trembling fingers, Tora touched the stone. "I saw something. Not about . . . what we talked about earlier," she said, glancing at Rana. "But something about the Ring of Obscurity. I can't quite understand it, but I saw a giant butterfly, and it was guarding the ring."

Usagi gaped. "We're going to Woodwing to look for the ring, and we've talked about how it's near Butterfly Kingdom. Maybe that planted an idea—"

Unconvinced, Tora shook her head. She looked at the Tree of Elements and bit her lip. "Forget what I said about surprises."

CHAPTER 10

BUTTERFLY KINGDOM

"RING MISSION, ON THE HUNT!" bellowed Goru. The trees around them quaked as he charged ahead. Tora laughed and sprinted after him, her travel pack bouncing on her back. They shifted into spirit speed and were quickly gone.

Inu raised an eyebrow at Usagi. "You said you all practiced stealth techniques while Saru and I were away."

"We did," Usagi said, grinning. "I didn't say that everyone did perfectly." She stifled a giggle. "He's going to alert the whole of Woodwing if he keeps that up."

More than two weeks had passed since the four of them had left Mount Jade to track down one of the two remaining lost Treasures. They had just left the town where the very last Tiger Warrior and his Heir had made their final stand, fighting to protect the townspeople against a battalion of invaders from the empire of Waya. Parts of Woodwing were still in ruins, and some of the Wayani soldiers had never left, becoming Guard for the Dragonlord and keeping order for him in Flower Song Province, once renowned for its perfumes and the kingdom's finest incense.

In the guise of day laborers from a neighboring village, Inu and Tora had made discreet inquiries in the town, while Usagi used her rabbit hearing to see if their questions had shaken loose any talk by the locals about the Ring of Obscurity. They made sure to steer clear of the Guard, not wanting to be questioned or suspected of having zodiac powers. Goru's sheer size drew a lot of notice, but the townspeople instantly took a liking to him. He used his strength to help people carry heavy loads, shore up fallen walls, put up buildings, and corral unruly animals.

His helpfulness soon paid off. The townspeople gave Goru warnings so that he could duck out of sight whenever a Guard patrol came through. And then, he returned with a new bit of information.

"Everyone tells me it's been impossible to enter Butterfly Kingdom these last seven years," he reported. "They swear that valley is haunted by the ghosts of the dead, and that their spirits have become butterflies." Goru gave a disbelieving chuckle. "These ghosts will attack when you enter the valley. Doesn't that seem odd?"

"Sounds like they're warning us away from that place. I doubt there are actual butterfly ghosts, but . . . maybe the butterflies are protecting something," said Tora. "I had a vision back at the shrine that an enormous butterfly was guarding the ring."

Usagi nodded. "There could be a connection."

Armed with that hope, they'd quietly left Woodwing and headed for the long rift valley that cleaved the southeastern part of the island. Insects of all kinds were found there, including fireflies, moths, and winged beetles, but especially butterflies of all shapes and sizes, which gave the valley its name.

Though Butterfly Kingdom was a fair distance from even Woodwing, which was the nearest town and an hour away on horseback, it was famous enough that in the days before the war, people used to travel a well-worn track to see the butterflies. Now that they'd left the town, Goru felt free to run along the old route with abandon, and after a while, Usagi and Inu joined in.

Their path became choked with wild growth, and they slowed to a walk. As they picked their way through riotous weeds and creeping vines, Usagi could see the rift walls rising up on either side of them into steep hills, cradling a long flat expanse that was the valley. And everywhere they looked, there was movement.

The trees and bushes seemed to dance with fluttering wings and flashes of jewel-like color. Clouds of purple and yellow filled the air, swirling past them like windblown flower petals as they ventured farther. The shrill drone of cicadas echoed off the valley walls, buzzing in Usagi's ears.

"Spirits," Goru exclaimed. He chortled as a dozen cream-colored butterflies settled on his shaved head, looking like a pulsating feathery hat. "If this is an attack, it's more of a tickle attack than anything else." He gently brushed a hand over his scalp, shooing them away.

Tora gazed about, entranced. She slipped her arm into Usagi's. "I don't think I've ever seen anything more beautiful."

Nodding, Usagi clutched her friend's arm. Her chest felt light and she couldn't stop staring. It was all so wondrous. If only her sister could see this place. Uma used to love chasing after butterflies—until she developed horse speed and became too fast for the fluttering insects. But now that the Dragonlord had her, had she become too hardened to appreciate these delicate winged beauties?

Usagi turned to Inu. "I've only read about the Ring of Obscurity and looked at drawings, but you've actually seen a Warrior wearing it. What should we be looking for?"

"It's been years since I've seen it," Inu said. Thinking, he ran a hand through his shaggy hair, displacing an errant butterfly. "It's got a huge amber stone ... surrounded by carved mother-of-pearl. I remember there was tortoiseshell on the band." He held up his thumb ring. "It's a lot bigger than this archer's ring. I got thumped with it quite a few times when I was misbehaving during lessons with Master Pom."

Tora snickered. "There were paintings of it at the Dragon Academy too. They made us memorize what it looked like and what it could do, but it didn't include thumping naughty Warrior Heirs."

"The 46th Tiger Warrior wasn't shy about knocking it on our skulls." Inu smiled wryly. "He was just as strict as the Tigress."

Usagi looked around the verdant valley, full of trees and bushy thickets dotting long rolling meadows carpeted in blossoms. The sun was giving in to the pull of the horizon. Before long, dusk would set in. "No matter how big Inu says it is, I don't know how we're going to find the ring here. This place is enormous."

"Look to where the butterflies are thickest," Tora said firmly. "That's what I saw when I fainted at the Tree of Elements."

At the mention of the sacred tree, Usagi stuck her hand in her pocket, where she was keeping the piece of ironstone that had fallen from its trunk. She fingered the stone's rough surface. She wasn't sure why she'd brought it, but it felt like a talisman of sorts—a piece of Mount Jade that might protect them on this mission.

Goru laughed. The butterflies had landed back on his head and gathered on his shoulders like a mantle. "Thicker than this?" He shook himself, and the butterflies dispersed.

"If it's truly here, we should be able to locate it, between all of our senses—my dog nose, Usagi's rabbit hearing, and Tora's tiger vision," said Inu. "We'll search till it grows dark, and if we don't turn anything up, we start again in the morning."

A look of longing came into Tora's eyes. "I bet if we'd brought the Mirror of Elsewhere, we'd be able to find it immediately," she muttered to Usagi.

"Good thing we brought the Apothecary—your face would be glued to the mirror otherwise." Usagi grimaced. "You're just feeling its pull. It's not like it would give us a map, you know. You still have to understand what it shows you."

As they walked farther into the valley, they found themselves in an overgrown holloway. The sunken path was lined with sheltering trees. From a vaulted ceiling of branches, butterflies hung in droves, some looking like yellow-green foliage, and others like scraps of bright ribbon. A few were brown and dull, looking for all the world like dead leaves, until they unfolded their wings and fluttered, showing flashes of iridescent purple. The air was heavy with the sweet scent of flowers and green, leafy growth, with a sharp undernote of decay. As Warrior Heirs and presumed leaders of the mission, Inu and Usagi took turns going off the sunken path to do some preliminary exploring, rejoining the group as they traversed along the holloway. On one such excursion, Usagi discovered the trickle of a stream that ran alongside the path, and refilled everyone's water gourds.

The sun went down and the light grew dusky blue. Butterflies settled onto every available leaf and branch, coming to rest for the night. Greenish lights began to wink in the air and the trees, becoming a constellation of fireflies. The valley wasn't terrifying at all. If anything, it was enchanting. "How could anyone possibly think these butterflies are ghosts?" wondered Tora.

"We might as well get ourselves settled," Inu suggested, and Usagi agreed. The holloway seemed a decent shelter, cool against the heat of summer and warm against the evening chill, with fireflies lending their shimmering light. They set up camp and laid out their bedrolls.

Usagi stretched out on the hard-packed earth, staring up at the winking fireflies and the patches of sky visible between the branches covering the holloway. Goru had begun to snore, and Inu soon joined in. She was drifting into sleep when Tora whispered her name. Usagi cracked an eye at her friend. "What is it?"

"I'm seeing a strange light in the sky," said Tora.

Pushing herself up, Usagi tried to look. "Where?"

"It's easier to spot if we move out from under these trees." Tora got up and beckoned Usagi a little way from their campsite, where the two boys continued to sleep soundly.

She pointed to the open sky. "It looks like fire."

Above them was a sea of black, speckled with white starlight like grains of salt on a swath of dark silk. A curved sliver of moon hovered like a silvery claw poised to slice open the sky. And as she followed Tora's finger, Usagi saw a glimmering golden light. Closer to them than any star, it was still just a bobbing speck. Could it be the ghosts the townspeople had warned about?

"What is that?" Usagi wondered. "I can't see much from here."

Tora's amber eyes were narrowed. "It looks exactly like a lantern, only it's not hanging from anything. It's floating—and I think there are words painted on it."

"A sky lantern!" Usagi had read about them in the shrine library. Back before the formation of the Twelve, when the ancient tribes of Midaga were constantly warring with each other, they used fire signals such as sky lanterns and hilltop torches to send messages. But such things hadn't been used in centuries. "Where do you think it's coming from? Could it have drifted here from Woodwing?"

Frowning, Tora shook her head. "I suppose. But the town isn't that close."

"Maybe it's a ghost like they said," joked Usagi, but she felt a shiver of alarm.

Tora snorted. She stared at it a while longer, then headed back to the camp. "I think we need to shoot it down."

Spinning on her heel, Usagi trotted after her. "Are you sure that's such a good idea? That could raise trouble if you get caught by whoever's sent that up. And what if you miss?"

"One—I don't miss," Tora threw over her shoulder. "And two, I won't get caught. I've got my spirit speed, and besides, I doubt there's anyone else in this valley. Look at this old path. No one's been here in years. I'm going to borrow Inu's bow so we can get a closer look at this thing."

Usagi was doubtful. "I don't know—Inu's not going to like you playing with his bow."

"Playing?" scoffed Tora. "I'm as good a shot as he is. He won't mind. If it bothers you, you don't have to come."

"You think I'm going to let you go after this by yourself?"

"Of course not." Tora's snaggleteeth glinted. "Why do you think I woke you in the first place?"

Quietly, they stole into the camp. Tora lifted Inu's bow and quiver from his belongings with careful movements, and Usagi grabbed her walking stick with its hidden sword blade. There was no telling what they might find, so it was better to be prepared. They left the two boys snoring in their bedrolls and set off toward the light in the sky. Using their spirit speed, they ran and bounded in the direction of the lantern, its golden flame shining like a beacon from a lighthouse.

Before long they drew close enough that it seemed to hover directly overhead. Usagi could hear the hiss of the fire that burned at the base of the lantern, propelling the paper balloon high in the air. They were far from the sunken path and the shelter of the holloway, closer to the rising walls that cradled the valley. "Now what?"

"Now we get this thing down." Tora looked up at the floating light and drew out the bow. Nocking an arrow to the string, she took aim and let it fly.

The arrow soared up into the dark. There was a ripping sound as the arrow punched through the sky lantern's fragile paper walls, jerking it aside. It began to list and lean, collapsing on itself, and within seconds the flame that had lifted the lantern began to consume it, licking at the paper with flaring, leaping tongues.

"It's burning up!" Usagi clapped a hand to her mouth as the lantern, now a ball of fire, began to fall. As it plummeted toward them, she and Tora shrieked and darted out of the way. The lantern crashed to the ground in a blaze of burning paper and bamboo, the thin frame crumbling as it burned.

Tora sighed. "Well, that didn't quite go as planned." She approached as the fire shrank and sputtered out, toeing the charred remains. The paper was burned clean off. There was nothing left to read.

"Did you get a look at what it said before you shot it?" Usagi asked.

"Not really." Picking up a burnt scrap of bamboo, Tora examined it dolefully. "Something about a wish or a prayer?"

She looked around, scanning their surroundings. "I wonder where this could have come from."

Usagi rubbed her rabbit pendant, listening carefully. The night air was still, and to ordinary people it would have seemed dead silent. But echoing in her ears were the clicks of insect jaws and their tapping legs, the swoosh of owl wings, the fluttering of moths, the movement of ground squirrels and other small animals in their burrows. Far off in the distance, Usagi could just make out the snores of Inu and Goru. At least they were still asleep.

And then she caught a more unfamiliar sound—a strange thrumming, almost like a very fast heartbeat. It was coming from somewhere deep inside the valley, even farther from where they were, and it seemed to call to her. "I'm hearing something. I think we should try to find it."

"Lead the way," said Tora, looking intrigued.

For a moment, Usagi hesitated. Should they wait for the morning, so their whole group could investigate together? It might be safer. But the thrumming sound was so curious—she felt the urge to find it right away, while she could easily locate it among the notes of the night.

Tora smiled. "I'll see for us in the dark. I've got a good feeling about this."

Slowly they traipsed toward the sound, as Usagi tried to pinpoint its source. At last she figured it was coming from deep in the heart of the valley and the direction of the holloway. Using their spirit speed, they raced toward the end of the sunken path, only to find it blocked off. Usagi drew her hidden blade and poked at the thick brush and hanging vines that clogged the old holloway, but Tora shook her head. "We're going to need help with this."

They decided to return to their camp and come back with the others in the morning. "Something's beyond this—I can hear it," Usagi said, sheathing her sword reluctantly.

She could barely sleep when they got back to their bedrolls, and when the sun peeked over the lip of the valley and the sky began to lighten, Usagi shook everyone awake.

"Tora and I found something last night," she announced. "Well, a couple of things. I heard a strange noise, and traced it to the end of this path, but it's blocked. We'll need to clear a way through to find out what it is, but I think it's important."

Goru rubbed his eyes and stared blearily at her. "What was the other thing?"

"A sky lantern." Usagi held up the charred bamboo frame. "Tora shot it down."

The Dog Heir sat up. "She what?"

"I borrowed your bow," said Tora with a cheeky shrug. "Hope you don't mind."

Sour-faced, Inu examined his bow, then grunted. He

turned his attention to the lantern piece, then gave a low whistle. "I wonder what sort of signal was being sent. Or who was sending it."

"Well, we didn't see anyone, and it burned up before we could figure out what was written on it," said Usagi. She bounced impatiently. "Can you get up now so we can go?"

After rousing out of their bedrolls and downing a quick meal, they set off. Urged on by Usagi, they sped down the sunken path with spirit speed until they reached the place that had stymied Usagi and Tora the night before. In the daylight, Usagi could see why Tora had insisted that they needed more hands. The holloway was impassable, sealed off by a wall of vegetation that extended outside the sunken path. The entire surface was covered in fluttering butterflies, like a bright silk tapestry come to life.

Goru began to rip out the thick vines while the rest of them hacked and pulled at weeds and brush. Butterflies flitted about them—so many that it was hard to see at times. At last an opening was created. Inu sniffed carefully and cocked his head. "I'm not smelling anything different," he said. "Just plants and insects. So many insects."

They slipped through one by one and found themselves in the middle of a lush wood. The thrumming was louder now, and Usagi surged forward. "Come on, it's this way," she said. Squeezing past closely grown trees and scratchy bushes, she led the others to the source of the sound, the hum vibrating in her ears. Butterflies were everywhere, even more of them than Usagi thought possible. It felt as if they were walking through drifting clouds of color.

"What's that?" Tora gasped.

They stopped and stared. Usagi squinted, trying to make out what Tora was pointing at. It was a hulking shape that at first looked like a fallen log, only it was streaked with silver and glistened in the sunlight. One end of it was attached to a massive tree, and it rested on the ground, dwarfing nearly all of them.

"Is that . . ." Inu swallowed. "A chrysalis?"

Goru stepped closer. "You mean to say there's a butterfly growing in there? But . . . it's nearly as big as me!" He peered at the shining, translucent casing, through which intricate wing patterns could be seen, as well as the folded limbs and body of a giant being. "Burping blisters—I think I see the ring."

"What?!"

"Where?"

With exclamations of shock, they crowded around. Goru pointed. There was a steady flutter beneath the surface, which seemed to be the source of the thrumming sound that Usagi had been hearing. And nestled inside the chrysalis, in what appeared to be a coil of rope, was an amber stone rimmed with pale mother-of-pearl.

"How in the world did it get in there?" Usagi wondered.

153

Inu got on a knee and reached out a tentative finger. "It must have been placed here by Master Pom for safekeeping. Judging from the size of the chrysalis, it's probably been guarding the ring all this time." He touched the translucent, silvery casing.

"By the gods," Tora whispered. "It's just as I saw on Mount Jade. How are we going to get it out?"

Reaching into his belt, Inu drew out a knife. "Easy. We'll just make a tiny little cut here and slip the ring out. It shouldn't hurt the butterfly one bit."

"Are you sure?" Tora nervously rubbed the scars on her arm. "In my vision . . . there was a giant butterfly, and it wasn't friendly."

The Dog Heir gestured to the giant form on the ground. "This isn't quite a butterfly yet. I won't hurt it—I'll just nick the shell. It's not going to feel a thing."

Curious, Usagi placed a hand on the chrysalis. It was cool to the touch, and she could feel the vibrations of the fluttering heart beneath the tough, glowing membrane. "I think it'll be fine," she agreed.

"Suit yourself, but don't say I didn't warn you," said Tora, backing away.

Inu's dark eyes crinkled. "I'll be careful." He took the tip of the blade and scored the chrysalis lightly, then went over it again with more force, until a small slit had been created right over the ring. He looked at Usagi. "Your hands are smaller. Can you fish it out?"

Nodding, Usagi leaned over and reached for the ring. The thrumming sound grew louder, and the ground at their feet began to tremble. There was a crack, and the slit in the silvery shell zipped along the length of the giant chrysalis. It split open, and the veined wings began to unfurl. A barbed leg shot out. Usagi screamed and they all scrambled back.

"Spitting spirits, we've awakened it!" cried Tora.

CHAPTER 11

THE KEEPER
OF THE RING

THE GIANT CHRYSALIS TREMBLED, and the split in the translucent silver casing grew even wider as a second leg poked out, jointed and covered in thick spikes. They waved about wildly, and Goru had to duck. Inu rolled out of the way. Usagi and Tora jumped back. Two prismatic round eyes, glittering and as big as platters, emerged along with a curling long appendage. It was the butterfly's tongue, Usagi realized—and it was wrapped firmly around the ring.

"How are we going to get the ring now?" she cried. Even as she spoke, the butterfly was prying itself out of its old shell, heaving and unfurling bit by bit.

With his knife still drawn, Inu warily approached the butterfly struggling to get out of the chrysalis. He reached for the ring. Another set of legs popped out and shoved Inu back. He stumbled and fell, and the butterfly cast aside the rest of its carapace and crawled out, looming over him, waving two knobby antennae as long as Usagi's arm.

Goru grabbed Inu and dragged him out of the way. Gaping, they all stood in a wide circle around the butterfly, unsure what to do next.

Though its wings were crumpled and just beginning to expand, the butterfly was already enormous, with a body that unfolded into segments thick as a tree trunk. They were dark gray and furred, and the undersides of the wings were pale and webbed with veins. They looked like giant dead leaves. But as the wings stretched out and began to beat, Usagi saw brilliant flashes of iridescent purple on the top side of the wings, which were edged in black and dotted with cream and coral spots. It was a butterfly known as the great purple emperor, but far greater than any she'd ever seen—and the Treasure was still clamped in its curled yellow proboscis.

"I don't want to hurt it," said Inu. "But we need to get that ring before it flies away." Slipping his knife back in his belt, he reached for his walking stick, where a metal claw on a long chain was stashed inside.

Flexing his hands, Goru stopped him. "Don't use that," he said. "I'll handle this, giant to giant." He took slow steps toward the butterfly. Its wings were now at their full expanse, stirring the warm summer air with each slow beat. "Nice fly-fly," he crooned. "Good butty-butt. Just give me the ring. No one wants to hurt you."

"Boils and blisters," Tora burst out. "That's no way to approach a butterfly." She yanked up a handful of wildflowers and shoved them into Goru's hand. "They love flowers—show these and maybe then it'll let you get close."

Usagi began grabbing for more. "That can't be enough. Look at the size of that thing."

But Goru had already shuffled closer, offering the blooms to the butterfly. The faceted eyes, as golden as the ring's stone, were trained on the flowers. Its antennae waved, and then the tightly curled tongue began to loosen, along with its grip on the Ring of Obscurity.

"It's working!" breathed Tora.

Goru brought the flowers closer, closer—and then he made a grab for it, throwing an arm around the butterfly's head and trying to pry the ring from its proboscis. There was a loud *whoosh* that seemed to come from the butterfly's entire body, and its hind legs stomped several times, while the barbed front legs flailed. One struck Goru, and a swarm of butterflies flew at his head, blinding him with their fluttering wings. Trying to wipe them from his face, he loosened his grip on the giant butterfly.

With a final push, the butterfly wriggled from his grasp and rolled its proboscis back into a tight coil. It launched into the air, flapping its massive wings and taking the ring with it.

"No!" Inu shouted. He reached for his bow.

"Stop!" cried Usagi. "Don't shoot it!"

Before he could nock an arrow, she took a great big rabbit leap, soaring into the air above them all. The butterfly was lifting higher with each beat of its wings. Usagi focused on its stout gray body as she began to fall, and landed on the butterfly's back. The great insect bucked and wobbled for a bit, but then continued to push its way into the sky. Usagi wrapped her legs around its abdomen and pressed herself against its furry back.

On the ground, the others shouted and screamed. Tora jumped and waved by the empty chrysalis, while Inu stood slack-jawed and Goru hollered through cupped hands. The butterfly flitted and darted, circling over the hidden forest, the ring still curled in its long proboscis. Usagi waved back. "I'll get the Treasure!" she called. She had no idea whether they heard her, but as the butterfly dipped and soared, there was no time to worry about it—she needed to stay on.

The butterfly pulsed beneath her, as if it were taking deep breaths. With each contraction of its body, its massive wings rippled through the air like enormous sails, speeding them through twists and turns that left her gasping. Usagi knew that butterflies didn't fly in straight lines like birds did, but it was one thing to watch an ordinary one flutter about, and quite another to be riding a giant one. It felt as if she was being tossed about the rapids of a rushing river.

With a few stirring beats of its colossal wings, the butterfly took off down the length of the rift valley, swooping and swerving over rolling meadows and clusters of trees. The landscape below shimmered, the colors of butterfly swarms shifting with their tremulous fluttering. As Usagi became more comfortable with the erratic pattern of the butterfly's flight, she sat up a little higher. A grin stole across her face. She was *flying.* Not even her rabbit leap compared to this.

Under the bright morning sun, the roar of the wind filled her ears, her hair whipped nearly out of its plaits. Usagi was still clutching a handful of flowers, though they were getting badly windblown. She stuffed them in her tunic, squealing as they wheeled through the air over Butterfly Kingdom. She could see everything from here—the long, tree-covered holloway, the hidden forest where they'd found the giant chrysalis, the rising walls of the rift valley, the streams that ran along the valley floor.

It was amazing, and a part of her didn't want it to end. But Usagi still needed to get the ring. She was getting tired, her arms and legs aching from hanging on for dear life. Her stomach was barely keeping up with the butterfly's unexpected twists and turns. Trying for the ring seemed impossible. Surely the great purple emperor had to stop and rest sometime. Otherwise, how was she to get down? She prayed to the gods that the massive insect wouldn't fly out of the valley to some unknown corner of the island.

At last, after flying the long span of the rift valley several times over, the butterfly circled back to its hidden forest home. *Please land,* Usagi begged silently. It felt like they'd been flying for hours. She spotted a glimmering pool deep in the heart of the trees, in the midst of a small clearing that grew larger as the butterfly dipped toward it. She braced herself as they alighted on a large boulder in the middle of the water. The butterfly's flapping wings slowed.

"Spirits." Usagi sighed in relief. It felt good to be near solid ground again, her stomach no longer flip-flopping with each unexpected turn. Now for the ring. She pulled the flowers from her tunic and examined them. Bruised and battered, they were all that she had, but were thankfully still fragrant. Stroking the butterfly's furry back, Usagi leaned forward and held the flowers over its enormous eyes. The butterfly uncurled its proboscis toward the blossoms as if to sniff them, the ring gleaming tantalizingly over its tip. Usagi held her breath. *Don't move. Have patience.* She mustn't make the same mistake Goru did. As the end of the long yellow tongue appeared before her, she slowly reached out and plucked off the ring. "Got it!"

The tongue lashed about wildly. Usagi ducked and thrust out the flowers. It batted away the blooms and the butterfly's knobby antennae twitched and gyrated, as if searching for the ring. Usagi balled a fist around the ring, then dove off into the pond with a splash. Kicking to the pond's edge, Usagi clutched the Treasure so hard her hand hurt.

Dripping wet, she staggered out of the water and turned

to look at the giant emperor butterfly. It remained perched on the rock, its shimmering spotted purple wings opening and closing like a heartbeat. Usagi stared at its golden eyes, seeing herself reflected a hundred times in the faceted globes. "Thank you for guarding the ring," she said. "I promise we'll take good care of it."

She didn't know if it understood her or not, but the butterfly's feelers waved, and it made no move to attack her. Slowly she backed away, and then darted into the trees, moving as quickly as she could through the undergrowth. The Treasure was theirs!

Usagi perked her ears, scanning her surroundings until she located the others. They had left the hidden forest and were out searching for her in the valley. She followed their worried voices at a brisk trot until she was standing at the edge of a rolling meadow. Usagi spotted Goru's tall bulk in the distance, and bounded toward them with spirit speed.

"There she is!" Tora cried.

"Thank the gods," said Goru.

Upon reaching them, she grinned and jumped straight into the air, high above their heads in celebration. She held up the ring. "I got it!" She bounced into the air again and twirled.

"All right, calm down and let us see it," said Inu with a laugh. He put away his bow.

Usagi clutched her heart. "I'm glad you didn't shoot," she said. "It's actually a very gentle creature."

"It looked like a monster," Inu admitted. "I wouldn't be surprised if the power of the ring made it grow like that."

"Just because something's unusually big doesn't mean it's a monster," said Goru self-consciously. He looked at Usagi. "Quick thinking on your part, Rabbit Girl. I thought I could wrestle it away, but scared the poor thing instead."

With a smile, Usagi put the ring in Goru's hand. "Well, I got to fly—and now we have the Ring of Obscurity!"

They gathered around to admire it. The central amber stone glowed like a miniature sun, cradled by mother-of-pearl that shone with an iridescent light, as if it were the arms of the moon. Now that they could look more closely at it, Usagi noticed twelve tiny animals of the zodiac carved into the mother-of-pearl. It was all set in a dark tortoiseshell band that gleamed with flecks of gold.

"Beautiful," Goru said. He began to polish it on his sleeve, but Tora and Usagi cried out, and Inu grabbed his arm.

"We'll be overtaken by clouds if you rub it," Inu reminded. "It has power. Let's wait till we get back to the shrine."

"Sorry, I forgot." Sheepishly, Goru handed it to Usagi. "Here, Rabbit Girl—why don't you hold it for safekeeping."

It was time to head back to Mount Jade. Usagi strung the ring on the chain around her neck, and tucked it under her collar alongside her rabbit pendant. They traipsed along the shaded holloway, butterflies fluttering all along their path, making their way toward the mouth of the valley. Usagi lifted her hand and let the butterflies land on her palm as she walked, thinking of the great purple emperor butterfly. It no longer had to guard the Treasure. It was free.

They emerged from the sunken path when Usagi's ears pricked. There was a rustling in a sprawling thicket nearby. "Something's in those bushes," she muttered to the others, pointing. "And I don't think it's ghosts."

Tora stopped, surveying the underbrush with narrowed eyes. Usagi clutched her walking stick close, and Goru flexed his fingers, frowning. Inu sniffed the air. "Half a dozen unwashed bandits," he growled.

A rock came sailing through the air and clonked Goru on the head, hard enough that Usagi gasped at the sound. His eyes rolled back, and he hit the ground like a felled tree, shaking the earth. "Goru!" Usagi cried.

Loud yells erupted and a group of thin, ragged men charged. Usagi and the others formed a protective circle around Goru's prone body as the bandits surrounded them. They weren't very tall but carried wooden clubs and hid their faces behind cloth kerchiefs—and they all had a tattoo of a butterfly inked on their wiry forearms. A few of the bandits clutched hefty stones and slings. "Give us your packs," ordered one, his voice thin and reedy. His eyes were a startlingly pale gray, almost silver. "Or we'll do the same to the rest of you."

Inu exchanged glances with Usagi and Tora. His hands

tightened on the sections of his walking stick. He shook his head. "You'll have to come and take them, I'm afraid."

"That's not very smart," warned the silver-eyed bandit. He nodded at the other bandits, and one of them twirled a leather sling over his head, launching a stone straight at Inu's temple. Inu ducked in the nick of time and pulled his hidden steel claw out of his walking stick. He threw it at the bandit's sling, hooking it. With a yank on his claw's metal chain, he tore the sling from the bandit's grasp.

A couple of bandits came at them, hefting their clubs. Usagi ran to meet them, throwing up her stick. She blocked their blows, then swung her stick in a wide circle, aiming to get them both. But they spun out of the way more quickly than she expected and she only grazed the shoulder of one, who yelped. The untouched bandit attacked her again, and Usagi barely managed to deflect the blow. These bandits were surprisingly strong and fast. Could they have animal talents of some sort?

She glanced over at Inu and Tora, and saw that the Dog Heir had faced off against the silver-eyed bandit, who was dodging all attempts by Inu to nick him with his sharp hook on a chain. Unusually, the hook appeared to swing back at Inu each time he threw it, hard enough that he had to duck. The silver-eyed bandit must have a metal gift.

Tora's fangs had come out, and she'd already clawed two of the bandits so that their sleeves were in bloody shreds.

But a third was sneaking up on Tora from behind. Usagi shouted a warning, and when Tora spun around, the bandit disappeared.

Usagi's mouth fell open, as did Tora's. The bandit had vanished into thin air. It was only the swish of a club coming at Usagi that jolted her out of her shock. She jumped straight into the air, higher than she meant to, and stared down at the group of bandits. They had zodiac powers, too. As she landed, she could see the surprise in the bandits' eyes, and they all froze for a moment. The disappearing bandit materialized, looking at Usagi with wide eyes.

Then Goru rose to his feet, roaring, and grabbed the bandits by the scruffs, crashing them together like cymbals and casting their limp bodies aside. Within a few moments, all six of the bandits had been knocked unconscious. Goru rubbed the raised bump on the back of his shaved head and glared at their attackers. "Let's tie these fools up," he growled.

Inu had a coil of rope, which they used to bind up the bandits. While they worked to tether them all together, a few of the kerchiefs over the bandits' faces slipped off.

"Gods' guts—they're all younglings," Tora exclaimed, pulling down the rest of their masks.

Usagi looked closer. "They're not all boys, either."

The lead bandit stirred and opened her silver-gray eyes. "No, we're not. But neither are you. Who are you?"

Cleaning the Ring of Obscurity is slightly more complicated, but not difficult if the number of activating strokes is kept in mind. Rubbing must be done with care.

Swish the ring in a bowl of lukewarm water, then pat dry with a soft cloth. The various parts of the ring may be wiped in a set number of strokes, then repeated as necessary. Do not exceed the number of strokes per set, or else the ring will be triggered to spew thick clouds of mist, dust, or smoke, depending on which section was rubbed. Therefore, wipe each part of the ring minimally.

A light coat of oil can be added for sheen.

ᴄ᷍ ACTIVATION STROKES ᷓᴐ

Amber: *Rapidly rub the stone twelve times to release yellow dust.*

Mother-of-pearl: *Circle the setting three times to produce white mist.*

Tortoiseshell: *Rub the band four times for black smoke.*

If the ring has accidentally been set off,
open all windows and doors and air out the room.

—Care and Maintenance, from *Warrior's Guide to the Treasures of the Twelve*

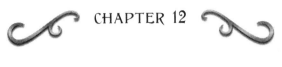

CHAPTER 12

GANG OF GHOSTS

GORU LOOMED OVER THE SIX bandits, younglings all. Except for the silver-eyed girl, the rest were still unconscious, their hands and feet trussed so they wouldn't cause any more grief. The rapidly swelling bump on Goru's head was turning an angry red from the rock the bandits had hurled at him. He glared at the bandit and repeated after her question. "Who are we?" His nostrils flared. "Who are *you*? How dare you attack us when we were just minding our own business?"

With a grunt and a grimace, the youngling sat up. Her hair was cropped short, and there was a growing lump on her forehead. She scowled and her eyes flashed. "You have no right to be trespassing here. The four of you may have zodiac powers, but so do we, and the Butterfly Kingdom is ours."

Goru folded his arms. "Says who?"

"We're not trying to stake out territory, if that's what you think," Inu interjected. "We were just passing through when you and your little band attacked."

The girl raised an eyebrow. "Oh really? You weren't running all over the valley, using our signal lantern for target practice, and trying to capture the emperor butterfly? Don't look so surprised—we saw one of you riding it, trying to bring it down."

Tora shifted uneasily. "That lantern was yours?"

"Yes, and you had no right to shoot it," snapped the bandit.

"We weren't trying to capture the butterfly," objected Usagi. "It was carrying something that belonged to us."

Rolling her eyes, the bandit scoffed. "And what could that possibly be? That chrysalis was sacred. You shouldn't have bothered it."

"It couldn't be helped," Usagi insisted. "We had an obligation to fulfill." Out of habit, she reached nervously for her rabbit pendant, but remembered the ring was attached. She scratched her neck instead.

Goru put a giant hand on Usagi's shoulder. "You don't have to explain anything to them. We got what we came for, and we'll be on our way."

"Hold on now," said the Dog Heir. "If someone came to our home uninvited and disturbed things, we'd be upset too." He bowed to the silver-eyed girl. "We're sorry. We didn't mean to scare you."

The bandit gave him a disdainful look. "We're not scared. We're the Ghosts of Butterfly Kingdom. Those who wander here fear *us*."

"Ghosts? You all seemed pretty solid when I knocked your heads together," snorted Goru. He paused and regarded her for a moment. "But folks in the nearest town did warn me that the valley was haunted."

Usagi had a realization. "Are you from Woodwing originally? Do the townpeople say that to keep the Guard away?"

The girl's silver eyes widened. "Yes," she admitted. "Our parents sent us here when the invaders started going after anyone with powers. They warned us to never show ourselves to the Guard and started spreading rumors about the valley being haunted so people would avoid it. You're the first ones to come through in a long time."

"That's pretty smart," said Tora. "I wish we'd had more people willing to cover for us in our hometown. All the younglings with powers ended up exposed."

"Even so, I'd be careful if I were you," said Inu. "The Dragonlord is still looking for younglings with powers, and he's doing much more than sending them to the mines these days."

"He's training them for his strike force," said Tora. "A growing number of Dragonstrikers out there are those with zodiac powers. They're a lot harder to fight off."

Nodding, Usagi added, "When we ran into some, we

barely managed to get away."

Goru tested the bump on his head and flinched. "And trust me, you don't want to become a Striker. They tried forcing me to join—and I saw nothing good about them."

The other younglings began to stir, and a couple of them groaned as they came to. Inu looked at them and gestured to Usagi and Tora. "We should free them."

"Here, let me," said Goru gruffly, and bent to untie the ropes that bound the younglings. But he got a little dizzy and reached out to steady himself. "Bumps and bones, whoever threw that rock has a good arm."

The silver-eyed girl cracked a smile for the first time. "That would be me. You can call me Miru."

They freed Miru and her companions. Head bumps and scratches were attended to with medicines from the Apothecary, while apologies and introductions were made all around.

"It's not often we meet others with powers," said a scrawny boy named Puli. Born in the year of the Tiger, he was the one with the talent for disappearing, seemingly into thin air. He grinned at Tora. "You gave us the toughest fight we've ever had!"

"I'd expect no less from a fellow Tiger," said Tora loftily, baring her tiger-toothed smile.

The younglings of Butterfly Kingdom, who called themselves the Ghosts, invited them to stay for a meal. They brought them to their encampment, a small sheltered bower deep in the valley, not far from where Tora had shot down the sky lantern.

Over a simple meal of boiled greens, roasted caterpillars, and a makeshift tea of flower petals sweetened with nectar, Miru explained that they hardly had any contact with the outside world, though sometimes meager supplies were hidden for them at the entrance to the valley. Each month, during the new moon, they would send up a sky lantern as a signal to their families of their survival. They painted their wishes and prayers on the lantern for good measure, in hopes that they would reach the gods. "When it got shot down last night, we knew there were intruders."

Tora dropped her head. "I'm sorry. I had no idea."

The girl shrugged and turned her silver gaze to Usagi. "When we saw you flying around on the giant butterfly, we really got worried. Part of the reason our parents sent us here was because of the Tiger Warrior and his Heir."

"They defended our province so bravely, may their spirits rest," Puli burst out. The scrawny Ghost gave a savage poke at the campfire with a roasting stick, sending up sparks. "The people of Woodwing will never forget, no matter how hard the Guards try to make them."

Miru's eyes grew steely. "Yes. Never forget." Taking a sip of tea, she continued. "The Tiger Warrior told our families that there was something of great power hidden in the valley, and we'd be safer here. We figured it was the emperor chrysalis—what else could it be? So we couldn't let you leave Butterfly Kingdom—at least not before we made sure you hadn't harmed the emperor."

Exchanging glances with Usagi and the Heirlings, Inu hesitated, then told the Ghosts of their true identities, and what they were trying to do. "We didn't mean to disturb the butterfly, but we had to get Master Pom's ring. It must be taken back to the Shrine of the Twelve."

The Ghosts were astonished. A sacred relic of the Warriors, in their own valley! They spent the rest of the meal asking the four of them questions. As darkness fell, the two groups huddled around the light of the campfire, exchanging stories. The Heirs and Heirlings demonstrated some kicking and striking techniques to help the Ghosts in their next fight.

"Can you imagine if all younglings with powers could join forces?" exclaimed Puli. "We'd never live in fear of the Dragonlord's men again."

With a snort, Goru touched his head where the bump had been. "You have Miru, the Ghost with the Good Arm. They ought to be in fear of you."

Smiling, Miru flexed her arm, and the wings of her butterfly tattoo seemed to flutter. "Any Guard who tangles with this will be sorry."

They examined the slings and clubs that the Ghosts had

used in their attack and dispensed advice on how to defend oneself when their weapons were limited. Usagi showed them some pressure points that could render an opponent immobile, much to Miru's delight. It was late when they finally collapsed around the campfire, exhausted.

As they slept around the embers of a dying fire, Usagi was awakened by the sounds of thrashing and whimpering. Tora was kicking about in her bedroll. She shook her friend's shoulder. "Wake up! You're having a bad dream!"

Tora's eyes blinked open, and she sat up, breathing hard. Sweaty tendrils of her unruly hair were stuck to her temples. "A vision," she said, dazed. "I think I had another vision of the future."

"What was it?" whispered Usagi. The rest of the camp was fast asleep beneath the trees, whose leaves quivered from Goru's snores.

Tracing the scars on her arm, Tora frowned. "I saw a worker in the Eastern Mines. He was running away with a hammer in his hand. It looked like the Conjurer. I followed him and wound up in a deep canyon of pale marble, where there was a banquet attended by faceless people. Then a lot of people were chasing me."

Usagi shuddered. "People without faces? What do you think it means?"

"I'm not sure." Tora lay back, thinking. "But that hammer is around the Marble Gorge. I just know it. If we go there, I think we'll find the Conjurer."

In the morning, they told Inu and Goru about Tora's dream. Inu frowned. "The Marble Gorge is in the next province over, but we'll have to pass by the Eastern Mines to get to it. It could be dangerous."

"Everything we do is dangerous," retorted Tora. "Since when has that ever stopped us?"

"Besides, wasn't the Conjurer first hidden near the mines? They were part of Tora's dream," said Usagi. "That must mean something, Inu. You said yourself that the gift of foresight is a talent she's developing."

Goru rubbed his giant hands together. "I say we go take a look. Tora saw the giant butterfly, after all. We should heed her tiger vision."

They prepared to leave the younglings' encampment. Since the Ghosts had only rock slings and wooden clubs, Inu offered them a few blades from his pack, some small enough to throw, and a sizable one that would be an effective weapon in Miru's hands, given her elemental gift with metal.

"We have a friend who's keeping other younglings with powers under his protection in a remote sanctuary," Inu told her. "It's a ways from here, deep in the central part of the island, but if you're interested in joining forces with others, it would be a good place to start. We can take you."

The silver-eyed girl hesitated. She looked at the other

younglings. A couple of them made faces and shook their heads. "Appreciate the offer, but we've managed to do just fine where we are. Someday we'll be strong enough to make our way back home."

"I'm sure you will," said the Dog Heir. He gave a crooked smile. "We'll be going, then. But if you ever change your mind, go to Sun Moon Lake. When you come across a man named Yunja, just tell him that Inu—born in the year of the Metal Dog—sent you." He gave Miru a formal bow.

She bowed back. "On behalf of the Ghosts, this Metal Dragon thanks you."

A cry went up from the younglings of the valley. "Great gods, look what's coming!"

It was the giant purple butterfly, soaring through the air like a flying ship with shimmering sails. The enormous creature dipped and dove, circling above them several times, as if to say goodbye. Usagi was half tempted to leap after it and try for another ride. She waved at it instead, touching the Ring of Obscurity at her neck. *Thank you*, she thought. The others exclaimed and shaded their eyes against the morning sun, watching the butterfly's fluttering dance in the sky, its massive wings stirring everything around them with a gentle breeze. Then the great purple emperor wheeled and flew off toward the hidden forest, deep in the heart of the valley.

"It looked like it was blessing you," said Miru, her silver eyes wide.

Usagi smiled. "Let's hope."

They said their goodbyes to the Ghosts of Butterfly Kingdom, and the Heirs and Heirlings set out from the valley.

"I wonder if they'll ever go to Sun Moon Lake," said Usagi. "They've been hiding in Butterfly Kingdom for so long. They're lucky the people of Wingwood protect them."

Inu tossed his shaggy hair out of his eyes. "They can't hide in the valley forever, and it'd be good for them to be with other people with zodiac powers. They even said so themselves. If they change their minds, they know where to go."

A thought occurred to Usagi. "You and Saru came across younglings with powers in the Dancing Dunes, and now we've discovered this group in the Butterfly Kingdom. There must be more younglings with powers hiding out there."

He nodded. "I wouldn't be surprised. The war might've wiped out most grown men and women with powers, but it couldn't eliminate powers in Midagians entirely. Some will always emerge with talents and gifts as they come of age, as they have from the island's earliest days. It's only smart to hide."

"If we find more, we should bring them to hide at Sun Moon Lake," said Goru. "They'd be on our side instead of the Blue Dragon's. Together we'd be so much stronger."

Usagi felt a prick of doubt. Even if they did take all the younglings they found to Yunja, what was that to the Dragonlord, who already had so many under his command? Maybe it would be better to leave them be, especially if they'd found a way to live undetected. It seemed risky to involve more people in their cause. So many things could go wrong.

Launching into spirit speed, they headed for the province of Copper Moon, hardly stopping as they leaped and ran in the direction of the Marble Gorge. Usagi bounded with zeal, covering ever-longer distances with each step. It felt good to soar through the air by her own talents, though she would never forget what it had been like to actually fly. On the chain around her neck, the Ring of Obscurity bounced and clinked alongside her rabbit pendant. The ring's weight was reassuring, reminding her that they had but one last missing Treasure to find. Once they recovered the Conjurer, they would be in the perfect position to go after the Treasures held by the Blue Dragon—and rescue the Tigress at last.

When it grew dark, they stopped to make camp and rest, eating the provisions they'd brought. Tora was quiet and listless, ignoring her salted strip of boar meat. Her tawny skin was ashen and her eyes were unfocused.

"You look like you're going to throw up," Usagi said, concerned. She brought out a sliver of dried manroot and urged Tora to chew it. "I know you don't like the bitter taste, but it will make you feel better."

With a grimace, Tora stuck the manroot in her cheek. "I'm not going to throw up. But my head feels like it's going to split open."

Goru rubbed his giant palms together and put them on either side of Tora's head. "Does this help?" His fingers covered her entire face.

"Not really," she said, pushing his hands away with a wan smile. She pinched her eyebrows together. "It's like something's trying to come out."

Inu frowned. "That doesn't sound good." He offered her some water.

As Tora drank, Usagi searched for something else that might ease her headache. She felt the ironstone in her pocket and had an idea. "Maybe what's trying to emerge is another vision. I brought a piece of the Tree of Elements with me—it's the chunk of tiger iron that fell out when you were having your vision of the butterfly. Do you want to hold it for a while and see if something arises?"

"I don't know, Usagi." A flicker of fear crossed Tora's face. "What happened at the Tree of Elements scared me."

"But the vision you had—it totally came true," said Usagi. "And I was there. You'll be okay. I won't let anything happen to you."

Inu and Goru exchanged glances. "Are you sure about this, Usagi?" asked the Dog Heir.

With an impatient sigh, Usagi held out the tiger iron. "Just try a little mind-the-mind and hold this. Trust me. I think it might help."

Tora winced and pressed her fingers to her temples. "All right." She took the piece of ironstone and cradled it in her palm. She straightened in her seat and closed her eyes. Her breath slowed. As Usagi and the others waited, Tora's eyelids began to flutter. Her forehead creased and her breathing became shallow. "Oh!" she exclaimed. A tear crept out from the corner of an eye and rolled down her cheek. After what seemed like an eternity, she took a shuddering breath and opened her eyes. Dazed, she blinked and smiled, the color returning to her face. "You were right, Usagi. It was a vision trying to surface."

"Well, what did you see?" demanded Goru.

Tora turned the tiger iron over and over in her fingers. "It was another vision of the Conjurer. I saw the hammer on a slab of white marble, surrounded by glowing blue light. It felt warm and safe. Like you'd feel when you're with family. And a voice was calling to me. It sounded almost like my father—but I think it was the Conjurer."

"The hammer was talking?" Goru sat back, puzzled. "So . . . is that it?"

"That, and my headache is gone," said Tora with relief. "I'm not great at explaining what I see. All I can say is we're definitely on the right track."

In the morning, they set off at the start of Dragon hour, traveling by spirit speed over hills and vales, by streams and lakes. As the sun crawled across the heavens, they crossed through untamed forests and swaths of grassland. Eventually the land grew rocky and barren, with little in the way of trees or vegetation to shield them.

They slowed to a stop. The sun was just going down, casting long shadows as it sank behind a plain dotted with colossal mounds around gaping maws in the earth. Wisps of smoke stretched toward the sky, weaving a hazy filter over the landscape.

"Is that what I think it is?" Usagi wondered.

Inu nodded grimly. "Yes. The Eastern Mines."

CHAPTER 13

SHADOWLANDS

THE SETTING SUN TURNED BLOOD red as it slipped through the thick haze that hung over the plain—a wide, flat expanse that went on for as far as the eye could see. Deep gashes in the earth shredded the landscape, and massive conical piles surrounded them, crusting the plain like giant barnacles. Towering plumes of smoke rose from smelting furnaces. In the distance, Usagi heard the clinking of hammers, rock being pulverized to dust, the crack of whips on human flesh, and keening shrieks of pain.

"The Eastern Mines are bigger than ever," said Inu. "And I can smell their poison from here." He pulled out a long cloth and wound it around his nose and mouth.

Goru sniffed, then shook his head. "I can't quite smell anything, but I see the smoke." Though the gray pall that blanketed the horizon, the sky was streaked with scarlet and gold, as if it were on fire. Dusk was setting in, and Usagi spied flickers of torchlight bobbing in the distance. She could hear the squeak of wagon wheels and oxen lowing as their carts were filled with extracted metals and precious stones to be transported on the Ring Road to the capital. Tora surveyed the landscape ahead and frowned.

"There are a lot of Guard around," she said. "We'd best keep our distance."

"How?" Usagi scratched her nose.

The Eastern Plains of Midaga were mineral rich and had supplied the kingdom with precious metals for centuries. Between the fertile fields of the Western Plains, called Midaga's rice bowl, and the abundant ore and gemstone deposits in the mines of the Eastern Plains, known as Midaga's vault, the kingdom had never wanted for anything.

But ever since the Blue Dragon had seized the throne, the crops of the Western Plains had been largely sent to neighboring empires as tribute, while the Eastern Mines had become not just a source of gold and silver for the Wayanis and Hulagans, but also a place for the Dragonlord to send his enemies and anyone suspected of being a threat to his regime. It was clear the mines had grown in size as thousands of Midagians were sent to labor in their depths. Never before had Midaga produced so much in riches. But none of it was for its people—and worse, its people were suffering for it.

Tora scanned their surroundings. There was little cover

out on the plain. "Lucky for us it's getting dark, but we shouldn't camp out in the open like this. We can better hide ourselves in those hills." She pointed.

They trudged along in silence, Tora leading the way in the fading light. Usagi had never been to this part of the island, but being sent to the mines had been a threat for nearly half her life, and she was unnerved to see them, even at a distance. The sounds of constant toil and suffering were all too clear with her rabbit hearing, and they tore at her with every step. She wished she could block them out the way Inu was trying to block out foul smells with his head-wrap. Usagi fumbled in her pockets for some cotton wool to muffle her hearing but came up empty. She gritted her teeth and marched on.

As they drew closer to the hills, Inu grew uneasy. He pulled down the cloth covering his nose and sniffed the air. "I smell death," he muttered, wrapping the cloth more firmly about his face. "Keep together and stay alert."

Usagi tightened her grip on her walking stick and kept her ears pricked. Nervously she felt for her rabbit pendant. Her fingers brushed the Ring of Obscurity, and she cupped her palm around it, comforted for a moment. If they got into trouble, at least they had something that might help them out of it.

The sky turned dark, with only a faint glimmer of light from the sliver of moon rising over the horizon. They reached the edge of the hills, the great mounds looming black in the night. There was something familiar about their shape, like so many giant sleeping turtles. Usagi gave an involuntary squeak.

Inu and the others turned. "What is it?" he asked.

"I think I know why you smell death," Usagi said. "These aren't hills. They're graves."

Tora gasped. "Just like the turtleback grave at home."

"There's one outside my town too," Goru said softly. The traditional rounded turtle shape of Midagian graves was still visible in mass graves created after invasion and war, but the graves were so large they were often mistaken for hills. Usagi hadn't seen one since she'd left Goldentusk.

But here, on the outskirts of the mines, was a whole host of great mounds. A giant graveyard, filled with who knew how many hundreds—or thousands—of dead. Usagi felt sick. How many people were worked till the point of collapse? How many were thrown away here?

They set up camp but spent a mostly sleepless night. Usagi found it hard to fall asleep, there amid the looming grave mounds, and the others tossed and turned as well. It wasn't until the moon was high in the sky that soft snoring broke out at last, but Usagi remained wide awake, even as she closed her eyes and prayed for sleep. When the hour of the Rabbit came, the dawn light turning the black turtlebacks gray, Usagi gave up. She decided to stretch her legs and got out of her bedroll.

The Dog Heir raised his head. "Where are you going?" Inu whispered.

Usagi gestured to the surrounding hills. "I can't sleep. I thought I'd take a short walk around."

"I can't sleep either," said Tora. She rolled over, yawning, and sat up. "Do you want some company?"

A groan erupted from Goru. "We're all awake. I don't think anyone can sleep well in this place. Let's just get going."

"The sooner we get out of here, the better," agreed Inu.

They packed up and set off, winding through the mounds. Unlike the giant turtleback at home, which was green with grasses and wildflowers, these were barren dirt hills littered with rocks and gravel. "Gods," Usagi said. She kicked a stone, skittering it out of their path. "I was always afraid of being sent here, but now I know why."

"We haven't even gotten a look in the actual mines yet," said Tora.

"Trust me, we don't need to," Usagi said. "What I've been hearing since we got here is horrible. Seeing it might be even worse."

Her ears pricked and she stopped in her tracks. "There's someone else here," she hissed. "Somewhere to the west."

Inu raised his head and sniffed. "By that far mound over there. How did I miss that?" He shook his head. "The stench of the mines and the graves is throwing me off."

With a stretch and twist like a cat just awakening from a nap, Tora stole a look in the direction Inu was indicating. She squinted. "I see him. A youngling. Huh. He's scraggly looking. Ox Boy here could squash him in an instant."

"Oi, be nice," said Goru mildly.

"It's a compliment. You could squash *anyone* in an instant," said Usagi.

"That's true," he admitted with a modest shrug.

"Can you see anything else?" Inu asked. "He seems to be alone."

Peering toward the westernmost hill grave, Tora frowned. "He doesn't look much older than we are. I don't think he's escaped the mines—he'd be skeletal if he had. He's not in any sort of armor, but he's got a sword. I don't like that."

"Maybe he wants to join us," Usagi suggested. "Maybe he escaped the mines a while ago and has been hiding here."

Tora considered. "Or maybe he's spying for the Guard."

"Let's see if he follows us," said Inu. "We'll keep going."

They trod on, Inu leading the way forward, while Usagi listened with her rabbit hearing and Tora used her tiger vision to keep track of the strange youngling. He was moving quickly, stepping lightly on the rocks and gravel that covered the hills as if he traversed them often. His feet barely made a sound, but every now and again his sword would rattle in its sheath, and occasionally there would be a small stony crunch or the clatter of an accidentally kicked pebble as he hurried to keep up with them.

"He's definitely following us," said Usagi. She glanced back. The sky was lightening as the sun began to emerge, and it was getting harder for the youngling to hide. Even she could see him now, crouching behind a pile of rocks, unsuccessfully trying to conceal himself. His hair was shaved down on the sides, but stuck up in longer spikes on top, protruding from behind the heap of rubble.

Tora rolled her eyes. "This is silly." She whirled and, in a burst of spirit speed, ran and leaped upon their stalker. He yelped and struggled, but Tora quickly overcame him. She called for the others. "Oi! Come look at what I've caught!"

As she approached, Usagi saw that Tora had him facedown on the ground, his arms pinned behind him. His cheek was mashed against a rock, and he winced as Tora grabbed him by the scruff. "Who are you and why are you following us?" she demanded.

Gritting his teeth, the youngling said nothing. Tora looked over her shoulder at Usagi. "Take his weapon."

While Tora continued to pepper him with questions, Usagi reached for the sword at his side. It rang out with a metallic zing as she pulled it out from its sheath. It was a fine one, made of the hardest steel, with a beautifully lacquered scabbard. The hilt was wrapped in glistening sharkskin and bound with gold thread. "Nice," she muttered, examining it.

It would have looked right at home on the weapons wall at the Shrine of the Twelve.

"Hold it to his throat," said Tora, who was crouched on top of their stalker, her feet firmly planted on his back. As Inu and Goru joined them, she scowled. "He's not answering any of my questions."

"Why should I when you're crushing me?" her captive grunted.

Tora glared at him. "You want to know what real crushing is? Here, Goru, let's have you sit on him!"

The youngling's eyes widened, but Goru just sighed. "I can do more than crush people, you know."

He nudged Tora aside and sat the youngling up, keeping a firm hold on him with an enormous hand. Though their captive was scruffy and lean, with spiky, unkempt hair and a faded scar on one cheek, he was well dressed in an embroidered tunic and pants of deep oxblood red.

"If he's not a spy, he must be a bandit," Usagi muttered to Tora. "Look at his clothes and his weapon. They have to be stolen."

With a curt nod, Tora examined the blade of the youngling's sword. "Agreed." She took it and pointed the sword at him. "All right, you sneak. I'm giving you one more chance to state your business. What were you doing, following us around? Are you spying for the Guard?"

An indignant look crossed the youngling's face. His scar

puckered. "I do nothing for the Guard."

"Were you planning on robbing us?" asked Inu. "That's unwise. I'm sure your sword is a sharp one, but you won't get much from us. Besides, you're outnumbered."

The youngling smirked. "Maybe, maybe not."

Tora gave the sword a little shake. "We're not jesting. Answer our questions or you'll never get this back."

He glanced up at the rising sun, and a mischievous gleam came into his eyes. "I don't really care if I get that back or not." The boy shrugged.

"Wait, what's happening to your tunic?" Usagi stared as the youngling's clothes began transforming before her eyes. The thick oxblood fabric faded to a nondescript gray and erupted in patches, while his pants developed holes at the knee and ragged hems. His sturdy felt-and-leather shoes turned into worn straw sandals, tied to his feet with scraps of rope.

The sword Tora held disappeared, and she jumped. "What . . . I was just . . . it's gone!" she spluttered, her hands grasping at air.

"Spirits!" exclaimed Goru, squeezing the youngling's shoulder so hard that he squealed like a pig. "Sorry."

Usagi's whole body tingled. They were close to the last missing Treasure! The hammer could create anything you wished for—but whatever it granted wouldn't last long, existing for a single cycle through the hours of the zodiac before vanishing. Looking at the boy in his rags, it was clear that his finery had come from the Conjurer, and recently. She tried to contain her excitement as she exchanged glances with Inu and the others. She could see they were thinking the same thing.

"You wouldn't happen to have seen a special hammer around here, would you?" the Dog Heir said carefully.

The youngling's eyes widened for a split second, then he shook his head. "I don't know what you're talking about." He pulled at his sleeves, which had become rather short, and avoided Inu's gaze.

"You do too," accused Tora. She flapped her empty hands. "How else do you explain your disappearing sword? It was right here."

The youngling shrugged. "What sword? I don't see any sword. Stop making things up." He pressed his lips together defiantly.

Tora's eyes narrowed and her lip curled, exposing one of her tiger teeth. She took a step toward him, but Inu stopped her.

"All right, then. Sorry about that," he said to the youngling. "There must have been some sort of mistake. We hadn't realized the Eastern Mines came this far west, and the fumes from the mines are addling our brains." He nodded at Goru. "Let him go." Goru looked puzzled but released his grip. The boy rubbed his shoulder with a grimace and got to his feet. With a wary gaze, he backed away a few steps. When Inu waved a dismissive hand, the youngling turned and ran off.

They watched him go. He looked back over his shoulder once, then sped up until he disappeared around a mound.

"Quick," said Inu. "We need to follow him."

They scrambled after their spy, launching into spirit speed until they were nearly on top of him. "There he is!" said Tora, coming to a sudden halt. The boy faltered and turned his head.

"Don't let him see us," hissed Inu, and they pressed themselves into the shadows of the grave mounds.

Goru's stomach growled, loud enough to sound like a disgruntled bear. Inu frowned and shushed him. "What?" Goru looked affronted. "We never had our morning meal!"

Reaching into her pack, Usagi pulled out a strip of salted boar. "Here."

"So small." Goru peered glumly at the wrinkled, dry sliver in his giant fingers. With a sigh, he popped it in his mouth and began to chew.

The scar-faced boy resumed his hurried trek to some unknown destination. Hanging back as far as they could, Usagi, Inu, and Tora used their animal talents to track his movements while keeping out of the boy's sight. They clambered over the rock-strewn slopes of the hill graves, threading through the mounds as the youngling jogged north.

Usagi was stunned at how many graves there were. They seemed to stretch on for at least a league, in sight of the Eastern Mines. The smoke from the smelters rose thickly in the morning air, and the towering slag piles loomed in the distance, even bigger than the grave mounds.

"Where do you think he's going?" she wondered.

"To the Conjurer, I hope," said Inu. "It was so obvious that his clothes and sword were granted by the hammer, especially when they vanished right before our eyes. That's the downside to getting whatever you wish for—any happiness it brings you won't last."

Tora scoffed. "If whatever I wished for didn't disappear on me, my happiness would stick around just fine."

Despite the youngling's threadbare clothes and tattered slippers, he strode over the rocky ground quickly, never seeming to flag. They followed him for hours, and even as the sun rose to its highest point in the sky, the scar-faced boy kept going. Usagi was impressed by his stamina.

Vegetation was starting to return to the landscape, and the grave mounds gave way to actual hills. Usagi picked her way past dense low scrub and dusty plants covered in prickles. There might be places to hide here. She wondered if they were getting close to his home.

They climbed up a ridge that afforded them a look at the plain. The Eastern Mines looked smaller now, the haunting sounds of mining and despair grown faint, and Inu had let the cloth around his nose slide down. Usagi detected the rattle of wheels just over the next ridge—the Ring Road was near. As they watched and followed the boy, he seemed to drop out of sight.

"Where'd he go?" asked a bewildered Goru.

Inu raised his head and sniffed. "He's still there. And a bunch of other people—not far from here."

At that, Usagi pricked her ears. Sure enough, there were voices.

"Look who's back! We were just going to send a search party after you."

"Stayed out too long, did you? Look, all your hammer grants are gone. Gods be good, Panri, you know better than that."

"Not my fault—I came across a bunch of travelers in the Shadowlands."

"They're talking about the Conjurer—and us," said Usagi.

Putting a finger to his lips, Inu whispered, "Okay then. Stay close and don't make a sound." Gingerly, they traversed a rocky path and drew near to what looked like a ravine. Peering over the edge, they saw it was an old abandoned rock quarry, full of marble scree and boulders. Clumps of bushes had taken root in the half-filled pit, and a pool of water had formed at the bottom. Around the pool were a few tents. The scar-faced boy they called Panri was hopping down, surefooted and quick, toward a small cluster of

195

people gathered outside the tents. They were all dressed in the oxblood finery that Panri had been wearing.

"I was going to see if they had anything worth taking," said the scar-faced boy. He reached the quarry floor and trotted to the group. "But all I got from them was a little information before I let them go. They know about the hammer."

"Information? More like a beatdown," muttered Tora. "We let *him* go." Frowning, she studied those listening to the boy as he chattered on. "Those people—they're not all younglings. Some are older." Her eyes narrowed. Then with a gasp, she lurched forward, knocking a rock into the ravine. As it clattered, the boy and his companions turned and looked up. The tallest was a man who looked well into his twenties. At the sight of them, he drew out a sword.

"Intruders!" he shouted. "Get your weapons—now!"

"We should go," said Usagi nervously. "They're not happy to see us." They backed away, all except for Tora, who stared down into the old quarry, frozen. Usagi tugged at her arm. "Tora, come on."

Tora whirled, tears in her eyes. "You don't understand," she choked. "The older one. I know that face and that voice. It's my brother."

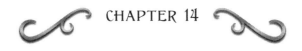

CHAPTER 14

THE PAINTED HOLLOW

WITH A TREMBLING HAND, Tora pointed at the tall young man at the bottom of the old quarry. He'd drawn his sword and was ordering the other members of his gang to find their weapons and take cover. Usagi couldn't quite see his face clearly, as his dark hair hung about his shoulders like a curtain. But Tora's face had gone pale. Her amber eyes were wide with shock, filled with tears threatening to spill over.

"It's Imugi—my second-oldest brother," she insisted. "He was nineteen when the Guard took him away." She hugged herself, rubbing the scars on her right arm. "I thought I'd never see him again."

Usagi couldn't keep her mouth from hanging open. "Are you sure, Tora?" She turned to the others. Both Inu and Goru gazed into the pit, their jaws slack as well. The scar-faced boy and his companions raced to take up positions behind boulders and slag heaps, while the man who was supposedly Tora's brother gestured at a young woman with a bow in her hand. He pointed up at them.

"What in the name of the Twelve?" muttered the Dog Heir. He backed away from the steep edge of the old quarry. "Tora, if that's really your brother, he'd better recognize you fast, because they don't look welcoming. Let's get out of here."

Tora turned on Inu, her teeth clenched. "I'm not going anywhere. Not until I talk to him." With that, she waved her arms and began shouting her brother's name. "Imugi! It's Tora! Your sister!"

Usagi heard a twang. "Duck!" she screamed, and yanked Tora down. An arrow whistled over their heads and richocheted off the stony hillside behind them.

"I don't think he's listening, Tora," said Goru. He shrank back as far as he could, but his bulk was hard to miss. "Can we go? I'm feeling like a target bale up here." He pulled his pack off and held it in front of him, but it barely covered his face.

"I'm going to *make* him listen." Tora scrambled to her feet and tried again. She shrieked her brother's name and then pointed to herself. "I'm your sister, you fool! Tora!" Another twang sounded. Usagi was about to shout a warning, but Tora saw it coming this time and dodged out of the way. "That is so rude! If Papa were here, he'd wring your neck! How dare you shoot at your baby sister?"

The man ordered his archer to hold her fire. He stared up at them. "How dare you claim to be my dead sister?"

"I'm not dead, you big oaf," Tora hollered back. "And you're the one I thought was dead!" She put her hands on her hips as she stared into the ravine, as if daring the archer to shoot. Then she took a few steps forward. "Good gracious gods, it's really you! Imugi, born in the year of the Dragon, ruled by the Metal element, from Goldentusk in the province of Stone River. I know it's you!"

The young man faltered. "Tora?" He squinted, and his eyes flew open. "No!" He broke into a run.

Usagi heard Tora begin to sniffle as she climbed down into the old quarry. Her brother scrambled up, meeting her halfway, and threw his arms around her. Tora burst into sobs, as did her brother. Overcome, they clung to each other and wept.

Glancing at Inu and Goru, Usagi thought their eyes looked suspiciously shiny. Or was it because her own tears were in the way? She quickly swiped her eyes, elated for her best friend, even as a stab of longing for her own family pierced her chest. How she missed Uma. Would she ever be able to hug her sister like that again?

Pulling apart at last, Tora and her brother examined each other, wiping away tears and laughing. He cupped his hands around her face in disbelief, while she reached up and tucked an unruly tendril of his long hair behind his ear.

Their words spilled out in a jubilant rush as they asked each other questions that had been bottled up for seven years. As they gabbled away, the others inside the quarry stood wide-eyed and stock still, some clutching their chests as if they'd received a shock. Usagi and the boys hung back, unable to do anything but smile as they watched their friend's reunion. Finally, Tora turned and waved up at them. "Get down here! You must meet my brother!"

Usagi swallowed the lump in her throat as she made her way down to Tora, followed closely by Inu and Goru. Her friend had always been stoic about the loss of her family, and never liked to talk about how she'd gotten the scars on her arm. Sometimes Usagi thought it was because Tora had already had some practice at hiding her feelings, for Tora's mother had died when she was a baby. Even before the war, her friend wouldn't speak of it. Tora's insistence on finding her father alive had been the first sign to Usagi of just how deeply Tora missed her family. The fact that one of her brothers had survived both the war and the Eastern Mines was surely a gift from the gods.

They joined Tora at the bottom of the old quarry, and met her brother Imugi and his companions, all former captives forced to work in the Eastern Mines. Usagi noticed that they all had the same scar on their face as the boy who'd been following them, a web of lines enclosed in an oblong shape that, upon closer examination, resembled the official seal on a document. "It's a brand they gave us," said Imugi, as Tora delicately touched his cheek. "It's supposed to make it easier to identify us."

"And harder to run away," said Panri, the boy who'd been their spy. "We'll always be seen as belonging to the mines now." Panri was a year younger than Inu, born in the year of the Boar. He pulled up his tunic to show his torso, which was covered in bristly hair. "A Guard shot at me once and the bullet just glanced off. I've got a pretty thick hide. But it doesn't extend to my face and neck, unfortunately." He grimaced, twisting the scar on his cheek.

They were invited to stay with the former mine captives, who called themselves the Miners. "Come to our camp and meet everyone," said Imugi. "We'll cook up something delicious to celebrate. I can't believe you've brought my sister back to me."

Goru looked at the tents in the quarry, puzzled. "This isn't your camp?"

With a laugh, Imugi shook his head. "We were just doing scouting runs. There are more of us, in a place not far from here—but it'd be near impossible to find without guidance."

Beaming, Tora slipped her hand in his. "Let's go."

Her brother led them through the old marble quarry. It was an extensive, winding chasm excavated in the earth, full of places to hide among the fallen boulders and slag heaps, with small nooks that provided good cover. As they went farther into the quarry, the walls of the old mine closed in and their route became increasingly narrow. Before long they were at a point that seemed like an impassable dead end. But Usagi's ears picked up the low whistle of wind, carrying the musty scent of dark and damp. It was coming from an opening in the rock, hidden by boulders placed in an alternating pattern. They squeezed through the makeshift maze, Goru with some difficulty, until at last they were fully underground.

"Watch your head," Imugi told Goru, who hunched over. They were in a lengthy, narrow tunnel, dimly lit with torches dipped in pitch. "We dug this—it goes right under the Ring Road. It takes us straight into the farthest corners of Marble Gorge."

Usagi caught her breath. She exchanged excited glances with Tora. It was just as Tora had envisioned. They would soon be in the Marble Gorge. It was famed for its beauty, the quality of the marble found around it, and for its size. Much of the sprawling network of its canyons was unmapped. The main entry point had long been closed off by the Guard, for fear that Midagians would try to hide there.

The ground grew uneven and treacherous, covered in a knobby carpet of pale veined marble that shifted with each step. Picking her way carefully with her walking stick, Usagi tried not to turn an ankle on the stones underfoot as she hurried to keep up. At last the air that whistled past them became cool and fresh, and a glimmer of light appeared in the distance, like a star in the night sky. After what seemed like hours in the dark, the tunnel spat them out into an immense gorge that stretched as far as the eye could see.

Jagged gray cliffs peeled away from them in all directions, standing in intricate formations that reached high into the afternoon sky. Tiny cavities pierced the walls surrounding them, creating a lacy, silver veil of stone. The sound of rushing water echoed through the air. Before long, they came upon a vast river. Usagi gasped. The riverbed was covered with white marble rocks, and the water tumbling over them was the turquoise blue of a peacock's feather, turning vividly green at the shallow edges of the river.

"The Peacock River," said Imugi. He smiled, displaying teeth strikingly similar to Tora's. "Takes your breath away, doesn't it?" It was even prettier than Sun Moon Lake. Usagi followed the others as they knelt on large rocks at the river's edge and dipped their hands into the clear green water. The cool liquid felt almost alive as it swirled around her fingers, and tasted deliciously sweet. Usagi splashed it on her face, washing away the dust, smoke, and sweat of their journey through the graveyard the Miners called the Shadowlands.

"Whatever you do, stay close to the river," warned Tora's brother. "There are countless ways of getting lost here, but the surest way is straying from the water."

He led the group along the riverbed, which wound and

twisted through the gorge like a giant snake. Tufts of bushes and other plant growth appeared, dusting the surfaces of the forbidding rock with patches of green. Usagi spotted a couple of hawks sailing overhead, tracing lazy circles in the blue sky. As she tried to take it all in, her legs fought to find stable footing on the marble stones that paved the riverbed, and her walking stick saved her from a spill more than once. But the majesty of the gorge kept her going, eager to see what sights were next. Just as her wobbly legs felt as if they were about to give out, Imugi took a turn and climbed away from the river, up a rough path.

"I thought we weren't supposed to stray from the river," said Usagi.

"You aren't," he agreed. "Unless you're headed to the Miners' Den."

He pointed to the towering cliff before them, where the dark maw of a cave yawned. It looked rather ominous, like the mouth of a stone giant, a jagged fringe of rock lining its lip as if it were baring its teeth for a bite.

"Not the jolliest-looking place, is it?" commented Goru.

Inu's dark eyes narrowed as he surveyed the cave entrance. "I wonder . . . could it . . . ?" he muttered.

The path steepened on the approach and Usagi's walking stick slipped a few times. She soon found herself nearly crawling on all fours. "It's definitely not easy to get to," she huffed, climbing behind Tora and the others.

Reaching the top of the path, Tora turned to give Usagi a helping hand and gasped. "Stars and spirits."

Usagi heaved to her feet and turned to look. All around them was a citadel of silver stone. The river sparkled below like a necklace of aquamarines and emeralds, the white marble banks an edging of pearls. The hum of the rushing river echoed from the floor of the gorge, punctuated by cries of the hawks drifting overhead.

"What a view!" Goru whistled. "You can see everything from here."

Tora's brother smiled proudly. "No worrying about surprise attacks." He ushered them into a cavern hundreds of paces deep, large enough to hold several of the Western Plains' biggest rice fields. Usagi stopped, awed. The arched rock ceiling was so high that she had to crane her neck to see where it began. A bright beam of sunlight poured from a cleft in the ceiling and splashed across the center of the cavern, illuminating a large ring of stones. A group of Miners, all sporting the same brand on their cheek, were sitting on the stones, talking and laughing. Upon spotting Imugi, they jumped up. "You're back! How'd the scouting go?"

"Look what we've brought back with us," said Imugi. He presented Tora, who was welcomed with exclamations of wonder, Usagi, who smiled and bowed, and Inu and Goru, who did the same. As they were introduced, Usagi counted nearly two dozen Miners of varying ages who were making the cave their home, all of whom had zodiac powers of some sort. A few were adults, though none much older than Imugi, who was twenty-six. The others were younglings in a range of ages, with the youngest at eleven. Other than the time she'd sneaked into the Dragon Academy to rescue her sister, Usagi had never been around so many with powers. She felt strangely at home.

Panri and the other scouts showed their visitors to a cozy nook where they could deposit their meager belongings. Tora quickly dumped her pack and walking stick and ran back to the circle of stones, anxious to be by her brother's side. Usagi and the boys took their time, setting up their bedrolls and wandering about the cavern, getting a good look before rejoining everyone.

Long wooden torches dipped in pitch were set in the walls, which were covered in paintings. Primitive lines and simple shapes in colors of reddish umber, chalk white, and charcoal black depicted figures in scenes of activity. Some were no bigger than Usagi's hand and others life-sized. She stepped closer to look. Though the paint was powdery and flaking off in places, she could still make out the forms— some human, some of animals. Usagi got the feeling the paintings were very old.

"It's as I thought," whispered Inu. He pointed to a tableau of three figures. One looked like a great cat with dagger-like fangs. Another appeared to be a horse, and what might have been a hare, long-eared with its haunches in midleap. The animals were running after each other, hunting. Or being hunted. "This is no ordinary cave—we're in the Painted Hollow. It's one of the sacred spaces of the Twelve." The Dog Heir's eyes flashed with excitement.

Goru leaned over them both to look. "I don't understand—I thought the shrine on Mount Jade was the sacred space of the Twelve."

"It is," said Inu. "But it's not the only place with meaning for the Warriors. One of the First Tribes used to live here in the Marble Gorge. Before there was a kingdom, or the Twelve—before this island even had a name—this cave was their secret gathering space, where they held ceremonies and special rituals." He nodded at the circle of rocks. "After the first Twelve Warriors of the Zodiac assembled, the Painted Hollow came under their guardianship—until the war."

Usagi looked over at Tora and the Miners, gathered at the stone ring. She counted exactly twelve boulders, shaped like giant claws rising from the cave floor. They reminded her of the curved jade bead that the Tigress had made to replace the missing piece in the Jewels of Land and Sea. "What a happy coincidence that the Miners found this place," she said. "It feels like a sign."

"It is a sign," agreed Inu. "Great things have happened here. The spirits of the Twelve are with us yet."

Goru smiled. "Let's hope they'll help us hunt down the last missing Treasure."

There was a flurry of new activity and excited voices around the circle of stones. Imugi and some of the other Miners were piling wood by the firepit at the circle's center. Tora turned and waved Usagi and the boys over. "We're going to have firepot!"

Her brother's snaggleteeth glinted. "What's more celebratory than cooking and eating together? It's been a while since we've had a chance to enjoy firepot." He looked over their shoulders. "Watch your backs—the pot is coming through!"

Panri and another Miner carried a battered iron vessel, so large and and heavy that they could barely walk. It looked like a former smelting cauldron, and was filled with water that sloshed and splashed with every step. "Here, let me," offered Goru, and lifted the iron pot easily out of their grasp. He placed it in the firepit, and Imugi stoked the fire with more wood. As the flames leaped and crackled, heating the water, everyone prepared ingredients for the meal.

Usagi helped with cleaning water spinach and cattail shoots from the river, wild tubers, and handfuls of mushrooms, chopping them down into small pieces so that everything would cook quickly. Goru and Inu cut wild garlic and onions, sniffling and wiping their eyes at the pungent fumes, until Inu couldn't take it anymore and went to help a couple of Miners with preparing game. There was a small haunch of mountain goat, which they shaved into the thinnest of slices.

"This isn't like the firepot we used to have for winter soltice celebrations," Tora remarked to her brother, rinsing off some foraged chicory stems and fern heads.

Imugi chuckled. "I'm sorry we don't have platters of beef and lamb, or your favorite sweet cabbage, or any fancy sauces. We've mostly had to make do with what we can find and hunt here in the gorge. But we supplement. A raid on a mine caravan gets us enough outside supplies for a while."

Usagi remembered the provisions in their packs. "Would you like some preserved dried boar?"

"That'd be a fine addition! It will make the broth taste even better." Imugi happily accepted.

At last, the water in the cauldron was bubbling merrily, steam rising in clouds. Salt and spices were thrown in, and feedsticks were distributed. Everyone crowded around the pot. "Let's eat!" said Imugi.

They dunked the prepared foods in the scalding water, and as pieces of game or wild vegetable cooked through, they were fished out with feedsticks and dipped in an improvised sauce of beaten eggs from the nests of cliff swallows. Usagi had enjoyed firepot feasts before—she still remembered helping her mother grind toasted sesame seeds for their dipping sauce, and swishing sheets of tender lamb through boiling water till they were ready to eat. But the sight of the Miners, their cheeks branded with identical scars, gobbling up hard-won tidbits of meat and laughing as they fought for the same cattail shoot in the pot—Usagi blinked back a sudden tear. They'd all been through so much, which made the meal feel special, even with the humblest of ingredients.

Before long, every last scrap and morsel had been cooked and eaten. Their faces were flushed and warm from clustering around the firepot. All that was left was the water, transformed into a bubbling broth smelling fragrant and savory. "I've got a surprise for us," Tora's brother announced. "In honor of my sister and her friends."

Panri approached the circle bearing an enormous bowl of steaming rice. The Miners all made appreciative noises, and clapped as the youngling upended the bowl over the cauldron and stirred the rice into the broth, rich with all that had cooked in it. The rice would absorb the flavors in the pot and thicken the broth, making a wonderful soup.

"Where did you get all that rice?" asked Tora, eyes round. Usagi wondered the same thing. Rice was hard to come by even in the Western Plains where it was grown, let alone the untamed Marble Gorge.

"We have our ways," said her brother with a mysterious smile. He gestured to Panri, who bent down. Imugi cupped his hand around Panri's ear. Focusing her rabbit hearing, Usagi listened in.

"Did you make sure the hammer is secure?" asked Tora's brother quietly.

"It's hidden in its usual spot," Panri murmured.

Imugi gave a grunt of approval. *"Good job. Thank you, Boar Boy."*

A shiver of excitement ran through Usagi. She leaned over to Inu and Goru. "The Conjurer is somewhere right in this cave," she whispered. "We have to find it."

CHAPTER 15

HUNTING THE CONJURER

USAGI PEERED THROUGH THE SMALL cavern, the only light from glow worms clinging to the rough stone walls. She kept her hand on Tora's shoulder as Tora used her sharp vision to lead them through an offshoot of the Painted Hollow. Inu and Goru followed closely behind, Goru bent nearly double to avoid hitting his head on the low ceiling. Something fluttered around Usagi's face and she squealed.

"Spitting spirits—I'm being attacked!" Ducking, she threw her arms over her head.

Tora snorted. "It's just a moth."

As the boys sniggered, Usagi straightened, her cheeks warming. She tossed her braids over her shoulders. "Laugh if you like. But don't come crying to me if something in these caves decides to make you its snack."

"It was your idea to go looking for the Conjurer," Goru pointed out. "We've been into four caves so far and found nothing but glow worms, a bunch of mushrooms, and plenty of rocks. No hammer." *Brraaaap.* A noxious smell wafted through the atmosphere. "Oh, sorry."

"Son of a wind god, Goru," growled Inu, pulling his collar over his nose. "Stop doing that."

Goru waved a giant hand, trying to clear the air. "I'm not the only one who's been having stomach trouble. You said yourself it's a sign that the rice was conjured by the Treasure."

"Too bad we can't conjure *this* away." Tora muffled a laugh. She hurried them forward. "Come on. The faster we get away from it, the better."

It was true that they'd all been having the same problem since the firepot meal. For Usagi, it was just the proof she needed to convince the others to go searching for the hammer: food produced by the Conjurer had the unfortunate side effect of giving the eater a lot of gas. Usagi had read that it was because the food disappeared midway through the body, leaving nothing but air. It made for a few uncomfortable moments as they explored the smaller caves that branched from the main cavern of the Painted Hollow. But it only confirmed Usagi's belief that Panri had used the Treasure to create the rice, and stashed the hammer somewhere nearby.

Tora had tried to get her brother to talk about the Conjurer, asking him where his fancy oxblood clothing had gone when he and the other scouts appeared in ragged, patched clothing. But just as he had avoided answering her question about the rice, he was cagey, even when she hinted that she'd seen Panri's clothes change right before her eyes. Finally, despite Usagi's warnings not to say anything directly, Tora had become impatient and asked him point-blank about the Treasure. "I know you have a powerful hammer. It creates whatever you wish for—but everything it makes disappears after a day. Can't you show it to me?"

But much to Tora's disappointment, Imugi pretended not to understand. "A hammer that grants all your wishes? What a fun dream tale. I'd wish for a palace and a herd of the finest horses. Maybe a few chests of gold. Or a suit of armor made of pure jade, straight from the sacred mount herself." He changed the subject, and a frustrated Tora stalked off.

"I don't know why he won't talk to me," she'd complained.

"I told you not to say anything," Usagi scolded. "Now he's going to be suspicious. I don't blame him for not trusting us—if you had something like the Conjurer in your possession, would you go around telling outsiders?"

"But I'm his sister!"

Inu had interjected. "We'll just have to go looking for it, like Usagi said."

So now they were roaming down yet another narrow corridor in hopes of finding a place where the hammer could be safely hidden. The Painted Hollow itself was an enormous cavern, where everything was in the open. It was in the connecting nooks and grottos where people could sleep undisturbed and find privacy. The Heirs and Heirlings had quietly wandered off and discovered that there was an entire network of smaller caves. Yet as they explored the system, nothing turned up. Then Tora's sharp tiger eyes had noticed a smear of charcoal at the entrance to the passageway they were in now. Usagi prayed they would find the hammer here.

Tora came to an abrupt halt, and Usagi bumped into her, followed rapidly by Inu and Goru. "Ow!" exclaimed Usagi. "What's wrong?"

"It looks like the end," said Tora. "There's a big boulder here. But there's also . . . a handle?" She tried pulling at a thick metal bar, then pushing. "I think it's supposed to move this rock—it's some sort of lever. But it seems stuck."

Goru rubbed his hands. "Here, let me. Stand back." He stepped up to the boulder, and with a grunt, wrenched it out of the way. The metal bar clattered to the ground.

"I think you were supposed to move the lever, and that would lift the rock away from . . ." Tora sighed. "Never mind."

As Goru set aside the boulder, Usagi saw that it had hidden a hole from which a soft blue light emanated. Goru peered inside. "Spirits." He turned. "I won't be able to fit through here, but you all should go in and take a look."

Squeezing through the hole one by one, Usagi, Tora and Inu found themselves in a small chamber. The ceiling was thick with glow worms, which shone with a bluish light illuminating the chamber's contents. Stacked along the walls were bags of precious gemstones and ingots of gold and other metals. "Great golden ghosts," breathed Inu. "There's a fortune in here."

Tora grabbed Usagi's arm. "My vision."

On a block of white marble sat a rough wooden box. Tora fell upon it but fumbled with the latch on the lid. She pushed it at Usagi. "My hands are shaking. You open it."

Trying to keep calm herself, Usagi pried the box open, revealing a roughspun drawstring bag. She untied the strings, her heart racing, blood rushing in her ears. She reached in and pulled out a painted wooden mallet. It was hard to make out the symbols in the dim light of the glow worms, but Usagi had no doubt. "It's the Conjurer!"

"Uh . . . can you all come out now?" called Goru. "We have a little problem."

Inu sniffed the air and grew tense. "We've got company," he muttered. Moving to the hole, he stuck his head out, then raised both hands. He glanced back at Usagi and Tora. "It's your brother."

After he climbed out, Tora followed. "Bring the hammer," she urged.

216

"Just like this?" Usagi looked at the wooden mallet. It was too bulky to shove under her tunic or hide in a pocket.

Tora's jaw set. "I want to have a good talk with Imugi about it." She slipped out of the chamber.

With a shrug, Usagi stuck it back in the bag and looped the drawstring around her wrist. She clambered through the hole to find Panri standing with a long sharp spear pointed at a resigned-looking Goru, and Imugi with a firm hold on both his sister and Inu.

"Want to tell me what you four were doing in our vault?" asked Imugi.

Panri glared at Usagi. "Stealing, obviously." He raised the spear he was pointing at Goru. "This isn't going to disappear, by the way. It's as real as you or I."

"Unlike the sword you were carrying?" growled Tora. She struggled against her brother's grip. "Let me go, you lump of stinky bean curd. I asked you about the hammer because we've been looking for it. Since you lied to your own sister, we had to find it for ourselves."

Imugi frowned. "How do you even know about it?"

With a shake of her head, Tora bared her snaggleteeth. "It's a long story. We'll tell you, but you have to tell us how you got it. And then *maybe* I'll forgive you for lying to me."

Her brother hesitated, then his own snaggleteeth gleamed. "Fine," he shrugged. He snatched the bag from Usagi. "Let's go."

With Panri still pointing the spear at them, they marched back into the main cavern. Some of the Miners looked at them curiously. "You can put that away now, Boar Boy," said Imugi. He strode to the circle of stones and bade them sit.

Fiddling with the strings of the bag, Imugi nodded at his sister. "You go first."

"You've asked how I escaped the Dragonlord, but I haven't told you everything." Tora gestured to Usagi and Inu. "It was really because of these two." She explained that Inu was one of the last Warrior Heirs to survive the war, and that he and the other Warrior Heirs had found Usagi and helped train her. "Thanks to them, Goru and I are now on Mount Jade, training to become Heirs as well."

Her brother was incredulous. "I can't believe it. I thought anything having to do with the Twelve was wiped out." He shook his head, then held up the bag. "So where does this come in?"

Tora gave a little bow in Inu's direction. "You're the senior Heir. Want to tell him?"

Describing the Treasures that had once been carried by the Circle of the Twelve, Inu explained they had become scattered by the war. A look of understanding dawned on Imugi's face. "You're saying this once belonged to the . . . the Ram Warrior?"

From the drawstring bag, he removed the mallet. Afternoon light filtered through the cleft in the ceiling, piercing the gloom of the cave. In that sunbeam, the mallet's bright colors seemed to glow. The twelve animals of the zodiac were lacquered on the wooden head, and the circular swirling symbol of the Twelve adorned the flat round faces. It truly was the Conjurer, before them at last.

Imugi rubbed at an invisible speck on the gleaming lacquer. "It was crusted in mud when I found it half-buried near the mines. I just thought it was a regular hammer at the time. But when I began using it, strange things happened— wonderful things. I started making my daily quota and more—no one else could keep up with my output. I helped a couple of other miners make their quota. Food and water would appear, lasting just long enough to keep us going. The food it makes can cause a bit of stomach upset." They all nodded, Goru most vigorously. Imugi's snaggleteeth glinted. "But we were starving, so we didn't care. We figured out that whatever we wished for would be granted to us by the hammer for a day.

"Eventually we grew strong and bold enough to make plans for escape," he continued. "The hammer granted us armor that allowed us to dress like the Guard, and weapons to protect ourselves. It was just a few of us at first, but once we were successful, we went back and helped others get out."

Led by Imugi, whose possession of the hammer had helped free them, the Miners made a home for themselves, first in the abandoned quarry, then in the Marble Gorge. Though Imugi's main power was a metal gift that had served him well as a blacksmith's apprentice, he did have some dragon tendencies—like an affinity for water. He couldn't control weather and bring rain like some Dragonborn, but he'd found the Peacock River and the cave. "We've been here ever since."

"You've taken good care of the hammer, and it's taken good care of you," said Inu. "But it needs to be brought back to its rightful home. Our mission is to collect all the Treasures before the Blue Dragon can get to them."

Tora's brother frowned. "We have a mission too." He told them that the Miners' main purpose was not mere survival. "We're the lucky ones," said Imugi. "We got out. There are many more prisoners still suffering."

In an effort to disrupt mining operations, Imugi said they'd been raiding mine shipments, diverting precious metals and gems from their ultimate destination. They'd also made attacks on the Eastern Mines, causing enough distraction with the Guard to give people the opportunity to escape. "We're not the only group out there now. There are other former miners who've scattered to neighboring provinces and are in hiding. They have zodiac powers too, and help us with selling the metal and gems from our raids. But we're the ones who've been able to do the most, thanks to this hammer."

Tora put her hand on her brother's shoulder. "Papa would be so proud of you. He always said that your heart was as big as Mount Jade."

Scrubbing a hand through his shaggy hair, Inu cleared his throat. "So . . . you're not willing to let the Treasure go?"

"How can I?" asked Imugi. He turned the Conjurer in his hands. "One of the biggest shipments from the mines is scheduled to pass by soon. We need this."

"So do we!" blurted Usagi. "The Blue Dragon has captured our teacher. We need all the Treasures to help her."

Rising to his feet, Tora's brother put the hammer back in the drawstring bag and secured it to his belt. He shook his head. "I'm sorry. You're welcome to stay a while longer, but I can't let you go with such an important tool."

"Why don't we help you with the raid?" suggested Goru. As everyone looked at him in surprise, he shrugged. "Maybe all you need is a few more people with zodiac powers instead of the hammer."

Imugi snorted. "I doubt it."

"But that's a great idea," said Tora, brightening. "I'd love to help with a raid."

The scar on Imugi's cheek puckered with his smile. He put an affectionate hand on top of her head. "All right, then. We could always use help. Now, I'm going to go fix the door on our vault. Want to assist me?" He excused himself with a bow and left, Panri and Tora following close behind.

At a loss for words, Usagi sat there in the circle of stones. She looked at Goru and Inu in dismay. "What now?"

Inu sighed. "Ox Boy's bought us some time, but we'll have to figure out a way to get that Treasure."

In the following weeks, Usagi and the others did their best to help the Miners around their encampment and prepare for the upcoming caravan raid. Tora followed her brother like a shadow. Her usual fierceness had softened, and she seemed happier than Usagi could remember. "Did you ever think Tora could be this sweet?" she asked Inu and Goru.

"If she hangs around her brother much longer, our Tiger Girl might lose her fangs and claws for good," joked Goru.

"I'm worried," said Usagi. "How are we going to get the Conjurer from him? And even if we do manage to get that hammer—is it possible Tora won't want to return to Mount Jade? What if she wants to stay here and isn't interested in becoming an Heir anymore?"

Inu twisted his thumb ring, considering. "It's not going to be easy," he agreed. "Somehow we need to take the Treasure back without angering the Miners. As for Tora, we can't tell her what to do. We can hope that she still wants to become the Tiger Heir. But if she decides she wants to stay with her brother, we have to honor that."

Biting her lip, Usagi nodded. She didn't want to lose her friend. But Tora looked so utterly content. "I'll ask her to convince him," said Usagi. "I just hope she doesn't forget our mission and what we came here to do."

The thought kept her awake that night. Usagi tossed and turned, staring at the ceiling of their sleeping nook, which glowed softly with the light of dozens of glowworms. In the dark, they gave off pinpricks of pale blue light, making the roof of the cave look like a starry sky. Usagi heard Tora tip-toeing toward her bedroll, and raised her head.

"You're awake," said Tora, sounding surprised.

Usagi squinted under the dim light of the glowworms. "You seem like you're having a nice time with your brother."

"I still have to pinch myself," Tora said. She unrolled her bedding and lay down with a contented sigh. "It's been wonderful to be with him again. To be with . . . family. Not that you and the Heirs haven't been great."

Reaching out, Usagi squeezed her friend's arm. "I know."

"He knows about my visions," Tora confided. "I told Imugi about it all, how I saw our father in one. And how they started after I got up Mount Jade, and how everything's been coming true."

Usagi drew back. "What did he say about that?" she asked cautiously.

"He's proud," said Tora. "He says he always thought that

I would be the one in our family to do the best if only I'd had the chance to attend school. He thinks I could become a Warrior Heir."

That was encouraging. Usagi relaxed. "Have you talked to him again about letting us take the Treasure back to the shrine?"

Tora shifted in her bedroll and was silent for a moment. "Err . . . no. Not yet."

With a frown, Usagi raised herself on an elbow. "You need to talk to him. He might listen to you. The Tigress—"

"Yes, yes, I know," Tora interrupted. "Usagi, I'm tired. Let's talk about this in the morning." She rolled over, and before long was snoring.

Lying back, Usagi felt for the rabbit at her neck and stared at the winking glowworms. The Ring of Obscurity clinked beside the pendant, and she wrapped her fingers around it, feeling the amber stone warm in her palm. Tora had seemed to deflate when she brought up their mission. A knot formed in Usagi's stomach. Was Tora going to choose her brother and abandon them?

The next morning, Usagi awoke to find that everyone else had long been up and about. "Sleepy Rabbit wakes at last!" said Goru as she stumbled out of their nook.

"I had trouble falling asleep," she replied, her voice froggy. She looked around—the cavern was near deserted.

Goru handed her a bowl and feedsticks. "A few of the Miners are out hunting, and some are scouting outside the gorge. The rest are preparing for the raid. Inu, Tora, and I are going to see what they have planned. So eat up, and come down to the river when you're done." He pointed to the firepit in the center of the cavern. "We saved you some millet gruel for morning meal. There might be some pickled snails left." He lowered his voice. "It's bland and the snails are rubbery, but it's not conjured food, so it shouldn't give you any problems." Chortling, he turned and strolled out of the cave.

Bowl in hand, Usagi approached the ring of twelve chiseled stones where the Miners liked to gather. Each pale, silver-veined marble boulder had a rounded squat base that narrowed and curved up like a claw, forming a perfect seat. Usagi could picture the members of the first Warrior Council sitting around the firepit in this circle of thrones, discussing matters of the kingdom. Sunlight poured from the great crack in the ceiling, illuminating the stones so they glowed.

Putting a few cooked snails in her bowl, Usagi helped herself to some steaming porridge from an iron pot sitting in the coals. She settled cross-legged on one of the marble thrones, the rough-hewn surface warm from the sun, and slurped at the hot gruel. Thinking of the first Twelve, she reached in her pocket and pulled out the ironstone from the

Tree of Elements. Tora had given the stone back to Usagi for safekeeping, uncomfortable with its powers. "What if it makes me see visions all day long?" she'd worried. Though Usagi had tried to calm her friend's fears, in the end she'd agreed to hold on to it.

Its stripes of red, black, and gold shimmered as she turned the stone in her hand. Tiger iron, it was called. Tiger iron was supposed to be full of powerful energy, able to give strength and stamina to the bearer, and speed healing. Tupa the Ram Heir had told her about it—before betraying them all to join the Dragonlord. Usagi still couldn't understand how people could turn their backs on their friends, but she would never forget it.

She closed her hand around the tiger iron. If only she could somehow give it to the Tigress. The old warrior had seemed so weak when they saw her in the Summoning. *Hold on, Teacher.* Usagi prayed that they would be able to rescue her soon.

Placing the ironstone before her on the marble boulder, Usagi looked around the circle. Supposedly one of the First Warriors had marked the Tree of Elements with pieces of tiger iron. What if they'd sat in this very spot? Usagi gave the stone a little spin and fished a bit of snail from her bowl with her feedsticks. It was chewy, like Goru had warned, but not bad. It reminded Usagi of clams.

Orange flames crackled and danced in the firepit. In the

distance, Usagi heard her friends showing the Miners how to use spirit speed, urging them to practice.

"You need to be running faster after setting traps for the caravan," hollered Inu. *"Anyone can run, but only those with powers can move three or four times as fast—more if you have horse speed. Don't let the Guard even get close!"*

She smiled to herself and hurried to finish her meal, anxious to join them. As she jumped up from her seat, she accidentally kicked the piece of tiger iron. "Oh!" Usagi watched in horror as the ironstone flew into the firepit. She scrambled to get it, but the heat of the flames was too much. Gods, if only she had a fire gift like her sister. Using her wooden feedsticks, she only managed to poke the rock farther into the flames and set the feedsticks on fire. "Scabs!" she swore, blowing frantically at the burning feedsticks.

It couldn't be wood. Usagi needed something long and metal that wouldn't burn. Her sword. She ran to get her walking stick and pulled out the blade. As she stuck the blade into the fire, sparks flew up. She grimaced. Inu would have a fit if he saw what she was doing to the sword he'd made her, but she couldn't just leave that rock in the fire—it was from the Tree of Elements.

At last she nudged the rock out from the flames. It lay there in the sand at the edges of the firepit, its stripes of red, gold, and black shimmering with heat. Then to her astonishment, the ironstone began to transform, just as if it were a chunk of wax. Its rough surface tightened and grew glossy. Edges rounded and bulged. The center twisted, lengthened and curled. Before her eyes, the piece of tiger iron became a perfectly polished curved bead, identical in shape to the clawlike boulders around her. It looked just like the jade piece in the Jewels of Land and Sea, only it was striped in the gleaming colors of a tiger's coat.

"Spirits," Usagi breathed. She waited for what seemed like forever for the bead to cool, then scooped it out of the firepit, where it sat winking in her palm. The others would never believe this. But as she looked wildly around the deserted cavern, surrounded by ancient paintings on the walls, it began to make perfect sense. This wasn't just the Miner's Den—it was the Painted Hollow, sacred to the Twelve, and it had just given her something special. She didn't yet know how, but this bead was going to help them. Usagi felt it in her bones.

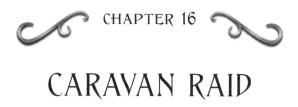

CHAPTER 16

CARAVAN RAID

THE DAY OF THE RAID arrived, and the mood in the Painted Hollow was tense. It was quieter than usual, the laughing and joking at a minimum, as the Miners prepared for an approaching caravan from the Eastern Mines. Tora's brother paced about with the Conjurer secured at his waist in its bag. He fiddled nervously with the drawstrings.

"It's been ages since we've hit a shipment," Imugi said. "But an especially large one will be coming through on the Ring Road tonight." The main thoroughfare circling the island ran past the hills abutting the abandoned mine where they'd first found the Miners. Caravans of ox carts and bullock wagons traveled the road regularly, accompanied by Guard.

"The key is, when we leave them alone for a long stretch of time, they get sloppy and careless. Because they think we've stopped," he explained to Tora and Usagi. "But we're constantly sending scouts to track their activity. That's how Panri wound up finding you."

"More like we found him," said Tora with a laugh. "Right, Boar Boy?"

Panri snorted. "Whatever you say, Tiger Girl."

"We'll do anything we can to help," Usagi told Tora's brother. They still hadn't figured out how to get the hammer from him, and Tora had changed the subject every time Usagi tried to discuss a strategy. Maybe if they helped make the raid a success, Imugi would be more open to letting the Treasure go.

They set out in the evening, the rising moon like a pale steamed bun, the white half circle just begining to puff. Leaving the gorge, they went through the long secret tunnel into the abandoned quarry and hiked through the surrounding hills until they came to a ridge overlooking the Ring Road. Imugi took out the hammer and closed his eyes, mouthing a silent prayer. Then he struck the ground, his expression purposeful, each blow producing something new.

Whack! A handsome bow and arrows appeared.

Whack! A box of explosives popped up.

Whack! A long firecannon materialized.

After hammering out weapons and supplies for the raid, he distributed them to the Miners, assigning each a task. "Lately the caravans have been starting out at odd hours, including the middle of the night," said Imugi. "It makes it all the more important to have scouts to alert us when the shipments come through." His eyes crinkled as he looked at the Warrior Heirs and the Heirlings. "My sister's tiger vision will be a great help here." He gave Tora several folded sky lanterns. They were made of four sheets of rice paper glued onto a bamboo frame, with a waxy piece of oil-soaked felt suspended in the frame's center. "When you see them coming, send up one of these as a signal, and we'll launch the raid. If you see danger and we need to retreat, send up two."

The Miners pulled cloth masks up over their noses to hide the telltale brands on their cheeks. With a wave, Imugi and his team quietly disappeared into the evening. "Be careful!" Tora called after them. She hugged the stack of folded sky lanterns and gave Usagi a brave smile, but her amber eyes were troubled.

"I had another dream last night," she confessed. "I can't make out what it means. I saw a massive fire, and then a great battle—but none of us were in the fight."

"That's not a bad thing." Usagi drew out the ring dangling at her neck. "There really was a giant butterfly guarding this, but it wasn't a monster. And you were right about the Conjurer—it was in the Marble Gorge, just as you'd said it would be. You even saw it in the hand of a miner." She grinned. "You just didn't know it would be your brother. Don't worry about the battle—your vision could be showing another happy surprise."

With a nod, Tora rubbed the scars on her arm. "Maybe."

They found a concealed spot on the ridge that gave them a good vantage point over the Ring Road, which stretched as far as they could see in either direction. In the distance, the deep pits and towering waste piles of the Eastern Mines were like festering wounds and pustules across the plain, edged by the ugly knobbled swath of the Shadowlands. The Blue Dragon had done so much damage to the kingdom and was still amassing power. He had Usagi's sister in his thrall and had turned a Warrior Heir to his side. Would resisting him change anything?

Usagi took a deep breath. Giving in would be worse. They had to at least try. The words of the Tigress came back to her. *"The conquest of a mountain begins with the smallest of steps."*

As the moon rose higher in the sky, the night air grew cool, portending the waning of summer. Not a soul could be seen on the Ring Road, and all was still. Usagi heard little beyond the usual night noises: animals rustling, insects crawling, moths fluttering, bats and owls diving and snapping after prey. The quiet dark weighed down her eyelids, and she found herself getting sleepy. Before she knew it, a rough hand shook her. "Usagi, wake up," Inu said urgently. "The caravan is coming. We have to warn the Imugi and the Miners."

Usagi snapped awake, embarrassed. In the distance came the sounds of clopping hooves, draft animals snorting, rattling wheels and marching feet, accompanied by the squeak and clank of Guard armor. "I hear them," she rasped, her voice thick with sleep. She felt a bit foggy-brained.

Tora and Goru unfolded one of the paper sky lanterns. Usagi fumbled for a firestarter. She held it near the oiled felt square at the mouth of the lantern and struck the metal against the flint until sparks appeared. But one flew up too high and hit the rice paper, and the lantern quickly caught fire before they could send it up.

"Spitting spirits," cursed Inu. He stomped out the flames. "Hurry, get another lantern ready."

With shaking hands, Usagi reached for another one. Inu picked up a still smoldering piece of the burned bamboo frame. "Give it here," he barked. He had Tora and Goru hold the top corners of the paper cube, and touched the glowing tip of the burning bamboo to the oiled felt. It flared with a bright light, becoming a hungry flame, and Inu snuffed out the burning bamboo. Hot air soon swelled up the paper lantern until it was bobbing and straining to float away. "Okay—let it go."

The glowing cube lifted into the night air, sending a light that could be seen all throughout the hills and, Usagi suspected, from the Ring Road. She could hear the Miners mobilizing and getting ready for the approach of the caravan. "I think the lantern has done its job—we should shoot it down," she told Inu.

The Dog Heir frowned. "Are you sure?"

"The caravan will see this too and know that we're here," said Usagi.

Inu reached for his bow and arrows, but Tora stopped him. "My brother didn't say to do that. He said to send up the lanterns when we saw the shipment coming, and that's it. I think we should leave it be."

Goru looked up at the lantern, floating ever higher in the sky. "I don't know, Tora—Usagi's probably right. If the others are seeing it, then maybe the Guard can too."

"With their ordinary vision?" Tora scoffed. "No, we should just follow orders."

Furrowing his brow, Inu crossed his arms. "Orders? We don't answer to Imugi. He's not our master."

Tora's eyes narrowed. "Maybe not, but he's the leader of this whole raid, and we're supposed to be helping."

"That's what I'm trying to do!" said Usagi. "It's just a matter of time before that lantern gets spotted by the wrong people. I can hear the others getting into position, so let's just cut that down now!"

As Tora hesitated, Inu reached for his bow again. But then Usagi heard a shout in the distance.

"It's too late," she said, dismayed. "They've seen it." She tensed at the sound of thundering hooves. "A mounted calvary is coming. We need to call off the raid."

Tora stood and peered into the distance. "Blasted blisters.

We have to send two lanterns up now to warn them off."

Usagi pulled out a lantern, then rummaged frantically through the pack. Her heart sank. They'd had three, but one had burned away because of her carelessness with the firestarter. "There's just one left."

They stared at each other, stricken. Then Inu took the lantern from Usagi. "The other one is still up. We'll launch this too—hopefully they'll get the message when they see a second lantern along with the first."

"Okay, but hurry," Tora said, watching the Ring Road. "There's a unit of mounted Guard nearing. They'll be here soon."

Usagi grabbed her firestarter, but Inu stopped her. "You'll torch the lantern again. Light the frame of the ruined one, and we'll use that," he ordered.

Biting back a retort, she showered the fragment of bamboo with sparks until finally it began to smolder. Inu snatched it up and lit the last lantern while Tora and Goru held it in place. As they released it, Usagi breathed a prayer to the gods that the Miners would see the lantern and understand. Her heart beat in tandem with the pounding of horse hooves. *Retreat, retreat, retreat,* she thought.

Confused shouts rang through the hills. *"Two lanterns! Stand down!"*

"No, there was one—and now there's a separate one—that means there's two caravans approaching!"

"Get the explosives ready!"

Burying her head in her hands, Usagi groaned. "The second lantern isn't working. They're not retreating."

"But they must," said Tora, alarmed. She turned. "I've got to warn my brother."

"No, Tora, wait! Come back!"

Goru started after her. He looked over his shoulder at Usagi and Inu. "Are you two coming or not? We can't let her do this alone."

They grabbed their belongings and followed. Tora moved swiftly in the dark, while Usagi, Inu, and Goru scrambled after her. Unfamiliar with the terrain, they repeatedly stubbed toes and nearly twisted ankles on wayward rocks as they tried to keep up. The sky lanterns had drifted high into the atmosphere, glimmering like stars as winds carried them off into the west. Usagi listened hard for the Miners, alerting Tora whenever she caught something.

"It sounds like they're proceeding with their plan," Usagi told her.

Tora groaned. "We need to get to the Ring Road. I'm sorry, I have to use spirit speed. I'll see you down there." She took off, leaving them to make their way on their own, without the benefit of her tiger vision. But the hour of the Rabbit was fast approaching, the eastern sky becoming pale, and gradually their path came into view. They were almost there.

A battery of explosions tore through the dawn, echoing across the hills. Usagi clapped her hands against her ears in a futile attempt to shield them from the percussive blasts. They were followed by shouts and the terrible screams of both horses and people.

"Quickly!" Inu urged, and they shifted into spirit speed. They arrived upon a scene of utter chaos. The Miners had set off explosions across the Ring Road at the sound of approaching horses but emerged to find that the caravan was not there. Instead it was a mounted cavalry of Guard, some of whom had been injured in the explosions, with spooked horses throwing their riders and racing off. The rest were engaged in beating the Miners with whips and the butts of their firecannon as they rode around them in circles, trying to round them up. Usagi looked frantically for Tora.

Dry brush along the Ring Road had caught fire from the explosions, crackling and popping as the flames consumed it. Against a wall of fiery light, Usagi spotted Tora's silhouette, defending her brother from a Guard whose horse had run off. Imugi was crumpled on the ground, unconscious. The gilt handle of the Conjurer gleamed beneath his arm, as if he'd fallen on it.

"Tora!" Usagi ran to help her, Goru and Inu hard on her heels. As a Guard galloped up to them, Goru raised an arm and knocked him off his horse. Inu had his bow in hand and fired arrows as quickly as he could draw them. As he struck approaching Guards, they would clutch their shoulders or knees, screaming, and tumble off their horses to the ground.

Tora glanced up, and her wild gaze met Usagi's for a brief moment before the Guard cracked his whip at her. She ducked. "Grab the hammer! We need more fighters!" Her fangs were out, and so were her claws. As the Guard tried to whip her again, she snatched the end of the whip and yanked it toward her. The Guard stumbled forward and Tora clawed hard across the Guard's face. "Hurry!" she screamed.

Usagi ran up to Imugi's side. He was bleeding from a cut to his head and was out cold. She reached for the handle of the Conjurer and pulled it out from under him. She remembered the vision Tora had told her about. With all her might, she beat the mallet against the earth, as fast as she could, wishing for deliverance from their attackers.

With each whack of the mallet, a mounted soldier on a horse appeared and trotted forward. They were in full armor, wearing metal breastplates and helmets, with leather armguards and shinguards, and their weapons were an even match for the Guard cavalry wheeling about on their horses. They immediately attacked the Guard. Shouts of confusion rang out as the Guard began fighting the intruders. Usagi pounded the mallet relentlessly, the driving rhythm creating a calvary that was even bigger than the one that had been sent out from the caravan.

As the conjured soldiers overtook the Guard, Goru lifted Tora's injured brother easily and disappeared into the hills with Tora at his side. Inu ran to the other Miners, who were frozen at the spectacle of Guard fighting a newly appeared army. "Come on!" he shouted, and grabbed Panri's arm, snapping him out of his daze. "Usagi! I think that's enough—let's go!"

Usagi paused, and the last mounted soldier sprang from the earth and galloped into the fray. Over the neighing of charging horses and the clash of swords, she heard a new sound. "The caravan is here!"

They turned and looked down the road. As the sun fully stretched its rays over the horizon, it illuminated a long line of wagons approaching. The first wagon driver's mouth was agape at the sight of the fire and the brawl. The Guard were close to being completely overcome by the soldiers of the Conjurer, and frantically called for help. The caravan Guard, some on foot, others on horses, rushed to help their comrades, ignoring Usagi, Inu, and the Miners entirely.

"Perfect," said Panri. "The Guard are so busy fighting, they're not going to bother with us. Let's go!"

"We'll take what's ours!" shouted a young woman. The other Miners roared. They took off for the wagons, which had lost their Guard protection.

For good measure, Usagi created another squadron, hammering the mallet until her hand was sore and her arm ached. "There!" she said, and looked in satisfaction as the last conjured soldier ran off. She stood up, mallet in her grip. She'd pounded until a shallow hole had formed in the Ring Road, and the Guard were now locked in a fierce battle, outnumbered by the army of the Conjurer.

"By the gods," said Inu, his eyes wide. He swept aside his shaggy hair with a chuckle. "Shall we give the Miners a hand?"

Usagi tucked the Treasure in her belt and grinned. "Why not?"

They raced toward the caravan. A couple of wagon drivers had been tied up and were sitting on the ground, looking on helplessly as the Miners heaved baskets of smelted metal and uncut gemstones off their wagons. A few Miners stood guard against any other drivers coming to the aid of their caravan mates.

Panri spotted them and waved them over. "Here!" He loaded their arms with heavy sacks. "Go, go, go!"

CHAPTER 17

FEAST OF THE HAMMER

DARKNESS FELL ON THE MARBLE Gorge, but inside the Painted Hollow, elaborately painted lanterns cast a warm glow, illuminating an enormous banquet. Dressed in sumptuous bright silks produced by the Conjurer, Usagi and the others joined the Miners for a night of festivities in the cavern, seating themselves on plump cushions strewn across a thick carpet. On low carved tables set before each person, plates of the finest porcelain and feedsticks of pure silver glistened, all of it created by the hammer.

"Spirits," said Goru, tugging uncomfortably at his cutsilk tunic, which featured a fierce, snorting ox stampeding across his back. He pushed up an intricately embroidered sleeve and took a cup of punch proffered by a conjured servant. "Err . . . thank you?" The servant bowed blankly and turned away, passing a quartet of conjured musicians playing lively tunes. Goru rubbed the back of his shaved head.

"This all seems like a bit much, doesn't it?"

Usagi smoothed the luminous fabric of her robes, which were cinched with a wide brocade belt of gold thread. "Oh, I don't know. I could get used to this."

"I didn't know you had such expensive taste," Inu teased. His shaggy hair had been slicked down and his clothes were made of shimmering watered silk in a refined shade of celadon green.

Grinning, Usagi looked around the lavish banquet. "I didn't either!" She spotted Tora by her brother's side. Though Imugi had been badly hurt in the raid, his injuries were easily treated thanks to the Apothecary. But Tora still fussed over him, checking his forehead and touching his arm every so often. Usagi's grin faded. The Conjurer was back in the bag at his waist. It was the first thing he'd asked for after he came to. Imugi had been so delighted by the raid's success and his rapid recovery that he wanted to create a celebration. When Tora had pointed out everything was going to disappear, her brother had laughed. "Yes, but we'll have enjoyed it all long before it does."

The chatter in the cave quieted as Imugi got to his feet. "To our honored guests, the Warrior Heirs!" he cried. "I wouldn't be standing here right now without you. We are grateful for your assistance, your bravery and ingenunity." He chuckled. "Creating a shadow Guard to fight the real ones was truly clever. We'd never thought to ask for people from the hammer before." Glancing at the expressionless musicians playing and vacant-eyed servants milling about, his snaggleteeth gleamed. He raised his cup. "The Miners will always be in your debt—and you are always welcome among us. Bottoms up!"

Bowing at the appreciative cheers, Usagi raised her cup along with Inu and Goru, and took a sip of chilled melon punch. It was sweet, almost too much so, leaving a cloying film in her mouth. She stared at Imugi's drawstring bag. How were they going to get the Treasure back?

They began to feast, eating food fit for royalty. Sweet whole crabs, briny oysters and quivering scallops glistening in their shells, all manner of juicy roasted birds, crisp suckling pig, giant lobsters cooked with aromatics, fresh prawns bursting with roe, tender braised meats in delicately crunchy potato cups, vegetables tied up in cunning purses filled with soup or carved to look like flowers, steamed puddings, translucent dumpling wrappers stuffed with various delicacies, soft rice cakes fried in savory spiced sauces, tangles of slippery long noodles, and warm bowls of rice simmered in rich broths and studded with nuts and dates. By the time they got to the sweets, Usagi wasn't sure if she could take another bite, but Panri urged her on.

"It's all going to disappear anyway," he said, slurping up a bowl of finely shaved ice drenched in sweet syrup. "Better stuff yourself while you can."

"Don't you get some . . . side effects after eating food from the hammer?" Usagi asked. She gave an involuntary little burp.

The youngling grinned and shrugged. "It's worth it. If you'd rather, there might be some millet porridge and snails left over from the other day."

"Maybe some of that iced jelly then." Usagi hiccupped. "And a couple of honey blossom cakes."

But after eating her way through every course, Usagi looked around the banquet, the tables littered with empty plates, picked-out shells, and bones sucked dry, and felt rather ill. She turned to Inu and Goru. "What are we going to do? We can't stay here forever—and we can't leave without the Treasure."

"Did Tora ever talk to her brother?" asked Inu.

"She promised to ask him again tonight." Usagi tugged at the gold brocade of her belt, which pressed uncomfortably against her full belly, and hiccupped. "I can't see him giving it up—not when it can do all this. And if it weren't for that hammer, we wouldn't have gotten out of that botched raid, let alone have turned it into a victory."

Goru leaned forward and lowered his voice. "Well then, we'll just have to take it."

"That might be tricky." Glancing across the stone circle, Usagi saw Tora making her way toward them. "Let's see if Tora got Imugi to agree."

Her face aglow, Tora plopped down beside them. She plucked an uneaten cube of dragon fruit off Usagi's plate and popped it in her mouth. "Isn't this all marvelous? Don't you wish we could live like this always?"

"It's lovely, but none of it is real," reminded Usagi. "We can't forget why we came. Did you explain to Imugi about the Treasure?"

A little of the light went out of Tora's eyes. "I did, but he hasn't had time to think about it."

"What's there to think about?" Inu demanded. "He can't keep putting this off. And we just helped them with their most successful raid ever. Let's just go talk with your brother now."

"Oh, all right." Reluctantly, Tora led them to Imugi. Most of the Miners had finished feasting and were either up and dancing as the musicians played or lazing on the rug and playing games like six sticks. Lounging on a cushion in posh silk robes, Imugi watched two Miners playing a game called containment, each trying to control the most space on a board with black and white stones, and commented on their moves. He beamed as Usagi and the others approached.

"Warrior Heirs!" He winked at Goru and Tora. "And Heirlings. How are you enjoying yourselves?"

Inu bowed. "Very much. May we have a word with you in private?"

"Of course," said Tora's brother. "Have a seat." He glanced

at the revelry around them and pulled out the wooden mallet. With a quick whack on the floor, an opulent tent with thick carpeted walls sprang up around them. Imugi grinned. "This way, we don't have to leave the party." He slid the mallet back in its drawstring bag and patted it. "This truly is a gift from the gods."

"We wanted to talk to you about that, actually," said Inu. "We need to return to Mount Jade—and I'm afraid we'll be needing the Conjurer."

Imugi sighed and slumped back on his cushions. "Yes, my sister mentioned it to me. But I'm afraid that's not possible."

"Not possible?" The Dog Heir frowned. "It belongs to the Warriors of the Zodiac. We're obligated to take it back to the Shrine of the Twelve. Our mission—and the future of Midaga—depends on it."

Imugi cleared his throat, fidgeting with the strings of the bag. "I understand your dilemma, but you have to understand that I'm responsible for all these people. We can't get by without the hammer."

"But what about the loot from the raid?" Usagi asked. She glanced at a bag of raw gemstones at his feet. It was one of many that had been brought back, not to mention baskets of smelted metal ingots. The new haul had stuffed the Miners' vault to overflowing. "You can buy what you need—you have enough for everyone to live comfortably several lifetimes over."

"Besides, you said yourself that the Miners owe us a debt," Goru pointed out. "Everyone at the banquet heard it."

The brand on Imugi's cheek jumped and twitched. "Without it, we wouldn't have escaped the mines. I'm sorry. I can't let it go."

Inu leaned forward. "If you give it to us, you will be giving the people of Midaga another chance. The horrors at the Eastern Mines won't stop until the Dragonlord is stopped. And the best way to do that is to keep the Treasures from him."

"Well, I'm not about to let him have it," said Imugi indignantly. "Besides, I was the one who found it."

"That doesn't mean it's yours," Usagi blurted.

There was a silence, and as Imugi's stare grew steely, Usagi felt her face flush, but she lifted her chin. "It's not," she insisted. "The Conjurer is one of the Treasures of the Twelve—and it needs to be returned."

"What, so *you* can use it?" Imugi shook his head. "The Twelve are no more. You call yourselves their Heirs, but what does that mean, really?"

"We're trying to restore the Circle of the Twelve," Inu said stiffly. "But it takes time, and training, and the right candidates." He turned his dark eyes to Tora. "And the Treasures."

She looked away, rubbing at the scars on her arm. Finally Tora straightened and moved to her brother's side. "You heard him," she snapped. "The hammer belongs to the Miners now."

Usagi, Inu, and Goru stared at her in disbelief. "What about our mission?" asked Inu softly.

"I don't know if it's my business anymore," Tora replied.

A panicky feeling pressed against Usagi's chest, making it hard to breathe. "Are you saying you're not coming back with us?"

"Wait, you have to come back," said Goru. "You're so close to becoming Tiger Heir."

A strange look flickered across Tora's face. She regarded them soberly. "My brother is everything to me. He's my family. All that I do is in service to my family." She looked at Imugi. "You know that, don't you, brother?"

Imugi's eyes reddened, and he took his sister's hand. "Of course I do. Nothing can sever our bond, but knowing that you want to be here makes me happier than I thought possible." He turned to Usagi and the boys. "You're welcome to stay with us as long as you like, but we cannot let the hammer go."

Dismissed with a wave, they exited the private chamber without the Treasure—or Tora. Usagi fought to keep from crying. In stunned silence, they walked through the Miners' revelry and went to their nook. As soon as they were alone, Usagi looked at Inu and Goru in despair. "Now what do we do?"

"Start packing," said Inu. "Since he won't give it to us, we'll need to steal the Conjurer—and we'll have to make a run for it as soon as we get it."

A tear slid down Usagi's cheek. It was just as she'd feared—her best friend had made a choice, and it wasn't them. "I knew this might happen, but I still can't believe she's staying."

Goru patted her awkwardly on the back. "We've all seen how happy she is to have found her brother."

"It's a blasted shame," said Inu. "But we can't force her to come back with us. That's not what becoming part of the Twelve is about."

They packed their meager belongings into their packs. The sumptuous conjured silks they wore would disappear within the day, so they changed into their own clothes of dark roughspun cotton.

"We'll wait until the hour of the Rat," said Goru. "I'll stand guard, and you two will go take the hammer from Imugi." He dug in his pack and brought out a small paper envelope. "Here—Rana gave me something. It's a bit of her paralyzing venom mixed with sleep powder. The effects only last a couple of hours, but this'll keep them from moving if they wake up."

Inu chuckled wryly. "That's brilliant."

A noxious smell filled their nook. Inu grabbed his nose and groaned. "Ox Boy. Forget the sleep powder—we should just have you fart in Imugi's general direction. It'll knock him out for days."

Goru smirked. "It's not me."

"Sorry," mumbled Usagi, reddening.

"Gods!" Inu pulled his scarf over his nose. "Just goes to show, the small and silent can be more powerful than the big and loud."

They took turns dozing while waiting for the moon to show itself through the crack in the cavern ceiling. When it reached the highest point, splashing the stone circle with moonlight, Goru shook Usagi and Inu awake. "It's time."

Stealthily they put on their travel packs. Usagi listened for signs of activity in the cavern and heard nothing but snoring and the tinkling notes of a soothing sleepsong. "Sounds like everyone's asleep," she whispered. They slipped through the cavern. The festive lanterns had dimmed, and all the Miners had either passed out amid the remains of the banquet or retired to their sleeping alcoves. The expressionless musicians of the hammer continued to play, and the conjured servants blankly went about cleaning up the mess, paying them no attention.

Inu took the envelope of sleep powder that had been enhanced with Rana's paralyzing venom and tipped a small amount into a hollow reed. He crept toward Imugi, who was sound asleep atop a pile of cushions, preparing to blow it in his face.

Usagi's ears pricked. Padding toward them, so quiet that her footsteps could only be detected with rabbit hearing, was Tora. Usagi whirled to see her friend holding something, but it was half in the shadows. Tensing, Usagi squinted, and then her eyes widened. She stopped Inu. "Wait!"

As Tora moved into the light, the gilt handle and brightly lacquered head of the Conjurer gleamed in her hand. Her eyes were red and puffy, but her jaw was set. "Let's go."

"Are you sure?" Usagi whispered.

Tora nodded. "If I stay here, I don't know how much things will change. This is just one Treasure. If we get them all . . ." She looked down, then took a deep breath. "Maybe everything can change."

With a look of relief, Inu squeezed Tora's shoulder. She handed him the mallet. "We better leave before my brother wakes up and finds this missing. I put a big bone in his bag, but it won't fool him for long."

They hid the hammer away in Inu's pack and hurried out of the cave into the dark gorge, led by Tora and her tiger vision. Usagi felt like a huge weight had been lifted, though she knew that Tora had left a piece of herself behind, just as Usagi had when she'd left her sister at the palace. Perhaps Tora's brother would be more forgiving than Uma. The

Miners had so much in riches now—surely they would be able to survive just fine without the Conjurer.

But they had hardly reached the river when Usagi heard Imugi's voice ringing in the distance. *"They've taken the hammer!"*

She could hear Miners scrambling to get out of the cavern. "Imugi knows we're gone," Usagi warned. "They're coming after us."

Goru cursed. "Squealing scabs."

They kicked into spirit speed, racing alongside the river. At the sound of shouts, Usagi glanced back and saw the bobbing of torchlight not far behind.

"They're gaining on us!" she cried.

Inu grunted and ran even faster. "Now I wish we hadn't showed them how to use spirit speed."

Reaching the tunnel that led out of the gorge, they darted underground and hurried through the long passageway. They emerged into the abandoned quarry and careened around cracked boulders and piles of shattered marble, all the while trying to keep ahead of the Miners. Usagi listened for their footsteps and urged the others on whenever their pursuers sounded too close. Her legs and lungs were beginning to burn.

At last they reached the path that they'd first taken into the pit. They clambered out and ran along old twisted roads that once led from the quarry to the Ring Road. They crested one ridge and sped down a curving trail, when Usagi caught the sound of something just ahead. "Stop!" she shouted. "Turn around!"

But before they could take another step, a figure landed before them, blocking their path. It was Imugi. Two more Miners jumped down from the steep hillside and joined him, torches in hand. Usagi turned and looked behind her—more Miners were rushing toward them. They were trapped.

"Tora!" Imugi's eyes blazed in the torchlight, and his fine silk robes from the Conjurer were torn and dirtied from his pursuit. "What's the meaning of this? I thought you were going to stay."

"I said that I was going to do everything I could in service to my family, and that's what I'm doing," said Tora. "If I become a Warrior Heir, maybe I can find out what happened to Papa. I told you—he could be in Waya right now, making swords for their emperor and the Dragonlord."

Her brother shook his head. "I'm sorry, little sister. I know you miss him. Papa was a fine blacksmith. But he— he's dead. I'm all you have left. Don't fool yourself."

Tora bristled. "How can you say that?"

"And what about this?" Imugi held up the empty draw-string bag that had held the Conjurer. "You know we need the hammer."

"No, you don't," said Tora. "You have a vault bursting with gems and gold—you'll be fine. Besides, look at how you're using the hammer. For ridiculous outfits and servants that are hardly human and fancy fake food—for what?"

"We didn't realize just how powerful that tool was until this raid," said Imugi. "We can create armies with it, Tora. If you really want to make a difference against the Dragonlord, stay here and help me take over the Eastern Mines. We'll have everything if we have the hammer. Stay, sister. Don't worry about your friends—we'll give them all the treasure they need."

Usagi glanced around. They were surrounded now, the path blocked by Miners both before and behind them. She peered to the side, where the slope dropped off steeply. In the torchlight, she saw a path running below.

"We don't want any jewels or gold," Inu said. "The only Treasure we need is the hammer."

Out of nervous habit, Usagi reached for the pendant at her neck, and was jolted as her fingers found the Ring of Obscurity. Why hadn't she thought of it sooner? She glanced at Goru, who saw the ring in her hand. She flicked her eyes to the side of the path and raised her eyebrows. Goru made to twist and stretch his neck as if it were sore, taking a good look in the direction she indicated. He gave a tiny nod.

Together they inched closer to Tora and Inu as they argued with Imugi. Tora pulled back her sleeve and shook her arm at her brother. "Don't ever say that I abandoned you—I got these scars trying to save you! Every day I've had to look at them and think about how I failed." Her voice broke. "I'm not going to let myself feel that way anymore."

Usagi had to act fast. She tried to remember what she'd read in the shrine's library about the Ring of Obscurity. Would dust, fog or smoke be the most effective? Dust, she decided. Fog might be risky. Though Imugi's dragon talents with water were slight, there was still a chance he'd be able to sweep it away.

Rubbing the amber stone as if she were trying to polish it, Usagi prayed to the spirits of the Twelve that it would work. They hadn't even tested the ring. What if it had been damaged? Or worse, what if it wasn't even the real Treasure? Her thumb passed over the pale stone once, twice, thrice— on the twelfth stroke, the ring vibrated, as if coming alive. A swirl of yellow dust shot out from the ring, billowing about them and stinging their eyes. Within seconds they and the Miners were enveloped in a churning cloud of powdery grit, unable to see anything beyond their own noses.

Usagi reached for Inu and Tora, with Goru right behind her. "Jump!" she choked, grabbing their hands. Together they leaped off the trail to the path below.

His Majesty was warned against using the Conjurer for anything that had to do with the body. Food, no matter how fine, would cause terrible indigestion, and altering one's appearance inevitably led to immense dissatisfaction. But the king did not listen, and ordered my sister-in-arms, Kuri the Ram Warrior, to take the hammer and create a great banquet for his birthday, and make him the most handsome man in the room. The results were predictably disastrous.

—From *Memoirs of a High Priest on Mount Jade,* by Ondori, 13th Rooster Warrior (Retired)

CHAPTER 18

THE NEWEST HEIRS

BRILLIANT RED MAPLE LEAVES LITTERED the stone tiles of the shrine courtyard like spots of blood on a jade slate. Usagi picked up a particularly vibrant one and placed the Ring of Obscurity on it. Set off by the crimson leaf, it glowed in the slanting afternoon light. She held it out to the others.

"That stone's the size of a dragonberry! It looks like one too, except it shines so." Admiring the ring, Rana's dark eyes sparkled.

Saru leaned companionably over Rana's shoulder and reached for the ring. "The First Tribes called amber 'tiger soul,'" the Monkey Heir said. "Doesn't it look like a bit of light from a Summoning, just before turning into a tiger?" She slipped the ring on a finger and splayed out her hand, where it gleamed. "Beautiful. You did well, all of you."

"If it hadn't been for Usagi's quick thinking, that ring

might still be flying around Butterfly Kingdom," said Goru, looking sheepish.

Inu chuckled. He grew serious as he looked at the Conjurer in Nezu's hands. "And we didn't need to use your sleep powder, Rana, because of Tora. Thanks to her, we have the hammer."

Ducking her head, Tora scratched behind Kumo's ears as the cloud leopard leaned against her with a rumbling purr. "I hope my brother forgives me," she said softly.

"You did the right thing. And he'll come to understand that." Usagi reached out and squeezed Tora's shoulder.

Tora sighed. "I hope so."

"I wish I'd seen Usagi on that giant butterfly." Nezu flashed a grin. "That must have been a wild sight!"

"It was an even wilder ride," Usagi told him. Her stomach did a little flip at the memory of the flight.

"Well, it paid off," said the Rat Heir. He turned the Conjurer over and ran a thumb across the lacquered images of the zodiac animals. "Now we have seven of the Treasures." He handed the mallet back to Tora. "You and Usagi should have the honors of placing these in the chest."

Saru took off the ring and put it in Usagi's hand, where it glistened atop the scarlet leaf. Following Tora, Usagi carried it into the Great Hall, trailed by the others. They gathered around the chest that held the Treasures and carefully deposited the ring and hammer in empty drawers.

Usagi stepped back, absently twirling the stem of the maple leaf. It felt strange to no longer have the ring's weight at her neck, but she was relieved to see it safely at the shrine with the other Treasures. She adjusted her rabbit pendant and gave its head an affectionate rub for helping to guard the Ring of Obscurity.

"What's our plan for the five missing Treasures?" Goru slid open an empty drawer. He peered into it as if an artifact would suddenly materialize like a wish granted by the Conjurer.

Nezu brightened. "We've been working on that." He took out the Mirror of Elsewhere. "While you were gone, Saru and I tracked all the Treasures in the Blue Dragon's possession with this. We took turns looking, of course, so we wouldn't get too attached."

"Oh, the mirror," breathed Tora.

With a gentle nudge, Usagi admonished her friend. "You don't need that—you've got your tiger vision."

"It's not the same at all," groused Tora. She gazed hungrily at the mirror in Nezu's hand. "What did it show you?"

"There were critical things we didn't know," Saru explained. "Like whether the Blue Dragon had locked up the Treasures at the palace, or deployed them with his Dragonstrikers. So we did some surveillance." She turned to Rana. "Snake Girl, would you mind getting the chart?"

With a nod, Rana ran off. She soon returned with a

rolled-up scroll and spread it across the sparring mats. They knelt around it. It was a detailed chart that listed the five missing Treasures—the Coppice Comb, the Bowl of Plenty, the Winds of Infinity, the Pen of Truth, and the Jewels of Land and Sea—and where each one had been on a particular date and time, as shown in the mirror.

"As you can see, the Treasures have been kept at the palace since we began tracking them. He doesn't let them off the grounds," said Nezu. He gave Usagi a wry smile. "That time we ran into the Strikers with the fan was very bad luck—my guess is that they were taking the Winds of Infinity to the Dragonlord when we ran into them."

Usagi could feel the heat rise to her cheeks as she remembered that awful day, but Saru seemed to read her mind and put a hand on her arm. "The good news is, because they're all at the palace, we can get them in a single mission," said the Monkey Heir.

As she studied the chart, Usagi saw a problem. "Spitting spirits, the Blue Dragon keeps three of the Treasures *on him!* How are we going to get the comb, the necklace, and the fan if he's wearing them?"

"That's the bad news," admitted Nezu. "But he's not always wearing them. He takes them off to sleep."

Goru whistled. "If they're in his sleeping quarters, that's hardly better. No one is allowed in his personal chambers except for his Dragonstrikers."

"What about the bowl and pen?" asked Tora, leaning over the chart. "It looks like they're kept in the Hall of the Golden Throne." She traced a finger over the marks counting the number of days the bowl and pen had been in one spot.

Saru nodded and took the mirror from Nezu. "He's got them under guard there night and day."

"I'm not so worried about those," said the Rat Heir confidently. "If we use the element of surprise, we can take on even Strikers. Our challenge will be getting the ones that the Blue Dragon carries."

Frowning, Usagi worried her rabbit pendant between her fingers. "That, and finding the jade bead that the Tigress hid." Without it, the Jewels of Land and Sea would remain broken, its powers lost.

That evening, Nezu laid out a table full of dishes for their return. It was far simpler than the banquet they'd had with the Miners in the Marble Gorge, but every bite was satisfying, from the eggs scrambled with bits of salted turnip to the bubbling stew of marinated boar meat spooned over a little steamed rice, fluffy and hot. There was an array of mountain vegetables, both pickled and cooked fresh, roasted sweet potatoes, and balls of minced lake fish and chives floating in a savory broth.

"The four of you are eating as if you haven't eaten for

months," marveled Nezu, watching Inu collect every stray grain of rice with his feedsticks and Goru tilt up his bowl to get at the last drops of soup.

Usagi scraped her plate for the remaining crumbs of fried egg. "The last big meal we had really didn't count."

Swiping a splotch of stew that had fallen on the table, Tora nodded and licked her finger. "It really didn't. We experienced the downside of getting exactly what you want from the Conjurer."

Saru wiped her mouth and smiled. "I'm glad that you're appreciating the simpler things here." She turned to Rana. "I think it's time."

With a twinkle in her eyes, Rana got up and hurried out of the dining hall. While the rest of them helped clear the table and wash the dishes, Nezu brought out candied persimmons and sugared chestnuts with cups of hot tea to wash it all down. After gorging at the Miners' conjured feast and suffering the effects for days, Usagi hadn't thought she'd ever want to touch another sweet, but it felt different eating real food. She was on her third chestnut when Rana returned with a cloth-wrapped bundle, bringing it to Saru. As the Monkey Heir began to untie its bindings, Usagi felt a surge of excitement, realizing what was about to happen. "Oh!"

As Nezu turned and winked, Usagi stuffed the rest of the chestnut in her mouth and hurried off to retrieve a small bundle of her own. When she returned to the dining hall, Saru held a handsome bow, along with a finely decorated quiver containing a set of well-oiled arrows. Tora and Goru were called to stand before everyone.

Tora looked a little uncertain as Saru faced her. "Do you accept the title of Tiger Heir, promising to uphold and defend the Way of the Twelve?" asked the Monkey Heir.

"What about Warrior Trials?" Tora asked in surprise.

Saru smiled. "Warrior Trials were traditionally administered by one's master. But since the Tigress is not here, and you've been learning alongside the rest of us, we Heirs have decided as a group that you are ready."

"Besides, what you did to get the Conjurer back was a great trial in itself," Inu added. "If that doesn't prove that you're worthy of becoming Heir, then nothing does."

Tora's hand strayed to the scars on her arm. Usagi caught her eye and nodded encouragingly. Tora threw her shoulders back. "Then yes, I do, with honor."

She was given the new bow, which curled compactly when unstrung, much like Inu's bow. "No more borrowing mine," said Inu with a mock scowl.

Laughing, Tora tested the string, pulling it and flexing the bow. "I won't," she promised.

"And now something from me—or the Tree of Elements, actually." Usagi stepped forward and handed her friend a

265

small cloth pouch. "Remember that chunk of ironstone that helped with your visions?" she asked. "I think it's time you started carrying it."

Tora opened it and pulled out a finely wrought gold chain, which Usagi had asked Inu to make. The tiger-iron bead dangled from its delicate links. Tora's eyes widened. "I don't remember it looking like this."

"I dropped it by accident into the firepit in the Miners' Den," Usagi confessed. "When I finally managed to pull it out, it transformed. The firepit's the center of the Painted Hollow's old ceremony circle, so some ancient power turned the tiger iron into this jewel."

Tora touched the bead with tentative fingers. Its stripes of red, black, and gold glistened as she examined it. "It's beautiful." She hesitated. "I'm a little nervous about carrying the ironstone. I worry that it'll give me constant visions."

"Wear it for a bit and see how you feel," Nezu said, flashing a grin. "If anything, it will help you master your tiger vision. You're an Heir now, so don't be afraid."

Nodding, Tora took a deep breath and slipped it on. After a bit she exhaled and smiled. "Thank you."

"Now for Ox Boy," said Nezu. Hunching his shoulders self-consciously, Goru shuffled forward.

"For Goru, you have shown that it's not a matter of mastering a physical weapon—it's a matter of mastering oneself," said Saru. "Your bravery, resilience, and willingness to help in every situation exemplify the qualities that every good Warrior must have."

Upon Goru's accepting the title of Heir to the Ox Warrior, they presented him with a metal chain belt attached to a round iron weight the size of a coconut. It was a power chain sized to fit him, and so heavy that Rana had to enlist Nezu and Inu's help to bring it into the dining hall. "You may prefer to use your fists, but it never hurts to have extra tools at your disposal," Nezu huffed as they dragged it in.

Goru lit up. "Bulging blisters! This will help me pack a punch."

He put it around his waist and hefted the weight in his palm like a juggler's ball. He was also given a coat of fine chain mail interlaced with rows of small iron plates. "I've been working on that for months," said Inu, smiling. "You're so big and strong, you're practically a weapon unto yourself, but with some extra protection, you'll be unstoppable."

With a grin, the new Ox Heir slipped on the metal jacket. "Bring on the Dragonstrikers," he roared.

"What about Snake Girl?" asked Tora.

Rana smiled. "I'll be next soon enough! Inu, you'll have to make me a coat of scales when the time comes!"

"That I will," promised the Dog Heir, chuckling. They raised their cups of tea and cheered the two newest Warrior Heirs.

"Six Heirs, one Heirling, and seven Treasures," exclaimed

Nezu. "Do you know what that means?"

Saru put her arms around Tora and Goru. "It means we're more than halfway to completing the Circle."

With Tora and Goru as Heirs, everyone's focus turned back to planning the final mission. Hard at work one day in the shrine's library, they went over dozens of old scrolls depicting the Palace of the Clouds. They noted all the changes that the Blue Dragon had made to the compound. From memory, the former Dragon Academy cadets sketched a map featuring new fortifications and building complexes that had been added, like the Academy and the Sunburst lockup.

"We lived and trained here," said Goru, stabbing the map with a thick finger. "In this part of the Central Court."

Rana pointed out the Inner Court, where the Dragonlord's quarters were located. "Remember this garden, by the royal residence? We escaped under the wall right in this far corner."

"And the Guard and Dragonstrikers are housed in separate barracks in the Outer Court," Tora said, inking them onto the paper.

The senior Heirs offered their own observations. "The bowl and the pen are kept at the throne hall, which is in the heart of Central Court," said Saru. The Monkey Heir circled the building on the map, then marked another building in the Inner Court. "The rest of the Treasures go with the Blue Dragon every night to his private chambers here. That's where he removes them to sleep. Our best shot at those will be at that time, but it won't be easy."

"So we'll aim for the Hall of the Golden Throne first," said Inu.

Leaning forward eagerly, Rana traced a path on the map. "I know a good way in . . ."

Usagi interrupted. "First we look for the Tigress," she said firmly. "We shouldn't let her languish a minute longer."

Nezu tugged on his whiskers. "But we'll still need to secure the other Treasures once we get there."

"Which includes the missing bead from the Jewels of Land and Sea," Usagi pointed out. "The Blue Dragon is desperate to find it. If we go after the Tigress first, we can rescue her and track down the Jewel at the same time."

Saru tilted her head as she considered the map of the palace. "I certainly don't want to delay Teacher's freedom any longer than necessary."

"But won't she slow us down?" Rana asked. "We'd still have to get the other Treasures. How would that work if Mistress Horangi is with us?"

A flush of anger rose in Usagi, especially when Saru nodded thoughtfully. Was she agreeing with Rana? How dare they even think that the Tigress would be a drag on the mission? She *was* their mission. Usagi was about to blurt all this when she saw Tora put a hand over the tiger-iron bead at her neck, frowning. Her friend squeezed her eyes shut as if she were in pain.

"What's wrong, Tiger Girl?" asked Nezu, looking concerned.

Goru peered at Tora. "I think she's having another vision."

"Spirits," said Nezu, impressed.

They waited with bated breath while Tora pinched the space between her eyebrows. Finally she opened her eyes, troubled.

"I saw Uma," she told Usagi. "She looked like she was in trouble—she was tangled in a Striker's fly-net somewhere in the wilderness."

Usagi sat bolt upright. "What? She's a Dragon Academy cadet. She's going to *be* a Striker. Why would they need to capture her?" She scrambled to her feet. "I have to check the Mirror of Elsewhere."

She ran out of the library, Tora on her heels. They raced into the Great Hall and Usagi skidded to a stop in front of the chest holding the Treasures. Yanking open the drawer with the mirror, she reached for it, heart lodged in her throat. Had her sister undergone a change of heart? Had Uma decided to leave the Academy? Had the Dragonstrikers hunted her down? Spitting spirits, she should have checked in on Uma sooner. It had been well more than a year since she'd laid eyes on her sister.

The image of Usagi's panicked gaze blurred, and then the mirror cleared. There was her sister, dressed in the cadet blues of the Dragon Academy. Uma's expression was as severe as her hair, which was tied tightly back in a flowing tail, but she was sitting quietly.

"I see her!" Usagi exclaimed. "She's not in a fly-net—that's good. But where in the world is she?" The image expanded to show her sister with a group of other cadets. They knelt in a long, grand room lined with twelve sets of imposing carved pillars painted in a riot of colors. On an altar across from the cadets, the Bowl of Plenty and the Pen of Truth were displayed, cradled in silk cushions. Two Dragonstrikers in full armor stood at attention on either side, firecannon on their shoulders. "The Treasures," breathed Usagi. "She's in the Hall of the Golden Throne."

Kings and queens once sat on the dais at one end of the throne hall, receiving subjects and conferring with the Council of the Twelve. Anyone who approached the throne platform would pass a niche that held the Summoning Bell. Now the Dragonlord had turned the bell niche into an altar for the Treasures and made the throne his own. The image of the Blue Dragon came into focus.

Usagi recoiled. She hadn't wanted to see the Dragonlord

since their last encounter, and had managed to avoid seeing him in the mirror until now. But she couldn't look away. The Blue Dragon sat on an ornate gilt chair in the middle of a dais, flanked by two carved golden dragons. He listened with his hooded eyes half-closed as ministers and Guard commanders knelt before him and gave reports. His chin was propped on one hand, but as he shifted, Usagi saw that across one high cheekbone was a strange mark—that of a hand, a pale imprint against his gray-blue skin. Her eyes widened. The Tigress had slapped him, right before their last battle, and her handprint remained emblazoned on his face all these months later.

On a silk cord at his neck was a black pearl and a white one—the Sea Jewels that were said to control ocean waves. But the Land Jewel was still missing. The Tigress had said she'd hidden the replacement jade bead away from the Blue Dragon, and it appeared that he hadn't yet found it. Usagi was heartened until she noticed the folded fan tucked in the front of his belt. "The Blue Dragon has the Winds of Infinity right on him, just as Nezu said," Usagi confirmed.

At his side, a small table held an elaborate tea set. There were multiple bowls for rinsing tiny cups used in tastings and ceremonies, and pots of tea brewed with different types of leaves at different strengths. He poured himself a splash of tea in a cup that would barely hold the Ring of Obscurity.

With long-nailed fingers, he held the cup delicately to his dark purple lips, looking over the rim. His hooded eyes stared at the Striker kneeling before the dais, helmet removed. With a jolt, Usagi recognized him. "Well, if it isn't two-faced Tupa," she muttered. "Hello, traitor."

"Oh, let me see," said Tora, reaching for the mirror.

Holding a hand up, Usagi brushed her off. "Wait—I'm not done."

As Tupa bent humbly, his gilded helmet in his arms, he said something to the Dragonlord. The Blue Dragon's gaze grew hard, and he hurled his teacup in a sudden movement. The cup whipped across the room and struck the bowing Tupa squarely on his shaved head. Usagi winced, even as she remembered the former Ram Heir having a skull hard enough to butt straw target bales without hurting himself. The cup shattered and porcelain fragments flew everywhere, including into the group of cadets sitting to the side. Her sister didn't flinch, even as a thin line of blood appeared on her cheek. The Blue Dragon stood and began shouting soundlessly at his Striker captain.

Usagi dropped the polished disk as if it burned. It tumbled to the floor and swiveled around and around on its knobby handle like a slowing top.

"What did you see?" asked Tora, her brow wrinkled with worry.

She told Tora about what she'd just witnessed, and seeing her sister cut by flying shards. "It didn't even faze her, and she was *bleeding*."

"Sounds about right," nodded Tora. "When the Dragonlord is your master, he can do whatever he wants. He can use you for target practice if he feels like it."

Usagi bit her lip. "That's terrible."

Glancing down at the tiger-iron pendant around her neck, Tora frowned. "So she's not stuck in the wilderness. I'm not sure what my vision was about, then." She bent and snatched the mirror up, and began polishing it on her sleeve. "Gods, I've missed this thing."

"You've been doing so well without it," Usagi reminded her. She took the mirror from her friend and put it back in the chest. "Try not to look in it for a little bit longer?"

Tora rolled her eyes. "All right." She sighed. "It's not like I'm great at reading what it shows me, either. I have a feeling that what I thought was my father in the mirror might have been Imugi all along." She took Usagi's hand. "Come on— let's go tell the others what you saw."

As they left the Great Hall, Usagi's dread grew. She had a dire feeling about the Tigress. No wonder the old warrior had appeared so unwell—the Dragonlord treated even Tupa, the head of his prized strike force, as if he were nothing. Could Uma still be devoted to the Blue Dragon after witnessing such treatment? Usagi felt the old ache for her sister resurface, sharper than ever. She had to take Uma away from that place, along with the Tigress and the Treasures. But with the Treasures either under constant guard or worn by the Blue Dragon himself, recovering them would be their biggest challenge yet, not to mention locating and freeing the Tigress. The task ahead seemed impossible.

CHAPTER 19

ENDANGERED TIGRESS

THE WINDS GREW SHARP AND chilly on Mount Jade as the Heirs and Rana prepared for their mission to the capital. It would be a tricky one. In Dragon City, there were five Treasures to recover—one of which was in pieces, with a crucial part hidden somewhere by the Tigress. Several of the precious artifacts were carried daily by the Blue Dragon. On top of which, his palace compound was heavily guarded.

Most importantly, they would be rescuing the Tigress herself. Everyone was needed for this mission.

Tora had had a vision that showed them bringing along the seven Treasures that were in the chest. "We each had one—I couldn't quite see who was carrying what—but a golden light surrounded us, almost like a shield," she recounted. "I don't always understand my visions right away, but the meaning of this one seems clear."

"We must have the power of all, to get all," said Saru. "It makes sense."

Nodding with the others, Usagi vowed to herself that they would bring every last Treasure back to the shrine. She'd never lose another one again.

Everyone agreed that each of them would assume responsibility for a single Treasure, and use its powers if needed. As they clustered around the chest in the Great Hall, Inu chose the Flute of Dancing Dreams, since he knew how to play and usually carried a flute around anyway. Nezu cheerfully volunteered to wear the belt again. Rana took charge of the pillbox. "I've been working on my venom talents, so I'd better carry the antidotes in case we need them."

"May I wear the tiger-soul ring?" asked Tora. The Ring of Obscurity glowed with golden light as she slipped it on her finger. Goru selected the Conjurer. It hung from the other end of his power chain, which he wore as a belt, the heavy iron ball tucked in a pocket. Dangling from the thick metal links, the wooden mallet looked like a little ornamental charm on him.

Saru turned to Usagi. "That leaves the Fire Cloak and the Mirror of Elsewhere. What would you like to be in charge of?"

"The cloak," she decided. She didn't want to say it out loud, but thinking about her last encounter with her sister made her realize it'd be better to have some fire protection.

Pocketing the mirror, Saru handed her the cloak with a smile. "As you wish." She helped Usagi into the Fire Cloak. It was light as a feather and whisper thin. Usagi noticed that she was instantly warmer against the wintry chill. "I don't think I want to take this off!" she exclaimed.

"If you come up against someone with a fire gift, you definitely won't want to," agreed Saru.

It was as if she'd read her mind. Usagi's stomach clenched. "I hope it doesn't come to that."

"It will," said Inu grimly. "Tupa's still captain of the Strikers, after all. If we make one mistake at the palace, I'm sure ol' Fire Ram will try to stop us." He pushed his shaggy hair off his furrowed brow.

An excited whistling in the doorway of the Great Hall caught Usagi's attention. *Kwa hee kwa hoo. Kwa hee kwa hoo.* "A forest angel!" Sitting there was a bird of many colors that she'd often seen around Sun Moon Lake, happily grubbing for worms and snails in the damp of the cloud forest. "What's one doing all the way up here?"

The bird flew into the hall and landed on the chest of Treasures. Its chestnut crown was the same color as Saru's hair, and it had a crimson belly, white chest, and wings in shades of brilliant blue and green. Its bright eyes peeked from a striped mask of black feathers like a little thief. Tied to its leg was a paper scroll.

"I think Ji's made friends with a few new birds," said Nezu. He removed the scroll and unrolled it. Scanning it, he flashed a grin. "Yunja's wondering when we're coming—he's more excited than ever about the project that they want to show us. Says he thinks it could help overthrow the Blue Dragon."

Inu barked a laugh. "That's a bold statement. I suppose we should find out what they've been up to—it's not a small thing to get a forest angel up here. Those birds don't usually get to these altitudes."

Smiling, Saru took the slip of paper from Nezu. "Then we'll stop and see them on the way to the capital. If they truly have something useful against the Dragonlord, it's worth checking out."

They wrote out a message for Yunja and attached it to the rainbow-hued bird. Fluttering its vivid wings, it whistled goodbye and flew out the massive doorway, back into the wintry blue sky.

As they left the Great Hall themselves, Usagi spotted the Summoning Bell across the courtyard and remembered the frail form of the Tigress. "I'm worried about Teacher. I know she warned us not to contact her, but it would be good to know how she is."

"She should know that we've recovered all the missing Treasures and are coming for the rest," Nezu said, stroking his whiskers.

"And that we're coming for her too," agreed Saru. "Teacher has been in captivity for so long. She needs hope."

So they gathered around the great bronze bell, and the Monkey Heir struck it with its hammer. A single note pealed, deep and rich, growing in strength till the vibrations shook the leaves of the nearby Singing Bamboo. As the bamboo sang in concert with the bell, they stood in a circle and waited, anxious. Would the Tigress appear? Was she in good health? Was she even still alive? Usagi fervently prayed that the Tigress would show.

The thrum of the bell had nearly dissipated when at last a tiny pinpoint of light appeared, winking like a firefly. After agonizingly long moments, it grew and twisted into shape, until it was a giant translucent tiger. To Usagi's alarm, the tiger barely gave off any light, and flickered like a candle guttering in the breeze. It wasn't standing, either—it was lying down, and looked asleep.

"Teacher?" she ventured. "Are you okay?"

The tiger's great head lifted, and its glimmering green eyes blinked open. "Young Rabbit," it said wearily. "My Heirs. It is dangerous to Summon me while I am kept prisoner by Druk. I thought I made that clear."

"Forgive us, Teacher," said Saru. "But we thought you should know that we've succeeded in securing the remaining Treasures."

The tiger seemed to glow a little brighter, and its large

ears swiveled forward. "That is good news indeed."

Inu stepped forward with the flute in his hands. "We have seven of the Twelve Treasures in our possession." He motioned to everyone to show the Tigress the items in their charge. Usagi shrugged off the Fire Cloak and held it toward the ghostly tiger so it could stretch out its neck and sniff it, along with the other Treasures. It gave a chuff of satisfaction.

"We know where the Blue Dragon's keeping the rest at the Palace of the Clouds," said Nezu.

"We're coming to get them—and we're coming to get you, Teacher," blurted Usagi. "Please keep your strength up."

The tiger's green eyes flared, and for a brief moment it struggled to push itself up on its forepaws. "Say no more. Druk has the Pen of Truth and could force me to reveal what I know. If he should learn that you have the rest of the Treasures and are coming, then he will be looking for you. He has always been skilled in the use of the Four Poisons: surprise, fear, doubt, and confusion. You must be on your guard."

"Well then," said Saru slowly. "I hate to tell you that Usagi spoke too soon. She desperately wants to come save you, as do we all, but we cannot go to the Palace of the Clouds in search of the remaining Treasures, because er . . . we're very busy training. And as for the Treasures that we do have— they will be kept safely here at the shrine. Isn't that right?"

Saru glanced around with a hard stare, and after a brief moment of confusion, they quickly nodded and agreed.

"We'll be staying right here and guarding the Treasures!" Goru bellowed, as if saying something louder would make it so.

The tiger flopped back down and coughed a chuckle. "That is a pity. The only thing that might help free me would be the power of the Treasures, as wielded by those with zodiac powers. But I forbid you to come. I know you always follow what I say without question." It coughed again.

"We shall obey," said Tora. "Mistress Horangi, we never met in person, but I'm . . ."

"And it is better for me not to know of any new developments or additions to your ranks," interrupted the Tigress. "Though I trust that all are trained with care, and practice with diligence, as always."

Usagi reached out and squeezed Tora's hand. "Of course. Anyone who joins us must have the heart of a warrior."

"Good," grunted the tiger. "One thing to remember. Though Druk has been expelled from Mount Jade, I do not think it will stop him from trying to attack once more—not when he has five of the Treasures and a growing number of troops with zodiac powers."

The Heirs exchanged alarmed glances. "But . . . if he was ejected before, how could he succeed now?" asked Inu.

"The mountain repelled his forces, which were made up

of foreign invaders," said the Tigress. "Since then, he has been conscripting Midagian younglings with powers. There is no telling what the mountain will do with them."

It hadn't occurred to Usagi that Mount Jade could ever be vulnerable to the Dragonlord. "Have you heard anything, Teacher, that would make you think that he's planning an attack sometime soon?"

The Tigress sighed. "Not yet, but as soon as he finds out that you have the rest of the Treasures at the shrine, he may try." She paused. "Mount Jade is not the only sacred spot to the Twelve."

"We understand," said Saru meaningfully. "We shall hold on to hope that we will be together again."

The tiger grunted. "Never let go of it. Hope feeds the strength we need to endure." Her head swiveled and her green eyes narrowed. The tiger's ears flattened. "I must go," she hissed. "They are coming!" Her ghostly form quickly melted away.

"Teacher? Teacher?" Usagi called, alarmed. But there was no answer, save for the mournful melodies of the Singing Bamboo.

They had no time to waste. The Tigress might soon be interrogated. They needed to rescue her as soon as possible and take back the Treasures in the Blue Dragon's possession.

Hurriedly, they packed up their tools, provisions, and weapons, securing everything at the shrine for their absence.

In the midst of all the activity, Kumo paced about the courtyard, occasionally going off into a corner and turning his back on everyone, sulking.

"I'm sorry," Tora told him, rubbing his ears. "I promise we'll be back again soon. We need you to guard the shrine while we're gone." With a grunt, the cloud leopard stalked off, tail lashing from side to side. Tora shrugged, her snaggleteeth glinting. "Grumpy cat. He'll be fine."

The seven of them, each carrying one of the Treasures, set off from Mount Jade. Snow had begun to fall at the highest elevations, and the chill air swept down on them as they descended the slopes. But Usagi barely felt it with the warmth of the Fire Cloak protecting her.

After several days speeding through the wilderness, they arrived at Sun Moon Lake. Usagi was eager to check in with Yunja and see how Ji and the other younglings were doing in his care. She was wildly curious about the project he wanted to show the Heirs. They found the hermit and his charges busy at work building contraptions like she'd never seen.

Inu poked at the frame of a giant kite on the ground. It was nearly as big as Goru, made of oiled barkcloth stretched across a thin wooden frame. "What in the name of the Twelve is all this?"

"Strap yourself onto that and you'll sail into the sky like you've got Rooster flight!" said the hermit. He puffed out his sunken chest. "Remember how you were wishing that all Midagians could join in fighting against the Blue Dragon?" He tapped his head. "It got me to thinking."

Yunja was putting his old carpentry skills to use in creating items that would give ordinary people something close to zodiac powers. There was a wooden horse without a head, but it had a seat and stirrups connected to four jointed legs. A rider could make the wooden horse walk by moving their own feet in the stirrups, which six-year-old Buta, the little boy born in the year of the Boar, was doing with ease.

"Would you look at that!" marveled Nezu, tugging on his whiskers. "Even without a horse or spirit speed, you can still cover more ground than you could on your own."

The hermit gave a gap-toothed grin. "That's the idea! I'm still working on free-flying, instead of being tethered to a kite. Rooster Girl doesn't have the powers of flight, but I'm trying to change that."

He pointed to Ji. Their young friend was wearing unwieldy wings made of a framework of reeds and woven matting. She ran back and forth, hopping like a sparrow trying to get off the ground, a look of intense concentration in her eyes. Yunja's three dogs were barking and racing in frenzied excitement over the visitors, but it wasn't until one nearly knocked Ji over that she noticed Usagi and the other Heirs.

"You're back!" she cried. Casting off the wings, she ran

over to Usagi and threw her arms around her. Ji's face had filled out and she no longer looked like the timid, frightened girl hiding in the shadows of Port Wingbow.

Usagi hugged her. "How have you been? Where are your birds?"

"Which ones? I've made so many bird friends here." Ji beamed.

"We noticed," laughed Usagi. "Your last messenger was such a colorful eye-catcher! But I meant the seagulls."

"Nabi and Neko? They're off somewhere, but they'll come when I call. When we get these wings to work, I'll get to fly along with them. Yunja's been building so many things, and we're the first to try everything out. And guess what? I've been learning to control my flame!" The little girl's words tumbled out in a rush. She excitedly showed them some of the other contraptions the hermit had been working on—a boat that could dive beneath the water's surface, allowing its occupants to breathe with bamboo tubing. A cart on wheels that needed no horse to pull it. And wooden birds the size of actual crows, with cavities inside their bodies to hold anything from pitch and gunpowder to messages.

"They don't fly very far—they travel farther if they're catapulted with a sling," said Yunja. "But if you ever wanted to send the Blue Dragon a message, one of these wooden crows would do the trick. Especially if it were stuffed with flaming manure." He cackled.

Saru smiled briefly, then turned serious. "We do want to send the message that he's not all-powerful. But he may lash out with even more force then." She explained how the Tigress had warned them of a possible attack on Mount Jade by the Blue Dragon. "He's after the Treasures, and the more younglings with powers that he adds to his troops, the greater the chance that he'll try to come to the shrine."

"Little does he know that we're coming for *his* Treasures," said Goru, pounding a great fist into his palm with a giant smack.

The hermit shook his head. "Once you get all the Treasures back, of course he'll attack the shrine," he growled.

"That's what we're afraid of," said Inu. He explained how in recovering Treasures all over the kingdom, they'd come across other groups of gifted and talented younglings in hiding. "There must be a way for us all to help each other."

Yunja stroked his beard. "If everyone worked to make things miserable for the Blue Dragon, we'd surely get our kingdom back. Gods' guts, what I would give to see all Midagians rise up."

"But even if it were just those with zodiac powers banding together, it would make a difference. We may need assistance in defending Mount Jade," said Saru.

"What about my birds?" Ji piped up. "They can carry messages to the other younglings."

They turned. "To all of them?" asked Usagi.

"Just tell me where they need to go," said Ji confidently.

Tora raised an eyebrow and nodded. "It's worth trying."

The Rooster youngling let out a shrill cry. After what seemed like an eternity of silence, Usagi heard a thin answering call, and looked up to see the twin gulls flying toward them. "Here come Neko and Nabi!"

Once the birds arrived in the clearing, Saru quickly wrote up messages for both the Miners and the Ghosts of Butterfly Kingdom on long strips of paper. Inu drew a map of Midaga in the dirt, showing Ji the location of the Marble Gorge and Butterfly Kingdom and describing what to look for.

Ji attached a message to each bird and murmured to them, stroking their feathers. "I hope they won't be mistaken for the Dragonlord's messenger birds. What if your friends try to shoot them down?"

"Oh, I wouldn't worry about that—they look nothing like pigeons," said Goru. "My only fear is that someone will think a seagull will make a good meal."

At Ji's look of panic, Usagi elbowed Goru.

"Never mind what Ox Boy says." Yunja chuckled. "Your birds know how to take care of themselves. Let them go."

With a kiss on their snowy-white heads, Ji threw each one into the air, where they flapped until they were high overhead. "Be careful!" she called. The gulls circled once, dipping their wings as they soared, then flew off. Saru wrote up another message to the Dunelings of the Dancing Dunes. Ji sent it off with a forest angel, the multicolored bird ascending into the sky like a flying rainbow.

Nezu flashed a grin. "Now come on. We've got some Treasures to go after."

CHAPTER 20

THE BUG PIT

USAGI SQUIRMED, TRYING IN VAIN to readjust her heavy suit of Dragonstriker armor. She gave up and hurried after Goru, disguised as the biggest roach of them all. The Ox Heir had created Striker armor with the Conjurer for each of them. Every step sent the lacquered leather plates clacking, and while the rattling had ceased to unnerve Usagi, it was still annoying. The worst part was the helmet, which sat so low on her forehead that she had to tilt her chin to get a good look at anything. But at least the Heirs could move through Dragon City undisturbed. People dodged out of their path as they strode through the streets of the capital.

More than a year and a half had passed since they'd last been here. In the dead of winter, drifts of snow edged the broad streets, pushed there by street sweepers clearing the marble paving stones. Trampled by crowds of people bundled up against the chill, the dirty gray piles were turning to slush in the midday sun. Vendors selling roasted sweet potatoes or sacks of warm chestnuts crouched by iron braziers filled with glowing coals and poked at their wares as the food heated on the hot metal. It smelled deliciously welcoming. But the ubiquitous tributes to the Dragonlord weren't. Dour portraits of Lord Druk scowled from windows, and his dragon crest was emblazoned on passing carts. Bronze statues stood watch over market squares and street corners. Here, the Blue Dragon was impossible to forget.

With a shiver, Usagi tightened her grip on the firecannon over her shoulder—her walking stick transformed by the Conjurer that morning, with her pack disguised as an ammunition bag. They had to complete their mission before the next morning, when the changes brought about by the hammer would disappear. The crowds parted as they walked by, looking at them uneasily. A group of Guard saluted as they passed. Saru saluted back, and Usagi and the others followed suit.

"Stay together, everyone," Inu muttered. They were approaching a watchtower, spilling patrols of Guard into the streets. A tall structure with many stories and tiers of curving tiled roofs, the Guard station had once been part of a shrine to the Twelve. As various patrols spotted the Heirs, clad in elite Striker gear and equipped with superior weapons, some Guard nodded and saluted, and others stared with bemused expressions. Usagi could hear them murmuring to each other.

"Will you look at the small one!"

"I didn't know Strikers came in pocket sizes."

"Har har har! Must be one of the Dragonlord's little freaklings that's been promoted. I don't understand how younglings can possibly be of any use to him, demon powers or not."

"They're talking about us," warned Usagi. "Just ignore them, whatever they do."

"Oi, little Dragonstriker!" teased a Guard as they passed. "Are you off to fight some freaks like you? Or heading back to the palace to Lord Druk's zoo?" He marched alongside Rana, chuckling. "So, a girl's one of the best, eh? Don't mess with her!"

Rana pursed her lips. Before Usagi or anyone else had time to blink, Rana turned and spat in the Guard's face. He began to scream and clawed at his eyes. "It burns! She's a demon! For the love of all gods, help me!"

Without saying a word, Rana spun on her heel and marched on. Usagi glanced back and saw the other Guards looking at them fearfully, while the one with spit in his eye had fallen and was rolling around.

"Spirits, Rana—you shouldn't have done that!" Usagi hissed.

Rana raised her chin, smiling slightly. "Maybe—but that

felt good. Besides, it won't blind him forever. He really should rinse his eyes though, if he's smart."

"Obviously he's not, or he wouldn't have bothered us to begin with." Tora snickered.

The Rat Heir turned and flashed a grin. "At least they know not to underestimate you. We can't all be Goru's size."

"Just be careful," Usagi grumbled. Couldn't they see? The last thing they needed was to raise the ire of Guards before they even got to the palace.

They moved on through the streets easily, their helmets obscuring their faces, and the armor deflecting any questions. By late afternoon they'd reached the palace district, where the streets grew narrow and crooked, winding up and about the hills that surrounded the Palace of the Clouds.

Perched on the tallest hill, the white marble walls of the palace gleamed. Usagi's stomach twisted in a knot. So much had happened since she'd last been inside those walls, and yet some things were unchanged. Her sister was still there, as were the remaining Treasures. The Tigress was there too. All were within reach, if they could pull off several big tasks by dawn.

They headed for one of the five smaller Element Gates, having decided against going through the main palace entrance, known as the Gates of Heaven. Though the main gate had more foot traffic that could serve as distraction, there were also more Guard on hand. The smaller gates, used only by workers and troops, would have fewer to contend with. For while their Striker uniforms would help them blend in, Goru's giant frame was unmistakable, and he'd grown quite a bit since living on Mount Jade. There was no blending in for the Ox Boy.

But as they drew closer to the Water Gate, which would take them into the eastern side of the Outer Court, Goru broke rank. "Wait—give me a moment." He ducked into a side alley, squeezing behind a wall of rice-wine barrels.

"What's going on?" asked Saru. "Are you all right?"

"I'm fine—I just got an idea," called Goru.

Usagi and the others exchanged puzzled looks. Then she heard a series of ringing taps. "He's doing something with the Conjurer."

Rolling his eyes, Nezu said, "I think we have enough armor, Ox Boy."

"Oh no," said Goru, so quietly that only Usagi heard it. She felt a stirring of alarm and headed down the alley.

"What's wrong, Goru?" Usagi glanced behind at the others, who'd followed, and shook her head. Something was off. The Monkey Heir's face creased with concern.

There was a pause. "Uh . . . I thought I might try to disguise myself a little further." Goru stepped out, and they all gasped. He was no longer giant. He'd taken the Conjurer and wished himself smaller—only he'd gone too far. He was barely the size of Rana, though stockier. His armor and power chain had shrunk along with him, and now the hammer looked quite large in his hand.

Thunderstruck, they stared at him in silence, unable to say a word. Sheepishly, Goru shuffled his formerly giant feet. "At least no one at the palace will recognize me."

"Wh-what . . . ," Inu spluttered. He towered over Goru now. Grabbing him by the scruff, he examined the tiny Ox Heir from head to toe. "We can't go in with you like this. Change yourself back!"

Shaking his head, Goru held up his hands. "I tried, but I only made it worse. Gods, those warnings in our manual were no exaggeration. More power means more problems."

"Then give me the Conjurer," said Inu. "I'll wish you back." He reached for the hammer.

Saru stopped him. "You could make it even worse," she said. "What if you accidentally wish him into being the size of a watchtower? It's not worth the risk." She looked around at everyone sternly. "This is why we're not supposed to use the hammer to change our bodies."

"At least this way we should be able to go through the palace gates without attracting notice," Usagi pointed out. "He'll be back to his usual size tomorrow."

"But we could use his usual strength and size *today*," Inu said, frowning.

The Ox Heir looked affronted. "I'm still strong, even if I'm smaller," he insisted. He turned around and grabbed a full barrel, its rice wine sloshing within. His arms couldn't fully reach around, but he hefted it easily and then balanced it on his fingers. "See?"

Nezu flashed a grin. "Well then. The Tigress always said a good warrior can adapt to any situation. Usagi's got a point. We can get in the palace more easily this way. It might be a blessing. No one who knew you at the Dragon Academy would notice you're back on the grounds."

Both Tora and Rana nodded vigorously, still looking stunned. "That's for sure," said Tora, slack-jawed.

They neared the Water Gate, a portal in the winding marble wall of the palace compound, barely half the size of the Gates of Heaven. The doors were open and manned by only two Guards, one on either side. Saru strode straight past them with a brief salute, and they saluted back as the Heirs passed through the gateway. Usagi kept her chin down and her expression stern, holding her breath till they were well away from the gate.

"That went better than I expected," she murmured to Tora. "They didn't even question us."

"Let's hope our luck holds up," Tora said.

They moved across the compound in formation, looking like a squad of Strikers on patrol, acknowledging the salutes of passing Guards with quick nods. Straightaway they proceeded to a part of the grounds abutting both the Central and the Outer Court, not far from the Guard barracks. A squat, round tower stood on a small rise, with long, low buildings bristling from it like spikes.

"There it is," said Goru. "The Sunburst."

Dark and bleak, the Sunburst hardly matched its name. It was built of bloodred brick, and a stand of wooden pillars stood before the Sunburst like a denuded forest. Many of them were covered in streaks and surrounded by blackened patches of earth. Usagi shuddered as she realized they were whipping posts.

"We'll split into teams to search the cell blocks," said Saru. "Tora, Goru, and Rana—you've never spent time with the Tigress, so you'll need to be paired with someone who knows her and can recognize her right off. Whoever finds the Tigress, get her out of confinement and say you're bringing her to the Dragonlord on his orders."

Nodding, Usagi and the others squared their shoulders and held their weapons at the ready. Her stomach tied up in knots as they approached the doors.

With a shove, Goru threw open the doors of the squat tower and swaggered in as if he were still a giant. Usagi and the others followed closely. Before them was a group of Guard clustered at an observation station, where they could look down the length of each building from their central vantage point.

"Rather brilliant design, actually," whispered Inu. "Fewer

Guards are needed to watch over the prisoners when you can see everything at a glance like this."

The Guards turned at their entrance and hastily stood at attention. One came forward and saluted. "How may we help you?"

"The Dragonlord has sent us to do an inspection," answered Saru crisply. "We are to examine every cell."

The Guard looked surprised. He had a large mole just above his left eyebrow, and it skated up his forehead. "Certainly. I can escort you through—"

"No escorts," Saru snapped. "We are under strict orders to make sure everything is secure, without you Guards trying to cover up any sloppiness."

The mole on the Guard's forehead dove for his nose. "I assure you, there is no sloppiness here. Not when we are guarding those the Dragonlord has special plans for."

"Special plans?" blurted Usagi. "What do you mean by special plans?"

Mole Face looked at her and his eyes narrowed. In that instant Usagi wished she hadn't said anything, but she stuck out her chin and stared back, demanding an answer. He hesitated, then shrugged. "I couldn't say. Some of them end up sentenced to the mines, but some he keeps for a while, and every now and again he pays a visit and takes them to the special room." He jerked a thumb behind him. "I don't ask, and I don't watch when Lord Druk visits. But it doesn't sound like much of a party." He sniggered, and the other Guards behind him guffawed.

"That's enough," said Saru sharply. "We'll take a look for ourselves, thank you."

They marched past the observation station, and Saru pointed them down the various cell blocks. There were five long corridors in all. The Monkey Heir paired Goru with Nezu and gestured to Rana. "Come with me." She turned to Usagi and Tora. "You two inspect this one. That leaves one extra. Whoever finishes their block first, take this center block."

Inu saluted and headed off to inspect cells by himself, sniffing for signs of the Tigress. Nezu and Goru started down a block of cells, while Rana followed Saru into another. Usagi stood beside Tora and stared down a long corridor. She glanced at Tora, who nodded grimly. "Here goes."

The air in the corridor was foul and musty, rank with the smell of human waste and unwashed bodies. Heavy latticed doors ran the length of the building, cells on either side of the long hall. Across each door hung a rope of iron bells, set to jangle in warning if the doors were ever disturbed. The cells were small and dank, with floors of hard clay brick and a fetid hole in the corner of each cell. The only light filtered through slits in the wall that could hardly be called windows, and from dusty lanterns hanging in the corridor.

Moving slowly down the line of cells, Usagi and Tora

peered into each one. As they clacked up in their Striker armor, listless huddled shapes stirred. Some of the prisoners raised their heads, but they were so thin and ragged that it was hard to say whether they were men or women. The pupils of Tora's amber eyes grew enormous as they gazed through the dim light for signs of the Tigress. "No, that's an old man ... not this one, too young ... definitely not her, let's check the next ... ," Tora muttered.

Usagi squinted through the thick wood slats of each door, occasionally making eye contact with haggard-looking prisoners, their faces drawn and despondent. Feeling a strange mixture of sympathy and repulsion, she hurried after Tora. She didn't know why they were in these cells, but Usagi doubted it was because they were bad people. If only there were a way to free them. She shook the thought from its perch. *Focus.* First and foremost, they had to find the Tigress.

As they neared the end of the corridor, the bells hanging from one of the doors began to jingle. The person inside was rattling the door. "Teacher?" Usagi murmured. A spark of hope propelled her to the cell.

A stringy-haired man pressed his bearded face against the wooden slats of the door. "Let me out!" he roared. "I'm innocent!"

Recoiling, Tora moved quickly on, while Usagi glanced back and saw the Guards at the observation station staring after them. She turned to the frantic prisoner. "I'm sorry, I can't help you," she said softly. "How long have you been in here?"

"Fifty-four days," he replied, and pointed to a set of neat scratches on the wall of his cell. "Fifty-five with the next sunset. And for what? All I did was laugh in the presense of Lord Druk—but I wasn't laughing at *him*." He bellowed it louder. "I wasn't laughing at him!" He began shaking the door again, the rope of bells jangling against the frame. Usagi worried that the Guards would come down to investigate the disturbance.

"We're looking for an old woman. About this tall?" Usagi gestured to her shoulder. "Her hair is white but there's a black streak in it."

The prisoner stopped shaking the door. "Is her face covered in scars?"

"Yes, that would be who we're looking for," said Usagi eagerly.

The man leered and tucked his long stringy hair behind an ear. "Might have seen her around."

"Where?"

"In the throne room for tea," he snarled. "The last lot of you dragged her off to the Bug Pit. Don't you talk to each other?" He shuddered. "They showed it to me once, and that was enough. Straightaway I sent apologies to the Dragonlord." He paused and raised his voice. "Even though I never laughed at him!"

"The Bug Pit—where is it?" Usagi pressed.

"What do you mean, where? It's in the next cell block!" His bloodshot eyes focused back on Usagi. "Rather young for a Dragonstriker, aren't you?"

Usagi thought quickly. "I just got promoted," she said. She turned to go, then stopped. "I hope the Dragonlord forgives you and you get out soon."

The sneer on the prisoner's face melted into surprise. "Me too," he said, and slumped against the heavy latticed door, looking tired.

Tora reached the end of the corridor and swung back. "The last few were empty. Did you learn anything? Poor man seemed pretty riled up about laughing."

"He said the Tigress was taken to the Bug Pit," said Usagi.

Frowning, Tora adjusted her Striker helmet. "Where's that?"

"In the next block, I think. Let's find out." Usagi headed for the Guards at the observation station.

They got back to the central tower right as the others did, looking grim and disappointed. Saru shook her head, Rana by her side. "All clear in Block Four."

"Same in Block One," said Inu.

Nezu pulled so hard at the whiskers on his upper lip, Usagi thought they were going to come out. "Block Two clear."

"Block Five also clear," Tora reported.

Usagi glanced at the Guards, who were watching them with interest. "There was a prisoner at the end of our block," she said casually. "He was a wreck. Said the last place on earth he wanted to go was the Bug Pit." She jerked a thumb down the last corridor, the one that they had yet to inspect.

A knowing look came into Saru's eyes. "Good." She turned to Mole Face. "Sounds like you have the prisoners properly cowed. The Dragonlord will be pleased."

The head Guard nodded and saluted, puffing out his chest.

"We'll just need to do one last inspection down this block," said the Monkey Heir. "And I want to check the Bug Pit."

"Certainly," the Guard said. "I'll unlock it for you."

"That won't be necessary," said Saru crisply. "Just give me the key and I can unlock it myself."

Mole Face hesitated. "We're not supposed to give the keys to anyone."

Goru frowned. "Do you give the keys to the Dragonlord when he comes?"

"Of course," scowled the Guard. "What's it to you, little one?"

"Little one?" The Ox Heir looked taken aback, then collected himself. Staring up at Mole Face, he growled, "Little or no, we're here as representatives of Lord Druk. I'm sure he'd be *very* interested to hear that his Dragonstrikers were prevented from carrying out their inspection." He held out his hand for the key. Had he been his usual size, it would have been as big as the Guard's head. Instead Goru merely looked like a small stout youngling in Striker armor. Usagi bit her lip. Maybe a tiny Goru was a bad thing for their mission after all.

The head Guard snorted. The mole over his eyebrow danced and his lips twitched. "All right, young Striker." With a shrug, he placed the keys in Goru's hand.

The Ox Heir jingled them triumphantly and looked at Saru. "After you."

They strode down the corridor, checking the cells, until they reached a heavy door at the end of the passageway. It was solid, with no latticework or bars to peek through, and locked with a heavy padlock. Inu sniffed. "Blisters. It smells terrible. There's something that reminds me of the Tigress, but it's hard to tell."

All Usagi could detect was the same rank odor as the rest of the cells. "Maybe the stink's just covering her scent?"

"Gods be good, let's hope she's okay." Saru took the key from Goru and unlocked it.

With a heave, Goru opened the door, revealing a small windowless chamber with an iron grate in the floor. It was empty, save for a bloodied tree stump, a stone basin, and a stool. A dozen beetles scuttled in the sudden light, slipping through the iron grate into the darkness below. Foul damp waves of air, full of putrid rot, wafted from the grate. Inu jerked back, gagging, while the rest of them held their noses and looked down.

Tora peered through the grate. "Gods' guts, it's truly a pit." She gasped and stifled a little shriek. "The ground is covered with bones and dead rats—and there are bugs and maggots all over."

"What do the bones look like?" Usagi felt as if she were about to throw up.

"Some are animal bones," said Tora. "But there are quite a few that are . . . not." She looked up at them with troubled eyes. "Didn't the Tigress carry a staff?"

Saru stiffened. "Do you see one?"

"Yes." Bleakly, Tora pointed into the dark.

"We have to go down there and check," said Inu.

The Monkey Heir reached in her ammunition bag and pulled out a fire starter and a candle. "I'll do it—I can climb."

"No, let me," said Usagi. "I'll jump down and back up in an instant."

As Goru yanked the grate off the top of the pit, Saru lit the candle and handed it to Usagi. "If you find any sign of the Tigress, let us know immediately."

"Oi! What do you think you're doing?" shouted Mole Face from the observation station.

"Go!" commanded Saru, and as Usagi leaaped down, Saru shouted back, "What does it look like we're doing?

We're inspecting the Bug Pit!"

Landing with a squish and a thump, Usagi held up the candle. The pit was deep enough to swallow an entire house, with no way of escape. Even if there were more than one prisoner in the Bug Pit, standing on each other's shoulders wouldn't be enough to reach the grate overhead. Usagi swallowed a scream as her candle revealed several large skeletons that clearly had once been men, surrounded by maggot-covered dead rats. The stench was overwhelming, and Usagi retched. *Just breathe through your mouth.* The ground teemed with cockroaches and scorpions underfoot, and her every step crushed dozens with a sickly crunch. Thank the gods for her Striker boots.

She spotted the staff just as Tora whispered down to her, "Look over to your right. It's by that piece of cloth—I think it's a robe." Usagi brushed off a giant centipede and examined the staff in the light of the candle. It was Horangi's. With a sinking heart, she looked at the crumpled robe on the ground, recognizing the rusty orange color of persimmon dye. But where was Teacher?

CHAPTER 21

HALL OF THE GOLDEN THRONE

"Is it the Tigress's staff?"

Usagi looked up at the anxious faces peering at her in the Bug Pit. Nodding, she held up the candle in the darkness so the other Heirs could see the long wooden stick in her hand. "Her robe, too."

She bent and picked it up, shaking off several scorpions. There was no sign of the old warrior's body, but the Tigress had clearly been down here. Usagi swallowed hard and clutched the robe close. It was torn and filthy, but she didn't care.

With another quick sweep around the deep, vermin-infested pit, Usagi checked to see that she hadn't missed anything beyond the skeletons that lay in crumpled heaps, all either clearly not human, or too large to be the Tigress.

"There's nothing else. I'm coming up. Stand back."

Usagi blew out the candle, then crouched and sprang straight out of the pit, back into the dank windowless chamber where the other Heirs and Rana were waiting with doleful faces. They crowded around as she showed them the robe and the staff. "What do you think this means?"

Taking the robe into her hands, Saru shook her head. "We might be too late."

"She's gone?" Usagi's voice cracked. Despair rose, threatening to spill over into hot tears. She blinked them back. "But it's the Tigress. She's survived so much else."

Tora put a hand on her shoulder. "Can we check the Mirror of Elsewhere?"

"Yes!" said Usagi, grasping at a tendril of hope. The mirror had showed Horangi alive when she'd been thought dead. Surely it would again. "We must make certain."

Saru fumbled with her Striker armor, then drew out the mirror. She gazed into it, then lifted her helmet to get a better view. Time seemed to stop as she peered at the polished bronze disk. Finally she let her helmet drop back on her forehead. "I don't see her."

"What do you mean, you don't see her?" Usagi refused to believe it. "What did it show you?"

The Monkey Heir's pale face was ashen. "I asked to see her and the mirror went dark. All I could see was myself, actually."

"What about the Land Jewel?" asked Inu urgently. "Can we ask the Mirror to show us that?"

With a nod, Saru went to check the mirror again. The sound of the head Guard's boots came echoing down the corridor. "Oi, you done with the Bug Pit? What's taking so long?"

Goru's expression rearranged itself into a snarl. "I'll hold him off." He trundled out of the chamber. "No, we're not done! We'll take as long as we like!" he bellowed. As he continued to berate the Guard, Nezu muttered to Inu, "Let's go back him up."

"Hurry," Inu told Saru. "Try to find the bead." He and Nezu turned and went to give the Guard a hard time.

Saru took a deep breath and closed her eyes. Then she held up the mirror and looked into it, her lips whispering a silent prayer. Usagi's restless fingers searched fruitlessly for her rabbit pendant, which was tucked beneath the plates of her Striker armor. Finally a look of recognition crossed the Monkey Heir's face.

"It's buried somewhere in the pit," exclaimed Saru. "We'll have to go back down and try to dig it up."

"I don't know if there's time for that," said Tora, nodding toward the corridor, where the irate head Guard was sounding increasingly bewildered.

Rana's eyes sharpened as she gazed into the dark hole. "I can find it with my earth gift. Jade from Mount Jade, right?

I just need a little help getting in there."

"I'll take you," said Saru. She hurriedly tucked the mirror away and put her arms around Rana's waist. "Hold tight."

"Breathe through your mouth down there," Usagi advised.

With grim nods, they jumped into the depths of the Bug Pit. While Usagi and Tora looked in after them, Saru lit another candle. Rana asked what Saru had seen in the mirror, and Saru described seeing first the bead packed in soil, then the Bug Pit itself.

"Hmm." Rana held out her hands, while Saru lifted the candle and looked around. The Monkey Heir kicked aside some bones, trying to clear the ground as she searched for a possible hiding spot.

Tora shook her head. "We're going to get kicked out before they find it," she muttered to Usagi. The boys were still haranguing the head Guard, which was making Usagi nervous. Silently she urged Rana to hurry.

A rumbling sound caught Usagi's attention, as if a horde of earthworms were tunneling through the ground. "I hear something," she told Tora. Before long, dozens of rocks came squirming out of the earth in the Bug Pit, almost as if they were alive.

"Oh!" exclaimed Tora, leaning forward. They tumbled across the floor of the pit, rolling over scuttling insects, and lined up before Rana. Saru raised the candle over the dirt-crusted stones, just as Tora pointed. "It's on the left," she hissed to them. "A jade bead!"

Rana swooped and grabbed it, and she and Saru bent their heads, inspecting it. They looked up and nodded. "This is it. We're coming up," said Saru. She put Rana on her back and climbed nimbly up the sides of the pit. They emerged into the windowless chamber, a flash of green clutched in Rana's hand.

"Quick, let's get out of here," said Usagi. "I don't know how much longer the boys can argue with old Mole Face." They dragged the heavy grate back over the entrance to the pit, and Rana stowed the bead away. Usagi stuffed the Tigress's robe into her pack and grabbed her staff. Then they left the foul, airless chamber and shut the door firmly behind them. Down the corridor, Goru, Nezu, and Inu turned from the red-faced head Guard, whose eyebrow mole was nearly crawling into his eye.

"We are satisfied," said Saru primly. "Thank you for your patience and accommodation, sir. We shall bring word to Lord Druk of the excellent conditions we found here."

As they filed past the spluttering Guard, Goru reached up and pounded the man on the shoulder, knocking him slightly off balance. "Good work."

Marching straight out of the Sunburst, they didn't say a word to each other until Saru had led them nearly to the Central Court. In a quiet cloister between buildings, they stopped to examine the jade bead. Its curves were still caked with dirt, which Rana quickly blasted away in a puff of dust. On her palm, the polished green stone seemed to glow, almost like the Tigress's eyes.

Saru's pale face shone. "You did it," she exclaimed, and hugged Rana.

Flashing a grin, Nezu patted Rana's back. "Well done, Earth Snake." As the others congratulated the Heirling, Usagi felt a stab of anger. Her knuckles turned white around the old warrior's staff.

"What about the Tigress?" she burst out. "Have you all forgotten? We're supposed to be rescuing her!"

Rana looked startled, and the smiles on the others' faces faded.

"I hate to say this," began the Monkey Heir, "but she didn't come up in the mirror, and we found her things in that horrible pit. I—I think she's gone."

Stubbornly, Usagi turned to Tora. "Can't you try using your tiger vision?" she asked. "Hold that ironstone pendant in your hand and find her!"

"I'm not a human Mirror of Elsewhere," said Tora, affronted. "My visions don't work that way."

A wave of frustration came over Usagi. "Why are you all fighting me on this? Does no one else care?"

Inu frowned. "What are you talking about? We all care. You're not the only one who wants to save the Tigress—and you're not the only one on this mission."

"We're here as a team, Usagi," said Saru. "No one's fighting you."

"Here," said Goru gently. He took the Tigress's staff from Usagi's grasp and transformed it into a miniature version of itself with a tap of the Conjurer. "This way we can take it with us—and give it to the Tigress if we do find her."

Nezu pulled at the whiskers on his lip. "Don't lose hope, Rabbit Girl."

Looking at their earnest expressions, Usagi was thrown. Had she misjudged everyone? She took the shrunken staff, now the size of a feedstick, and tucked it in her pack next to the Tigress's robe. For months, she'd feared being left out, alone, and isolated, but her friends were there all along. Chastened, she took a deep breath. "You're right. I'm sorry. I just . . . forget sometimes. So what *can* we do?"

Inu's somber gaze met hers. "We honor Teacher's wishes and get the rest of the Treasures."

As the early dusk of winter fell, the shimmering orange sun slid below the horizon like a bright coin into a temple offering box. The curving eaves and carved figures adorning the buildings around them were growing shadowy and dark. There was no time to argue or even to mourn. They had to get to the Bowl of Plenty and Pen of Truth. Usagi nodded. "Let's go."

They hurried for the Hall of the Golden Throne at the heart of Central Court. It was the tallest building there, raised on a tiered stone foundation with carved balustrades, overlooking an expansive square. Usagi's ears pricked. "The Dragonlord is still holding court inside," she told the others. They ducked below the wooden platform of the covered walkways edging the courtyard. Usagi tilted an ear toward the high open doors of the entrance, framed by brightly painted pillars and an elaborate scrim.

"The increase in production was not what I'd hoped, Commissioner." The Blue Dragon's voice was low and even.

"My lord," quavered the man. *"We have instituted double shifts for everyone. But without more food, workers have been collapsing."*

With her rabbit hearing, Usagi caught the tinkle of several rice grains going into a metal bowl. Then she heard a rattle and stifled gasps as the bowl filled up with rice, multiplying what had been placed in it. It was the Bowl of Plenty. *"Here,"* the Blue Dragon said casually. *"Take this back to your workers."* There was a sudden patter of rice grains skittering across a wooden floor. The Blue Dragon must have flung the bowl's contents to the ground. His voice dropped to a growl. *"Tell them that the mines are next—see if that doesn't get them going."*

She shook her head and told the others what she was hearing. "If anyone could be cruel with the Treasures, it would be the Blue Dragon."

"Not for long," muttered Nezu.

Saru peered out at the darkened sky. "Change will be coming soon."

Through the Mirror of Elsewhere, they'd determined that the watch guard for the Treasures was changed every hour, with a new team of four Strikers relieving the old. The changing of the guard would give them their best chance to slip in.

The sound of a temple bell echoed through the palace compound, struck by the temple in the Outer Court to signify the start of Rooster hour. It was the time of day when the cock came home to roost, the hour when the Dragonlord would dismiss his petitioners and advisers—and leave the throne hall to have his evening meal.

Goru shifted uncomfortably. "Never thought I'd hear that bell again. It's so strange to be back." Rana and Tora nodded in silent agreement. As the ringing of the hour faded, they watched and waited in the shadows.

"He's leaving," said Tora. The Dragonlord emerged from the building, followed by a retinue of attendants. She hissed out a breath. "They're coming this way. Duck!"

They dove and held as still as they could, hardly daring to breathe. The footsteps of the Blue Dragon and his entourage sounded on the wooden walkway above. Usagi recognized Tupa's swaggering stride accompanying the Dragonlord and stiffened, remembering their last encounter. Her heart pounded so hard she thought it might rattle her armor on its own. As the footsteps of the Striker captain and the Blue Dragon disappeared, she gave an all-clear sign and everyone exhaled.

"Good thing I made myself so small," Goru said, lifting his helmet and wiping his brow. "I don't know where I could have hidden if I hadn't."

"We would've grabbed the hammer and shrunk you ourselves," said Tora with a glint of her snaggleteeth.

Reaching into her pack, Rana doled out packets of sleep powder. "I added a touch more venom to buy us time. If anyone wakes up sooner than expected, they'll still be paralyzed for a good while."

"We'll make our move just before the changing of the guard," said the Monkey Heir, pocketing hers. "Everyone ready?"

Usagi's ears pricked. "The next watch is approaching. Three hundred paces. They'll be here in a few minutes." The timing was important—they had to take them out quickly and with as little commotion as possible, so that the Guards and Strikers inside the throne hall would not be suspicious, and anyone near the Hall of the Golden Throne would see nothing unusual.

Quietly they split up and moved into their planned positions near the grand entrance to the building. They lay in wait. The clatter of the Dragonstrikers' armor grew louder as they drew near, four roaches in their dark leather plates. *Click clack. Click clack.* Their boots rapped against the raised wooden walkways around the courtyard, and they stepped for the open doors.

Just before they reached the building, Inu, Goru, Nezu, and Saru slipped out and began marching alongside them. "What in the—" spluttered one, and the roaches came to a startled halt.

Nezu flashed a grin. "Hello." He shoved a handful of sleep powder into the face of the nearest Striker and caught him as he fell. Inu, Goru, and Saru did the same for the other three. Only Goru misjudged the distance and fell short. The sleep powder blew harmlessly away and the roach raised his fire-cannon, opening his mouth to yell.

"Oh no, you don't!" Goru lunged and punched him with a swift uppercut. The Striker fell back, out cold, collapsing on the walkway. "Scabs, that was close. Would've been nice to be my regular size for that."

"Let's get them out of sight," Saru told the boys.

As they began dragging the Strikers away, Usagi hustled Tora and Rana into the Hall of the Golden Throne. "Get ready," she murmured. Saru left the boys to deal with the knocked-out Strikers and quickly joined them. They moved in formation through long galleries, marching to the throne room as if they were the new watch team, passing Guards and servants.

Would anyone here notice that they weren't actual Strikers? Usagi willed herself to breathe slowly, as if she were practicing mind-the-mind. *Concentrate. You are a Striker.* The Treasure watch stood at attention in the deserted throne room—two Dragonstrikers at the doorway, and two more flanking the altar with the Treasures.

But as Usagi and the others entered, the roaches by the door seemed to know something was wrong. "Halt," said one. She frowned. "Who are you?"

"We're here to relieve you, of course," said Saru, sounding offended.

Taking a step forward, the Striker reached for her firecannon. "I don't recall ever seeing you. What's the watchword for the day?"

Usagi's heart sank. Watchword? They'd never thought there might be such a thing.

Saru shot her and the others a look. "It's 'Now'!" said the Monkey Heir, and sprang at the Striker. She threw the sleep powder in her face, and the Dragonstriker coughed and squinted, fumbling with her weapon before collapsing to the floor, unconscious.

The other Striker aimed his firecannon at Tora. But just as he was about to fire, Rana reared back and spit in his face. With a curse, he grabbed at his eyes. Tora pounced and shoved a palmful of sleep powder into his nose and mouth. He gave a muffled cry before falling silent and going limp.

Usagi heard the two Strikers by the altar move to attack. Powder clutched in each hand, she whirled and leaped to them in a single bound. Before they could react, she threw the sleep powder squarely in their faces. The Strikers coughed and sneezed once before stiffening. Their eyes rolled up, revealing the whites, and the roaches hit the ground with a thud.

"Get the Treasures!" Saru urged, nodding to the altar. She dragged the first Striker away from the doorway, and Rana followed with the second.

Usagi seized the pen and bowl, sticking them deep inside her fake ammunition pack. "We need the replacements!"

"I have them." Tora pulled a hammered metal bowl and enameled brush pen from her own disguised pack and placed them on the altar. Goru had created them that morning with the Conjurer, right before they entered Dragon City. They looked exactly like the real Treasures, down to the nicks and scratches the ancient items had gathered over the centuries. "There. Now if anyone happens to look in, they won't see that they're missing till we're long gone."

"Get the roaches by the altar," Rana reminded them. "They'll come to in a couple of hours."

"Tie them all up," said Saru. "And move them out of sight."

They quickly bound and gagged the four Strikers and dragged them onto the dais. An enormous, painted folding

319

screen backed the throne, so they pulled the Strikers behind it to hide them.

"All right, let's go," said Saru, and they hurried out of the Throne Room. As they started through the innermost gallery, they were met by Goru. "Did you get them?" he asked.

Usagi patted her bag. "Right here." The Pen of Truth was back in her hands at last, as was the Bowl of Plenty, tucked beneath the Tigress's robe. An old knot of guilt in her shoulders loosened.

"I'm going to hammer out a few fake Strikers for the throne room," Goru told them. "It's all well and good that we have the fake Treasures in there, but if they're unattended, it will raise alarms."

Saru nodded. "Good idea." They slowed their pace, delaying their exit, till Goru rejoined them. Then with a brisk step, they slipped out of the hall and reunited with Nezu and Inu in the shadows of the courtyard.

"How'd it go?" asked the Dog Heir.

"It was close," replied Saru. "There was a watchword that we didn't know about. We had to take them out with Rana's sleep powder."

Nezu tugged at his whiskers. "Spirits. These were the easy ones. We can't even get to the other Treasures till the Blue Dragon goes to sleep."

"We should get ourselves to the Inner Court," said Saru.

"It's early still, but he'll be retiring to his chambers after evening meal."

Only three more Treasures to go. They began crossing the palace grounds in tight formation, returning salutes from passing Guards and Strikers.

Then Tora muttered, "Oh no," and pulled her helmet down lower.

"What is it?" Usagi whispered. She heard a familiar voice in the distance and stumbled. "Never mind. I hear them." It took all her strength not to call out or start running toward the voice.

A group of Academy cadets was approaching, and one of them was her sister.

CHAPTER 22

THE BLUE DRAGON'S LAIR

"QUICK," SAID TORA. "WE CAN'T let them see us." With an abrupt turn, they filed behind a building, waiting for the Academy cadets to pass. Rana, Tora, and Goru pulled nervously at their helmets. As former students at the Dragonlord's Academy, they ran the greatest risk of being found out if their old classmates got a good look at them.

Usagi reached for her silver rabbit pendant, but it was behind her armored breastplate. As the cadets drew closer, teasing and bantering, she could hardly breathe, hearing her sister's voice among them. She homed in on Uma's conversation and realized her sister was talking to Jago, the little boy from their hometown of Goldentusk. His rooster flight and capture was what had led them all here.

"Don't pay attention to them," Jago said. *"They've always been*

jealous. They're just looking for an excuse to pick on you."

Her sister sighed. *"Thanks, Jago, but maybe you shouldn't walk with me. Those bullies will make you pay for it."*

"I don't care," Jago said stoutly. *"You've always looked out for me."*

"Well, I'm looking out for you now. Run ahead. I'll wait here for a bit."

Usagi's brow furrowed. She knew she needed to stay out of sight. But it sounded like Uma was in trouble. Unable to stop herself, she peeked around the corner. Down at the other end of the building, Uma stood alone, watching as Jago marched ahead with the rest of the cadets. She looked just as she had when Usagi had glimpsed her in the Mirror of Elsewhere, dressed in severe cadet blues, her long hair tied in a high tail. But her sister was taller now, Usagi could see, and she seemed sadder, too.

If only Usagi could run to her, give Uma both a hug and a good shaking, and make her realize how mistaken she'd been for placing her trust with the Blue Dragon and his minions. Was she no longer one of his star cadets? Why? How were they mistreating her at the Academy? Usagi leaned farther out, trying to get a better look.

"Get back, Usagi," hissed Rana. "What are you doing?"

"It's Uma," she shot back. "She's right there."

"Rabbit Girl, let her go. I know you miss her, but we've got to stick to the plan," said Nezu.

Usagi scowled. "I know the plan! Can't I just look at my own sister for two seconds?" She waved them off impatiently, rattling her armor. Uma turned her head. Usagi ducked back behind the corner. *Scabs.*

"Er . . . she might have seen me," Usagi admitted. "We should go." But as the others began to move, her rabbit ears detected the rapid patter of Uma's feet speeding toward where she'd spotted movement. Alarmed, she urged Rana and the Heirs to run. Just as her sister was nearly upon them, Usagi impulsively stepped out before her.

Uma came to a violent halt. "U-Usagi?"

Though Usagi's Striker helmet sat low on her head, there was no hiding her identity. She raised her chin and looked Uma in the eye. "Hello, little horse. How you've grown. Is everything . . . are you okay?"

"What are you doing here? And why are you dressed like a Dragonstriker?" Uma's wide eyes were bewildered, and a mix of emotions flitted across her face—shock, anger, relief, fear.

Usagi faltered. "I—I needed to see you. It's been too long." She heard the others stealing away. Hopefully they would be able to get to the Inner Court as planned. "Uma, surely you don't want to stay here still? Come away with me. I promise you'll be better off."

"Better off?" Her sister frowned. "How can I believe that? You've lied to me before."

Usagi saw the suspicion in Uma's eyes and recognized her mistrust. It felt as if she were gazing into a mirror. "I never meant to deceive you. But I understand why you think you can't believe me. I know what it's like having someone you trust lie to you. All I can do is promise to be honest, and prove what I say through my actions."

"You're still with those rebels, then?" Uma glanced around, but no one was in sight.

Hearing her friends' footsteps fading well into the distance, Usagi felt something release. "They're the rightful Heirs to the Twelve, Uma, and so am I. Remember all the stories Mama told—that I used to tell you and Tora? Midaga was once so different. It can be that way again."

Uma shook her head. "I hardly remember Mama. And those stories . . . they were nice tales, but Lord Druk is in charge now." She took a deep breath. "It's best to do what he says. What choice do we have?"

"We all have a choice," said Usagi. "We can go along because it seems easier, or we can resist when we know something is wrong. And what he's done, what he's doing— it's wrong. You must know that, deep down."

Turning her head, Uma bit her lip and didn't say anything. Usagi tried again. "I've seen and heard some things around here, Uma—I don't want to see you mistreated."

Her sister crossed her arms. "I'm fine. They're just . . . testing me."

"You haven't been fine." Usagi looked at her sister pleadingly. "Don't stay here."

"Running away isn't going to fix things," said Uma. She squeezed her eyes shut. "Lord Druk's forces get stronger every day—he'll hunt every last traitor down. There's no escape for the disloyal. Being on the winning side is power. It's the only way forward for Midaga." She spoke rapidly, as if she were reciting something that had been drilled into her. Opening her eyes, she looked at Usagi. "Besides, not everyone here is so difficult. Like Jago. Remember him? Or have you been too busy with your new friends to recall your old ones?"

"Of course I remember Jago! I can't believe you'd think I wouldn't."

Uma shrugged. "Then you know I can't leave him behind—he needs me."

Putting her hands on Uma's shoulders, Usagi tried to keep her voice steady. "I know I can't force you to see what I do, or to come away with me, but I only want the best for you. I think of you every day."

In silence, Uma stood unrelenting. Usagi sagged and embraced her sister. "I hope you'll be able to understand and forgive me someday," Usagi whispered. "You'll always be my baby sister."

For a brief moment she felt Uma slump, then she tensed and pushed Usagi away. Her eyes narrowed. "So are the others here too? Tora? Goru and Rana? If they get caught, the Dragonlord will make them pay."

Usagi hesitated. She'd promised not to lie, but she couldn't let her sister jeopardize their mission. The burnt fragment of her old wooden rabbit pendant, the one that their father had carved and that Uma had burned in a fury, seemed to warm in the rabbit-shaped locket beneath her breastplate. What should she do?

If she wanted her sister to trust her, Usagi would need to trust Uma too. With a deep breath, she admitted that she was on a mission, but didn't elaborate. "I said I'd be honest with you, and so I am. But if I tell you any more, it could be dangerous—for you and for others."

Her sister stared at her, then backed away. "Doesn't matter. I think I know what you're here for, and it's not me." She glanced around. "I'm warning you, there's no peace for the wicked. Where the king sleeps, the floors sing." She took another step back. "I'm going to the Academy now. I'll tell Jago that I saw you"—her breath caught—"in a nice dream." Whirling, Uma ran off before Usagi could say another word.

Usagi stared into the gathering darkness. Her sister was gone. Was she letting Usagi go? Or would she raise an alarm? But what Uma had said about the floors singing sparked a bit of hope. She needed to find the others right away and tell them.

The moon emerged like a luminous eye, keeping a cool

gaze on her as she hurried to the Inner Court. Lanterns and torches flared to life as workers lit them around the palace grounds. No one looked twice at her, dressed in her Striker armor. As she neared the former royal residence halls in the Inner Court, she heard someone whisper her name. It was Tora, calling from a path leading to the gardens. Following her voice, Usagi slipped into the grounds. In the moonlight, the bare branches of manicured trees looked like lacy black fringe embroidered on the sky.

She remembered this garden well—through here Usagi had escaped the palace in the dead of night, tunneling through the wall with Rana and Goru's help. Now they and the other Heirs had taken refuge in an ornate open-air pavilion overlooking a crescent-shaped pond. As she drew closer, Usagi saw that it was twin to the one at the Shrine of the Twelve. Even in the dark, she could tell it was identical to the Tigress's Nest on Crescent Lake, with a gilded roof and the animals of the zodiac sculpted into twelve brightly painted pillars.

Inside the pavilion, she was met by Tora and the others, all of them relieved to see her, yet angry. Contrite, Usagi immediately apologized.

"What in the name of the Twelve happened back there?" barked Inu. "How did you get away?"

"I didn't tell her details, but my sister knows I'm here on a mission, and she didn't try to stop me," said Usagi. "She won't leave the Academy, though I tried to convince her.

And she also said something interesting: 'Where the king sleeps, the floors sing.'"

"She told you about the warning system?" Frowning, Nezu pulled at the whiskers on his lip. "Why would she do that?"

"Wait, what warning system?" asked Rana.

"The cricket floors," chorused Tora and Goru.

Looking out across the pond to the complex that once housed the king and his family, the Monkey Heir pointed. "'No peace for the wicked' is an old saying about the floors in there. They're rigged to chirp with every step, remember?"

"Oh right—that's why we need the Belt of Passage," Rana said.

"The cricket floors were installed by the Warrior Council generations ago, so that no one can sneak up on the king while he sleeps," Nezu told her. "Not that it helped poor King Ogana, may his spirit rest."

"We should move forward with the mission," Usagi urged. "Given Uma's warning about the floors, I get the feeling she isn't going to say anything about seeing me."

"Either that, or we could wind up in a trap," said Inu doubtfully.

"There's only one way to find out," Usagi replied. "I don't want to abort the mission now, do you?" They all shook their heads, including Inu.

Tora's snaggleteeth gleamed. "Let's finish this."

Usagi prayed that their plan would work. They'd studied the layout of the palace grounds for weeks, especially the royal residence. In the shrine library on Mount Jade, there was one detailed scroll from a hundred years ago that featured the royal family in their private chambers—the king in the North Wing, the queen in the South, and princes and princesses in the East and West Wings. Each well-guarded wing contained dozens of rooms linked by long corridors. Not much had changed here after the Dragonlord had taken over. Even in Striker uniform, it would be a challenge to get in and out with the Treasures.

They watched and waited, shivering and stamping in the cold night air, until activity around the Inner Court ceased and windows grew dark. "It's time," said Saru.

In groups of two and three, they struck out for the former royal residence halls, now guarded by the Dragonlord's elite forces. None of the other roaches seemed to notice as they joined in patrolling the quiet central courtyard of the four connecting buildings. The grand residences loomed over them. The moon had climbed above their high peaked roofs, casting its glow on the elaborately decorated ridgelines teeming with zodiac animal guardians. It was nearly the hour of the Rat—the Blue Dragon sure to have retired by now to his chambers in the North Wing, its entrance flanked by Strikers.

Saru and Rana made the first move, marching toward the former hall of the queen. The Dragonlord had given it over to favored advisers, and it was lightly guarded compared to his own. They slipped through the South Wing's unattended entrance, followed not long after by Goru and Inu. When Usagi, Nezu, and Tora reached the doors, they stole through and joined the others. The corridors were empty and quiet, dimly lit by sconces along the wall and stately lantern fixtures hanging from the ceiling. As a unit, they began moving through the building. To Usagi's dismay, a chorus of chirping crickets erupted, their every step announced by the rigged floorboards.

"Stop! The whole building will hear us," Usagi hissed. "There's no way we'll even get close to the North Wing without notice."

Nezu flashed a grin. "Time for the belt." He took off the Belt of Passage and whipped it toward the end of the hall. The belt stretched into a long bridge of rope and wood planks that ran the length of the corridor, suspended just below the gilded rafters above their heads. "See? We won't have to touch the floors." He gave Tora a boost.

Reaching down from the bridge, Tora grasped Goru's hands, pulling while Inu and Nezu grunted beneath his weight.

"He's smaller but he's not any lighter," gasped Inu, straining to lift Goru.

Goru smirked. "Never judge a person by their size."

Saru swung onto the bridge with Rana in tow, and Usagi hopped up. Once Inu and Nezu joined them, they crept down the hall. The bridge creaked and swayed but was far quieter than the singing floors below. Usagi's heart raced as she listened for approaching servants or Strikers, but the only other sounds were their booted feet tiptoeing along the wooden slats of the bridge, and the occasional rattle of their armor.

At the end of the bridge, they looked through a painted lattice panel framing the entrance into the adjoining wing. It was thankfully empty. Nezu had them hang from the lacquered frame. "Don't touch the ground—I'll make this quick." Clinging to the top of the doorjamb with one hand, he pulled at the bridge, which snapped back into a belt, then threw it across the length of the next corridor. They swung back onto the bridge and hurried through the hall in relative silence.

At last they reached the juncture between the West Wing and the North. Peering through the ornamental divider framing the doorway, they saw pairs of Strikers stationed at intervals all along the hall, the entrance to the Blue Dragon's private chambers at its midpoint. Tora counted. "There are at least eight sets of Strikers here."

"We can take them," Goru scoffed. "They have no idea that we're coming."

Quietly, they came off the bridge and Nezu snapped it back into a belt. He clipped it around his waist and reached into his disguised pack for a handful of blades dipped in Rana's paralyzing venom. "Get ready for the next phase," he warned. As the others pulled out hidden blades or sleep powder, Usagi opened her pack and saw the Tigress's robe and the Treasures from the throne room. She grabbed sleep powder and blades, then firmly lashed the pack closed. She was taking no chances with its precious contents.

Peeking around the corner where the wings adjoined, Nezu set his sights on the two roaches flanking the end of the corridor. He took two disk-shaped blades and held them between his fingers. Aiming carefully, he flung the blades. They spun from his hand in opposing directions, hitting each Striker in the neck. Both roaches jerked, their eyes wide, and began to fall.

"Go!" he ordered, and Usagi and Saru entered the hall. The floor chirped loudly as Saru ran forward and began flinging blades. Usagi leaped to the far end of the corridor. A shout went up as she passed over the heads of several teams of Dragonstrikers. The cricket floorboards squealed as she landed before two roaches guarding that end. She threw sleep powder in their faces, and as they slumped to the ground, the nearest remaining roaches started for her, drawing their swords. At the other end of the hall, Saru, Nezu, and Tora were taking out Strikers with hidden blades and sleep powder. The whole corridor was filled with a cacaphony of shrieking floorboards. Usagi positioned two star-shaped blades in her fingers, then let them fly. She managed to nick both approaching roaches, although one lumbered for a few steps more before collapsing at her feet.

The corridor quieted for a brief moment. Usagi looked up. All the Strikers in the long hallway had been taken down. But inside the royal chambers, Usagi could hear the Blue Dragon's deep voice, demanding to know what was going on, and the clacking of Striker armor and footsteps. She waved frantically at Inu and the others. "The Blue Dragon is up—and he knows there've been trespassers," Usagi warned. "More Strikers are in his chambers."

"Earplugs in," called Inu.

As they reached for earplugs Rana had made from special clay, Inu pulled out the Flute of Dancing Dreams. Usagi jammed the clay in her ears and felt a heavy silence settle around her. She could still hear her own breathing, the sound of her swallowing, even her heartbeat, but the chirps of the cricket floors were muffled into nothingness. She raced toward the other Heirs just as four more Dragonstrikers stormed into the hall from the Blue Dragon's chambers. Usagi skidded to a stop, face-to-face with Tupa, the captain of the Dragonstrikers. His eyes widened and he opened his mouth to speak just as Inu put the flute to his lips and began to play.

Within moments, the former Ram Heir and the other roaches sank to the ground. Tupa toppled like a felled tree, while the others curled up as if they were napping in a cozy bedroll. Usagi resisted the impulse to kick Tupa. Hopping over him, she rejoined the others.

Goru bent over Tupa's prone form and nudged him with a toe, then gave an all-clear sign. Tora's snaggleteeth gleamed, and Rana's dark eyes seemed to sparkle. With a flashing grin, Nezu waved them forward. Saru gestured to Inu to lead the way. They followed, their ears safely plugged, as his fingers moved up and down the flute in a soundless tune. The cricket floors could have been as loud as the Summoning Bell, and it wouldn't have mattered.

Even so, Usagi's stomach clenched as they entered the Blue Dragon's chambers. They moved cautiously into a series of grandly furnished rooms, filled with exquisite furniture and paneled with opulent silks and carved screens of pure jade.

When they happened across the Blue Dragon, Usagi bit back a scream.

All Heirs must learn to play at least basic notes on a standard flute before attempting to play the Flute of Dancing Dreams.

While anyone who can play a simple song can access the powers of the Flute of Dancing Dreams, only skilled players can achieve utmost control. If one can play a flute well, then playing the Treasure will allow one to exert their will on individuals and large groups at the same time. Even the smallest actions can be controlled by a very good flutist.

—Requirements of the Treasures, from *Manual for Warrior Heirs*, 17th edition

CHAPTER 23

TAMING THE DRAGON

IN THE MIDDLE OF A richly decorated antechamber paneled all in gold, the Blue Dragon sat upright on the floor, his platform bed in the room beyond. His eyes were closed as if he were simply doing mind-the-mind, and his chest rose in even breaths. But one hand gripped a fan that Usagi immediately recognized as the Winds of Infinity, and the other clutched a drawn sword, as if he had been caught on his way to join a fight.

Eyes wide, Rana pointed and mouthed, "Sleeping?"

The Monkey Heir glanced at Inu, who was playing the Flute of Dancing Dreams more intensely than ever. Drops of sweat glistened on Inu's nose. Saru approached the Dragonlord and touched his arm. He didn't respond. With a grim smile, she nodded.

The Blue Dragon was clad in a dressing gown of dark silk, which pooled around him on the floor. He was gray-blue and his skin waxen, as if he were starved for air. His dark hair was pulled in a topknot away from his face, his cheekbones so prominent they were almost skeletal. His lips were purple to the point of black, and a disfiguring handprint on his left cheek—planted there by the Tigress—stood out in stark white, mirroring the pearls on a cord at his neck. A walnut-sized black pearl nestled next to an equally large white pearl—the Sea Jewels that were part of the Treasures! A dark blue vein throbbed in the Dragonlord's neck, and his eyebrows were scowling black slashes.

Usagi shuddered, remembering how he'd looked when she'd refused to join his Dragon Academy and had tried to protect the Tigress. He'd looked at her as if she were nothing but a bug to be squashed and disposed of. "We'll find a use for her . . . for Master Douzen's experiments," he'd said casually, as if torture were an obvious solution. And then he'd threatened to cut the Tigress open. With hot eyes, Usagi stared at the Tigress's handprint on his cheek. Was that all that was left of her? What had he done to her? Had she wound up as fodder for experiments, tortured and tormented till the old warrior finally gave in to death?

The Dragonlord remained unmoving as Saru carefully pried his long-nailed fingers from first his sword, then from the Winds of Infinity. She looked up and gestured for the replacement fan.

Tora jumped as if she'd been kicked. She rummaged

frantically in her pack and pulled out the fake Winds of Infinity that Goru had conjured with the hammer. She bent over the Blue Dragon and placed it in his hand, while Saru stashed the real one away in her belt. The Monkey Heir removed the pearls and put them away as well. Tora found the replacement Sea Jewels in her pack and fastened the silk cord around the Dragonlord's neck, her hands trembling.

But where was the Coppice Comb? The Blue Dragon was not wearing a belt, and the dressing gown had no pockets. Usagi ran to the bedchamber and found a golden chest by the Blue Dragon's bed. She searched its drawers and quickly found the comb. She waved at Tora and held it up, and Tora rushed over with the one created by the Conjurer. She placed it where Usagi pointed and shut the drawers while Usagi tucked the comb with the other Treasures in her pack. Her whole body tingled with a strange thrill. They'd done it—they'd gotten hold of all the Treasures.

She glanced over at Inu. Beneath his Striker helmet, his shaggy hair was damp with sweat, plastered to his forehead as he played with all his might. Spirits, if he got too tired to play, they'd be done for. Usagi made sure the Dragonlord's chambers looked untouched, and joined the others, who were staring at the Blue Dragon with a mixture of disgust and fascination. Nezu was seething, his hands clenching and unclenching. Usagi saw that the Dragonlord was utterly helpless in that moment, and a thought struck her.

Here was an opportunity. This could be their chance to change everything. They had all the Treasures on them, and he would not be able to fight back. They couldn't simply leave without doing *something*—like sickening him with Rana's venom, or taking him prisoner. As Nezu reached for something at his belt, Usagi moved to help, thinking he sought to tie down the Dragonlord. Then she froze. Nezu's hand shook as he raised a knife.

Usagi scarcely breathed, watching to see what Nezu would do. If they *could* end things once and for all, shouldn't they? The Blue Dragon had destroyed the old way of life on Midaga, he was responsible for the deaths of entire villages, and so many were still suffering because of him. The moment stretched nearly to the breaking point as Nezu summoned the strength to act. Then Saru placed a hand over his clenched fist. She took the knife from him, and Nezu sagged, looking ashamed. The Monkey Heir gestured at them to leave the chambers. Inu was still playing the flute, but his dark eyes flashed with anger and he stopped playing long enough to point at the Dragonlord and mouth the words, "Do it."

Saru shook her head and pulled at Inu's arm, trying to get him to come along, but Inu shrugged her off and pointed furiously at the knife, then at the Blue Dragon, sitting there grayish blue and still as a long-dead corpse. As Saru hesitated, Inu grabbed for the knife himself, the flute in his hand forgotten. Usagi's heart pounded, feeling as if it were beating its way out of her chest. The Dog Heir was going to kill the Dragonlord.

The Blue Dragon's eyes opened, dark as a storm. Inu recoiled in shock, then recovered and lunged, but he was too late. The Dragonlord sprang to his feet. His gray-blue face wore a rictus of fury. He knocked Inu's arm away, sending the knife flying right into the wall, its blade sinking deep. Inu brought the flute to his lips, but the Dragonlord already had his fingers in his ears. He stood smugly, eyebrows raised, as Inu frantically played the Flute of Dancing Dreams. Then his sneer turned into a snarl and he lashed out with a kick, striking the flute out of Inu's hands.

The Treasure skittered across the floor and the Blue Dragon whipped around and hurled a second kick at Inu, straight into his jaw, sending him flat.

Goru lowered his head and tackled the Blue Dragon, who stumbled. He quickly braced himself and pushed back, reaching down and grabbing hold of the Ox Heir. Roaring, he lifted Goru's small, stocky frame over his head and threw him. Goru flew across the room and crashed into the carved gilt panels, splintering them into gold bits and sawdust.

The Dragonlord started for the flute, but Rana dove on it before he reached it. His purplish lips curled in an amused smile. With a flourish, he snapped his fan open. He waved it over Rana, but nothing happened. The Dragonlord's grin disappeared. He flapped the fan harder. Loose strands of Rana's hair that had come uncoiled puffed gently about her face.

The Blue Dragon stopped and stared hard at the fan. With a look of rage, he ripped it apart and swiftly kicked Rana in the stomach. Her face crumpled and she curled into an agonized ball. The Dragonlord swooped down for the flute and then stopped. He reached over Rana and picked something up. Straightening, he held up a curved green bead and a look of wonder came into his eyes.

"No!" Usagi shouted. The Dragonlord looked over at her and his eyes gleamed. He said something, but with her earplugs in, she couldn't hear anything but her own panicked breathing.

Tora jumped onto his back, her fangs bared, and sank them into the back of the Blue Dragon's neck. He jerked up, mouth open in a roar that none of them save Inu could hear, and tried to pull Tora off. His long black nails raked across her face and blood began to run down her cheeks, but she held on. As the Blue Dragon thrashed about, trying to get Tora off, Nezu and Saru drew their swords, looking for an opening to attack without hurting Tora.

Usagi lunged for the flute and snatched it up. She ran to Inu, who was struggling to get up, his mouth bleeding. His eyes widened at something over her shoulder, and she turned to see Tupa and three other Strikers running into the Dragonlord's chambers.

The former Ram Heir quickly surveyed the room. His eyes met Usagi's for a brief second and hardened. As the other Strikers fanned out behind him, he pointed at Usagi and Inu, directing his men to them and to Goru and Rana, who were staggering to get up. Then he advanced on Saru and Nezu, who had the Blue Dragon surrounded.

Pressing the flute into Inu's hands, Usagi looked at him and wordlessly begged him to play. He put the Flute of Dancing Dreams to his bloodied lips, but the two Strikers heading toward them remained wide awake, their swords drawn. Inu shook his head—he was having trouble.

Out of the corner of her eye, Usagi spied the Dragonlord's sword on the ground, which Saru had set aside after prying it from his hands. She grabbed it just as the two Strikers charged, and deflected their attack, their blades colliding with bone-rattling crashes. She gritted her teeth and swung the sword at first one, then the other Striker, attempting to hold them off as Inu kept trying with the flute. Finally he gave up and pulled out his Striker sword, then leaped into the fray. With the Dog Heir fighting beside her, Usagi found a surge of strength. They slashed ferociously at the two roaches while Saru and Nezu clashed with Tupa.

The Blue Dragon finally managed to pull Tora off his

back and promptly flung her across the room. Usagi saw her coming too late. Tora slammed into her and the two of them crashed to the ground. The wind was knocked out of Usagi, and she lost the Dragonlord's sword. She grimaced as she tried to get up. Her walking stick, disguised as a firecannon, was strapped on her back, digging painfully into her spine with every move. Tora was on top of her, blood dripping from the scratches on her cheeks.

Usagi looked at Tora and made a quick polishing motion, rubbing the top of her hand. Tora's eyes widened in understanding. Her thumb went to work on the ring she wore, rubbing back and forth across the dark tortoiseshell band. After a few seconds, thick choking smoke shot out from the Ring of Obscurity in all directions, shrouding them in a dark cloud that rapidly filled the chamber.

Coughing, Usagi pulled out her earplugs and grabbed Tora's hand. They ducked low and ran out into the corridor, followed closely by Inu and the others. The floors chirped loudly as they ran down the hall, which was lined with the motionless figures of Strikers they'd attacked with blades and sleeping powder. If only the effects of the flute lasted as long.

"Can you play at all?" she asked Inu.

"Mmmphf," he answered. A dribble of blood trickled from the corner of his mouth. Gods, had the Blue Dragon broken Inu's jaw? It was clear he could no longer access the flute's power.

She gestured to the others to take out their earplugs. "Inu's hurt and can't play. We need to get out of here, now." She looked at Rana, who was hunched and holding her stomach, and Goru and Tora, who both sported bloody wounds. "Can you run?"

"I'm fine," said the Ox Heir, gingerly touching the cut on his head, and Tora gave a grim nod.

"I can carry Rana," offered Saru.

Rana waved her off with a wince. "I'll be fine. But the jade bead." Her dark eyes were stricken. "The Dragonlord took it."

Another round of chirps sounded behind them, and Usagi looked back to see Tupa and his three Strikers emerging from the Dragonlord's chambers in a cloud of black smoke. "Tupa's coming!"

"We're in no shape to go back for the bead," said Saru. "Run!"

They stampeded down the hall, sending up a cascade of chirps from the cricket floors. They sped through the North Wing and burst out of the building into the courtyard. Roaches patrolling its perimeter halted in confusion, staring at the seven Strikers running out of the Dragonlord's residence—several with blood on their faces.

"Don't stop," Nezu ordered.

As they ran, shouts went up, and Usagi heard the pounding of booted feet, followed by Tupa's voice issuing commands. "They're raising the alarm," she warned. "Go!"

The urgent clanging of bells sounded, answered by ringing in the Central and Outer Courts, alerting the entire palace to intruders. They took off at spirit speed, racing out of the enclosed courtyard. As they turned for the gardens, Tora stopped them, her pupils enormous in the dark. "There are Guards heading there now."

"We'll storm the Earth Gate," Saru told them. It was the only side gate in the Inner Court, positioned directly on the other side of the palace complex from the main Gates of Heaven, and their nearest option. But it could only be reached if they crossed the entirety of the Inner Court. With Tupa and other Strikers on their tail, they shoved past Guards on night watch and leaped over passing servants in their scramble to escape.

Usagi tracked the rhythmic thump of boots in pursuit. A spasm of fear ran through her at the growing sound of clattering Striker armor. "More Strikers have joined in the chase," she warned. "With spirit speed."

The moon was past its apex in the sky, its cool light reflected by the pale marble wall of the palace compound. The rise of the wall loomed closer as they leaped and sprinted with all their zodiac powers. Goru lumbered ahead of them like a charging bull, tossing aside anyone who dared get in their way. Soon the wooden doors of the Earth Gate were in sight, painted with a pattern of mountains and flanked by two Guards.

Upon spotting their approach, the Guards scrambled to block the gate and aim their firecannon, but Usagi and the others were upon them before they could blink twice. Bellowing, Goru wrenched their firecannon away and threw himself against the doors, bursting them open. They streamed through, racing into the narrow hilly streets of the palace district, following the twisting lanes that led toward the rest of the city.

CHAPTER 24

FLIGHT TO MOUNT JADE

AS THEY TORE DOWN THE slopes, going as fast as their spirit speed would allow, Usagi glanced back at the palace on the hill. Its white walls gleamed coldly in the moonlight. Heaviness overcame her, pulling at her legs as she leaped. The Tigress was gone, and they'd lost the jade bead she'd tried so hard to keep from the Dragonlord. And what would become of Uma? Though they had all the Treasures otherwise, the mission felt utterly incomplete.

Yet there was no time to dwell on it, for the clatter of Striker armor began to echo in the streets after them. At this late hour of the night, the streets of the capital were far less crowded, but there were still carts and wagons to hurdle, people to dodge, and Guard patrols to avoid. They raced through the hilly palace district and reached the city flatlands. Saru steered them into a dark and deserted lane.

"We need to change," she said breathlessly. "And take care of injuries."

Tora frowned. "Shouldn't we wait till we're out of the city?"

The Monkey Heir shook her head. "The Dragonstrikers are looking for roaches on the run. They won't notice us as ordinary people. And if we're going to take a moment to change, then we ought to fix those cuts. You'll all run faster if you're not bleeding."

Inu mumbled something through his swollen lip. Rana pulled out the Apothecary. "Here!" She gave Inu a wad of yarrow and other herbs to put in his mouth. She selected a vial out of the pillbox and shook it onto a cloth. She stanched the bleeding from the cut on Goru's head, then wiped away the blood dripping into his eyes.

He flinched, then relaxed. "That feels better." Goru smiled. "Thanks, Snake Girl."

Tending to Tora's wounds, Rana dabbed at the scratches the Blue Dragon had slashed on her cheeks and smoothed a salve over them. "This should prevent scarring," she said.

"That's good—I have enough scars as it is," said Tora with a wry smile. "But what about you? You must be terribly bruised."

Rana nodded and rummaged through the pillbox. She mixed two powders with a small bottle of liquid into a paste, then put the concoction on her tongue. She grimaced and swallowed. "Scabs, that's bitter," she gasped.

"Wash it down with some water," advised Nezu. He tipped his flask into Rana's cupped hands, and she drank gratefully.

Inu spit out the herbs he'd been chewing and rubbed his jaw. "That was quite a kick the Blue Dragon had. I'm glad there's no permanent damage."

Flashing a grin, Nezu peered at Inu's face and raised his hand. "We'll see about that. How many fingers am I holding up?"

Saru rolled her eyes. "Goru, can you conjure us some clothing that will help us blend in?"

The Ox Heir reached for the Conjurer and regarded each of them with pensive eyes. Then he nodded to himself and tapped each person lightly on the shoulder with the mallet.

Tap! Usagi's armor transformed into the clothing of an old peddler woman. Her helmet became a shawl about her head, and her pack a basket of sweet potatoes.

Tap! Tora found her outfit changed into that of an old man, her unruly hair tucked beneath a cloth cap. Her pack morphed into a bundle of firewood on her back.

Tap! Inu and Nezu became ordinary Guard, their armor reduced to simple iron breastplates with leather arm and leg guards. The bug-like horns on their helmets melted away, and they were left with plain iron headgear.

Tap! Saru's armor was turned into the stiff brocaded silks of a wealthy Hulagan woman, and Rana's armor became the simple hemp garments of a maidservant.

Tap! Goru changed his armor into the robes of a squat traveling monk, his shaved head covered with a round straw hat. He grinned from beneath the wide brim. "How's that for disguise?"

They looked at each other and smirked.

"We won't be able to use spirit speed till we're out of the city," said Saru. "But the Strikers aren't going to pay much attention to us now."

After they'd added a bit of face paint, their disguises were complete. They moved back out into the streets, walking in pairs or singly, keeping each other in sight. As shouting Strikers ran past, searching for the whereabouts of the palace intruders, Usagi and the others strolled unnoticed out of the city gates and onto the Ring Road.

Once they were far enough from the city on a deserted stretch of road, they were free to launch into spirit speed. They ran and leaped in the dead of night, heading away from the capital as quickly as they could.

When the sun peeked over the horizon, they plunged into the wilderness and began their journey back to Mount Jade. In the refuge of a wooded glen, they stopped by a stream to rest and get their bearings. Usagi took out the Tigress's robe and shrunken staff and examined them carefully, but they yielded no clues.

"You'll want to be careful with that staff," advised Goru. "It'll spring back to its regular size in a few hours."

Usagi smiled. "As will you."

The Ox Heir took off his straw monk's hat and rubbed his shaved head. "It can't come soon enough. I used to wish I weren't so big, you know. I stick out, everywhere I go. People always stare." He looked down and fiddled with the Conjurer on his belt. "There have definitely been some advantages to being smaller. But I miss being me."

"We'll take you at any size," said Tora. "And thanks in good part to you, we have all the Treasures!"

Rana's face fell. "We don't have *all* of them," she lamented. "We only have the Sea Jewels, which are supposed to control the tides. The Dragonlord took the Land Jewel, which is supposed to access the power of Mount Jade. Without it, the pearls are useless."

"We'll figure out a way to get the jade bead back," Saru promised. "The full power of the Treasures can't be accessed until the necklace is restored. But the bead is no good to the Blue Dragon by itself, and he has none of the other Treasures now. The Tigress would be proud."

Usagi felt a stab of sorrow. She hugged the old warrior's ragged robe close and clutched the shrunken wooden staff tight. She would bring them back to the Shrine of the Twelve and put them in a safe place, with the hope that somehow, some way, they would be needed again.

The Treasures from the palace were brought out. Saru tied the Sea Jewels around Rana's neck. "Don't worry. Someday this necklace will be complete."

Reaching into her peddler's basket, Usagi pulled out the Bowl of Plenty and handed it to Nezu. "You should be in charge of this."

He cradled it like a pet and crooned at it. "Hello, old friend. I've missed you." Flashing a grin, Nezu polished off an imaginary speck on the bowl before tucking it away.

Usagi offered the comb to Inu. "Are you sure?" asked Inu. "You kept the comb safe for years."

"I'm sure," she said. But Inu wouldn't hear of it and made her take the Coppice Comb. Though Usagi knew now that it hadn't been created by her father as she'd first thought, a warm feeling still came over her when she slipped the carved wooden comb, so familiar and dear, under her belt. She handed the Pen of Truth to Tora. "I think it'd be better if you carry this." With a glint of her snaggleteeth, Tora accepted.

Saru held up the fan. "Inu, why don't you take this instead? Or Goru—would you like to carry it?"

The Ox Heir waved it off. "I'm fine with the Conjurer. Inu's been an Heir for far longer—the fan should go with him."

"Now that I can play the Flute of Dreams again, I've got all I need," said Inu. He rubbed his jaw. "You're the senior Heir, Saru—you should keep the Winds of Infinity."

With a nod, the Monkey Heir tucked it in her belt. With the exception of Goru and Inu, both carrying a single Treasure, each of them would safeguard two Treasures back to Mount Jade. "When the circle of Warrior Heirs is complete, we'll each be responsible for just one item," said Saru.

"Imagine that. Twelve Warrior Heirs," said Nezu, smoothing the fuzz on his upper lip. "And the Treasures of the Twelve—united on Mount Jade. We'll change the course of Midaga yet."

Soon their clothes and weapons returned to normal, and Goru was happily giant once more. Usagi carried her walking stick in one hand and the Tigress's long staff in the other, anxious to get back to the shrine. Speeding through hills and valleys, through farmland, orchards, scrubland, and forest, they came within sight of the Midagian Alps after several days. The bristling ridge of mountains was the spiked backbone of the island, crowned by its highest peak, Mount Jade.

In the midst of winter, the sacred mountain was cloaked in a thick mantle of snow, like a queen wrapped in her furs. The green of evergreen trees and jade stone outcroppings dotted the white snow like embroidery and beading on a royal cape. It was the hour of the Horse, the sun directly overhead, and the mountain glowed with welcome.

"Almost home," said Nezu with a grin, and Usagi felt her spirits lift somewhat. Though she longed for both her sister and the Tigress to be with them, she was glad that at least the Treasures would be back to their rightful place at the shrine, to be protected and to protect, until both the necklace and the Warriors of the Zodiac could be restored.

As they neared the Sea of Trees, a deep and impenetrable forest at the base of Mount Jade, Tora stopped short with a gasp. Usagi turned and the others halted. "What's wrong?"

"Usagi," Tora said urgently, grabbing her by the arm. "I . . . I don't know what to think—but Uma's there."

"What?" They stared at Tora. "Where?"

Tora pointed. Usagi squinted. In the distance, just outside the Sea of Trees, stood a small figure, alone.

"How can that be?" wondered Inu.

Though she hardly dared hope, Usagi knew to trust Tora. Her tiger vision was unfailing. "My sister has horse speed, and she knows where Mount Jade is—the Blue Dragon required all his cadets to study maps of the kingdom. She must have managed to get away!" Breaking into a run, Usagi sprinted toward the figure, then sprang into her rabbit leap, her feet as light as her heart. Her sister was here!

Closing the distance with just a few bounds, she landed right before Uma. With an overjoyed squeal, she reached out and squeezed her sister's hands. Uma squeezed back weakly. She was pale and exhausted looking, with dark circles beneath her eyes. Her usually neat hair was still tied back but disheveled, as if she'd run all night and all day to arrive at Mount Jade before them.

"You came!" Usagi said happily. She threw her arms around her sister. "I'm so glad. I wasn't sure I'd ever see you again. Thank you for letting me go—and for the warning about the singing floors. As soon as you mentioned them, I knew you couldn't possibly want to stay with the Dragonlord." She couldn't stop from babbling, the words pouring out. There was so much to say to Uma, so much to show her. "I've been worrying this whole time about how to find you again. But now you're here!" Pausing to take a deep breath, she pulled back to look at her sister more closely.

Uma's eyes were filled with tears, and her lower lip trembled. "Usagi, I'm so sorry."

"No, no, I'm the one who's sorry." Usagi tried to soothe her sister. At the sound of approaching footsteps, she turned to see her friends approaching. Usagi waved them over with joyful abandon. "Everyone will be so thrilled. A youngling of the Horse year has yet to join our ranks. I was always hoping it might be you. Now you'll get a chance, the mountain goddess be praised!"

Shaking her head, Uma looked down. "No, it's not that." Her voice was barely audible as a tear trickled down each cheek. Her eyes, dark and wet, met Usagi's. "This is all a trap."

As she stared into her sister's eyes, a cold shock went through Usagi like an icy wave. Every last hair on her arms stood on end. Pricking her ears, she realized it wasn't just the sounds of the approaching Heirs that Usagi was hearing—they were surrounded. She whirled in a panic, just as Rana and the other Heirs drew close.

"Usagi!" said Inu urgently. "I smell danger."

"It's an ambush!" she shouted just as a loud explosion went off.

CHAPTER 25

WRATH OF THE DRAGON

STICKY FLY-NETS CARTWHEELED THROUGH THE air, and a roar went up as dozens of Strikers threw off hiding screens of woven bamboo laced with branches, grass, and other greenery. They had been lying in wait just before the Sea of Trees. Usagi yanked out her sword as the others reached for their weapons. As the fly-nets spun toward them, they ducked and rolled out of the way. But Uma remained motionless, just staring at her feet, and was hit with a net. It knocked her down in a tangle of tacky rope. Usagi scrambled up and stood over her, fighting a rush of anger. Her sister had deceived them after all. Uma's dark eyes met hers.

"I had no choice, Usagi," she said. "They forced me to be the bait."

Her words gave Usagi pause. She examined her sister's face and saw no satisfaction, no resentment or fury—only sorrow and regret. Then Tora shouted her name.

"Tupa and the Dragonlord are coming!"

The line of Strikers approached steadily, weapons drawn. Some had firecannon, others carried swords, and several had long spears. Tupa sauntered behind them, emerging from the shadows that edged the Sea of Trees, followed by the Dragonlord, resplendent in a full suit of plated armor. Even from a distance, a pale hand-shaped mark could be seen on his cheek.

Usagi looked back down at her sister. She raised her sword and Uma cringed, her eyes growing wide. Uma opened her mouth to cry out, but before she could utter a sound, Usagi brought her blade down and swiftly cut the ropes of the flynet. She yanked hard at the sticky strands, leaving an opening for her sister. "Stay low, whatever you do," she told Uma.

Whirling, Usagi ran to join the others, who stood shoulder to shoulder. She held her sword tightly, her heart pounding as she got into position next to Tora. There was no time to create armor for themselves with the Conjurer—not when there were several dozen Strikers advancing, about to charge them at any second. At least she had on the Fire Cloak, and the Coppice Comb was tucked in her belt. If the Blue Dragon wanted the Treasures, he and his forces would have to fight for them.

As the Strikers came to a halt, the once and former Ram Heir strolled up. Tupa was similarly clad in shiny black lacquered armor, but his horned helmet was tipped in gold. On a strap around his neck was his firehorn, a curved ram's horn that spewed flame. Stroking his goatee, Tupa gazed at their small band. A broad smile split across his face. "Brothers and sisters! You should never leave without saying goodbye. What happened to your manners?"

Inu's nostrils flared. "We could say the same for you," he growled.

"We're not your brothers," spat Nezu.

With a chuckle, Tupa touched the shoulders of two Strikers. "Our bait's about to get loose—go fetch her," he ordered.

"Yes, Captain!" The Strikers ran forward and grabbed Uma, who was trying to get out of the fly-net. Usagi watched helplessly as they hauled her back and dumped Uma at the Dragonlord's feet.

The Blue Dragon looked down at Uma, his lips curling as if she were an errant strand of hair in his soup. "You should have reported them when you had the chance. I've long suspected you had a loyalty problem." Turning away, he paced a few steps behind the line of Strikers, his dark eyes raking over Usagi and the others. In one hand, he carried a paddle-shaped fan made of solid lacquered iron. "So. The Tigress's Heirs are still at it. You thought you could come into my palace, my chambers, and steal from right under my nose. There's a level of audacity there, I'll grant you that." His voice was deep and booming, echoing against the wall of trees behind him. "But audacity and foolishness are two sides of the same coin. Did you really think you were going to get away with it?" He chuckled, and Tupa's broad smile grew even wider.

"It's not your palace, Druk," said Saru. The Monkey Heir spoke quietly, but her chin was set and her eyes blazed. "Not your chambers, and not your Treasures. None of it belongs to you. You're the one who stole."

The line of Strikers tensed, and Tupa's smile disappeared. "How dare you speak to Lord Druk this way?" he hissed.

"What do you younglings know?" the Dragonlord said evenly, though the mark of the Tigress's hand on his livid face grew even paler. "I won't have my plans for Midaga delayed." He slapped the paddle fan against his palm for emphasis, making a metallic thwack. "Hand over the Treasures at once—and I'll let you keep your lives."

"Right, because you're so good at keeping your vows and promises, Druk," said Nezu.

Usagi saw that behind the line of Strikers, her sister had pushed herself into a sitting position, half-tangled in the fly-net. Fury coursed through her. "Yes—especially to those who serve you. Look at Uma. She believed in you—and you let her suffer. Even now, you're just using her."

The Blue Dragon smiled, his purple lips stretched over teeth as white as the mark on his face. "You say that as if it's a bad thing. To be an instrument for a greater purpose is an honor."

"Through suffering, she becomes stronger," Tupa interjected. "I thought I taught you that, Usagi."

A hot flush rushed to Usagi's cheeks, and her fingers tightened on the handle of her sword. "All you taught me was how little to trust anyone—you the least of all."

Tupa's eyes narrowed, but the Dragonlord waved his paddle fan.

"Enough. You will never outnumber us, and your powers are easily equaled—and surpassed—by my new Dragonstrikers. This can be quick and painless, or it can be the last thing you ever do. Your choice." The fan smacked against his palm repeatedly, like a threat. *Thwack. Thwack. Thwack.*

Usagi's heart pounded with the slap of the fan. They wouldn't be treated with mercy if they handed over the Treasures. They had to do whatever they could to keep them from the Dragonlord. She glanced at the others and saw that they felt the same. "For the Tigress," she whispered. "For Midaga. For the Twelve."

"For the Twelve," murmured the others. They faced off against the line of Strikers, the Blue Dragon and Tupa, with Uma still trapped beyond them in the fly-net.

Nezu waved his sword. "Come get the Treasures, you stinking blue toad!" With a stealthy hand, the Rat Heir uncorked the drinking gourd at his belt.

"Send in your little roaches," Goru hollered. The Ox Heir hefted his power chain, casually letting the heavy metal ball

364

swing, though it could easily crush a man's skull with one blow. Hidden in his giant palm was the Conjurer, attached to the other end of his chain.

Her pale face looking determined, Saru tilted her moon blade at them, the curved edge shining in the sun. Meanwhile Inu had his bow and arrows ready, as did Tora. Usagi glanced at her friend and saw that Tora's tiger teeth had lengthened into fangs. The Tiger Heir gripped her bow and nudged Rana slightly behind her. "Stay close, Snake Girl. You don't have any weapons."

"Oh yes, I do," said Rana. "Don't you worry about me. I'm not afraid of them." She raised her voice and waved the Apothecary. "Come and get this!"

The Blue Dragon rolled his eyes. "This is tiresome. Shut them up now, Captain."

"Attack!" roared Tupa, and the line of Strikers surged forward, sending up a racket of clattering, rattling armor.

"Hold your ground," shouted Inu. "No one move. Saru, the fan! Steady, everyone . . . hold steady. . . ."

As the Blue Dragon's forces got close, Saru whipped out the Winds of Infinity. Snapping it open, she slashed the fan through the air. A gust of wind knocked down every Striker like an invisible hand, and behind them, the Dragonlord and Tupa staggered, barely able to stay on their feet.

"Get UP!" Tupa roared at the Strikers. Grabbing his fire-horn, he blew a torrent of flame at Usagi and the others.

Nezu pulled a stream of water out of his canteen, turning it into a shield that kept the fire at bay.

Several Strikers scrambled up and aimed their firecannon. Tora's keen vision caught a glimpse of what was in the barrels. "Bullets incoming!" she screamed.

Goru smashed the Conjurer on the ground, and a giant iron shield sprang up, as big and wide as the Ox Heir. He planted the shield before them just as the Strikers began firing. Usagi and the others crowded around him as a hail of bullets peppered the thick metal.

"We need to hold off fighting them one-on-one as long as we can," panted Nezu. "There's too many of them, and they all have powers."

A bullet clipped the edge of the shield and hit the ground by Usagi's feet. Wincing at the unrelenting clatter, she pressed closer to Saru. "Spirits save us, we're too exposed," said the Monkey Heir. "We have to get into the Sea of Trees."

Over the barrage of bullets, Usagi caught the approach of footsteps and rattling armor. "Watch out, they're advancing!"

Two Strikers appeared, running at them from either side. Rana reared her head back and spit at first one, then the other Striker. They scrabbled at their eyes and sank to their knees, screaming.

The torrent of bullets ceased. More Strikers charged, the rattle of their armor growing louder as they approached.

"We can't hide any longer," cried Usagi. She reached into her pack and grabbed a handful of hidden blades that had been dipped in Rana's paralyzing venom. Then she launched herself straight up, ascending into the blue sky.

Soaring so high that the Sea of Trees appeared to be a deep green carpet, she glanced down and saw the Strikers running to surround them, looking like a horde of shiny black beetles scuttling toward a meal. As she began to descend, Usagi threw the blades with a practiced flick of her wrist, stopping several roaches in their tracks. When she returned to earth, a young Striker who looked to be about her age raised his sword and sprang right at her, his leap much like hers.

Usagi raised her own blade, blocking the Striker's swing with a clang. He landed on her, knocking her to the ground. With a grunt, Usagi flung him off and bounded to her feet. She struck at the roach, but he rolled out of the way and her sword bit into the soil. Yanking it back out, Usagi faced the young Striker with rabbit talents. He scrambled up.

"Just hand over that cloak," he said, hefting his blade. "You don't want to die over a stupid piece of clothing, do you?"

"Do *you?*" retorted Usagi. Over his shoulder she saw Tora and Inu firing arrows right and left. But two of the Strikers were fast enough to pluck them out of the air before they could reach their targets. Rana was having better luck. She spit burning venom at anyone who got too close, and had unleashed a handful of glittering white crystals that Usagi recognized as sand from the Dancing Dunes. The sand swirled about the heads of a couple roaches, pelting them hard enough that blood trickled down their exposed faces. Nezu and Saru were working together, using the Winds of Infinity and water from Nezu's canteen to defend against Strikers and fireballs from Tupa's firehorn.

The young Striker before Usagi scowled. Setting his jaw, he charged. As he tried again and again to strike Usagi with his sword, each blow would glance off hers, Usagi parrying his blade with her own. Then he spun in a different direction, and with a heave, his blade cut across as if he meant to chop her in two.

Usagi leaped up out of the way. As she landed, she swung down on him. He threw up his sword, smashing it into hers, and for a moment their blades rattled as they pushed against each other. The roach began to tire and bent farther and farther back while Usagi pressed as hard as she could. At last he gave a determined grunt and kicked her. Usagi heard a crack and felt a searing pain as his powerful rabbit kick connected with her leg.

As he darted free, she fell to the earth with a gasp. Looking across the battleground, she spotted the Blue Dragon, standing impassively with his arms crossed, watching as his Dragonstrikers fought the Heirs. But where was Uma? The fly-net was an empty tangle of charred rope behind him, her sister nowhere to be seen.

Usagi's ears pricked as she heard the approaching footsteps of the young Striker. She turned and feebly swiped her blade. He struck it with his own, so hard that her sword slipped from her grasp. The point of his sword moved to a mere whisker from her throat.

"Give me the cloak," he ordered.

Raising her hands, she tried to get up, then collapsed with a cry. "My leg!" It throbbed with a stabbing pain and her shin felt as if it had shattered. In desperation, she looked around for help.

But Goru was fighting half a dozen Strikers on his own. With his shield he deflected their cannonfire, then smashed their weapons to pieces with his power chain before knocking them to the ground. Meanwhile, Saru and Nezu were beating back another line of Strikers by hurling stinging sprays at them with the fan and water from Nezu's flask. But some of the roaches had gifts of their own and managed to deflect the water back at the Rat Heir and the Monkey Heir.

A familiar growl caught Usagi's attention, and she saw a blur charging out of the Sea of Trees. It was Kumo. The cloud leopard streaked toward Tupa and pounced on the former Ram Heir. As Tupa wrestled with the big cat, some of his fireballs began to burn the vegetation where they came to rest. Bushes flared bright with orange fire, a clump of tall grasses smoked and crackled, and the trunk of a small sapling smoldered before going up in flame.

On another front, Rana had managed to blind the Strikers who had super speed, allowing Tora and Inu to shoot their arrows without interference. The Tiger Heir hit several Dragonstrikers in the gaps between their armor and leg guards, crippling them. Usagi felt a sudden prick of sympathy for them, for she was just as hobbled now, and there was no one to help her but herself. She glared at her attacker. "I'm not giving you anything. You'll have to take it. If you can."

The young Striker looked at her with something like pity. Then he reared up and stomped on her other leg. There was a loud crack and a blinding pain ripped through Usagi. She screamed louder than she ever thought possible.

Tora turned and her amber eyes blazed. "You leave her alone, Tuzi!" she shrieked, and launched an arrow at the young Striker. It glanced off his helmet, and as he ducked, she quickly shot another one that struck him squarely above the knee. He yelled in shock and collapsed, writhing. Tora ran up to Usagi with Rana close behind. "Are you okay?"

"He broke my legs," gasped Usagi. "I—I can't get up."

Rana reached for the Apothecary. "I can fix it. Tora, cover us."

As Tora stood guard, shooting arrows at anyone who dared approach, Rana took out the pillbox and quickly rummaged through it. She poured drops from a few vials into a mix of powders, combining them into a pungent black paste, and scraped it all up with a mother-of-pearl spoon. She handed it to Usagi. "Take this."

The paste was so bitter that Usagi gagged and nearly threw up, but Rana was firm. "You have to swallow it! Don't breathe—just hold your nose!"

The vile taste remained in Usagi's mouth and was so strong that she forgot about her excruciating pain for a moment. Then she realized that the pain was slowly ebbing from her legs, and it felt as if her bones were vibrating. Her shins became itchy and she reached down to scratch, but Rana held her back. "Don't touch!"

As the young Striker continued screeching in pain, Tora snapped at him to be quiet. "Or I'll shoot your other knee!"

"Traitor!" spat the Striker.

"Evil tool!" she retorted, and let fly an arrow at another Striker aiming her firecannon at them. The arrow struck the Striker's arm and she jerked the firecannon upward. It went off, and a fly-net went soaring straight into the air. As the Striker struggled to dislodge the arrow from her arm, the fly-net came crashing back down on her in a web of sticky rope. Tora spied the cloud leopard fighting Tupa and gasped. "Kumo!" She raised her bow, then grunted in frustration. "Can't get a clear shot." She loosed the arrow at a charging Striker instead, who dropped his sword and grabbed his thigh with a howl.

As Usagi's bones knit together, a wave of heat cascaded through them. The itching became more like burning. She gritted her teeth and tried not to scream.

Though a good number of Strikers were down, Usagi's friends were still terribly outstripped by the Dragonlord's troops. Inu, Saru, and Nezu were surrounded by a circle of Strikers, while Tupa had managed to get on top of Kumo, even as the cloud leopard twisted, clawed, and growled, trying to clamp its jaws around the Striker captain's throat. Tora shot an arrow at Tupa, but it only grazed his helmet, knocking a gold-tipped horn askew. "Spit and spleen!"

Goru knelt behind his giant shield. He took the Conjurer and pounded it on the ground as fast as he could. With each beat of the wooden mallet, an armored Guard emerged. The Guards were all identical, clad in metal and carrying curved swords. They immediately swarmed the Strikers, distracting them enough to draw fire away from the Heirs. Several set upon Tupa, and he let go of Kumo and began fighting off their attack. Tora immediately called for the cloud leopard to run. "Into the Sea of Trees, now!"

Shield in hand, Goru ran over to where Tora and Rana were protecting Usagi. "We need to get you to the forest too, Rabbit Girl. Can you get up?"

"Her bones are still healing," said Rana, putting a hand on Usagi's shin. "Can you carry her?"

With one arm, Goru scooped Usagi up, taking care not to

jostle her. "I could carry all of you, actually."

"We can carry ourselves," countered Tora.

The Monkey Heir, Nezu, and Inu swiftly joined them, now that the conjured Guards were doing the fighting for them. "Once we get into the Sea of Trees, we have a better chance," said Saru. "The Blue Dragon is afraid to go in there."

In that moment, Goru's shield disintegrated into a pile of iron shavings, leaving them all exposed. The Ox Heir let out a yelp of surprise. Usagi looked over and saw the Dragonlord's lip curl with satisfaction. Rubbing his hands slowly, he fixed his gaze on the conjured Guard, then flicked his fingers. One by one, the false Guard crumbled into powder and blew away. He turned and strolled toward them, his dark eyes focused on Goru, and raised a palm. Usagi heard the clink of a chain, then saw to her horror that the heavy metal ball on Goru's power chain was floating up, lifted by an invisible hand. With a sharp snap of his wrist, the Blue Dragon smacked the air. "Watch out!" Usagi cried.

The iron ball flew at them. Goru tried to duck, raising his free arm. The ball grazed it and glanced off his forehead, hard enough that his head snapped back. He teetered for a moment, then crumpled to the ground. Usagi was still cradled in his other arm. She wriggled free and got unsteadily to her feet. Her legs were wobbly, but they were holding, and the burning itch of her knitting bones had subsided considerably. "Come on, Goru," she pleaded, trying to get him back up, but he groaned and didn't move.

Tora and Inu both strung arrows to their bows, but the Dragonlord chuckled. "Really? Go ahead," he sneered. Glaring, Tora fired hers, but he waved a hand and it went wide. Inu quickly followed with his shot, and the Dragonlord waved it aside, laughing harder.

Clutching her sword, Usagi stumbled forward, her legs buzzing as if they'd fallen asleep. With a twirl of the Blue Dragon's fingers, her blade twisted into a tight knot. "You'll give me that cloak if you don't want to end up like your sword," he growled.

Usagi stared at the useless clump of metal in her hand. Gods' guts, his metal gift was strong. But she wasn't going to give him anything, even though her legs felt like quivering bean curd and her weapon was destroyed. Hidden blades wouldn't work against him. The only other thing she had with any power was the Coppice Comb. She began to reach for it, then stopped. What could it do but bring forth a stand of trees—in full view of the man who wanted that very comb? It was too risky. Nor could Saru use the Winds of Infinity—with its metal ribs, it would surely be snatched up by the Dragonlord. Already the power chain was slipping from Goru's waist, the Blue Dragon trying to pull the Conjurer to him. Usagi dropped her ruined sword and grabbed at the power chain, tugging it back.

The others joined her, all of them taking hold of the power chain. But Rana had a better idea, and her fingers began working at the leather thong that tied the wooden mallet to the chain. She slipped the Conjurer off and stuck it in Usagi's pack. "Let him have it!" Rana cried.

At once they let go, and the power chain went flying. The enormous ball barreled at the Dragonlord's head, but he stopped it just before it reached him. His face grew indigo with anger. Bellowing, he hurled the power chain at them, and the ball streaked through the air, trailed by the long heavy chain. The links wrapped around all of them except Goru, who was out cold on the ground, and drew them tightly together, like a bundle of firewood. As they struggled to free themselves, the Dragonlord and his Strikers approached.

CHAPTER 26

ZODIAC RISING

AS THE CHAIN BINDING THE Heirs grew tighter and tighter, the Dragonlord and his remaining forces closed in around them. In the face of the Dragonlord's immense power with metal, their weapons were either destroyed or useless, and they were outnumbered to boot. The Blue Dragon would finish them off and get the Treasures after all. Usagi struggled against the thick links of the power chain as it pressed her against the others. It was getting harder and harder to breathe. In the shadow of Mount Jade, it seemed that all was lost.

Then Usagi heard the growing thunder of what sounded like hundreds of running feet. She turned her head. "Someone's coming."

Tora's eyes widened. "Is that . . . my brother?"

Masses of people were approaching—some at spirit speed, and others on horses and contraptions made of wood and bamboo. With a shock, Usagi recognized the grizzled, leaf-littered form of Yunja and his barkcloth-clad charges from Sun Moon Lake. Ji's seagulls swooped in circles above them, flying alongside a flock of fierce black crows.

Next to Yunja's crew was a small band of younglings, wiry and tough, carrying slingshots in their tattooed arms. "The Ghosts of Butterfly Kingdom," Usagi breathed. "They got the message we sent!"

A quintet of younglings Usagi didn't recognize ran alongside the Ghosts, but she heard Saru cry out. "Inu, the Dunelings are here!"

"What?" Inu craned his neck and sniffed the air, then yelped in surprise. "And the Miners!"

Nezu let out a whoop. "We have reinforcements!"

Sure enough, Panri the Boar Boy and an army of other scar-faced Miners raced for the clearing, all with weapons that looked like the spoils from caravan raids. Leading the charge was Imugi, Tora's brother, sword in hand.

Tora's eyes filled with tears. She bared her fangs at the Blue Dragon. "You see, Lord Druk? You may try to use our powers for your own ends, but not all Midagians will bend to your will."

The Blue Dragon looked out at the approaching horde, many of them younglings and lightly armed, all of them ragged. He burst out laughing, his teeth white and sharp against his dark lips. He turned to Tupa. "You know what to do."

The former Ram Heir saluted, grinning. "Yes, my lord." He barked at the other Strikers. "Fall in! Counterattack! Take your positions!"

As the Strikers ran off, the Dragonlord squeezed the chain tighter. "Poor fools," he said softly. "Your friends have come too late, and they'll pay for choosing to side with you. You've lost everything."

Usagi squirmed, laboring for breath as the chain contracted. She thought of her parents, and then of Tora's father, of the Tigress, of her sister. Where Uma had run off to, Usagi didn't know, but she realized that she'd lost her sister long before this day. So many they loved were gone. Beside her, Rana's mouth worked, as if she were chewing something. They locked eyes and Rana nodded.

"We have lost everything," Usagi gasped, repeating his words. She glanced at her friends and all those who were fast approaching, coming to join their fight. She fixed the Dragonlord with a hard stare. "And we have lost nothing."

Rana let loose with a stream of venom, striking the Blue Dragon squarely in the eyes. As it met his skin, his flesh curdled with a hiss. The Dragonlord opened his mouth and roared long and loud, his screams of agony and fury reverberating throughout the clearing. The charging Strikers and rebel groups all faltered, nearly coming to a stop, but Tupa shouted at the roaches to keep going.

Goru's power chain loosened as the Blue Dragon clawed at

his face, and Usagi and the others broke free. Rana bent over Goru, still passed out on the ground like a giant mountain. She brought out a tiny vial from the Apothecary and waved it under his nose. The Ox Heir's eyes opened, and he sat up with a start. He saw the Blue Dragon howling and clutching his eyes, and a grim smile stole over his face. "Nice work, Snake Girl," he said, and grabbed his power chain.

They surrounded the Dragonlord, while the Miners, Ghosts, Dunelings, Yunja's younglings and other assorted rebel elements from around the island clashed with the Dragonstrikers. The air was filled with the cacophony of battle—shrieking attack birds, rattling armor, weapon strikes, firecannon blasts, and fists coming to blows.

Meanwhile, the Dragonlord was blindly reaching for anything of metal. Usagi felt her rabbit pendant rise from her neck, and she frantically tugged it back. Goru grabbed the metal ball on the end of his power chain and clutched it close. Saru gasped as the Winds of Infinity and her moonblade sailed out of her grasp. Leaping, Usagi snatched the fan out of the air, but as the Dragonlord increased his pull, she found herself getting dragged along with it. Her still-fragile legs screamed with pain.

Out of pure desperation, she pulled out the Coppice Comb and threw it on the ground. Trees rumbled out of the earth, surrounding them, and obscured the Blue Dragon from view. She braced herself against the tree trunks. As she struggled to keep hold of her pendant and the fan, she heard the Blue Dragon stagger into a tree. *"What's this?"* he growled. *"A sudden stand of trees—it must be the Coppice Comb."* Immediately the tug on her necklace and the Winds of Infinity ceased as the Dragonlord dropped to his knees and began searching for the comb.

Usagi limped out of the coppice and found the others. She handed Saru the fan. "What do we do now?"

"Make sure he doesn't get a hold of that comb, for one," said the Monkey Heir. "As soon as you pull it from the earth, he'll be exposed. We'll have to watch for his metal gifts and hit him with everything we've got."

"His powers were even calling to this stone," said Tora. She felt for the ironstone pendant at her neck and stiffened. A strange look crossed her face, and she hurriedly pulled it off. "Rana, give me the Sea Jewels."

With a look of confusion, Rana took off the silk cord that held the two giant pearls around her neck. As Tora strung the tiger-iron bead between them, Usagi could hear the Blue Dragon rustling in the copse of trees. "Hurry—I've got to retrieve the comb."

"Go," said Saru, hefting the fan. "We'll cover you."

Hobbling, Usagi went right to where she'd thrown the comb, its wooden teeth biting into the soft earth. The Dragonlord was nearly upon it, his eyes half open and oozing with tears and pus. Her heart hammering in her chest, Usagi pulled it out and the trees disappeared back into the ground, leaving her face-to-face with the Blue Dragon. His skin had bubbled into pale grayish blisters wherever Rana's venom had touched it. He saw Usagi and his blue visage contorted into a snarl. He lunged for the comb in her hand. Gritting her teeth, Usagi vaulted out of the way with her rabbit leap.

The Monkey Heir whipped the fan in the Dragonlord's direction, knocking him flat with a gust of wind so big that it rippled over the battlefield, throwing the fighting Strikers and rebel Midagians off balance. Goru swung the power chain in a circle, whipping it faster and faster, then slammed the immense ball straight into the Dragonlord's stomach. The impact cratered the earth around him. But the Blue Dragon had caught the iron ball just in time. He got up with a roar and sent it aloft. As the ball began to drift high over their heads, Goru struggled to hang on to its chain. The Ox Heir's feet scrabbled at the soil, then raised on tiptoe.

"Let him go!" Nezu growled, and unleashed a volley of water balls in the Dragonlord's face. Each orb of water exploded on contact, filling his nose and open mouth. Goru fell back to the ground, and the iron ball tumbled out of the air, striking the dirt so hard that it half buried itself. Tora and Inu took advantage of the Blue Dragon's distraction to fire arrows at him. They struck his plated armor, but he remained standing. With a howl, the arrows burst from him, flying back at the Heirs. Goru heaved himself in front of them.

"Goru!" Usagi cried out as the arrows hit his body. Goru turned around, unhurt, and gave his chain-mail jacket a jiggle, shaking the arrows onto the ground. The Ox Heir gave her a brief smile. "I'm okay, Rabbit Girl."

But within seconds, the Dragonlord was at it again, gathering up metal objects with his powers. Nezu's sword flew to him, as did all of their arrows, while the ball on Goru's power chain broke out of the earth and began sailing through the air. Their packs bristled with the points of hidden blades trying to get out. Saru hung onto the fan with both hands, digging her heels in the dirt, while Goru himself began to slide toward the Blue Dragon, carried along by his chain mail.

"We can't use anything that has metal in it!" Rana clapped a hand over Tora's ironstone bead, clacking between the Sea Jewels as it rose and tugged at the silk cord around her neck. She dug in her pocket and unleashed the white sand from the Dancing Dunes. They swirled around the Blue Dragon's blistered face and stung him till he let go of their metal items. Blood ran down his cheeks, shockingly scarlet against his blue skin and the white mark of the Tigress's hand.

Tora rubbed the Ring of Obscurity, and a jet-black plume of choking smoke emerged. With the Winds of Infinity, Saru directed the smoke so that it hung all about the Blue Dragon like a storm cloud, swirling around and around. "It'll only be a matter of time before he tries to take the fan again," she shouted.

"The Conjurer!" Usagi remembered it was in her pack. Pulling out the wooden mallet, she hammered out wooden shields and weapons of wood with sharp stone blades.

Lost within the black smoke, the Dragonlord bellowed for his captain. Tupa was still fighting Tora's brother, who was holding his own along with several Miners. The Striker captain called for a couple of roaches to go after Imugi and the Miners, then raced for the Heirs and the smoke that contained the Blue Dragon, charging at spirit speed.

With a roar, Goru lumbered toward Tupa, who lowered his head and smashed into Goru so hard that the Ox Heir was thrown fifty paces back. Usagi and the others grabbed their wooden shields and stone spears, but Tupa looked at them and guffawed. He raised his firehorn to his lips and blew a stream of fire, incinerating their shields and weapons to ashes. The stone blades fell to the ground and shattered.

As he smirked at them, a wave of wrath surged through Usagi. She grabbed Nezu and swept a corner of the Fire Cloak over him. "Let's give Brother Ram a proper welcome home, shall we?"

"Wait!" said Tora. "I'm coming too."

"And me!" said Rana. She and Tora slipped under the Fire Cloak with them.

The former Ram Heir was calling to the Dragonlord through the cloud of black smoke. "My lord, I'm here!" He aimed his firehorn at Saru, who was controlling the smoke with a steady fanning of the Winds of Infinity. As he began to blow, Usagi cried, "Now!"

The four of them ran at the Striker captain. He turned his firehorn and a searing stream of fire enveloped them. Usagi kept the Fire Cloak tightly closed. The shimmering, translucent fabric protected them from the licking flames, and they advanced closer. From under the cloak, Nezu directed water from his canteen to meet the fire in a blast, driving the stream of flame back until the water flooded the firehorn and into Tupa's mouth. As he coughed and spluttered, Rana stuck her head out and spit her blinding venom in Tupa's eyes. Tora rubbed the Ring of Obscurity and a cloud of gritty yellow dust poured from the amber stone, filling Tupa's nose and stinging his face. The Striker captain began to scream.

"Enough!" howled the Dragonlord. With a great yank, Usagi felt her rabbit pendant snap from her neck. The silver necklace strained at the inside of the Fire Cloak, while the ironstone bead at Rana's neck rose once more and pulled toward the Blue Dragon. Through the translucent cloak, Usagi saw the Winds of Infinity slip through Saru's fingers and the Blue Dragon's long-nailed hand reach through the black smoke and catch it. With a single wave, he blew away the cloud of smoke.

"Oh no," whispered Usagi.

The jaunty notes of a flute struck them then, and suddenly it didn't matter that Usagi's legs were still wobbly, for she and everyone else within earshot began dancing. On the battlefield, the Strikers were clacking and rattling in their armor, the Miners were stomping, the Ghosts were kicking, the Dunelings were spinning within cyclones of sand, and Yunja and his younglings skipped about. Cries of confusion filled Usagi's ears.

As she danced, she saw that Goru was up on his feet, lumbering around half-conscious, and the Striker captain was whirling uncontrollably. Half-blinded by Rana's venom, Tupa strained mightily for his firehorn. But though he nabbed it, he only managed to blast a few errant fireballs as he spun past the Blue Dragon. The Dragonlord shimmied and swayed, though his ravaged face was a mask of pure rage.

The only person not dancing was Inu, playing the Flute of Dancing Dreams. He tootled merrily, forcing the Blue Dragon to deposit the fan on the ground, and twirling him away. Inu danced Saru to the fan and bent her down in a bow, allowing her to snatch the fan back up while the Dragonlord and his Striker captain danced helplessly in the clearing by the Sea of Trees. Tupa's arm wound back and punched the Dragonlord's nose.

"Forgive me, my lord!" bleated Tupa. The Blue Dragon's fist collided with Tupa's chin, and the Striker captain's arms began wheeling. The two of them threw repeated punches at each other, even as a horrified Tupa apologized after each blow.

Usagi heard a low growl, and then Kumo raced back out of the ancient forest. Unaffected by the Flute of Dancing Dreams, he pounced on the Blue Dragon's back, tearing and slashing with his teeth and claws. All the while, the Dragonlord danced and bellowed, unable to escape the grip of the cloud leopard. He fell to the ground, kicking his legs to the flutesong, while Kumo sank his fangs into him.

"Inu, get us to the Sea of Trees," called Saru.

Nodding, the Dog Heir changed his tune slightly and Usagi found herself and the other Heirs doing a lively step toward the edge of the forest. Then he stopped playing and everyone jerked to a halt. "Now!" Inu shouted.

They dove into the trees, Kumo running after them at a full gallop. Out in the clearing, Tupa rushed to help the Blue Dragon up. "My lord!"

"My Treasures!" he screamed, bleeding and scratched, his face unrecognizable beneath its wounds. He stabbed a long-nailed blue finger in the direction of the ancient forest.

Tupa flinched and bowed. His face grim, he hurried toward the Sea of Trees. Usagi heard him muttering to himself.

"This is madness," Tupa seethed. *"There's no way I can get all Twelve Treasures back by myself."*

Tora rubbed the Ring of Obscurity, and a huge billowing mist filled the trees. "That ought to help hide us." She glanced at Rana, and her snaggleteeth gleamed. She pointed at Rana's throat. "Look!"

The tiger-iron bead, nestled between the giant pearls that were the Sea Jewels, had begun to glow. Saru gasped. "It looks just like the Land Jewel, only it's—"

"Ironstone from the Tree of Elements," finished Tora. "It may not be jade, but it's still a gift from the sacred mount." They stared at it in wonder. Here among the ancient trees of Mount Jade, the necklace seemed to be restored. "Give it a try, Earth Snake."

Rana's dark eyes sparkled, and she closed her hand around the curved stone, glowing red, gold, and black. Taking a deep breath, she shut her eyes. After a moment, the earth began to rumble, then jolted.

"Earthquake!" exclaimed Nezu.

Usagi looked at the giant trees around them. As the ground shook harder and harder, they swayed and creaked dangerously, groaning as waves of movement rippled out from the forest. She put an arm around Tora and a hand on the nearest tree to steady herself. The great dragon spruce pulsed beneath her palm, grounding her. As she found her footing, her legs received a surge of strength.

The earth bucked, flinging the Dragonstriker captain out of the forest, where he landed with a hard thud at the feet of the Blue Dragon. The shaking stopped and Tupa got to his hands and knees with a groan.

"I'm sorry, my lord," he panted. "I can't even get close."

"Torch it!" the Dragonlord howled. "Use your fire gift and burn it all!"

"But I . . ."

"Just do it!"

Staggering to his feet, Tupa brought his firehorn to his lips and blew. A stream of fire erupted toward the edge of the forest but didn't quite reach. With a growl, the Dragonlord grabbed Tupa by the back of his neck and marched him forward, then cupped a long-nailed hand around the firehorn. The fire burned hotter and brighter, and extended in a long arc till it licked at the first line of trees. A high-pitched sound hit Usagi's ears. "Merciful spirits—the trees are screaming."

"How do we make it stop?" With an anguished glance at the flames, Rana reached for the ironstone bead again. Hurriedly, she murmured a prayer to the mountain goddess, squeezing her eyes tight in concentration.

An even bigger jolt rippled through the ground, and a wave of earth rose up, like a giant worm was tunneling right below its surface. It barreled toward Tupa and the Blue Dragon, throwing them off balance and halting the stream of flame from the firehorn. Their eyes widened as a torrent of dirt and rocks swallowed them up, faster than they could run. Everyone watched as the Blue Dragon and his captain disappeared from the clearing, their screams quickly muffled as they were folded into the earth. And then all was still.

The pearls for the Treasure were gathered by the seamaids, the most skilled divers in Midaga, who with their water gifts searched the depths of the ocean for hours. The white pearl could bring in the tides, while the black pearl could send them out. The jade bead was shaped from stone found on Mount Jade. Bestowed by the mountain goddess, it would enhance the necklace-wearer's own talents, and give them the ability to move the land. When the jewels were strung together and blessed upon the mountain, their full power was realized—much like the Twelve Treasures themselves.

—From *Treasures of the Twelve: A History*, a volume in *Legends of the Twelve*

CHAPTER 27

A NEW JEWEL

THEY STARED OUT AT THE clearing. Dust from the disturbed ground settled, falling back to earth with a sigh. No other movement could be detected. The Blue Dragon and his second-in-command had been absorbed into the bowels of the earth. Usagi listened for signs of life, for heartbeats or cries beneath the ground, but heard nothing. "They're gone."

A great cheer went up across the battlefield as the rebel Midagians realized what had happened. In a panic, the remaining Strikers turned and ran as fast as they could. Some had already seen an opportunity to flee and were far into the distance.

Overhead, the branches of the outermost trees in the guardian forest smoldered. The thick mist from the Ring of Obscurity had provided enough moisture to keep them from entirely going up in flames, but some were badly singed. Nezu put out the remaining embers with the water from his canteen, while Usagi went around from tree to tree, using her wood gift to help them heal. Meanwhile, Rana hurried onto the battlefield with the Apothecary. With the restored and newly powerful Jewels of Land and Sea still around her neck, she tended to the wounded Midagians—both ordinary and those with zodiac powers—who'd come to help defend Mount Jade.

A tearful Tora rushed out from the Sea of Trees and ran into the arms of her brother. All was forgiven between them.

Now, on the scarred patch of earth where the Blue Dragon and Tupa had been swallowed up, former prisoners from the Eastern Mines, the Ghosts of Butterfly Kingdom, Yunja's band of talented younglings, and Midagians without zodiac powers from the town of Woodwing all danced in celebration. They didn't need the Flute of Dancing Dreams to move their feet. Their kingdom was finally free!

In the early dawn light of Rabbit hour, Usagi approached the Steps of Patience and heard the melodies of the Singing Bamboo welcoming her and the other Heirs back to the shrine. A lump came into her throat. After all they'd been through, she'd feared never hearing the bamboo's song again. She took a deep breath and began climbing, thinking of the previous day's battle. After a night of celebrations and rest with those who'd come to fight with them, the Heirs had taken their leave, anxious to return to the Shrine of the Twelve. They were invited by Imugi for a proper feast in the Painted Hollow, sometime in the months to come, and promised to meet again very soon.

But their mission would not be fully complete until they got the Treasures back to their rightful place at the shrine, and so Usagi tried to take each step as fast as she could, while being careful not to skip a single one. In her haste, her legs, healed but still tender, began to ache, and sweat dripped down her face onto the Fire Cloak. As she slowed, Inu caught up to her. "How are you holding up, Rabbit Girl?"

"I can't wait to get back," Usagi said. "I only wish . . ." She stopped, leaning on the Tigress's staff. "I'm glad we got all the Treasures, but I wish we'd found Teacher."

The Dog Heir nodded. "She should've been here to see us complete her most important assignment."

Usagi bit her lip. She didn't say it, but she also wished to know what had happened to Uma, who'd disappeared in the midst of the fighting. Usagi had asked Yunja and the other rebel Midagians to keep an eye out for her sister. She didn't see how Uma could survive by herself in the middle of the wilderness, let alone the Sea of Trees, which had driven away many from the flanks of the sacred mountain. Usagi prayed that she'd somehow gotten to safety.

At least the Dragonlord and Tupa weren't around to hurt her—or any youngling—anymore. Usagi pulled her rabbit pendant from her pocket and rubbed at it.

Inu cocked his head. "What happened to the chain?"

"The Blue Dragon broke it."

"Of course." He inspected it with a grunt. "I'll fix it. We'll have to make you a new blade, too. Good thing you've got Teacher's walking stick until then."

Usagi smiled in spite of her struggle to climb. "Teacher always said, 'Even the strongest are tried by the Steps of Patience.' I don't think she was only talking about these."

The others passed them at a faster clip, all eager to be home. As Usagi and Inu neared the top of the staircase, he frowned and sniffed the air. He stopped and Usagi turned to look at him. "What's wrong?"

Nezu and Tora squeezed by and rushed off into the Singing Bamboo, while Inu kept sniffing. A strange look came over his face and he raised an eyebrow. "We have company."

Usagi heard a yelp, then Tora's voice filtered from the courtyard. *"Oh, my stars and spirits! Usagi!"*

The urgency in her voice jolted Usagi. She hurried up the last few steps and ran through the swaying bamboo, swept past the twelve guardian lanterns, and burst into the main courtyard, only to fall to her knees.

There, before the Summoning Bell, stood Uma, petting Kumo's great furry head. Her hair was an even more disheveled mess, and her Dragon Academy uniform was filthy and torn. But she was alive—and at the Shrine of the Twelve.

Her wide brown eyes met Usagi's, and she gave her a shy smile. "Oh, at last. I've been waiting for hours!"

"How...?" Usagi gawked at her sister in disbelief. "You—you came up here all by yourself?"

With a modest shrug, Uma nodded. "Everyone was so busy fighting, it was the perfect time to slip away. I was going to hide in the forest, but then I saw this lighted path and I couldn't help but follow it." She fingered a big hole in her tunic. "There were a couple of tricky parts. But I figured it out." Beside her, the cloud leopard nudged her arm, and she resumed scratching its furry ears.

As the others exclaimed in astonishment and bombarded Uma with questions, Usagi got to her feet. Shakily, she embraced her sister. "I can't believe you're finally here."

"Do you forgive me?" whispered Uma.

Usagi's heart swelled, easing a ragged ache borne for so long, she'd nearly forgotten its presence. "Only if you forgive me," she said, hugging Uma tight.

The Monkey Heir smiled at them both. "You know what this means, don't you? The mountain goddess has chosen the next candidate for Heir to the Horse Warrior. Looks like we've got a new Heirling."

"The Welcome Song," an old Midagian tune traditionally sung before feasts, echoed off the walls of the Marble Gorge. Winter was giving way to spring, and the Heirs had come from Mount Jade to celebrate the Spring Festival in the ancient meeting place of the first Midagian tribes, by invitation of the Miners.

Tora sat happily by her brother's side, clapping and singing. Imugi's snaggleteeth matched Tora's as they smiled at each other. He and his followers had pledged to join the Heirs in reestablishing order in Midaga, and the last few weeks had been busy.

After the Blue Dragon disappeared, the capital was thrown into chaos as his advisers sent search parties throughout the kingdom to look for Lord Druk and Captain Tupa. Most of the Dragonstrikers with zodiac powers denounced their former roles. Some turned up in their old hometowns and provinces, while others wound up joining with rogue groups of talented younglings like the Miners and the Ghosts of Butterfly Kingdom. The Dragon Academy was dissolved, and many younglings returned to their families to much relief and rejoicing. Only Strikers without powers and Guard were left, without a master to serve. Some had gone on a looting rampage, which had to be stopped by ordinary Midagians and groups of rebel younglings around the kingdom.

With the help of the Treasures, the Heirs were beginning to put things to rights. Bringing all Twelve Treasures back to the shrine on Mount Jade had strengthened their individual powers as never before, and the very mountain itself seemed charged with energy. Soon, they knew, they would find Warrior Heirs for every branch of the zodiac. "Once the Circle of the Twelve is complete, the Shield of Concealment will return," said Saru confidently. "Until then, we help the people of Midaga fight back against the remnants of our oppressors, and when the shield is back in place, the Guard and their ilk can be expelled from the island. They will never be able to find their way back again."

Rana had been made the Snake Heir for her bravery in the ambush by the Blue Dragon and his Strikers and for burying him with her earth gift, which had been enhanced by the Jewels of Land and Sea. Tora, who was steadily learning to access her visions without the tiger-iron bead, was pleased it had gone into restoring the Treasure. "It sure makes touching the Tree of Elements worth it. Maybe surprises are a good thing after all."

For Rana's ceremony, Usagi had helped fashion a fine weapon—a hollowed length of wood that served as both a walking staff and as a blowstick. In a removable top section of the stick, she'd added compartments for storing poisoned darts. Inu made Rana a cuff bracelet that sported a latched container. It held grains of sand from the Dancing Dunes, which Rana could turn into a stinging whirlwind. "I think it will serve you even better than a jacket of metal scales. That was a brilliant idea, turning the sand into a weapon," he told her.

"I got the idea from the Ring of Obscurity," said Rana. Her dark eyes sparkled as she slid the bracelet onto her wrist, and Uma leaned over to admire it.

As the most junior youngling on Mount Jade, with finely developed horse speed and fire gifts, Uma was now the official candidate for Heir to the Horse Warrior. Other younglings with horse talent among the rebels had expressed interest in becoming candidates themselves. But Uma wasn't worried. "I got through both the Dragon Academy and the Running of the Mount—no one's going to beat me!"

A formal invitation was extended to Tora's brother to join them as Heir to the Dragon Warrior, but he declined. "The Miners depend on me," he explained. "I'd rather we help you from our corner of the kingdom. But if you're looking for good candidates, Panri's got the fighting mettle of a wild boar and a bulletproof hide, and that silver-eyed Dragon Girl has potential." He nodded at Miru of the Ghosts, who'd impressed everyone when she arrived in the Gorge on the back of the emperor butterfly. The young Ghost had managed to tame the giant butterfly after it had carried Usagi around Butterfly Kingdom, and often flew it around the island.

Yunja and his little band of younglings had arrived at the gorge in their strange contraptions, which they proudly showed to all who'd congregated there. "If those of us with powers can help those Midagians without, why not?" said

Yunja, patting the horseless cart they'd come in. "Make every Midagian more powerful, and we'll never fall to outsiders again!" They'd sent their headless horses back with the townspeople of Woodwing, who reported that the wooden steeds had cut down on precious travel time for young and old alike. They'd also made progress on free-flying, using constructed wings of bamboo and woven reeds to glide a fair distance. Ji had flown to the Marble Gorge on them, accompanied by her seagulls. She and Miru delighted in soaring through the towering cliffs on her wide, woven wings and the giant butterfly.

Now they were all gathered in the Painted Hollow, around a feast assembled by everyone in attendance. "No more fake food here," said Imugi. "This food will truly satisfy." There were roast ducks with crackling-crisp skin, an enormous roasted boar on a spit, seasoned sticky rice steamed in bamboo and lotus leaves, grilled fresh-caught fish, and plenty of wild greens, foraged mushrooms, and starchy roots fried into a delicious tangle. It was simple but filling food, brought and prepared by all of them together, and Usagi thought it was just as delicious as anything she'd ever tasted from the Conjurer.

Upon finishing their meal, Inu, Nezu, and Saru brought out instruments to play music. The Dog Heir promised, to hoots and teasing, that his flute was an ordinary one. Several of the Miners picked up their instruments, and rounds of singing began anew. As Goru and Rana got up and danced, Usagi noticed that her sister and Tora were nowhere to be seen in the cave.

Slipping out, she saw that they were a short distance away, sitting on a ledge overlooking the winding ribbon of the Peacock River. Beside Tora, Kumo rested, his broad head raised just enough to survey the gorge. His ears swiveled as Usagi came up and settled herself between her sister and best friend.

"Did you get any of the sweets?" she asked. "I was going to save you both some honeycomb from the clifftop hives. The Miners say that the honey from those bees gives you beautiful dreams and visions. But I think Goru ate the last piece."

"He can have all he wants. This is my dream right here," declared Uma. "We're not hungry, we've got each other, and we're safe. I don't need honey to make it beautiful."

Tora's snaggleteeth glinted, and she rubbed Kumo's broad velvet nose. "I get plenty of visions. And these days, they're all full of reunion." She glanced back over her shoulder at the cave, its walls echoing with singing and laughter. "I'd say that's sweet enough."

With a sigh, Usagi put her arm around her, and draped the other around her sister. Uma looked up at her. "What do you suppose Mama and Papa would think if they saw us now?"

Usagi gazed out over the gorge as the sun slipped toward the horizon, throwing a final band of gold against the deepening blue of the sky. The Silver Sea, a broad swath of stars, spread across the heavens like a celestial spill of milk. She spied a pair of stars that seemed to glow green. As they twinkled at her, Usagi smiled, thinking of the Tigress. "They would be proud."

The sounds of music and voices floated from the cave, joining with the roar of the Peacock River's tumbling rapids. It created a wild song that harmonized with the love vibrating in Usagi's heart. She looked at Uma and Tora, and they grinned at each other. Together, they could do anything.

Above them, the stars shone bright.

ACKNOWLEDGMENTS

I'm so grateful to be able to continue the story of the Warrior Heirs, and to bring a second book into the world. It could not happen without the work and support of a whole host of people, all of whom are Treasures in my eyes.

My thanks to Josh Adams for being the best agent and cheerleader a writer could ask for. Your belief in me keeps me going, and is a light in the dark fogs of doubt. All my appreciation goes to you, Tracey, and Cathy. I am so proud to be part of the Adams Literary family.

Endless gratitude to my editor, Kristen Pettit, for seeing the potential in my clumsy early drafts. If this story achieves any liftoff at all, it's because you gave me both the guidance and the space to run with it. Thank you for helping me reach for the skies.

Kudos and credit must go to the crack team at Harper-Collins. Praise and thank-yous abound to Clare Vaughn for taking care of the details; to Molly Fehr and Alison Donalty for the beautiful book design; to artist Sher Rill Ng for gorgeous cover art that took my breath away; to copy editor

Maya Myers for your meticulous attention; to production/ managing editors Jessica Berg and Gwen Morton for making everything run smoothly; and to production manager Kristen Eckhardt for staying on top of it all. Thank you to the marketing duo of Robby Imfeld and Emma Meyer, and publicists Kadeen Griffiths and Maeve O'Regan, for getting the adventures of Usagi and the Heirs in front of more eyes and into more hands. Thanks also to Kate Morgan Jackson and Suzanne Murphy. I'm so fortunate to be in such formidably capable hands.

Since the publication of the first book, I've met and heard from many who grasped what I was trying to do, and I am beyond grateful for your words of support and for championing *The Twelve*. A special shout-out to the wonderful folks at Owl Crate Jr. for showing it so much love, and to the Junior Library Guild, for its recognition. To the readers, librarians, bloggers, Bookstagrammers and booksellers—I thank you from the bottom of my heart.

To my friends in the writing community and beyond— thanks for being there along every step of the way, including your encouragement when this was all just a seed of an idea. Thank you for nurturing its growth, celebrating its fruition, and sharing it with the world. My humble gratitude to Paula Yoo, Erin Eitter Kono, Ken Min, Elizabeth Barker, Aurora Gray, Arti Panjabi Kvam, Hilary Hattenbach, Lilliam

Rivera, Elizabeth Ross, Josh Hauke, Kristen Kittscher, Jason White, Mary Shannon, Frances Sackett, Helena Ku Rhee, Sherry Berkin, Rita Crayon Huang, Mike Jung, Jessica Kim, J.R. Krause, Brandy Colbert, Elana K. Arnold, Evelyn Skye, Naomi Hirahara, C.B. Lee, Cindy Pon, Lisa Gold, Laurie Zerwer, Erin Kieu Ninh, Oliver Wang, Joven and Leslie Matias, Stefanie Huie, Emily Liu, Kathee Lin, Roger Fan, Carol Young, Peter Kim, Mayumi Takada, Eileen Kim, Johanna Lee, Phil Yu, Harry Yoon, Emmie Hsu, Rosa Yan, Leonard Chen, Judy Moon Kim, Tiina Piirsoo, Darcy Fleck, Trish Dacumos, Harry Lin, Ryder LinLiu, Allie Chiu, Leslie Lehr, Francesca Lia Block, Jim Thomas, Kim Turrisi, the Novel 19s crew, the UCLA Extension Writers' Program, SCBWI, and so many others. Writing is a solitary occupation, but because of you, I never feel alone.

Family is my foundation and my fuel, without which I could not pursue my dreams. Immense hugs to Amanda, Nicole, Lindsey, and John Paul, who inspire me every day. To my sister, Wendy, and brother-in-law, Dennis, eternal thanks for your unconditional love and encouragement. Thank you to the extended Chang clan for your embrace: Karena, Carl, Timothy, Joshua, Dave, Christina, Kadence, Tiffany, Harvey, Amelia, Steve, Virginia, and Grace. To Koo and Rosa Pak, and to the memory of Steven, my love always. To Aires, Pauline, Mimi, and my other Hou and Lin relatives, thank you for cheering me on. *To-siā*.

And as ever, my biggest thanks to my parents, Paul and Martha Lin. Without your faith in me and unwavering support and confidence, I wouldn't be here today. I love you.